Pippa Roscoe lives in Norfolk, near her family, and makes daily promises to herself that *this* is the day she'll leave the computer to take a long walk in the countryside. She can't remember a time when she wasn't dreaming about handsome heroes and innocent heroines. Totally her mother's fault, of course—she gave Pippa her first romance to read at the age of seven! She is inconceivably happy that she gets to share those daydreams with you. Follow her on Twitter @PippaRoscoe.

Amanda Cinelli was born into a large Irish-Italian family and raised in the leafy green suburbs of County Dublin, Ireland. After dabbling in a few different careers, she finally found her calling as an author after winning an online writing competiton with her first finished novel. With three small daughters at home, her days are usually spent doing school runs, changing nappies and writing romance. She still considers herself unbelievably lucky to be able to call this her day-job.

PLAYING THE BILLIONAIRE'S GAME

PIPPA ROSCOE

THE VOWS HE MUST KEEP

AMANDA CINELLI

MILLS & BOON

PLAYING THE BILLIONAIRE'S GAME

PIPPA ROSCOE

For Sareeta Domingo, who saw how much
I was inspired by *The Thomas Crown Affair*
and encouraged me to run with it.

And for Hannah Rossiter, who helped me
to ensure that it was the best it could be.

My sincerest thanks to you both.

xx

CHAPTER ONE

INTERVIEWER ONE: *Ms Keating, you understand that this interview is being recorded for internal Bonnaire's purposes only and that you do not need a lawyer present?*

MS KEATING: *I'm afraid that hasn't convinced me that I don't need one.*

INTERVIEWER ONE: *But you understand the statement that I have just made?*

MS KEATING: *Yes.*

INTERVIEWER ONE: *Then, if you would, can you please explain how you came to believe that the painting in question was a fake?*

MS KEATING: *As I have already explained, the painting I assessed in Sharjarhere was most definitely not a fake.*

INTERVIEWER ONE: *But you have stated that the painting, Woman in Love, up for auction after a private viewing at Bonnaire's London gallery and damaged on the night of June the twenty-first, was a fake?*

MS KEATING: *[brief pause] Yes. That specific painting was a fake.*

INTERVIEWER TWO: *And you claim that this was a different painting from the one you assessed, certified and valued in Sharjarhere and attributed to the painter Etienne Durrántez, owned by Sheikh Alham Abrani?*

MS KEATING: *Yes.*

INTERVIEWER TWO: *Why is that?*

MS KEATING: *Because I'm very good at my job.*

INTERVIEWER ONE: *We'll get to that later. For the moment, can you explain the circumstances under which you identified the damaged painting as a fake?*

SIA KEATING HAD been breathing hard even before the harsh ring of her phone broke through the nightmare that held her in its grip. She'd been fighting a losing battle with the stranglehold her sheets had around her arms and neck.

Several days later she would wonder if that moment hadn't been prophetic somehow. She'd woken with a feeling of dread. One that seemed to deepen the moment the words reached her from the mobile phone she pressed to her ear.

'Sia, we have a problem.'

Her heart dropped so quickly she wasn't able to form a response for David, the head of Scientific Research. Partly because his nickname in the department was the 'Art Detective' and as much as she liked the bespectacled, calm-toned man, there was only one reason an art valuer got a phone call from him.

'The Abrani painting. It's been damaged.'

Sia flung back the covers and pushed her hair out of her face, concern for the beautiful piece cutting through the fog from her nightmare. 'How?'

'There was apparently some kind of altercation at the gallery.'

'Galleries don't have altercations,' she replied, confused. She cast a look at the clock by her bed. It was two o'clock in the morning. But he'd said the painting was only damaged? If so, then why was David calling *her*?

'They did tonight. But the painting…there's a problem. Could you come down and take a look at it for me? Something's not right.'

For the entire journey between her little studio flat in Archway and the gallery in Goodge Street, Sia's heart pounded with fear. The kind of fear that heralded the termination of careers. David might just as well have proclaimed the apocalypse had come. Because 'something's not right' could really only mean one thing. And as the tube rattled its way along the tracks one thought reverberated in time with the clicks and clacks.

It's not a fake. It's not a fake. It's not a fake.

It couldn't be. The painting she had valued two months ago in Sharjarhere was not a forgery because she double-checked, triple-checked her work. Always. She *had* to.

Sia bit back the mounting nausea swirling in her stomach. For most art valuers, one or maybe even two forgeries were to be expected. For as well trained as most valuers were, con artists were better, more dedicated, even harder working. They had to be, they got the bigger payout, Sia thought ruefully. Until they were caught.

Sia's mind veered dramatically away from the last time she had seen her father in jail. The way he had looked at her from across the table in the visiting room of Brixton Prison, a sheen glistening in his eyes, his body angled slightly to the side, Sia couldn't help but wonder if he'd purposely arranged himself like a Vermeer. As if everything, his whole life—in *hers*—had been a forgery.

It's not a fake. It's not a fake. It's not a fake.

She ran through the valuation. It had been a bit of a rush as she'd been covering for Sean Johnson, who had fallen ill at the last minute. Even now she felt slightly guilty about the joy she'd felt at having been chosen to replace him *and* the uncharitable belief that his sickness might have been alcohol-related.

No matter how good she was, how accurate, precise and detailed, she'd been passed over for evaluations like this again and again. At first, she'd put it down to being the newbie. Then she'd put it down to being paranoid. And three years in and still missing out on some of the big jobs? She'd been forced to realise that her—or, more accurately, her *father's*—reputation was once again taking its toll on her life.

So she'd been determined to ensure that this valuation was *perfect*. She'd arrived at the palace in Sharjarhere from Athens, where she'd helped her friend Célia d'Argent and Loukis Liordis with an auction that raised an inconceivable amount for charity. Had she been riding so high on her contribution to the charity that she'd missed something at the palace? She shook her head, drawing a slight frown from a fellow tube passenger, even at such an ungodly hour in the morning.

No, she'd gone through each stage of the valuation process: the signature, the artistic style, the paint, the canvas. She'd removed the frame, checked the backing, the details were all correct—variations in the paint levels and thickness, the blacklight showing nothing untoward.

And her gut. The natural instinct she'd been born with telling her that she was in the presence of a true Etienne Durrántez, one of the twentieth century's most famous artists. It didn't matter to Sia that she knew the painting would fetch more than one hundred million pounds. It didn't matter to her who would spend such an impossible amount of money on the painting. It was the painting itself.

The unknown woman stared at the viewer with that same indefinable sense of inner knowledge as the *Mona Lisa*. The secret smile of, as appropriately titled, a *Woman In Love*. The swathe of long dark hair was impressive even to Sia, whose tumble of thick Titian waves were so noticeable she almost always swept them up into a bun at her neck. A slash of red across her lips was worn with pride, not arrogance, confidence, not false bravado, and it had made Sia want to have known the mysterious woman. To understand where her sense of admiration sprung from, not for the painter but the model.

Sia had been so drawn to the painting that there was absolutely no way that it could have been a fake. The signature, the artistic style, the paint, the canvas…she thought, checking through the assessment. And the provenance.

Her breath caught for just a second. She'd not been shown the provenance. Her manager had informed her that she needn't ask after it because the paperwork had already been forwarded to Sean. And even as she'd begun to question the unusual chain of events she'd heard it. The sigh.

It was one that she'd heard so many times in her three years at Bonnaire's. She could almost picture her manager now. Overweight, red-cheeked and always slightly sweaty, the man practically defined 'old boys club'. It was the kind of sigh that would usually precede some kind of patronising comment about her youth, gender, looks or inexperience.

The rage that had roared in her ears had almost blocked out his disappointment in having to remind her that she had been given an opportunity here and instead of making a mountain out of a molehill she should, essentially, keep her pretty mouth shut and get on with it. Yes, he'd actually said that.

And now, as the tube pulled into Goodge Street station, she was mentally kicking herself for toeing the line rather than following her instinct, trusting her gut. Trusting *herself.*

She held her coat tight against the unseasonal bite of the night-time gust of wind as she picked her way past take-away boxes and black bin bags towards the back entrance of Bonnaire's, waved her security pass over the sleek black electric reader and pulled the heavy door open.

Usually, at two-forty-two in the morning the white-walled offices would have been completely empty. But tonight at least fifteen staff were present and through the windows of the glass-lined meeting rooms she could make out at least two company directors, one of whom was shouting into a telephone, the angry words clearly audible from this distance.

Ducking into the stairwell that would take her three floors below ground to the extensive lab that took up an entire level, her heels tapped frantically on the concrete staircase as she ran to where she knew both David and the painting would be.

She ignored the stares of the lab assistants as she went straight to the long bench David used. She glanced to the

X-ray room at the back, the red light remaining dark, showing the machine was not in use.

David was at the computer, already going through the images from the infrared and ultraviolet tests before calling up the X-rays. The moment he caught sight of her, he ushered away a few more technicians from where they were staring at the damaged painting and beckoned her over.

The moment she caught sight of the painting she couldn't help the gasp that fell from her lips. Her instant reaction was shock and horror—red streaks poured down the painting, the consistency of wine, but the alcohol had begun to mix with the paint beneath it. Slashes of what had once been raven-black hair now dribbled down the palest of cheeks and the long silver necklace worn by The Woman in Love now pooled downwards towards the painting's frame in a way that most definitely wouldn't have happened if it had been the original painting. The real one. The one that had been valued at over one hundred million pounds.

'It's fake,' she exclaimed.

'Yes.'

She collapsed into the chair in front of the painting. 'This isn't the painting I valued. David—it's not. I wouldn't have made that mistake. Have you checked the photographs from my file?'

David paused before leaning against the table, facing her with a grim expression.

'I…they haven't given me access to the file.'

'But that's…' Sia trailed off. 'How are you supposed to evaluate against the initial assessment?'

'Sia, look, I think you should know that—'

But Sia wasn't hearing David. She was looking at the small video capture in the bottom of David's computer screen.

'What's that?' she interrupted.

David cast her one last concerned look before turning back to his screen.

'Security footage from the incident. It looks as if two guys got into a bit of a fight near the painting.'

Sia was unable to prevent her hand from pressing against her lips in shock at the sight of the fight that had broken out between the two men, causing a glass of wine to be thrown with unwavering accuracy against the painting.

'Is that Savior Sabbatino?'

'Yes, and his brother Santo.'

Sia bit back her shock. The Sabbatino brothers were more likely to be seen on the cover of a scandal rag rather than security footage. The implications of the damage to the painting, the seller and the gallery were beginning to spin beyond the realms of imaginable.

'Can you go back?' she asked David of the footage. Something was niggling at her and she couldn't quite tell what it was. She watched the footage again and again—the wine hitting the painting, the shock rippling out not only from the Sabbatino brothers but the attendees of the private viewing as each person turned their head, watching with horrified fascination the damage to such an expensive piece of…piece of…

There it was again. It was precisely because he was the only person in the whole room who didn't turn his head. Instead of being drawn to the moment like a driver passing a car accident, he had his back turned and was taking a sip of his drink with something that looked, to Sia, like the ghost of a smile.

It was a man she would have recognised anywhere. Just like any other red-blooded woman, whether or not they had a penchant for billionaires with bad reputations.

INTERVIEWER ONE: *So you immediately suspected Sebastian Rohan de Luen?*

MS KEATING: *Sheikh Alham Abrani was very clear in his instructions. The painting would never be sold to Seba—Mr Rohan de Luen. He had made many offers to purchase the painting in the last ten years, all of which had been far above the asking price, and had been refused each and every time.*

INTERVIEWER TWO: *Mr Rohan de Luen is a duke, is he not?*

MS KEATING: *His father was the Duque de Gaeten in Spain before being stripped of his lands. However, because this happened after Seb—after he had been titled at the age of eighteen, he was entitled to the... well, to the title, I suppose.*

INTERVIEWER ONE: *But on the night you believe you discovered the painting was a fake, he had not been anywhere near it?*

MS KEATING: *He was present at the private viewing.*

INTERVIEWER TWO: *But the CCTV footage shows that throughout the entire evening he was nowhere near the painting. In fact he remained behind to give a witness statement to the police, who were called in case any charges were to be brought against the two gentlemen involved in an altercation that damaged the painting.*

Ms KEATING: *Well, he would hardly hold up his hands and say, Me, me—I did it, would he?*

INTERVIEWER ONE: *[clears throat] And when you took your concerns to your superiors...?*

Sia could feel the nails of her fingers pressing crescents into the softness of her palms and knew they'd leave a mark.

'But I've told you, this is not the painting that I valued in Sharjarhere.'

She'd gone straight from David's lab to the executive offices, five floors above. She didn't know what she'd expected, but her manager's response was not it.

'Ms Keating. Please, I'd love to hear what is more plausible. That you were mistaken in your valuation or that you valued a true Durrántez, which was then somehow stolen and replaced with a fake painting on the way to Bonnaire's London gallery, which was then so unlucky as to have been damaged in a one-in-a-million altercation that caused wine to be spilled on it?'

Sia wasn't stupid. She knew what it looked like, could understand it seemed an almost unbelievable chain of events, but she knew what her gut was telling her. And, she cursed silently, she knew that she would never have valued a fake painting. It was the only thing that her father had given her before his arrest and incarceration. The ability to spot a forgery from a mile away.

'If I could just share the photographs I took in Sharjarhere with David then—'

'We have already spoken to Sheikh Abrani, who has apologised profusely for any confusion.'

Sia frowned, because she doubted if the determined, overly confident and deeply arrogant man she had met

when evaluating the painting had ever apologised to anyone in his life. There was simply no way he would have
admitted to even accidentally attempting to sell a fake
Durrántez.

'But—'

'The file has been sealed and will remain that way until
we can finish our internal investigation. And until then,
Ms Keating, you are being placed on suspension, during
which time you will not speak to anyone—*anyone*—of
your suspicions. You will have no contact with either Bonnaire's staff, the press or the Duque de Gaeten.'

The blood drained from Sia's face. Suspension? No contact with her colleagues? Sealed file? None of this was
making any sense whatsoever. She could understand why
Bonnaire's might want to keep the damage of a painting—
even a fake one—quiet until they had been in contact with
the seller and the prospective buyer. But they had already
spoken to Abrani. Everyone had decided that the painting
was a fake, but they were wrong. The painting *had* been
stolen, the thief was getting away with it and the only person being punished was her.

Her already dented reputation and her very young career were at stake. Everything that she'd worked so hard
for. Everything that she'd fought for.

She closed her eyes, refusing to allow the tears she felt
pressing against the back of her eyes to fall in front of
her manager. No, she'd learned a long time ago not to let
them see her cry.

At first it had been her aunt, who had never liked the
fact that her seven-year-old niece was being foisted upon
her while her wayward sister lurched from one man to
another in the wake of her husband's imprisonment. The
strict, dark and deeply conservative home of Eleanor Lang
had been a short sharp shock to a little girl who'd been

given pencils and pens and all but told to 'have at it' on the walls of her father's studio. How on earth was a seven-year-old to know that there was a significant difference between the white paper her father had spread across his studio walls and the magnolia paint that covered her aunt's sitting room and hallway?

After that, it had been the children at school. Her hair would have been target enough had the newspapers not been full of photos of her father—the most notorious art forger in England. Ever. Mothers refused to let their children near her, and teachers eyed her as if she would steal the shoes from their feet if they didn't watch her closely enough.

And while her aunt had given her food and board, there was little money for anything else. So when Sia hadn't had her head in her books, feeling an illicit pang as she traced her fingers over images of paintings she had once seen her father delight in copying, she had held down two after-school jobs, knowing that, whatever shape her future would take, it would have to involve university. Because it would have to be *proper,* it would have to be beyond reproach. It would have to be something that no one could take away from her.

But they had taken it away from her. Even when she'd followed the rules. Done everything perfectly and absolutely right. As the reality of her suspension began to sink in, so did the maths. She might have held down two after-school jobs as a teenager, but her university education had cost her greatly. She had debts of nearly twenty-eight thousand pounds that her position at Bonnaire's had barely managed to scratch the surface of. And even a month's suspension could seriously damage her credit history, let alone her housing.

As nausea rose in her stomach, the grainy black and

white image of Sebastian Rohan de Luen, smirking into his whisky rose in her mind. She knew that he was involved as sure as she knew a real painting from a fake. And she was going to do whatever it took to prove it.

INTERVIEWER TWO: *So, despite direct orders from your manager, you approached the Duque de Gaeten.*

INTERVIEWER ONE: *[low laugh] And how did that go down?*

It had taken Sia less than twenty-four hours to decide her course of action and track him down. The man had a social media page that was as effective as Google Maps, so it wasn't finding him that had taken the most time. No. It was finding her courage. Her plan was simple. Seduce him, find the painting, steal the painting. Or re-steal it anyway. Sia tucked her morals away on that front. Because surely it couldn't be illegal if she was returning stolen property?

No, she decided. It wouldn't. Even if she did benefit from it. Because surely if she returned the painting, the *real* painting, she would prove that she hadn't made a mistake and Bonnaire's would reinstate her. She would *prove* that she was good at her job.

That she was nothing like her father.

She shook the thought from her head as she approached what looked to be just another row of impossibly rich houses in Mayfair, each fronted with two Ionic columns either side of a sleek, shiny black door with a bronze lion's head door knocker. In fact, only the door with the large suited man in front was in use as, beyond the door, the partitions between the houses had been knocked down and the entire row had been converted into one of London's most sought-after private clubs.

When she'd discovered where Sebastian would be she'd known that she'd need help. No way would she have been allowed within fifty feet of the place—even with her surname. But her friend Célia on the other hand... Even before she'd married Greek shipping tycoon Loukis Liordis, Célia had a company with a reputation that would have opened many doors, including this one.

'Even if I get you in, *chérie*, you're going to have to look the part. And, of course, you always look incredible, but you need to look...*rich*.'

Sia's heart had sunk a little at her friend's declaration.

'This is important, *oui*?'

'Yes.'

'*D'accord...*'

Two hours later Sia had walked, wide-eyed, towards the green domed doors of Harrods where she met a lovely woman called Penelope who had been instructed to provide her with a complete outfit, hair and make-up for that evening and discreetly send any bill back to Célia.

She'd spent the next three hours in a complete daze. Dress after dress were given to her to try on, each one more beautiful than the last. When she had first conceived of her hare-brained scheme she had imagined herself in black, her hair pulled back into an efficient bun at the nape of her neck, her make-up simple. Something espionage-ish.

But now, as she looked down at the slash of silk peeking through the rich cashmere coat, she felt a tendril of excitement. Penelope had described the dress as teal and Sia had bitten her tongue. It wasn't teal at all. The colour was more closely Prussian blue, her—and her father's—favourite colour. She'd never once worn it, but when she'd seen in the mirror how well it complemented her pale skin and made her light auburn hair glow like gold she'd been speechless.

The stylist had batted Sia's hands away when she'd insisted on having her hair up and then accused her of committing some great crime, which had made Sia blush more than necessary. So she'd sat back and let him have her way. Sia's hair had been spun into large, seemingly careless waves that softened features that she'd been told far too many times were 'strong' in a way that clearly meant 'masculine'.

By the time she'd reached the suited man by the sleek black door of Victoriana she'd half convinced herself that all of that preparation had been for nothing and she'd be turned away, despite Célia's involvement, and was almost breathing a sigh of relief that she could simply go back home and curl up on the sofa, when the man greeted her by name and the door swung open, inviting her in.

She bit her tongue as she was greeted by a young woman dressed in a pair of tweed breeks and a contrasting waistcoat over a white shirt. Sia found herself looking around for a riding crop, such was the effect. Victoriana indeed.

Sia's coat was taken and she was led down the corridor towards what could have been called a drawing room but was so large that the word simply didn't do it justice. Along one side was a marble bar that stretched the entire length of the room. Behind it stood barmen and women, dressed similarly to the girl presently guiding Sia towards a seat, who was explaining the different rooms spinning off from the hallway behind, words like *library, billiard room, morning room, orangery*…all of which disappeared into the gentle hum of the conversations of the people.

Sia soon found herself deposited into a beautiful mahogany stool lined with a worn green leather seat at the bar, in front of a man looking expectantly at her with a broad smile.

'What's your poison?'

Sebastian Rohan de Luen, she thought.

The barman interpreted her silence as confusion and pressed on, not unkindly, with another question. 'What flavours do you like?'

'Ginger. Rum,' she decided. Not usually much of a drinker, Sia decided that some Dutch courage wouldn't go amiss. But she would stop at the one. Because instinctively she knew that she would need *all* her wits about her.

While the barman created her cocktail Sia scanned the room, trying not to show her surprise at the number of famous faces she saw. A TV star sat with the male model currently gracing Piccadilly Circus's illuminated advertising boards. A politician was pressing far too closely into someone he really shouldn't have been, and a news presenter was having a heated debate with a foreign dignitary.

But all of them faded into the background the moment that she caught sight of the tall, dark figure in the far corner of the room, bending slightly as if to hear what the beautiful woman he was talking to was saying.

She had found the Spanish Duke, but felt as if she were the one in the trap—not him.

She couldn't pull her eyes away. It was as if she'd been set alight and was painfully conscious of everything—the feel of silk against her skin, the gentle hum of voices around her, the way that the light glinted on the large red jewel on the necklace of the woman he was talking to. But, aware as she was of all those things, nothing was more prominent than him.

His profile was powerful. The faint trace of stubble marked a proud jawline, framing his features, and matched the thick waves of burnt umber coloured hair on his head, making her hands twitch reflexively. Even in the shadowed lighting of the corner where he and his companion stood, she could see the almost honeyed colour of his skin, rich and tempting. The exquisite cut of his clearly expensive suit outlined broad shoulders, a flat stomach and firm thighs. And, for the first time in what felt like for ever, she itched for a sketchpad. She wanted to trace the outline of his features, copy them, fill the page with the impression of...

She saw him still. It was an almost imperceptible absence of movement probably unnoticeable to anyone, but she had been so focused on him it blared at her like an alarm.

Unerringly, Sebastian Rohan de Luen, lifted his head and gazed directly into her eyes. Her heart missed its next beat, her breath caught in her throat and she nearly cursed when she saw the same ghost of a smile she recognised from the security footage from Bonnaire's.

He might be the most handsome man she'd ever seen, he might own a dozen four-star hotels around the world, he might be titled, but he was also the man who had singlehandedly destroyed her career and her future.

And she wasn't going to let him get away with it.

CHAPTER TWO

INTERVIEWER ONE: *And you say that he approached you?*

MS KEATING: *Is that so hard to believe?*

INTERVIEWER TWO: *If you could just answer the question.*

MS KEATING: *He approached me.*

SEBASTIAN ROHAN DE LUEN, raised the cut-crystal glass of whisky into the air, clinking it against the champagne flute, and relished the feeling of pure unadulterated pleasure running through his veins.

'To a dish best served cold,' he proclaimed, before taking a very welcome mouthful of ice-cold peaty alcohol. 'I couldn't have done it without you, so thank you.'

He looked into a pair of dark eyes outlined with thick kohl and most likely devastatingly attractive to anyone other than him. But he'd known Aliah for far too long and for that entire time they'd been united by one goal to the exclusion of all else. And that had clearly altered the usual dynamic he engaged in with women. Objectively, she was incredibly beautiful, but...

No. Nothing.

'And I wouldn't be here without you, so thank *you*,' Aliah replied sincerely.

'Dare I ask what you're going to do with your new-found freedom?' Sebastian asked before taking another sip of his drink.

'I have some business to attend to.'

'How suitably cryptic,' he observed wryly, genuinely uninterested. They had both played their part. Now it was time to…

'And you?' Aliah's melodic voice slid into his thoughts. 'Back to Siena? Or will you be visiting Maria while you're in town?'

Sebastian couldn't help the way his lips curved into a smile at the thought of his younger sister. Even if she had recently done the last thing he'd ever expected and run off with a Swiss billionaire on the eve of his best friend's engagement party.

'Maria has found herself a husband and is presently living on the edge of Lake Lucerne,' he managed to say without betraying his distrust of Matthieu Montcour, his *very* new brother-in-law.

'Oh. That's lucky.'

'Is it?'

'Some might say. Is she well?' Aliah asked, her genuine interest for his sister lessening his anger for the moment.

'She's nearly eight months pregnant, so I'm guessing that she is.'

'That's wonderful,' she said, and Sebastian didn't miss the note of longing, or the slight sheen that dusted the edges of her dark eyes. 'Uncle Sebastian, now that is a sight I'd like to see.' Aliah's smile was both mocking and envious, the shadows hinting at the unhealed wounds from the recent separation from her own family. 'Indulge them and appreciate them,' she commanded.

'I do,' Sebastian replied honestly. 'That is why it had to happen now,' he said, his grip momentarily tightening on the thick glass. 'Before Maria's child is born. A fresh start and the past behind us.'

'I'll drink to that,' she said, gently tapping the rim of her glass against his.

As the amber liquid burned down his throat Sebastian wondered if that feeling of peace would come now that everything was as it should be. A feeling that he'd been chasing for ten years that nothing and no willing woman had been able to appease.

With his father finally settled with his stepmother Valeria in Rimini, each happily making the other's life a living hell, and Maria with Matthieu Montcour, it felt as if it was the first time that he'd had no responsibilities. The world was his oyster. His hotels were doing incredibly, the opening of the Caribbean flagship was less than a week away—an event that would allow him to wrap up all loose ends from the Bonnaire's situation. Maybe then he'd find that sense of...

'I lost you there for a minute,' Aliah said.

'Never,' he replied, forcing a smile to his lips as it came time to say goodbye. 'If you ever need anything, I mean it. Anything. Let me know.'

He leaned forward to let her kiss him on the cheek. It was a chaste kiss from a friend. And it was most definitely *not* responsible for the sudden slap of adrenaline and arousal that cut through him when he looked over Aliah's shoulder and caught a glimpse of the woman sitting at the bar, her gaze locked onto him like a laser beam.

'Seb?' Aliah asked, the husky tone of her voice barely cutting through the power of whatever it was that had him in its grasp.

Ignoring her question, he stared deep into the pair of

startling blue eyes as they clashed with his and he felt it like a punch to the solar plexus. For a moment he simply felt awed. A rich, almost terracotta-coloured swathe of gentle curls poured over slender shoulders and dropped almost halfway down pale-skinned and very toned arms. Silk in a regal blue sheathed a body from neck to ankle that made his mouth water. For all of the scantily clad women Sebastian had encountered in the last ten years, this one was the definition of modest, but she alone held the power to undo him. And when his eyes returned to hers, to take in the arch of high cut cheekbones and a mouth made for sin, he couldn't help but pause. There was something about her... And then it dawned on him.

Oh, he was in trouble.

And he couldn't for one minute bring himself to regret it.

Because this? This was going to be fun.

Sia barely noticed the waiter place her drink before her as she watched the Duke return to his conversation as if her entire world hadn't shifted on its axis. Forcing her eyes away from him, she turned to the drink and blinked at it for a moment, having quite forgotten what she was supposed to be doing.

A blush rose to her cheeks and she hated it, hated *herself,* for in that moment—the brief pause before he'd smiled—Sia had forgotten everything. The potential loss of her job, the stolen painting, the fact she was sure that Sebastian Rohan de Luen, was at the heart of the entire mess. No. For that brief moment she'd been struck by an attraction so powerful that she'd almost forgotten her own name. A mistake, she promised herself, she'd not make again.

Reaching for her drink and letting the sweet spicy taste wash her lapse of judgement away and the sharp sting of alcohol bring her back to the task at hand, she realised that she hadn't counted on him having company. Stunning company at that. Casting a quick glance back towards the darkened corner where the handsome couple were still discussing something discreetly, she couldn't help but appreciate the woman's beauty. The way his body was angled beside her was almost protective and for a moment Sia tasted the bitterness of jealousy on her tongue. Not for her, or him, but what they seemed to share. There was something vaguely familiar about her, but Sia couldn't quite place her. It was hardly surprising that a man with Sebastian's roguish reputation was with a celebrity of some sort.

Frowning, she thought over her plan which, she now saw, had more holes than a sieve. What had she been thinking? That *she* could play *him*? *Seduce* him even? The blush returned to her cheeks with a vengeance and embarrassed tears threatened at the corners of her eyes.

And that slight blur to her eyes was the reason she didn't immediately notice that the Duque de Gaeten had crossed the room and come to stand beside her.

'It's a crime.'

The sensual tone of his voice rippled across her skin but it was the words that sparked outrage in her heart. Which was why it took her a moment to gather herself, to stifle the fury welling within her, before she could respond. That this man chose to refer to a crime… Did he know who she was? Was he playing the same game as she? A thin blade of anger cut through any concern. It made her mad. It made her bold.

'What is?' she asked, no trace of the heat in her veins or the pounding of her heart.

'For a woman as beautiful as you to be sitting alone.'

'The greater crime, surely, is the badly delivered line which has left me feeling somewhat cheated. I had expected more from, reportedly, the most renowned play-boy in all of Europe.'

'Renowned? You have me at a disadvantage. You clearly know me, at least by reputation.'

'Henri.' The name slipped from her tongue as if it hadn't been more than twenty years since she'd been called by it. And when he repeated the name back to her, as if feeling the word on his tongue, it sent shivers down her spine.

'You don't look much like a Henri.'

Perhaps she didn't. But Sia knew one thing very definitely. Sia Keating would never be able to do such a thing. Sia Keating was the good girl. She didn't put a foot wrong, never complained, never spoke out, was never angry... Anger was passionate and passionate was too much like her mother. But Henri? Her father's nickname for her, the shortened form of her middle name... Henri might just be able to pull this off.

'Oh, really? What *do* I look like?'

My downfall.

Thrusting aside the errant thought, Sebastian cast a long, slow pursual from the golden halo of her hair to the point of her diamond-encrusted blue heels and back again. He knew that the gaze was insolent and tried to cling to that feeling instead of succumbing to the simple desire to relish her. She was exquisite.

He challenged any man to refute the allure of her hair. Stunning long, honeyed, golden tendrils fell in waves down her back. This close, he could see that her make-up was subtle, allowing an incredible innate beauty to shine. The sheen from the silk glowed beneath the subtle lighting of the room, the shadows showing the shapely outline of her legs, crossed at the knee, legs that were so long Sebastian thought she might actually stand face to face with his six-

foot frame. The slash of silk across her collarbone perfectly displayed a long elegant neck and the sleeveless cut
showed off arms that were slender but shapely. There was
a concealed power to both her body and the whip-smart
mind he could tell was running through myriad possibilities and reactions to the words that would next come
from his mouth.

It had been on the tip of his tongue to say something
crass. It was what she expected of him, it was exactly what
he'd set himself up as being, but then he caught the look
in her startling blue eyes.

There, beneath the false bravado, because it clearly was
false, was something else. Something that pierced a conscience he professed not to have. It was too much like the
way his sister had looked at him—not that there was anything brotherly in his thoughts about the woman in front of
him. No. But it was the vulnerability beneath the defiance.
It was worthy of more than he had planned to offer her.

'Biondina,' he eventually replied.

Obviously the same pale skin, auburn hair, but there
was also something similar about the eyes. Not now, not
from the moment that he'd come to stand beside her, but
before then. Just after he'd said goodbye to Aliah, setting
her on the path towards a much happier future than she'd
ever been offered by her father.

He'd stood watching the way a golden curl swept down
her arm as she reached blindly for her drink. He'd wanted
to know what she was thinking, because her mind hadn't
been on the present, he was sure of it.

'Excuse me?'

'By Frederic Leighton,' he answered, returning to the
present at her question.

'I know who painted *Biondina.*'

The offence in her tone, the pure indignation, pulled

his lips into a broad smile. 'Oh, do you work in the arts?'
he asked, all mock ignorance. The tease was too easy for
him, and she was a terrible actress who seemed only to
remember after the fact that she wasn't Sia Keating.

There was something in his tone…something that made Sia
feel that he might be toying with her. Playing her even? If
he had stolen the painting, then in all probability he would
have researched Bonnaire's. It was a possibility she hadn't
had the time to think through before now and if she had
then, rather than letting her tongue run away with her, she
might just have owned up to being Sia Keating in the first
place. But she'd said Henri and now some deeply hidden
sense of mischief was winding within her. The desire, the
need to challenge him. To *best* him.

'I work for Bonnaire's,' she said, watching closely for
his reaction.

'Isn't that some kind of art dealership? Like Christie's?'

Mentioning their main competitor was just mean and,
despite her suspension, she couldn't help the bloom of loyalty unfurl in her chest.

'Yes, but better,' she replied condescendingly—a tone
she didn't think she'd ever used before.

'Wasn't there some kind of scandal there recently…?'
She watched, fascinated, as he clicked his fingers twice
as if trying to remember. 'Ah, I know. Didn't a painting
get damaged at an auction?'

She was so surprised that he'd taken the conversation
there that no words came.

'Or was it a fake? Or was it both?' He shrugged, the
smile on his face seemingly one of bemused ignorance, yet
to Sia it was like a red rag to a bull…until Henri took over,
transformed the fire of helpless fury striking her silent into

determination and action. She matched his tone and manner, joining in with the playful flirtation with the truth.

'Both apparently,' she said easily. 'Though may I tell you a secret?'

'Of course,' he replied, leaning in as if for her to confide.

'I don't think it was a fake,' she mock whispered behind her hand. 'At least, not before it was stolen and replaced with a forgery,' she concluded.

'Now that *would* be a scandal,' he said, as if impressed by the idea. 'Though I can't imagine for one minute an art house with a reputation like Bonnaire's would be willing to admit to such a thing,' he all but taunted.

Behind her smile, Sia's jaw was clenched with anger. Because he was right. They weren't. And that was why she was there, engaging in some insane cat and mouse game with an international playboy. Sia would have walked away, but Henri dug her heels in. Henri was the girl who had drawn on walls, who had laughed until she'd cried with her father, who had dressed up in the beautiful turquoise silks her mother had left all over their home in Peckham, who at the age of six had worn bright red lipstick and walked in too large high heels. It was time to see what she could do now as an adult.

'I'm surprised that a hotelier has his fingers on the pulse of the international art scene.'

Sia had to bite her lip to keep the smile from spreading, seeing the outrage that crossed Sebastian's features at the word 'hotelier' and at how easy it had been to pierce that clearly healthy ego of his.

'My hotels are four-starred, the restaurants have Michelin stars, celebrities beg to stay in my penthouse suites. I have one in every major European city, more off the beaten track internationally and at least two that are so exclusive they are not even known to the press, one of which is on an island.'

Despite herself, and the arrogance with which the information was delivered, Sia was impressed. Because, if the articles she'd managed to read online before coming here tonight were right, Sebastian's family had been exiled with little more than the clothes on their backs.

'And Leighton comes into this…?' she asked, as if bored of his list of achievements.

For the first time since he'd appeared at her side, Sebastian seemed to bite his tongue. 'Family heirloom.'

'You had a Leighton as an heirloom?' she blurted out, unable to keep the awe from her tone or prevent her eyes from widening.

'We had a couple,' he said, shrugging, as if they'd just been lying about the house.

'Anyone else I should know about?' she asked, almost forgetting the game.

'My father had a penchant for the Italian Renaissance—Giotto, Fra Angelico, Filippo Lippi… But my…mother preferred twentieth century artists. Rothko, Klee, Francis Bacon.'

Sia was so awed at the idea of growing up with authentic paintings by the artists he'd named, she'd missed the way that he'd stumbled over the reference to his mother. Without realising, he'd evoked her childhood fantasy and she imagined walking down grand mahogany hallways with the masters hanging on every wall. But she couldn't prevent herself from asking, 'Etienne Durrántez?'

'Amongst others,' he replied, without taking his eyes from her. She'd been watching closely for any sign, the smallest of movements, but there had been none.

Had she got it wrong? Before making the call to Célia she'd spoken to an old university friend who'd gone to

work at Interpol. She'd not heard anything on the grape-
vine about a stolen Durrántez, and clearly Sebastian had
no need for the money. She couldn't even begin to fathom
why he might have wanted the painting. But he clearly
had wanted it enough to make several public and incredibly generous attempts to buy it. Though she'd not found
any record of him trying to buy any of the other Durrántez for sale. There must have been something in particular
about *that* painting.

'I have a table. Would you care to join me?'

Sebastian half expected her to say no and half resented
the slight burst of adrenaline he felt when she inclined her
head and gestured for him to lead the way. Sebastian might
have recognised her but, beyond knowing that Sia Keating had been sent by Bonnaire's to Sharjarhere as a last-
minute replacement to evaluate the Durrántez, he knew
nothing. There'd been little or no point doing a check on
her by that stage. Besides, she was sure to be just as corrupt as the rest of them. She'd arrived at the palace, done
her job and left. If he'd known for even one second that
she'd be as feisty, playful and smart as she'd proven herself to be in just a short conversation he might have done
things a little differently.

Because she was proving to be a worthy adversary. An
adversary it would be worth knowing a little more about.

Victoriana had been a favourite of his ever since he'd
leased his apartment in Mayfair. Very few people knew
about either the club or his apartment and he liked it that
way. His sister had liked to think that she was completely
independent in her little flat in Camberwell, and Sebastian
knew how important it was for her to feel that way. But
he'd been looking after her since she was eight years old

and he wouldn't stop just because she'd wanted to come to London for art school.

He caught the eye of one of the staff, who nodded in return and proceeded to lead them to a more private area of the members only club. He gestured for Sia or Henri—he sensed there was something about that name that gave her confidence somehow—to precede him and when he, in turn, joined the procession he instantly regretted his courtesy. The demure high necked dress's secret caused him to inhale sharply. From how she'd been sitting, he'd not seen this angle before and now it caused an arousal so acute he was momentarily wordless and witless. The silk fell from her shoulders into a deep cowl that apexed at the base of her spine, revealing inches and inches of smooth creamy skin and showing clearly that Sia was bare beneath the silk. His mouth watered and he clenched his jaw against the need he felt coursing through his veins. And if the gentle sway of her hips was anything to go by, she knew exactly what kind of effect she was causing.

He knew from previous visits that he had approximately forty steps to get his raging libido under control before they would be directed to their table and he was going to need every single one of them. Because, instinctively, he knew he'd need all of his brain cells to tackle the dilemma that was Sia Keating.

They were shown into the Orangery, which would during the day look out onto an exquisite garden, cultivated and completely secluded. But, at this hour of the night, the outside was nothing more than a deep dark cocoon held at bay by the glass panes encased in white painted leadwork. Fairy lights hung from the ceiling, reflected in the windows, creating a canopy of thousands of stars above them.

The garden had been brought inside with hanging baskets of strings of pearls, strings of hearts, long trailing ivy and many more vivid bursts of green, the names of which Sebastian could hardly guess at. Every time he came in here, it never failed to impress him. But, within the large high space, there was more that really drew the eye. Huge bird cages in distressed white, old forest green and black, of all different shapes, some classically rounded at the top, some square—one even had tiers and a swinging perch— filled the space. Ivy grew around the ironwork, winding through and around the bars of the cages, giving the people inside them a feeling of privacy and secrecy.

Large enough to fit tables and chairs, some even large enough to fit groups of eight or ten, they were quite incredible and, from the look in Sia's eyes, almost the very last thing she'd expected. They were shown to one of the smaller cages, with cushioned seats on either side of a small round table clinging to the curve of the bars.

Two glasses of champagne were placed on the table and the discreet waiter disappeared. As she took one side, he took the other. Sebastian couldn't shake the feeling that they were combatants on opposite sides. Because he didn't think for one minute that it was a coincidence that she had referred to Durrántez, using a name which he knew to be fake, appearing the same night as he in a private club when he knew her salary would barely cover a drink, let alone membership to Victoriana.

Oh, Sebastian knew *all* about the backroom deals Bonnaire's pretended not to do and he'd hardly been surprised when the Sheikh had chosen them to fence his ill-gotten painting. But the moment the Sheikh had agreed that the painting had been a fake all along, Sebastian thought it done and dusted. Victory in his grasp. Revenge against Abrani for him and the others.

The last thing he'd expected was for Bonnaire's to send in some Mata Hari in a blue silk dress.

'We were talking about art. I'm curious,' he said, and he meant it, 'what is it that you *value* in an artist?'

Sia tried to prevent the tug of a frown at his choice of word. Surely it was her imagination. But as her mind picked over the possibilities her subconscious supplied a word that surprised her and spoke far too much of a past she wanted to leave behind.

'Authenticity.'

'A woman with a good eye then,' Sebastian returned without missing a beat.

'I'll take that as a compliment from a man with a good eye.'

The smile that broadened his lips was pure sin and Sia was horrified to find that she liked it.

'My friend?'

'She is truly beautiful,' Sia replied honestly.

'As are you.'

It took everything in Sia to hold his gaze. To not shrug off the easily given compliment, shy from it or deny it.

'You don't think so?' he asked, sounding genuinely intrigued and cocking his head to the side as if observing something fascinating.

'I think it is irrelevant in the presence of a beauty like hers.'

'Ah. Well, impartially, I can see your point but, as an old family friend, I do not quite see the allure. To me, your beauty shines brighter than anyone else in the room.'

And Sia hated that his assurance took the bite out of the strange nauseating jealousy she'd felt swirling in her stomach. But it did make her plan easier, not to have to compete with another woman.

A plan she was seriously beginning to doubt. And, for just a second, she allowed herself to wish that this was as simple as what it seemed to be: a handsome, charming man finding her interesting and beautiful. It was a yearning that took her by surprise. Sharp, sudden and acute.

She'd never had time for boys or, later, men. At school her goal had been university, desperate to get away from the cold, staid clutches of her aunt's house. And at uni? Just feeling the money slipping through her fingers each moment she was there had been enough to forge a single-minded focus she'd not really ever let go of. So she'd spent her Friday and Saturday evenings in the library and her nights alone in her bed and if it had made her feel a little lonely then so be it. Because she'd got her degree and a job that she loved for the most part and she was happy.

It was the touch of the pad of his thumb across her cheek, the way that his finger angled her jaw that brought her back instantly. It sent a cascade of sparks across her nerve-endings, lighting her pulse and kicking an extra thud into her heart. For just a moment she hoped he would kiss her. At the look in his eyes as he gazed at her mouth, she fooled herself into thinking that he might want to.

'Eyelash,' he said by way of explanation, pulling the rug from beneath her.

She couldn't do this. There was something about Sebastian Rohan de Luen that was more than just the arrogant playboy art thief and that made him dangerous. Too dangerous.

'I should go.'

CHAPTER THREE

INTERVIEWER TWO: *After all that, you just left?*

INTERVIEWER ONE: *I don't understand. You didn't even ask him if he stole the painting?*

MS KEATING: *But Bonnaire's doesn't think there was a painting to steal.*

INTERVIEWER ONE: *No...but you do. That's why you were there, isn't it?*

MS KEATING: *Yes.*

INTERVIEWER TWO: *So why did you—*

MS KEATING: *If you would let me finish?*

SIA COULDN'T EVEN look at Sebastian.

'I should go.'

'But do you want to?'

Yes. No. She honestly couldn't say any more.

He'd levelled her with such a look, one that she felt down to her toes. It was one that spoke of challenge and temptation. Sia would have run for the hills, but Henri?

While Sia was a combination of all the things that had happened *after* her father's arrest, Henri was all the things from before. The passionate, reckless, thoughtless parts of her mother and the intensely focused, creative, calculating parts of her father. Henri had been locked up for far too long and now she wanted to play.

She felt the sharp sting of arousal as his gaze locked onto her lips and desire rushed through her bloodstream, reaching parts of her body she barely recognised. She both welcomed and feared it, torn between the two. Never before had she felt such a thing.

'What I want has very little to do with it.'

'How strange,' he said, cocking his head to one side as if to inspect her from a different angle. 'I don't think I do that very often.'

'Do what?' she asked, genuinely confused.

'Self-restraint.'

The arrogance with which he said it, the sheer ego of the statement itself made it near impossible for Sia to keep her mouth closed against the shock. But she couldn't help the question that fell from her lips.

'You don't have self-restraint?'

'It's not that I don't have it. It's just that I don't need it.'

It was as if she had been drenched in ice-cold water. Any thread of attraction she thought she might have felt had been effectively doused by his…she internally growled…infuriating arrogance. Was this why he thought he could take the painting? Because he *could*? Because there was no reason that he could see *not* to? Given all the things that it had cost her, she was fuming.

She took a sip of champagne from the glass on the table between them to buy herself some time. She was so mad she could have walked away. And quite possibly would have, had it not been for the suspicion that it was exactly what he'd intended her to do.

Sebastian could see that it was working. He might have intensely disliked pretending to be the pampered, pompous playboy but it was better than what had passed between them moments before. When he'd touched her cheek with the pad of his thumb and felt a shower of fireworks across his skin.

It had been enough. Enough to know that whatever it was between them, it needed to stop. Especially if he was to find out what it was that *she* wanted from him. Because for a moment there he'd wanted to kiss her almost as much as he'd ever wanted the Durrántez. And that was inconceivable.

He took a sip from the champagne flute and looked around the Orangery. Anything to momentarily dull the impact of Sia Keating's stunning beauty. Was it only a few months ago in Paris that his best friend, Theo Tersi, had accused him of being jaded? Sebastian nearly choked on a laugh at the memory of it. He'd imagined it would take a few more years of indulging in a debauchery he'd welcomed with open arms a scant three years ago.

Though Sebastian wasn't sure what the Greek billionaire vintner would make of his current situation. Especially since Theo had developed something horrifyingly close to a moral code since he'd married and now had a child on the way. And not just a child, but a *royal* child. Who would have thought it? Theo Tersi, husband to a queen, soon-to-be father to a princess.

Still, although Sebastian had not exactly been lying when he'd told Sia he didn't need self-restraint, it didn't mean he was unfamiliar with the concept. In fact, he'd been overly familiar with it from the age of eighteen when his world had broken apart and his father had refused, or been incapable, of doing a single thing about it. Having spent his late teens and early twenties pulling his family from the ashes of financial ruin that had crashed down upon him and his sister Maria with such suddenness it felt as if nothing would ever be real and lasting in his life ever again, he had spent the following few years amassing an empire that rivalled anything the Dukes du Luen had ever before seen in the history of their nobility. During that time the fact that he'd also provided a roof over his father and stepmother's heads and a quite intentionally separate roof for him and his little sister, for whom he'd all but become a guardian, had left him feeling that he deserved to let off a little steam.

So he had. In whatever way he'd wanted, with whomever he'd wanted.

Although admittedly in the last few months, ever since the masked ball in Paris he'd accompanied Theo to, he'd not indulged. Perhaps that was why Sia Keating was having such a dramatic impact on him. Not because there was anything significant about her specifically—other than her beauty, of course—but simply because it had been quite some time since he'd lived up to his debauched reputation.

If he wasn't careful, he'd end up like Theo. Married and with a child on the way.

Just like his little sister.

But he *was* careful. He'd shouldered enough responsibility to last a lifetime. There were just three people left on his list until this whole Bonnaire's thing was completely resolved, and then it would be just him. Free to do as he wished, completely. And he chose to ignore the image that flashed in his mind of Sia Keating in a pool of royal blue silk sheets.

Which was presumably the only reason the question he asked came out of his mouth.

'What do you do for fun, Henri?'

I honestly don't know, would have been Sia's reaction. But Sebastian had asked Henri, so she answered.

'You mean besides having a drink with a notorious playboy?'

'Are you trying to tell me that you've had drinks with *other* notorious playboys?'

This time the mock arrogance and outrage in his tone lifted her lips into a reluctant smile. Because, for some reason, for all its apparent mockery, his reaction had felt so much more real than his insistence that he had no self-restraint.

'Are there so many of you?' She dramatically shuddered. 'Women be warned.'

'No, I can assure you. There are none like me.'

And Sia was beginning to think that he was right. There was something about the directness of his gaze, the way that his features almost seemed to relax when he was telling the truth. As if thankful for the brief respite from having to hold a mask constantly in place.

Sia turned her attention back to the question, feeling a slight ache in her heart as she did so. When was the last time that she'd had fun? When had she laughed until she'd cried, when had her stomach ached with joy and her chest heaved with an air so light it could have been helium rather than oxygen? Since she'd taken the job at Bonnaire's she'd worked all hours she could, desperate to prove her worth. To prove that she wasn't her father. Her salary hadn't left much over after rent and travel, food and basics. The offset was that she travelled with work, she supposed—Sharjarhere, Greece, Istanbul, New York to name just a few. But in that time the few friends she'd gathered from school or university had gone their own ways. A few work colleagues had stuck—Célia in particular. But she was now happily married and working on starting a family. But even with Célia it had been a close friendship, but perhaps not one based on fun exactly.

'It hurts that you have to think so hard to answer that question.'

Sia looked up to find him studying her once again, but this time sincerely, not for show, with his head angled towards his shoulder. She couldn't quite take the whiplash change of direction their conversation was taking. One moment full of tease and taunt, the other full of painful introspection.

'It is getting late. You have responsibilities? Work in the morning, I would imagine.'

The query hit a little too close to home. It felt a little as if he were pushing her, taunting her as if somehow he knew about her suspension and, despite the notion being fanciful, she couldn't help the bitter words which fell from her tongue.

'And what would you know of responsibilities?' she bit out, the acidity painful on her tongue.

He shrugged his shoulders. 'Very little. After all, apparently I'm the most notorious playboy in Europe.'

'So humble.'

'I don't believe in humility.'

'Really?'

'In most it is a lie and in others it is simply the desire to be considered worthy which, in itself, is hardly humble. I have neither the need to lie nor the desire to be considered worthy.'

'Because you don't think yourself worthy?' Sia asked, genuinely curious.

'Because I don't care how people consider me.'

'Not even the most beautiful woman in the room?' she asked ruefully.

'Oh. I *know* how you consider me,' he said with such a self-satisfied smile she had a strong urge to wipe it from his lips.

'And what would that be?'

'You consider me overly arrogant, purposely obtuse, careless and thoughtless. But I'm incredibly handsome, you can't help but be entertained by my charm and you're curious to see if there's a deep well of inner turmoil that could possibly redeem me.'

Well. He had her there.

'May I tell *you* a secret?' he asked, seemingly intent on using her words against her. She nodded and stilled as he moved towards her, one arm braced against the bar and the other at the back of her chair. As he leaned in, his lips close to her ear, she breathed in an aftershave that made her mouth water and her pulse race.

'There isn't,' he whispered, sending a chill down her spine as he promised no redemption.

As enticing as it was—the promise of hedonistic, ir- redeemable pleasure—she didn't fully believe it. So, be- fore he could lean back, before she could question her own intention, she turned her head ever so slightly, and this time it was her lips at his ear when she whispered, 'I don't believe you.'

'Really?' he said, leaning back and questioning her. Al- though the smile was steady on his lips, there was a dark shadow twisting in his eyes.

'Yes,' she said, locking her gaze with his. 'I'm very good at spotting fakes.'

* * *

The accusation struck a nerve he honestly didn't think he had. It made him angry. Oh, he'd been called fake before, but not in the sense that she had meant it. That Sia Keating, of all people, might just have seen behind his carefully constructed façade was untenable.

But, if he was being honest with himself, it wasn't her words that had struck deepest. It was that moment when she had turned to him, her lips barely a second from his and he'd wanted so much to take them with his own, to press against them, feel them, taste them.

Which was the only conceivable reason for him to say, 'You're not the only one, Sia.'

He watched as her head jerked back slightly as if she'd been struck and clenched his jaw against the wave of guilt. He abhorred violence against women, even verbally, and although no harsh words had been spoken a gauntlet had been thrown down. And now he'd started he just couldn't stop. 'But being able to spot fakes is a nice touch, given your occupation. I have to say, Bonnaire's has gone up in my estimation, sending such a tempting morsel my way.'

'I don't know what to be more offended by. Being described as a "morsel" or your assumption that I'm here because of Bonnaire's. I assure you, Mr Rohan de Luen I am here for myself.'

'I may have been exiled, but I'm still a duke, Ms Keating,' he said with all the imperiousness he didn't feel in that moment.

'Forgive me, *Your Grace*, a slip of the tongue,' she said insincerely.

He stifled a growl of arousal before it could reach the back of his throat as his mind suggested colourful displays of what he would very much like to do with her tongue.

'If you are here for yourself and not on Bonnaire's business, then why the use of a fake name?'

'If you knew it was fake, why entertain the deception for so long?' she quickly returned.

He could have pushed for an answer to his question—part of him wanted to, but now was not the time. Instead, he answered hers. 'Perhaps I wanted to see how far you would take it.'

'All the way,' she replied, determination flashing in her eyes.

'And, just so there isn't any misunderstanding, what does that look like to you?'

'To prove that you stole the painting.'

'Ah,' he said, for a moment regretting the images her accidental double entendre had thrust into his mind. 'The painting which I believe Sheikh Abrani has himself stated is a fake?' The careless tone of his own voice was barely audible over the pulse pounding in his ear. Bonnaire's, the Sheikh…they had done as expected. Hidden within the lie and taken the hit. But Sia? Now the gloves were off and she'd admitted her true intention—an intention that went far beyond what he'd have expected a corrupt Bonnaire's employee to have admitted. If the painting had been valued by Sean Johnson this wouldn't have been a problem at all. But Sia Keating was a new player and as such all the more dangerous for them all.

'But it wasn't,' Sia ground out, repeating her insistence that the painting she'd valued wasn't a fake.

'And you are sure that you didn't just make a mistake?'

She scowled and Sebastian thought that for a moment he saw more than just professional ego shimmering in her eyes.

'Very. You stole that painting and replaced it with a forgery. I have absolutely no idea why you would then have arranged for the painting to be damaged in a way that revealed the whole thing, nor why Abrani would claim it to have been a fake all along. And, to be honest, I don't care. But I *know* you did.'

'How?' he asked, genuinely curious.

'In the last ten years you have made twelve offers for that painting. Each one has been turned down. You have shown zero interest in any other Durrántez painting, yet *this one* clearly holds a fascination for you. At the private viewing, of every single person there, you alone did not watch in fascinated horror the damage being done to a painting valued at one hundred million pounds. And why? Because you knew it wasn't worth even a fraction of that.'

'That's what you've got? A hunch and the fact that I was more interested in my date than a painting?'

'It's enough for me,' she said mutinously.

'Good for you. But what is it that you think you can threaten me with? You can't go to the Sheikh—he has admitted to owning a forgery. You can't go to the police. No one has reported a theft. And the fake painting was damaged before it was sold, so no crime has been committed,' he concluded, shrugging his shoulders.

'I could go to the press,' she said, anger sparking in her eyes like fireworks.

'And you'd just look like someone who is trying to cover up a professional mistake through desperation and lies,' he said in a tone that was painfully patronising to his own ears.

'I could steal it back.'

He ground out a laugh and, as he expected, it ignited the rage within her. 'You'd have to find it first.'

'You think this is funny?' she demanded.

He hardly did, but he needed her to think that.

'I've been suspended. So you didn't just steal a painting, Your Grace, you stole my job, my career, my future. Everything that I've worked towards for my entire life.'

Sebastian felt as if he'd been slapped. Bonnaire's had sent probably the *only* person with integrity to Sharjarhere and because of him she stood to lose her job. Guilt fought with his own personal need for justice and in that moment Sebastian had the horrible feeling that there was no way that they would both walk away with what they wanted.

He could have sworn in that moment that he felt the tide of injustice wash against him from where she sat. Injustice, betrayal, loss. He knew those words. Knew that anger.

'So if it takes me a year—ten years—I'll find the proof. Because there's *always* proof. You didn't do this by yourself, you couldn't have. I will track down everyone that helped you, every single person you've spoken to in the last six months. I will visit every single place you've been in the last six years. If you try to move the painting I will know about it. If you try to sell the painting I will hear about it. You might be a billionaire businessman with contacts around the world, but I have lived and breathed art since I was born. And I will use every single contact I have to make sure that I get my hands *back* on the real Durrántez.'

'That's quite the speech,' he commented drily despite how impressed he was. While part of his mind worked through the implications of her words, the other recognised just how incredible she had become in that moment. It was as if with the challenge, in her desperation, she had risen from flames and become a phoenix—glorious, golden, bold beyond belief and utterly enthralling. Everything in him wanted to reach for her, to hold her to him, to clutch that power to him.

Everything apart from the fact that if she did as she

promised it wasn't just he who would pay the price. Each person involved had known what the implications were. Each person had made their decision freely. But they had also put their faith in him and his plan. The plan he'd assured them would come off without a hitch. Never would he let anything happen to them because of the one truly selfish thing he'd ever done.

Sia Keating uncrossed her legs and stepped from her chair around to the opening in the cage. It felt oddly like a portent of things to come. Unable to stay behind, he stood and met her head-on. Something primal roared within him and satisfaction uncurled in his gut as she stood, as he'd predicted, almost face to face with him.

'I am going to find out exactly what happened, who helped you and tell the world,' she promised him, golden sparks firing in her eyes captivating him as she stepped past him.

Once again, the sight of her backless dress taunted his arousal. The incredible pride stiffening her shoulder blades made him smile in appreciation even as he thrust all thoughts of expectation from his mind.

He reached for her wrist, encasing it firmly but gently, and pulled her back round to face him, cutting off the view that had sent him into a sensual torment.

'You're playing a dangerous game,' he said, his tone darker and harsher than he'd intended.

'You started it,' she replied, but there was nothing childish about the huskily delivered accusation.

That he really couldn't deny. Nor could he any longer ignore the only possible solution he'd been able to come up with. It was risky, but it could work.

'I have an offer.'

'You think you can buy me off?'

'Why would I need to buy you off?'

'Because you stole the painting.'

'I haven't said that I did. But neither can I have you running around making such accusations. It's not exactly good for business,' he sniffed, aiming for both nonchalant and irritating.

'Which business? Art thief or hotelier?'

'If I am guilty of your accusation, then both, I would assume.'

He could practically feel her frustration crashing against him like the tide. Good. Perhaps she'd be so incensed that she'd agree to his crazy proposition. Despite the fact that he was making this up on the spot, Sebastian had always been a goal-orientated quick thinker. This was what he was good at and what most people, who believed the carefully constructed careless playboy façade, took for granted. Thinking through the options, there was only one sure-fire way to know just how dangerous Sia Keating was.

Keep your friends close and your enemies closer.

'What if I gave you fourteen days?' he asked.

'Fourteen days of what?'

'Unfettered access to my life. Twenty-four hours a day for fourteen days, and if—at the end of it—you have not found your proof then you give up. Walk away and never think of it again.'

'Two weeks?'

'You should consider yourself lucky. Two days is my usual tolerance for female company.'

'I'm not your usual choice of female companion,' she returned so quickly he had to suppress a smile.

'I'm beginning to see that.'

'And if I *find* proof? Find the painting?'

He smiled, dark and predatory. 'If I am inept enough an art thief to leave either proof or painting lying around for you to find, then you are welcome to them.'

* * *

Sia couldn't believe what she was hearing. Not only did he clearly believe that she was incapable of doing what she'd said, he was also teasing her with every word. She fisted her hands so hard she knew she'd leave crescent marks in her palms. She wanted nothing more than to prove him wrong, prove him guilty.

She wasn't stupid. She knew that she didn't have the funds or the contacts to investigate him with the same depth as he was suggesting. But neither was she naïve enough to think it would be that easy.

'What does this "access" entail?' she asked cautiously.

'You can accompany me wherever I go. You can be by my side for business meetings and events, breakfast, lunch and dinner if you wish.'

'You said twenty-four hours a day...' The question came out of her mouth before she'd had time to properly think it through.

'You are more than welcome to join me for the nights, Ms Keating. My bed is big enough, I assure you.'

'As is your ego, clearly,' she bit out.

Rather than being bruised by the put-down, Sebastian seemed instead to relish it.

'My properties are large enough. There are plenty of spare rooms. That is, if you don't trust me not to do a midnight flit with the stolen painting.'

'I don't trust you as far as I can throw you.'

'Wise, Ms Keating, wise,' he warned.

'Which is precisely why I don't believe that you would make it this easy for me. What is stopping you from simply lying your way out of this? What makes this better than me investigating on my own?' she demanded.

He seemed to give the question, and her, some thought. His eyes assessed her once again—not the heated open perusal of before but more thoughtful, calculating—and it made her feel worthy.

'I'll allow you one question a day that I will answer with complete truth, no matter the question.'

'Just one?' she asked, buying herself some time, surprised by the addendum to their deal.

'It's more than I've given any other woman in my life.'

And she believed him. She hadn't been lying when she'd told him that she could spot fakes and forgeries. Her childhood had been built on it. Her career had been defined by it. And now her future would depend on it.

This was her only chance. It was more than she could have hoped for really. She wouldn't have been able to sustain Henri's persona for more than one night. It was too... tempting? She shook that thought away and focused on what Sebastian was offering.

'Okay. I'll do it.'

'It will mean a large upheaval of your life for the next fourteen days,' he cautioned.

'That...won't be a problem,' she replied, heat still simmering across her skin from her suspension.

'No...husbands or lovers to get insanely jealous and come after me with a pitchfork?' There was a teasing tone in his voice but his eyes held no spark of humour, only dangerous curiosity.

'No, but it's worth noting that I have my own pitchfork.'

'Good for you.'

His apparent support only infuriated her more. 'You don't want your lawyers to draw up any legally binding documents?' she asked, slightly surprised that he hadn't demanded she sign a million non-disclosure agreements.

'I'm happy with a gentleman's agreement.'

'You are hardly a gentleman.'

'Then perhaps *your* lawyers would be so obliging?'

Her silence said enough.

'Thought as much.' From his pocket he removed a sleek white embossed card and offered it to her. In a glance she took in the address and contact information for Sebastian Rohan de Luen.

'Then I will see you at nine tomorrow morning.'

She felt his retreat from the room the way that warmth dissipated as the sun set and her fingers closed around the stiff card in her palm.

Game on, Sebastian. Game on.

CHAPTER FOUR

INTERVIEWER ONE: *So, let me get this straight. The Duque de Gaeten, invited you to...what? Live with him for two weeks and you said yes?*

MS KEATING: *Yes.*

INTERVIEWER ONE: *After you told him you believed he'd stolen the painting?*

MS KEATING: *Yes.*

INTERVIEWER ONE: *Knowing that you were looking for proof of the stolen painting?*

MS KEATING: *Yes.*

INTERVIEWER TWO: *[sotto] What was his house like?*

INTERVIEWER ONE: *[clears throat]*

INTERVIEWER TWO: *[louder] I mean, in which of his houses?*

SIA LOOKED UP at the mansion in front of her with a strange sense of déjà vu from the night before. Once again, she was looking at a shiny black door with a bronze door knocker, only this wasn't a lion's head, it was that of a stag.

She could still back out. She didn't *have* to do this. Only…he had taken everything from her. She'd put her past behind her and stepped towards a new future. If she didn't prove to Bonnaire's that he had stolen the painting, that she had been right, she would never work in the industry again.

She'd lost so much. She refused to lose this too.

Which was why she found herself being led down a black and white checked marble floor towards a lower level of the Knightsbridge townhouse by the uniformed butler who had answered the door. Whilst still trying to hide her natural disapproval towards Sebastian for having an honest-to-God butler, she frowned a little as the air began to turn warm and she could have sworn she caught a faint trace of chlorine. She followed the butler into the room beyond the door and the scent dramatically increased as she inhaled a gasp of shock.

The butler retreated with little acknowledgement of her surprise, apparently used to such a reaction, leaving her standing beside a pool the colour of a cloudless summer's sky. The entire basement seemed to have been covered in sandstone, up-lit in a way that made it feel both warm and secretive. Along the length of the pool, the stone curved into arches with lush green vegetation that veiled the faint traces of chlorine somehow.

The sound of lapping against the edges of the pool drew her attention back to the water to where she could see a powerful shape gliding towards her. She was speechless as Sebastian broke the water of the deeper end of the pool, thrusting wet hair away from his face, his eyes—almost the same colour as the water—locked on her without shame or embarrassment or even any intent that Sia could discern, making her even more uncomfortable. He placed his hands on the side and drew himself out of the pool with the kind of grace that she was envious of. And then she had no thought for grace.

The last time she had seen a man in a swimming costume it had been on Brighton beach, their shorts had been baggy, their legs were like twigs and definitely turning that particularly British shade of burnt.

In tight-fitting thigh-level shorts Sebastian was none of those things. Well used to assessing pieces of art, her eyes went to work over every single inch of his body. She couldn't help but watch as water dripped from the hair he had swept back, onto his shoulders, running over muscles that spoke of more exercise than just swimming. She followed its progress over the dips and turns as it fell over pecs and abdominals that made her ache to touch. His hips were tapered just slightly, but not too much, making her deeply aware of his masculinity. She tried to retain objectivity, observe purely professionally, but she just couldn't. She might have studied the human form more than most doctors, followed the direction of paint across scenes of sensuality so incredible they'd been preserved for hundreds of years, traced her hands over cool marble sculptures... but she'd never seen this much of a man in real life and couldn't help but blush. It was almost painful as it spread over her cheeks and she bit her lip from...what, she honestly couldn't say. He was overwhelming. And by the time she raised her eyes to his, sparkling with more than a little awareness, she knew he knew it too.

'We like to keep the temperature warm in here,' he said, reaching for a towel, still not breaking eye contact, 'for obvious reasons. There are costumes you can borrow any time you like.'

'I'd rather not wear your girlfriend's cast-offs,' she replied, surprising herself with the acidity in her tone. But Sebastian? No, he seemed to find her response amusing.

'The costumes are for guests. My girlfriend wouldn't need one,' he said, turning and offering her a view of his back that made her want to dig her nails into the defined musculature there. She tried to shake off whatever spell he'd cast on her as he wrapped the towel around his waist.

'Breakfast?' he asked, walking past her back to the door towards the main part of the house, his bare feet leaving quickly drying watermarks where he stepped. She suddenly had the strange desire to place her own foot within the imprint, to follow in his steps, to slip into this strange world of butlers, indoor pools and swimming naked that was most definitely not hers.

Sebastian was aware of Sia behind him as he stalked through the halls of his London apartment. It had never bothered him before, going straight from the pool to breakfast, he'd never cared that his feet were bare, his skin half dry, his hair still wet. But there was something about Sia... so buttoned-up and fully clothed that he was conscious of it all. Not *self*-conscious—no, his ego was far above such things. But he still reached for the white robe that his butler had left for him beside the table where breakfast had been placed.

He'd hoped that last night he'd imagined it. The power her beauty had on him. Tried to convince himself that it had been a trick of the light, or the shock of her intention, even the challenge that she presented. But no. It was still there. That unwavering sense of...electricity, energy arcing between them. And he couldn't tell if she could feel it. Sometimes it seemed that she could and sometimes not.

He gestured for her to sit before he took his own seat. He ran his eyes over the breakfast table. A steaming pot of coffee, fresh fruit, croissants, a selection of meats and even a few boiled eggs. He nearly laughed. He wondered what Sia would say if he told her that he usually just had toast.

He doubted that she'd believe him.

'Coffee?' he offered. He was already pouring her a cup before she'd nodded her agreement.

'So, is this what you do all day?' she asked. 'Swim, eat and luxuriate?'

'You want to know what I do?' he asked and, in doing so, pointed out the rather presumptuous, slightly defensive tone of her question, before playing right into her preconceptions. 'As little as possible.'

Which, of course, was a lie. He'd worked through the night, finishing only at six that morning, dealing with a crisis in the Hong Kong hotel. In truth, he was exhausted, running on fumes and his hundredth cup of coffee in the last eight hours. Not that he would let her see that for a second.

Sia, in contrast, looked like a breath of fresh air. She wore a crisp white buttonless V-neck shirt tucked into high-waisted, wide-legged blue wool palazzo trousers. Given that, perhaps she had just been hot in the pool room. He got the distinct impression these were her work clothes. They were high quality and looked good on her— they'd have to, of course, especially if she were meeting sheikhs, royals, billionaires and whoever else might have their hands on hundreds of millions of pounds' worth of art. But they didn't necessarily feel like her.

He had to drag his eyes away as she reached for the coffee. The sight of her slender wrist, skin that had seemed pale in the pool room now, in the natural light, looked like honeyed cream, and thoughts of the deep tan of his own rough skin next to hers nearly unmanned him.

Instead he focused on the small holdall at the doorway to the room.

'Is that all you brought?' he asked without thinking.

It was the absence of movement that made him realise. Most people moved, flinched, reacted to a wound—verbal or otherwise. Sia seemed different, but in her silence he heard her response like a shout. *It's all I could afford.* And he felt like an ass.

'I'd like to look around.'

He gestured for her to do so and Sia was surprised. 'You don't want to…' she shrugged '…give me a tour?' The idea that she'd be let loose in his home was both a surprise and slightly frustrating. 'I can just thoroughly investigate the entire apartment?'

'I have nothing to hide,' he said, taking a sip of his coffee.

'*Here.* You have nothing to hide *here*,' she replied, unable to keep the disappointment from her voice.

He quirked an eyebrow in question.

'You have, as you've been quite proud enough to declare—a large number of hotels around the world, at least three residences, one in London, one in Siena and the other in New York. It is highly unlikely that you would offer me complete access if you had the painting here. However, in case you are attempting a double bluff, I'll just take a turn,' she concluded as she pushed back out of her seat.

'By all means. And when you are done investigating, Benjamin will show you to your room. In the meantime, I have some very important luxuriating to be getting on with. But if you need me, I'm yours.'

His last words repeated on a loop in Sia's mind as she made her way up the ridiculous amount of steps in the five-floor mansion that Sebastian called his London apartment. Despite her words about a double bluff, she knew he'd never offer her access like this if there was even a hope that she'd run into the painting. So it was unlikely that was here.

But as she walked the hallways lined with expensive art collections, priceless antiques and furniture, her disappointment gave way to awe, which in turn gave way to confusion. It just didn't feel like him. It was incredible but staid, old, *moneyed*. It didn't speak of the charming, game-playing playboy. There was no sense of *fun* in the décor. She had half expected to find a painting from the *Dogs Playing Poker* series hanging on the wall in between a Rembrandt and a Vermeer, but there wasn't one.

And all this space… What did one person *do* with it? She pushed open another door into another empty bedroom. Each one was perfectly made up, clean, immaculate, as if waiting to be filled, and suddenly it struck her as a very lonely house.

Down another flight of stairs, the smooth curved banister cool beneath the palm of her hand, and it looked just like the two floors above it. Barely taking note of the impressive paintings on display any more, Sia wondered if Sebastian had grown numb to their beauty in the same way she felt herself becoming, and almost laughed. Less than a few hours in his world and she had stopped caring whether the next painting was a Picasso or a Degas. Though, even as she thought it, she peered around, hoping that it actually *might* be a Degas.

Smiling at the turn of her own thoughts, she pushed open a door that she quickly realised was not like the others. The sheets on the bed weren't turned down with almost military precision, but were crumpled in a heap. The pillows still bore the impression of being recently slept on, and the air still held the scent of aftershave that was unnervingly familiar. A sound should have drawn her attention to the slightly open doorway in the corner of the room but she couldn't tear her eyes away from the impossibly large bed. She was in the midst of calculating just how many people it might be feasible to get on it when the flash of something at the edge of her sightline drew her gaze.

Once again, the man had a towel around his waist and far too much delicious skin on display. His muscles rippled as his arm towel-dried his hair and the breath caught in Sia's lungs.

'We really must stop meeting like this.'

She practically squeaked as she fled the room in a burst of shocked frustration made only worse as Sebastian's laugh chased her down the corridor.

It was strange having another person in his house. He never entertained his female guests here, despite what he'd said to Sia in the pool room. So, having Sia move independently around his space left him feeling...out of sorts. He'd been halfway through his dinner when he'd realised that she might have wanted to join him, his food sitting uncomfortably in his stomach until Benjamin informed him that Sia had asked to have her dinner in her room.

Reluctantly, he had to concede that he really hadn't thought this through. Yet it had been the only way to ensure that the people who had helped him—who *he* had helped—had his protection as much now as ever. So, reaffirming his conviction in his decision, he'd instructed Benjamin to invite Sia for a drink.

And as Sebastian looked out across the London skyline from the luxurious roof terrace, he turned his mind to the puzzle that was Sia Keating. He was surprised that she hadn't yet asked her question. He'd thought it might have been the first thing she'd say to him. She was clearly gutsy enough to have approached him in Victoriana, even to have accused him outright of the theft of a painting worth over one hundred million pounds. But she'd blushed like an innocent in the pool room, and run from his room as if the hounds of hell were on her heels. And the only real distinction between the two had been the use of the alias Henri.

'It's a beautiful home you have here.'

Still dressed in the same white shirt and wide blue trousers, there honestly didn't seem to be a wrinkle or hair out of place as she walked towards where he sat as the sun hovered lazily on the horizon as if reluctant to leave.

He stood, gesturing for her to take a seat at the table opposite him. Her eyes seemed to soften momentarily at his manners, until his response checked hers.

'This isn't my home.' He hadn't meant for it to sound so sharp. It gave away too much and she knew it.

'Then what is?' she asked as she sat in the seat, briefly smiling at Benjamin as he poured her a glass of wine.

'Is that your question?' Sebastian asked as Benjamin retreated.

'Not the one you have agreed to answer truthfully, no.' Her eyes settled on his with a confidence he found somewhere between Sia and Henri.

'My primary residence is in Siena,' he said, answering her original question. 'It was the first property I bought after leaving Spain.'

'Do you miss it? Spain?'

There was a pause while he chose whether to answer her or not.

'Yes. It is a strange thing to know that you will never be allowed to go home.'

'When was the last time you were there?'

'I was eighteen. My father made a bad choice of who he wanted to go into business with. But he also convinced a few other noble families, and not just in Spain, to invest in the same deal. So when the deal…fell through we weren't the only ones to lose everything. The shame it brought, not just to our family or the other investors, but the royals was immense. And because my father was the main investor and the one who encouraged the others to follow his lead, we were exiled.'

The bare facts did not convey what had happened but he could not stop the images from that night pouring into his mind. He felt the shock of it all over again. Remembering how men had come to his home, ripped things from the rooms and the walls, while Eduardo had sat in his chair, glass of wine in hand, ignoring Valeria, who was screaming obscenities at him. Maria had been standing at the top of the stairs in her nightdress, scared out of her mind, not knowing what was going on. Sebastian had practically shoved the men out of the house while they'd threatened to come back with the police and legal documents, which he'd told them to do.

Realising that his father was incapable of doing anything, there had only been one way forward. In less than twenty-four hours Sebastian had contacted lawyers, taken inventory of all their estates and what was left after the Spanish government had seized their property. With the help of a few remaining staff, he'd got Maria packed and told Valeria to take care of herself and her husband, as a man ticked off the only items they were allowed to leave with—possessions from their mother's estate from before she'd married Eduardo.

Not that they'd remained with the family for long. Over the next few months Sebastian had been forced to sell everything that wasn't nailed down. The only thing he'd kept was for Maria—their mother's necklace, which she never took off. He'd kept nothing for himself. In part because there'd been only one thing he'd wanted from his childhood and, nearly twenty years later, he'd finally got it.

'It was hardest on Maria,' he finally said, his voice gravelly as if roughened by tension. 'She was only eight when it happened. Having to leave her friends, her school...it was difficult.'

Sia felt an empathy with his sister. She herself had been seven when her entire life had changed. But she couldn't help wondering...

'And what about you?' she asked.

'Is *that* your question for today?'

'No,' she replied, oddly frustrated with the constraints on their conversation.

She felt his eyes on hers for a moment before he turned to take a sip from his glass—a red, she noted, while she had white wine. She watched as his throat undulated as he swallowed a mouthful of the rich alcohol, strangely hypnotised by the movement. She'd known that, until Benjamin had arrived with Sebastian's invitation, she'd been hiding. Even now she felt a blush threaten to rise on her cheeks at the memory of Sebastian in his room, at his presence even now.

The evening's gentle breeze soothed her heated skin and she looked out across a skyline of London she'd never seen in person before. Above the table was a crisscross lattice with clematis winding through it. Large old-fashioned light bulbs gave off a gentle glow and the large terracotta pots of shrubs and sweet herbs worked to make her forget that she was in the heart of one of the world's busiest cities.

'Why Henri?' he asked, pulling her back to the present.

Sia thought about not answering, just like he had, but she needed him on side for when she did ask her question.

'Henri is short for Henrietta—my middle name. My father used to call me Henri when I lived with them.'

'What happened for you not to be living with your parents?' he asked, the light of curiosity shining bright in the blue depths of his eyes.

'You mean you didn't have someone behind the scenes run up a file on me?'

He shrugged. 'Where's the fun in that? We have fourteen days in which you are determined to thoroughly investigate me. Perhaps I could do the same.'

Something she chose to ignore arced between them—a kind of energy, or electricity even—but it faded into the background as the realisation that he might not know who she was began to dawn on her.

'You really don't know?' she asked out loud. The narrowing of his eyes was the only response he gave, clearly not enjoying being in the dark. 'My father was John Keating.'

The narrowed eyes turned into a deep frown and Sia began to suspect that when Sebastian was quiet he was at his most dangerous.

'As in...'

'The most famous art forger in Europe? The man whose estimated profits were beyond ten million pounds? The man who was shopped to the police by his wife? *That* John Keating. Yes,' she replied, nodding. 'You see, I'm quite used to being in the company of infamy.'

As she said the words intended to bruise his ego a double-edged sword opened up a wound she'd thought had healed a while ago. Despite that, she pushed on. 'After my father's quite public arrest and the shocking scandal of my mother's betrayal, my Aunt Eleanor took me in. She is the opposite of her sister, Michaela. Conservative, steady job, never married—though I think taking care of me managed to scare away the few suitors who might have managed to get past her strong inclination towards disdain. But she took me in when she had very little money and no real obligation,' Sia concluded, still firm in the belief that she owed her aunt a great debt.

'She was your family, of course there was obligation,' Sebastian said, as if such a thing was as true to him as the sky was blue. But, for Sia, she wasn't so sure, because if it *were* true then her relationship with her mother might have been different.

'She put me in a good school and she gave me the boundaries that had been missing from my life with John and Michaela.'

'Where is your mother now?'

'Probably passed out in the bed of a married man.'

From the uncharacteristic look of shock on Sebastian's face, she could tell that her response had surprised him. But Sia had spent years compartmentalising her feelings about both her mother and her father, and it had been years since she'd actually seen her mother in person.

'Of all the careers you could have gone into, why art evaluation?'

'It's in my blood,' she answered immediately, as if there had never been any other option.

As Sebastian began to draw the information she had revealed together, painting his own picture of what it must have been like to try and pursue a career in a world where her name was not only infamous but linked to a man who had made it his life's work to deceive people like her future bosses... Not only was he incredibly impressed, he was also angry.

Angry because it wasn't supposed to have been Sia who had valued the painting. No, it should have been Sean Johnson, a man who *had* done enough to deserve whatever punishment Bonnaire's would lay upon Sia. Sebastian couldn't help but rub his jaw. Once again, the acrid taste of guilt on his tongue blotted out the heavy Bordeaux. He'd really messed things up for Sia Keating and presently he couldn't quite see a way for him to make it up to her without losing everything that he'd worked towards.

'Ask your question,' he stated.

'Why would Sheikh Abrani say that his painting was fake when it wasn't?'

INTERVIEWER ONE: *What kind of question is that?*

MS KEATING: *One he wasn't expecting.*

INTERVIEWER TWO: *Why didn't you just ask him where the painting was?*

MS KEATING: *He would have found a way round it.*

INTERVIEWER TWO: *But he promised to tell you the truth.*

MS KEATING: *[sighs] He would have said,* In a crate, *or* Somewhere safe, *or* I don't know—*which could easily have been the real answer if he'd asked someone to take it off his hands for a while and not tell him where it was being kept.*

INTERVIEWER TWO: *Huh.*

INTERVIEWER ONE: *So why did you ask about the Sheikh?*

It was honestly the very last thing that Sebastian had expected to come out of her mouth. He'd been curious to see what direction she would take and had certainly given her enough credit to know that she wouldn't be crass enough to come straight out and ask if he'd done it.

But that she'd veered so completely from what he'd expected, planned and prepared for her to ask... *That* was clever.

'I'm not sure how I would know the answer to that question,' he hedged.

'Take a run at it,' she said coolly, just as the wind picked up in the leaves on the plants placed at either corner of the roof terrace.

He looked across the skyline, unseeing of the shapes that interrupted the night sky, the way that lit windows merged with stars, the moon shining down on them all, and instead picked his words carefully.

'The Sheikh won't admit to the theft because it's in his interests also for there to be no fuss about this.'

'Why?'

'If there is a theft investigation then the police would be involved and they would discover that the Sheikh is hardly a pillar of the community.'

'But the theft has cost him one hundred million pounds,' Sia said, apparently appalled by the loss of an inconceivable sum of money.

'So, imagine the amount he's protecting from a criminal investigation. These days they're a little more hot on state representatives taking bribes and making backroom deals than they once were.'

'What do you mean?'

He sighed, not having imagined the turn the conversation would take that evening. 'What do you know of the Sheikh?' he asked.

'I met him only that once, when I was in Sharjarhere to evaluate the Durrántez.'

'What did you think of him?'

* * *

Sia searched her mind, unable to shake the feeling that this was some kind of test.

'I was only introduced to him and then he...' she shrugged '...left. I can't say that he filled me with warmth and joy, but he didn't have to.' Only that wasn't quite the truth. Now that she forced herself to look back and consider what he had been like, she remembered that she hadn't liked the way that he had treated his staff, nor the feeling that had permeated the walls of the palace. A feeling that was very much like fear, or the expectation of it at least.

'Let me tell you a little something about the Sheikh. Like many rulers, he is well educated, obscenely rich, incredibly well connected, which of course has absolutely nothing to do with the first two. On the surface he appears to be open-minded, fairly interested in ecological developments, was one of the first to sign the Paris Climate Agreement, and has an incredible breeding programme for his thoroughbred racehorses which also seeks to support endangered animals.'

'What's not to like?' she asked, even though she knew that something was coming. Something she almost didn't want to know.

'What's not to like is that *beneath* the surface he is a despot who brings his full force down upon someone's head if he deems that person to have offended or simply not done as was asked. His vengeance is cruel, bordering on psychotic, and there are areas beneath his palace where family members are kept and abused for his pleasure. Their crime? Wanting to leave the country. Four of his daughters were married in political alliances before they were sixteen, and the youngest only managed to escape this fate by the fact he literally gambled away her hand in marriage.

And that, Sia, was considered a *good* thing by his daughter. It was her only lifeline to freedom.'

'But that's…inconceivable.'

'Why, because you met him? You spent a few hours in his home? Because Bonnaire's would do business with him?'

'I can't believe it,' she said, even as his words were beginning to settle into a place that clicked with something already there in her mind.

'Sia, if you are so good at spotting fakes, look at me and tell me whether I'm lying.'

She didn't want to raise her eyes and meet his. Because she knew what she would find. And suddenly she was angry. Angry at Sebastian. If it hadn't been for him, she wouldn't have known about theft, forgery, nepotism, trapped family members, forced marriages and possible backroom deals at the company that employed her.

'You should go to bed. You've had a long day and will have another long day tomorrow.'

'Why?' she said, suddenly feeling the late hour of the evening against her skin.

'Because tomorrow we're going to the Caribbean.'

'What?'

'You don't have to come. But I'm keeping to my offer, for you to be my shadow for fourteen days. And my business doesn't stop for you, Ms Keating.'

'But I thought your business was doing as little as possible.'

'It is. I just like to be surrounded by exquisite beauty while doing it.'

How could he turn her feelings around with a carefully constructed and perfectly delivered line? Because whether *she* was the exquisite beauty he'd easily mentioned or the Caribbean, Sia couldn't say—not to mention her frustration at effectively being sent to bed. But she was beginning to see the pattern with Sebastian. He gave both truths and lies in equal measure so that she never knew where she stood with him.

Sebastian stayed outside for at least an hour after Sia departed. She might have been mad at him—it wasn't that hard to tell with her—but he'd had to send her away. He'd seen how the dawning realisation of what she'd got herself into had begun to chip away at her defences and he couldn't watch them crumble. She was going to need her armour—every inch of it—for what was coming. Because he simply could not afford to hold back.

CHAPTER FIVE

INTERVIEWER ONE: *So let me get this straight. The reason you didn't answer our calls was because you got on a plane with the man you believed to have stolen a painting from Bonnaire's and flew to the Caribbean?*

MS KEATING: *I believe he stole the painting from Sheikh Abrani—but yes.*

INTERVIEWER TWO: *Wouldn't you have?*

INTERVIEWER ONE: *[sotto] That's not the point.*

MS KEATING: *I thought it possible that the painting might be there.*

INTERVIEWER TWO: *And was it?*

WIND BUFFETED SIA'S hair, whipped at her thin long-sleeved T-shirt and almost managed to push her back an inch from where she stood beside the folded down steps to a private jet. But she braced herself against the wind, just as she ground her teeth together to prevent herself from slapping the smirk from Sebastian's handsome face.

The reason for the smirk was presently resting by his feet. The wooden crate, approximately twenty by twenty-four inches, also happened to be the exact measurements of the Durrántez painting *Woman in Love*.

'Are you sure you don't want to see inside of it?' he taunted.

'No, I'm fine, thanks.'

But she did. She *really* did. And he knew it. She couldn't work out whether he would be either that reckless or that arrogant to wave the real painting in front of her. But she would lose if she did look and lose if she didn't. At least by *not* doing so she could cling to the belief that it made her seem as if she didn't care.

Despite the traces of aviation fuel on the wind, there was something startlingly fresh about being in the middle of this flat, sparse private airfield outside of London. And Sia had to acknowledge that she felt much more awake and refreshed than she would have thought.

She'd imagined that in spending the night in Sebastian Rohan de Luen's townhouse she would have tossed and turned into the early hours, her mind whirling. But the moment her head had hit the pillow she'd fallen into a deep dreamless sleep. Before being woken up by Sebastian's servant. Or house man? She still didn't know what to call him.

All of which had meant that she hadn't spent the night wondering whether she should or shouldn't be going to the Caribbean with a suspected art thief, a confirmed international playboy. She'd been in too much of a daze to do anything other than agree when he'd first told her. And this morning?

If she said no she'd return to her flat in Archway, with no job for a month—and in all probability no pay either—and she'd be no closer to proving that she hadn't made a mistake. No. The only way she could ensure her professional reputation remained intact was to find the painting, and the only way she could do that was to follow him wherever he went.

She purposefully turned away from Sebastian, who was looking more attractive than anyone had a right to in a pair of aviation sunglasses, jeans that lovingly hugged his thighs and a dark blue long-sleeved Henley. Despite the casual look, everything exuded more money than she could earn in a month. She was on the verge of asking what they were waiting for when three dark, sleek town cars pulled onto the runway in an almost hypnotising procession.

They pulled up in a line beside the small jet and a man got out of the back of the middle car with a large black duffel bag handcuffed to each wrist. Sia watched, incredulous, as the man nodded to Sebastian, walked up the stairs, deposited the bags apparently in the back of the aeroplane and returned to the back of the middle town car, upon which all three of the sleek vehicles resumed their balletic procession and left the airfield.

'I don't believe you,' she tossed over her shoulder as she approached the stairs.

'What?' Sebastian asked, clearly finding it difficult to keep the laughter from his voice.

'You did that on purpose.'

'I don't know what you mean.'

'I don't think there's anything in those bags more important than kitty litter,' she ground out.

'To a cat owner without kitty litter they'd be pretty important,' he said, following her up the stairs and into the cabin.

As she poked her head into the surprisingly spacious area in the cabin and she rolled her eyes at the ridiculous duffel bags, each strangely strapped into a seat, her mobile phone vibrated in her pocket for the fourth time that morning.

'Please,' said Sebastian, 'don't let me stop you.'

'It's fine.'

'Are you sure? It could be important. And you won't be able to answer it in flight.'

She retrieved her phone and switched it off in front of him. But the problem was that she knew it probably was important. It had to be for Bonnaire's to have called her four times in the last hour and a half.

But they had suspended her. They had suspended her, and it didn't feel right. After the conversation with Sebastian the night before, she'd played the last meeting with her boss over and over again in her head. Why hadn't David been able to access her folders from the initial assessment? Why hadn't Abrani had the authentication papers to hand? He'd said he'd passed them onto Sean, but it was highly irregular to separate the papers from the painting. And she'd not seen them when she'd got back to Bonnaire's. And now she couldn't access the files to see if they had ever been there. But if they weren't, if they never had been…then Bonnaire's and Sean would have knowingly auctioned a painting without authentication papers, which was not exactly illegal. But the certificate of authentication acted like a sales receipt. It meant that they couldn't be sure that the Sheikh had come by the painting through legal means. And Bonnaire's shouldn't have been doing business under those circumstances. But they had.

'Please, sit where you like,' he said, cutting into her thoughts, before heading towards the cockpit.

She looked about her, trying to work out where she should sit. She waited for a moment for Sebastian to return from speaking to the pilot, but he didn't. Frowning, she gingerly made her way towards the cockpit and knocked on the door.

'Enter.'

'What do you think you're doing?' she demanded the moment she caught sight of him sitting in the pilot's seat.

'Flying us to the Caribbean,' he said with a smile that she was sure had dropped a few panties in its time.

'Ah...no. No, I don't think so.'

'You're more than welcome to follow on a commercial flight. I can have Benjamin book you a seat. You'll only be about fourteen hours behind me, but I'm sure you won't mind,' he taunted.

She was going to need a dentist by the time these fourteen days were up, she was clenching her jaw so much. She cast an eye across the vast number of little lights, some of which were flashing, some white, some red, all of which were too many for her to take in.

'I am a fully qualified pilot. We have blue skies, calm winds and should have a good flight time.'

The space was small, even with the two pilot seats and...steering wheels, not that she thought they were actually called that.

'Sia.' His tone called her attention back to him. 'I can fly this plane. And I promise you, if you want to get the commercial flight—'

'No. No. I...ah...' she laughed a little '... I trust you. In *this* I trust you,' she said, realising that she did.

'I'm sorry.'

'Why?'

'That must have hurt.'

She couldn't help but slap him on the arm, an action that momentarily surprised them both.

'You're welcome to stay,' he said, levelling her with a gaze she felt to her toes.

She looked at the seat, trying to figure out how to even get into the thing, and realised that she'd already made the decision. There was a feeling of excitement edged with a little healthy fear and something not too far from adrenaline running through her veins as he helped her into the seat and the harness.

She watched, fascinated, as he spoke into the microphone attached to the earphones, communicating with whoever he needed to about taking off. The gentle forward movement as they began to head towards the runway seemed slower than a walk but, before she knew it, they were picking up speed and approaching the runway and she couldn't take the smile from her face, even if she couldn't loosen her grip on the arms of the seat. Sebastian took them faster and faster and never had she been more conscious that they were two little people inside a slightly bigger construction of metal and technology and, just when she would have shouted for him to stop, the wheels left the tarmac and they soared.

It took everything in her not to whoop, biting her lip, clenching her hands. None of it worked. When Sebastian looked across at her his smile, pantie-dropping or not, was one of pure joy.

What do you do for fun?
Let billionaire playboys fly me to the Caribbean.

Sebastian was still smiling as he pushed down the steps of his private jet and gestured for Sia to precede him. In truth, the flight had been much more enjoyable than expected, once Sia had relaxed. She'd refused his invitation to take the controls, but he suspected she might agree next time he offered. It'd been clear she had enjoyed it too.

Not that there would be a next time, he reminded himself firmly. They had thirteen days left and he couldn't lose sight of the threat that Sia posed for each and every one of those days as she pursued her investigation into the Durrántez painting. That alone meant he needed to keep her at arm's length.

But all of those thoughts disappeared as he caught sight of Ajay, his manager. He'd been looking forward to this moment for the last eighteen months and now the Caribbean hotel was on the verge of opening.

He had one duffel bag in each hand, which he unceremoniously threw into the back of the pick-up-style truck waiting beside the small sandy runway, before walking over to take the man in a strong embrace.

'It's good to see you,' Sebastian said sincerely, seeing the warm smile on his friend's face.

'And you, Sebastian. And you.'

'How are they?'

'The cabins are perfect and all finished, just in time.'

'Not the cabins, Ajay, your family,' Sebastian said, rolling his eyes.

'They're good too. Tia is teething, which is always fun.'

Sebastian turned to make an introduction, finding Sia looking at him with the ghost of a smile on her lips and intelligent assessment sparking in her eyes.

'Sia, allow me to introduce Ajay—a man without whom none of this would be here.' Ajay appeared embarrassed at the praise, but Sebastian had meant every word.

Sia stepped forward and greeted him warmly, 'It's lovely to meet you.'

'Likewise. However, I'm afraid that we do have a little business to touch on before you can relax until the party this evening.'

'There's going to be a party?' Sia asked him.

'Yes. It's…' Sebastian paused, choosing his words carefully, feeling that familiar sense of mischief he couldn't seem to stop around her. 'It's a pre-opening gala for VIPs,' he concluded, avoiding the confused look Ajay was giving him. 'Come on,' he said, opening the door to the Jeep for Sia. He was tempted to take the long way round, extending the short fifteen-minute drive to nearly twice that, but, checking his watch, realised they didn't have the time. Reluctantly, he pulled onto the main road—a laughable description of one of the only three roads on the island which he owned and where he'd decided to build his most recent hotel.

As the road drew closer to the shoreline, through the dense palms, flashes of azure-blue sea could be seen, golden sugary sand beckoned and sparks of fuchsia, purple and yellow from the exotic flowers exploded in his peripheral vision. In the mirror of the Jeep he caught Sia staring, her head turning from one side of the car to the other, eyes wide with wonder as the air through the open window played with the trails of her hair. He knew the feeling. He'd had that same sense of awe the first time he'd come here and knew that he had to have it.

The heat was bearable, having passed from the rainy season a few weeks before and, inhaling deeply, Sebastian felt a wave of relaxation pour over him in spite of the requirements for that evening. In too short a time they pulled up in front of the reception and Ajay jumped from the seat and was opening the door for Sia.

Sebastian had seen pictures of the reception centre going up, and now that it was complete he was impressed, but it was the centrepiece inside he was desperate to see.

'Are they up?' he asked Ajay, who nodded, his eyes shining with equal anticipation. 'How do they look?' Sebastian couldn't help but ask.

'See for yourself.' Ajay gestured and Sebastian couldn't help but race up the stairs of the only two-storey building on the whole island so that he'd have just a few moments to himself to appreciate the dramatic impact of the commissioned pieces before sharing them with Ajay and Sia.

And those moments…they were needed because, as he inhaled with awe, he realised that what Astou Ndiaye had created was nothing short of incredible. Then he heard Sia's footsteps behind him and he turned to see her reaction.

Sia was speechless.

She'd followed Sebastian's swift departure at a more sedate pace, instead taking in the way that the building's thatch of rushes blended beautifully with the palms and larger trees it nestled within. Casting a quick glance further down the stony road, she could see glimpses of entrances to equally discreet buildings in a similar style. And as she pushed open the cool glass door, frigid from the power of the interior air conditioning, she peered into the gloom and came to a sudden stop.

The reception area was spacious and reached up to the ceiling above the second-floor balcony wrapping around the open area. In the middle of the ground floor stood a beautiful dark wooden desk, polished to perfection. But that was not what Sia was staring at. Two breathtakingly large paintings hung either side of the desk, from the ceiling above the second storey all the way to the floor.

Each easily more than ten metres high and maybe seven or eight in width, the impact of the abstract paintings was both powerful and humbling. There was something almost baroque about them, Sia decided, like Poussin's mythological paintings—it was as if through the shapes and splatters, the drama of the paint Sia could almost see the mountainous pile of bodies from a war between angels and demons. Yet, within the heady mix of colour and texture, there were no figures, no humanity, just a broiling clash and energy that made her blood fizz as she was looking at them. As if they called her, challenged her to act, to reach, to want...

But, beneath all that, there was something niggling at her. Something vaguely familiar? She shook her head, unsettled by the feeling.

'You don't like them?' Sebastian asked.

'No, actually, I love them,' Sia replied. 'I just...can't place the artist.'

'Astou Ndiaye. She's Senegalese, living in France.'

'They are incredible pieces,' Sia concluded, realising that she'd neither heard of the artist nor remembered seeing a painting by her before.

'Yes, they are. A recent commission' Sebastian replied, not looking at the paintings but her. 'Bad news, I'm afraid,' he said, tucking something large under his arm, the action finally serving to tear her attention away from the paintings.

'Yes?'

'You're stuck with me. The accommodation is fully booked out for the VIP event this evening.'

'Wait...what?' she said, having to jog after him as he made his way out of the reception area and down a stone pathway overhung by large green leafy palms, so thick they almost blocked out the sun's rays.

'It's just that the accommodation was arranged a month ago. I had hoped that there may have been a cancellation, but it seems tonight my hotel is *the* place to be.' Despite the fact that Sebastian was walking ahead of her, Sia was sure that she could hear a tone to his voice. A sarcastic one. 'But we're both adults,' he continued, 'and I'm sure we'll cope.'

'Cope with what?' she asked as they rounded a corner,

Sia having to duck out of the way of a palm she suspected he had swung her way on purpose.

'One bed.'

'What?' Sia demanded and had to pull up short to prevent herself from marching straight into the back of Sebastian.

He turned, grinned at her and announced, 'Here we are,' with a shrug and walked straight up the stairs of the most incredible 'cabin' she'd ever seen. 'Are you coming?' he asked, standing at the top of the short steps that led up to decking wrapping around an open-fronted Caribbean bungalow.

This playful Sebastian was new... Not new as such, just carefree rather than taunting. Or at least that was how he seemed. Her feet dragged unaccountably as she followed him up the steps, until she turned to look out at the view and, once again, Sia was speechless. In front of her lay a crescent-shaped bay, sweeping around to her right. On one side of the decking was a small, square but surprisingly deep pool that looked as if it merged with the sea on the horizon. On the other side was a hammock stretching lazily from beneath the thatched awning to a post at the far corner of the decking.

The riot of colours that greeted her were so intense and overwhelming she had to remind herself to breathe. She huffed out a laugh. Only three days ago she had been at her desk in her one-bedroom flat in Archway, peering through the gloom, desperately trying to find the man who had caused her to be suspended from work. The same man who had flown her halfway round the world, *himself*, and was sharing his accommodation with her.

'Do you like it?' she heard from behind her. And perhaps it was because she hadn't seen him, wasn't distracted by his mask, that she could sense the underlying plea in his tone. He wanted her to like it. And she couldn't bring herself to lie.

'Yes. Very much,' she said, turning to find him standing much closer than she'd expected.

'Good,' he said, only it came out as a whisper that she felt against her lips, lips that she instantly bit down upon to stop the tingling from spreading.

Looking past him, she couldn't help but be drawn into the cabin. Large beautiful wooden ceiling fans hung low and swung silently, creating a gentle but welcome breeze. A huge bed dominated the space, surrounded by mosquito netting that looked more pretty than functional. To the left, out in the open, was a claw-foot white enamel high-backed bath facing out to the view behind her.

'It is a couple's cabin,' Sebastian explained. 'The toilet facilities are in the only room with a door, behind the bed.'

Sia picked up the brochure from a wooden table with gold inlay and eyed the condensation-covered ice bucket and its bottle of champagne warily. But not as warily as the pair of binoculars also on the table.

'Bird-watching?' she asked, her tongue working around the double entendre.

'As you can see, there is no direct view into anyone else's cabin, so it really is for the wildlife.'

She walked towards the large, dark wooden object that he'd carried with him from reception.

'And this is…?'

'A screen. You will want to bath and to dress.' Her raised eyebrow seemed to bruise his ego. 'I'm a playboy, not a monster.'

'Duly noted,' she said, unfolding the intricately carved wooden teak screen. It was a marvel of artistry, much like the entire hotel. She was focusing on the small details because it helped. Helped her to ignore the current spinning beneath her skin at a rate of knots. The entire cabin, aside from the toilet, was open-plan and, as much as she tried not to, her eyes kept returning to the impossibly large bed.

'I'll be sleeping on the hammock. Outside,' he added.

Sia turned and hid the slight tinge of disappointment beneath a smile.

'But your dress won't arrive for another hour, so—'

'Dress?'

'I wasn't sure that you had packed one, so I took the liberty.'

That he was right didn't make him any more…any more…right. And she hated that he was right.

'So,' he continued, 'I'm going to get washed and changed.'

He was looking at her and seemed to be waiting for something but… 'Oh. Of course. I'll be outside,' she said awkwardly when she realised he was waiting for her to leave.

Shaking her head, hoping that it wasn't a smile she saw across Sebastian's face from the corner of her eye, she made her way out to the decking, her back firmly against the wall of the cabin. She exhaled a shaky laugh at her own foolishness and locked her gaze on the stunning horizon, purposely focusing on the feeling of excitement fizzing through her veins and not the aching thrill she was beginning to get whenever she looked at Sebastian.

She wanted to take this all in. She might have been to some far-flung and incredible places but each and every one of them was for work. Holidays with Aunt Eleanor had been to caravan parks at the end of long drives. Lovely, but very English—sunburnt moss and grass verges, sandy dunes that tipped down into a cool grey sea. This, the Caribbean, was almost the opposite. Everything seemed electric, even the colours, and Sia found it strangely stim-ulating rather than relaxing.

Being here was so completely different to her life in London, her one-bedroom flat and her almost constant working hours. Or, rather, what she'd *made* of her life in London? She had gone from university to the only place that had offered her a job and her gratitude had bordered on desperate, taking whatever valuation they'd given her, going wherever they told her to, working whatever hours they'd needed. All those things? That had been on her. The shape of the hole she'd forced herself into was one of *her* design. Perhaps, when all this was done, she should think about that design a little more. Maybe it wasn't the right fit any more.

Breathing past the dull ache in her chest, she looked up to find the most beautiful bird soaring through the sky. She turned to ask Sebastian what it might be, when her eyes took in the sliver of space between the wooden screen and the mirror behind the bath.

Words screeched to a halt on her tongue as her eyes clung to the taut muscles of his shoulders and neck as he angled his head further back to make room for the razor he was drawing delicately beneath his jaw.

Shirtless, his trousers hanging low, the top button un-done, leaving the corners of his waistband open like a book, the contours of his abdomen were almost perfec-tion. Side on, she could see the groove running from his hipbone to deep beneath the waist of his trousers.

All she wanted to do was run her fingers over his skin, to outline the rise and fall of his muscles, to feel the warmth of his body, not smooth and cold like marble, but warm and rough and real. There was a breadth and a power to him that he concealed beneath expensive suits and pithy remarks. There was something thin about the impression that gave—insubstantial. But here, now... Sia had to plant her feet on the decking to stop herself from walking forward. There was strength and a sense of something immoveable. Something thrilling. Her body began to heat from deep within, radiating outward in pulses that made her want to clench her thighs together. And suddenly all she wanted was to be the focus of all that strength and power. He angled his head to the other side, and she watched as he drew the razor from his throat upwards and she could no longer hide from the pure desire coursing through her veins.

Sebastian felt it. The moment her gaze struck his skin. It had been a spark that jolted his heart, his pulse and his arousal at the same time. For just a second his hand shook, he nearly nicked his jaw but pulled away just in time. He took a deep breath and relished it, inhaled the electricity he could feel. He was hyperaware of every movement, conscious of every turn of his head, almost every hair the razor's edge covered.

He delayed it until he couldn't resist any longer. He wanted to see her, wanted to glean something, anything, in her reaction in that moment. Was she aroused like him? Did she feel every inch of her skin and senses? She *had* to, surely. Only mutual attraction burned this brightly.

The moment his eyes met hers in the mirror he was very glad he'd put his razor down. It had been like a tsunami, one giant wave crashing over him and drawing him under, pounding against him with shocking force, all of which suddenly disappeared the moment she dropped her gaze.

He was playing with fire and he knew it.

It took him the next twenty minutes to get himself under control. By which time he was ready and the package from Reception had arrived.

He stepped out onto the decking to find her looking out at the horizon again.

'Your turn,' he said and at first he thought it funny the way she avoided his gaze. Until he realised that it was most definitely not. Because, this close up, he could see that it wasn't the act of an experienced tease, it wasn't a play at being coquettish.

That was innocence. Pure and true. And he felt it like a slap to the face. Tangling with the enemy was one thing, but that? Not his style. He preferred women who knew the score, a few nights of incredible pleasure...but after? A very happy and equally willing *adios*. Easy, enjoyable but, most importantly, short and simple.

And there was nothing simple about Sia and nothing short about what he wanted to do with her. So he ignored the urge to turn and discover whether she had closed the gap in the wooden screen or left it open for him, the thought firing his blood and his determination to leave Sia Keating the hell alone.

What felt like only seconds later, the sound of heels on the wooden decking drew him round and he had to bite his tongue to stop himself from heaping praise on her. From head to toe she was exquisite. He'd chosen the dress knowing that it was different to her usual style, but she looked... *Like everything he'd ever wanted.*

He shook the thought from his head and instead said a different truth. 'You should always dress like this.'

It was turquoise in colour, thin shoulder straps led to a V that hugged her breasts and dropped into a beaded bodice that was reminiscent of art deco in design. Flashes of turquoise-coloured square sequins flashed in the setting sun, nestled next to gold sequins so pale they matched Sia's skin, giving the impression of bare skin. Waterfalls of silk fell from her waist which swayed with each step she took towards him.

He could have bitten off his own tongue. He never should have bought this dress for her.

'It's hardly suitable for the office. It's very beautiful *and* generous, but I'm not sure it's me,' she said, fanning out the skirts around her legs.

'It is bold, courageous and sensual, which makes me wonder if it's the office that doesn't suit? It certainly reminds me of the woman I met in Victoriana,' he said truthfully.

'That wasn't me.'

'Are you sure about that?'

'Absolutely.'

'Well, that is a shame. Because *Henri* was impressive, passionate and powerful. Who stole that from you, Sia?' he couldn't help but ask.

'The deal is that *I* ask *you* the question. We had no agreement on me answering yours.'

He could see that she was hurt and angry. He knew that he'd pushed a button, but her retaliation was swift, harsh and, once again, it caught him unprepared.

'So, tell me what you see when you look at the Durrántez painting,' she demanded.

'My mother.'

Both the speed and his answer seemed to surprise them both.

'Literally or figuratively?'

He breathed in, needing a moment to secure a smile full of charm across his lips. 'One question per day, Sia. You know that.'

CHAPTER SIX

INTERVIEWER ONE: *What was this gala? I don't re-member seeing anything in the newspapers.*

INTERVIEWER TWO: *You said it was for VIPs?*

MS KEATING: *Yes, it was. Very important people.*

SIA TRIED TO shake off the mess of her thoughts as she followed Sebastian back towards the hotel reception on the high-heeled shoes he'd somehow managed to secure *in the right size*. In part she'd brought it on herself. Her question had been born of her own hurt, her own frustration that Sebastian saw something in her that she'd never seen in herself but wanted to. Had *always* wanted to. But she'd also wanted to know why the Durrántez was so important to him and his answer had only confused her.

A confusion that swirled around her like the skirts of the most beautiful dress she'd ever worn. But, no matter how wonderful it made her feel, how…sensual and bold—just as he'd said—she still didn't feel as if it suited her. Henri, perhaps. But not Sia, Bonnaire's art valuer. If she would ever be that again. *If she even wanted to be.*

She matched Sebastian's pace as it slowed to a stop, where he greeted some guests also making their way to the reception area. She didn't recognise the faces of the people that passed, but everyone was smiling and happy. She felt Sebastian's arm at her back as he guided her up the steps beside him and through the doorway.

The reception area had completely changed in the last few hours. Strings of fairy lights led from above the entrance to the opposite side of the room, as if guiding the guests towards the beautiful terrace area beyond. Unable to resist, Sia followed the others towards the steps out onto a back garden area that she had missed on their first visit.

Even more lights hung in a canopy above the garden and it was as if the stars had come closer just for them. Large broad-leafed palms interspersed with purple allamanda and jasmine created a beautiful, scented border for the party. Waiters in loose linen uniforms slowly circled the guests, offering flutes of champagne, pitchers of fresh fruit juice and platters of delicious-looking canapés.

And as she looked about her, Sia realised that, although everyone was dressed in finery, it wasn't the kind of obscene wealth she'd have imagined of a highly exclusive private event on a Caribbean island. One strange difference was that the guests genuinely seemed to be happy to be there, as if they actually knew each other rather than being there simply to be seen before finding somewhere else more important to be.

'Sia, you look beautiful,' Ajay said sincerely by way of introduction.

'Thank you.'

'I don't think she likes it,' Sebastian stage-whispered to his hotel manager, seeming to return to the funny self-deprecating figure he tended to become around Ajay, as if the awkwardness they had shared had disappeared like clouds on a summer's day.

'I do,' Sia said immediately, not wanting to seem ungrateful, but couldn't help feeling self-conscious as Sebastian once again seemed to gaze at her from head to toe before turning back to Ajay.

'Is it time?'

'Yes, sir.'

With a smile flashed in her direction, Sebastian left them and headed towards the decking area, stopping at the top of the stairs and waiting until everyone naturally grew silent.

'There is one thing that I like to do before the opening of every one of my hotels. It started with my first and has continued on from there. I like to bring *the* most important people together. You,' he said, offering his hands to the guests, and as she looked around the beaming faces she saw more than just happiness. She saw pride.

'You have worked beside me on this endeavour—contractors, suppliers, staff. This night is to say a huge and deeply heartfelt thank you for everything that you have done and have achieved. Tonight, I have brought in staff from other hotels around the world, not only to serve you, but for them to see what incredible things you've done. Tonight, you are the guests, the *first* guests of this hotel. So eat, drink, enjoy the cabins and the entertainment. I don't want to see any of you before at least midday tomorrow!'

A huge round of applause, a wave of laughter and a cheer rippled out across the small crowd, but Sia only had eyes for Sebastian. *The most important people, indeed.* Ajay cast her a knowing smile and led her to where delicious plates of food were being served while Sebastian stopped to shake hands and give thanks to some of the guests.

As Sebastian looked around he felt pleasure in their success, a thrill in seeing all the changes to the designs he'd made to ensure the buildings worked harmoniously with the backdrop. He remembered wrestling with the first architect—a very intelligent and experienced man, but his heart had been in chrome and steel, not in working sympathetically with the setting, local materials or even local experts. When Ajay had introduced his cousin, Sebastian knew he'd found the right man for the job.

The hotel had been done right and perfectly. But—Sebastian managed to stop himself from shaking his head—he thought he'd feel more... Just *more*. Here he was, with everything he'd ever wanted. Revenge had been taken against the Sheikh, his sister was happily married with a child on the way. His father and Valeria were safely in Rimini doing their own thing. But from the age of eighteen he'd done everything he *had* to. Then, in the last three or so years, anything he *could* do. But as he looked out to where the sea stretched beneath the stars, dark shapes twisting in the moonlight, he couldn't help but wonder if this was what he really *wanted* to do.

Instinctively, he was drawn back to the gathering, the cascade of laughter he recognised as Sia's and was suddenly, and completely irrationally, jealous of Ajay, who was a very happily married man and father of two.

She would make an incredible mother.

The thought popped into his head and caught there. He could see it in his mind's eye—her gently casting circles over a baby bump, a little more pink to her cheeks, the beautiful red-gold hair flowing down her back. The image was so pure, so true, it was as if he knew it was in her future—something she not only wanted but deserved. But, just as strongly, Sebastian knew it would not be in his. He'd experienced that heavy weight of responsibility, knew what it took to protect and safeguard that family and three years ago had decided he was done.

At eighteen, he'd been a teenager who'd sold his family belongings to keep the roof over his and his sister's heads. While his father and Valeria had sailed around Greece for months on end, Sebastian had gone to school plays, parent teacher conferences and spent every spare minute ensuring his first hotel was a success. And then the second. And the third. In the first five years of their exile he'd barely slept more than four hours a night. And not just because of the fact he worked all the hours God sent, but because of the fear. The fear that it could all be taken away again in the blink of an eye. The fear that nothing in this world was really lasting.

The sound of a glass breaking drew him back to the present, as highly efficient staff descended to resolve the situation. His mind refocused and he looked back to where Sia stood, taking a canapé from a silver tray on the table at the side and smiling up at Ajay with pure joy. No pregnancy bump, no thoughts of future family or responsibilities.

There was only now, only this moment and Sebastian couldn't resist the urge to show her just how much fun that could be.

'I hope you didn't mind Sebastian's joke,' Ajay said, pouring a little more champagne into her glass.

'I don't think it *was* a joke. These clearly are very important people to the hotel and to the island,' she said with a smile, unable to stop herself from swaying to the beat of a song played by an unobtrusive DJ. Because that was the thing about Sebastian—he seemed to play on expectations, both living up to and undercutting them at any given moment so that she never really knew where she stood with him. Never know what was real and what was not. She'd told him that she was good at spotting fakes, but she was beginning to doubt it when it came to him.

'We were so thankful to hear that Mr Rohan de Luen had closed the deal on the island. The first prospective buyer had plans to develop almost every inch of it. Our island isn't as big as some of the others, so the sale could have meant the loss of jobs as well as housing. But Sebastian found a way to make it work for all of us.'

'I'm surprised. For someone who generally seems very happy to brag, he's been particularly tight-lipped about all this,' she said, casting an eye over the large courtyard.

'Men don't brag about what's important to them,' Ajay leaned into confide.

'Which is why you'll never hear about his incredibly beautiful wife and two delightfully perfect daughters,' Sebastian leaned in to interrupt. 'May I?'

He held his hand out to Sia and she was genuinely concerned he was asking her to dance.

'I don't—'

'No one will start until I do and I'm not dancing with Ajay.'

'Yes, but I *can't*.'

'I don't believe that for a second. When was the last time you danced?'

'When I was seven?'

'Well, that's just plain stupid.'

'Stupid?' she asked, half laughing. 'You are trying to get me to dance with you by calling me stupid?'

'Is it working?' he asked, charm sparkling in his eyes and a smile that was horrifyingly irresistible. 'Please?'

She'd have liked to blame it on the gentle buzz in her veins from the two glasses of champagne, or the way the natural heat from the Caribbean had already sunk into her body, easing what felt like years of tension, but as she placed her hand in his, allowed him to lead her to a small flat area squared above by large bright bulbs, she knew it wasn't any of those things.

'You've been swaying to the beat of the last two songs, so I know you have rhythm,' he said, looking at her in a way that she turned away from. A blush rose to her cheeks at the thought he'd been watching her for that long. 'But if you're happy for me to take the lead?'

Sia nodded, incapable of untangling her tongue long enough to respond. And then she wished she'd refused, as he swept his arm around her waist and drew her into the warmth of his body. With barely an inch of space between her chest and his, his thighs brushing against the skirts of her dress, moulding them between her legs, he guided her around the space. She felt it, that need welling within her, pulsing within her chest, creeping up to her throat as if desperate to…to…she honestly couldn't tell. Sebastian's hand flexed against the base of her spine as if he were struggling with the same thing—a build-up of electricity that needed to be released.

She let him move her body around the dance floor and she felt as if she were floating, light as a feather, completely at his mercy and it was wondrous. His grip was secure but not tight, powerful yet restrained, and she wanted more. His steps began to slow and she couldn't resist looking up at him as he looked down at her, the gentle puff of his breath on her lips, the way that his gold-flecked irises retracted to make space for enlarged pupils, his arm around her waist drew her against him just that bit closer and her heart felt as if it might explode. She wanted him to kiss her. So much it hurt. It actually hurt.

And just when she thought he might, just when he'd begun to close the distance between their lips, he paused…

And a round of applause exploded around them like gunfire, shredding the moment just as effectively.

Sia bit her lip against the seesawing of her emotions and thoughts. After all, he had told her his purpose was to gather other guests to dance and she managed a smile at the couples now filling the dance area. So anything she'd thought might have been about to happen? Just in her imagination.

Smiling gamely, she called to Ajay and asked him to dance. Thankfully, the music was much more upbeat and the fun, simple twirls he guided Sia into were easier to manage. Every now and then she'd catch a glimpse of Sebastian at the side of the dance floor, her eyes drawn to him by the feeling of his gaze tracking her every move, but each time she raised her face to his he was facing the person he was talking to. So she cast off the feeling and instead focused on determinedly enjoying herself.

He'd held her in his arms and he shouldn't have. Because now he knew what that felt like he'd never forget it as long as he lived. It was like holding a live wire. Exhilarating, terrifying, humbling and addictive. She'd been avoiding him ever since the end of the first dance and he knew why. It was much safer for her to think that it had all been for show. It hadn't, of course. But safer for her to believe that.

Because he was almost one hundred per cent sure that if he got one taste of her it would most definitely not be enough. Gritting his jaw, he told himself firmly that Sia Keating would remain untouched for the next twelve days before he sent her on her way. Perhaps with a quiet word in the ears of a few well-placed people in the art industry. She needed to get away from Bonnaire's and their sullied reputation.

Ajay was leading a smiling and seemingly happy Sia

from the dance area back towards him. He wished he had a camera in that moment. She looked younger, the flush on her cheeks healthy and the shine in her eyes? Just incredible.

'I declare the evening a roaring success,' Sebastian said with a tilt of his champagne glass in Ajay's direction.

'Yes. The staff—'

'Guests.'

'The *guests* will remember this for a long time, Sebastian. It was a good idea.'

'I think we should do it once a year, not just for the opening,' Sebastian said, feeling the rightness of it the moment the words were out of his mouth.

'For Christmas?' Sia asked.

'It's a big season for us,' Ajay replied, unsure.

'March is fairly quiet. And we could get staff from other hotels to cover and, in return, we cover them, which would also allow staff to see how other hotels around the world are run.'

'See?' Ajay said, smiling, bumping his shoulder against Sia's and once again accidentally twisting a knife in Sebastian. 'He says "we".'

Sia nodded knowingly and Sebastian couldn't tell whether he was happy or irritated that they had been talking about him.

There were still a few guests dancing and milling around, but Sebastian was eager to go. He told himself he wanted to find a moment of quiet, away from the music and the hum of conversation around him, but he knew that wasn't true.

After a few more goodbyes than he'd intended, Sebastian led Sia back to the path away from the guests still partying. It was dark but the walkway's pale stones shone in the moonlight, leading them safely back to the cabin. He ducked under low-hanging palm leaves and held them out of the way for Sia. But when he didn't feel her following he turned to find her looking up at the stars, wonder on her face, lost in a private moment he didn't want to disturb.

'It's almost otherworldly, isn't it?' she asked, surprising him.

Casting a look up to the velvet sky, the bright stars nestled in the smoky swirl of cosmos, 'Very different to London?' he couldn't help but ask.

'Just a tad.'

'Where in London do you live?' He had been honest with her when he'd said he'd not looked into her or her background. It was almost novel—learning about someone only by what they said and by what he trusted.

'North. Archway. It's handy for work.'

'But?' he asked, sensing some hesitancy there.

'I'm a South London girl at heart,' she said, finally turning her face from the heavens to his, grinning with a strange kind of home town pride. 'I grew up in Peckham with Mum and Dad and then later, just up the road in Forest Hill with Aunt Eleanor.'

'Why did you have to live with your aunt? Wasn't it only your father who was arrested?'

'It was decided that it would be better for me to live with her.'

'Decided by who?' He hadn't missed either the pause or the clipped tone to her voice, but couldn't help but ask.

'Everyone.'

'Including you?' he asked, incredulous, thinking if he could have just one minute, thirty seconds, ten, five even with his mother again he'd sell his soul for them. He'd come to a stop while she'd continued walking and she was now ahead of him. Even so, he didn't miss the sound of breath puffed between her lips.

'Yes. Mum is a complicated person.'

'But—'

She turned on him then, spinning round as if all the pent-up frustration and hurt that he'd missed in her tone was finally escaping.

'I get my hair from *her*,' Sia practically spat, hating the bitterness in her own voice but unable to stop. 'I got my name from my dad, but my hair from her. I don't look like her in any other way. Nose, eyes, face shape...' she gestured to herself '...that's the Keating side. But the hair?' She huffed out a bitter half laugh. 'She always said that she gave me the one thing that made me stand out.' As Sia spoke the words a childhood hurt rose up within her. That horrible scarring feeling that she wasn't enough on her own, in her own right, that everything she had was dependent on and because of her mother. She couldn't see past the memories and thoughts to find Sebastian. She was lost to it now. 'I tried to dye it once. Brown. It didn't work that well,' she said flippantly of one of the most excruciating moments of her teenage years. 'It turned into this kind of sludgy, streaked mess. I thought Mum would lose her mind. But she didn't even notice.

'There was quite a lot my mother didn't notice when I lived with them,' she pressed on, unable to stop now. 'Bedtime, I could stay up as long as I liked. Mealtimes, whenever and whatever I wanted, as long as I could get it for myself. School was an if and when thing,' she said, shrugging, 'which for my mother was very little of the "when". I learned my trade at my father's feet. Even at the age of seven I did a mean Pollock,' she said honestly and bitterly.

'And Mum had one focus in life—Dad. She loved him. She loved him more than anything else in this world. She saw only him. And when he didn't see her, when he would spend weeks lost in front of his canvases, locked in the

studio day and night… It hurt her. Broke her. Initially she
would rage. Throw anything she could get her hands on—
glasses, plates… There was a particularly close call with
a kitchen knife once,' she said with a wobbly laugh as if it
had been humorous rather than terrifying. 'Oh, the things
she would scream at him.'

You're a photocopier! Good for nothing but copying.
You're not even an artist. Piss artist, more like.

Sia shivered at the memory, the shrieking South London
accent cutting through the beautiful warmth of the Caribbean and reminding her where she came from. She felt the
sheen of tears in her eyes covering a pain so close to the
surface, like the shimmer on an over-inflated balloon, and
she vaguely wondered if it was about to burst. Perhaps it
already had and she just hadn't noticed.

'The neighbours called the police one too many times
and she spent a few weeks in prison. Dad barely noticed,
but he was there to pick her up. After that, she tried a different tack. She thought she could make John Keating jealous,' Sia scoffed. 'There was this party, very bohemian.
Mum had draped silks over cheap lamps, candles everywhere. It was a miracle the place didn't burn down. She
was all over the shop, flirting desperately with men, trying to provoke some kind—any kind—of reaction from
my dad. And the most painful thing about it all was that
I could see, *everyone* could see, that he just didn't care.
He didn't laugh, he didn't get angry. He may as well have
just told the men that they could have her,' she said, pressing her lips together against the hurt cry of her childhood
wanting to get out.

'You asked me who stole my passion?' she said, finally
turning to Sebastian, seeing him in the present and not
hidden by the past. '*She* did. My mother. She taught me
that passion was selfish, cruel, mean and hysterical and,

in the end, utterly pointless. So forgive me if I don't live like you. *Love* like you. It's because even if I took the risk to, the fact that I could end up even remotely like her? Not worth it. Ever.'

She turned round and would have stalked off had Sebastian not slipped his arm around her waist and held her against him to prevent her from leaving.

'That wasn't passion, Sia. What your mother felt, what motivated her actions…it wasn't passion,' he said gently, as if trying to soothe her, unconsciously evoking the very thing they were talking about and the last thing she wanted.

'Please…' she begged, hoping that he would stop, wanting him to continue, to say something that would lessen the pain of her heart breaking—for the past and the present.

She heard him sigh as if he'd lost some internal battle. Felt his head bend, as if in defeat, to rest on her shoulder, leaning ever so slightly into the crook of her neck.

'The Latin origin of passion…it means to suffer. To endure. Passion is a suffering that you take on yourself for what you want. It has nothing to do with inflicting that suffering on another.'

And then he let her go.

CHAPTER SEVEN

SEBASTIAN PUSHED OFF the wooden post with his foot, sending the hammock gently swaying beneath a spangled night sky, and cursed himself. He wasn't quite sure what for, only that he knew he deserved it.

The full moon was so large and so bright it could have passed for that hour just before dawn, but at the last check of his watch it was barely one-thirty. With everything half lit, it felt half real... *A time for fairies and magic,* his mother would have whispered in his ear and he smiled sadly at the memory.

With one arm behind his head and the other hanging lazily down to where the ice-cold bottle of beer he'd retrieved from the outside fridge sat gathering condensation from the heat of the night, his eyes watched the sky, his mind skipping over the possibilities and infinities of the world. His lips curved into a half smile as he saw the bright burn and tail of a shooting star slash across the darkness as his unconscious mind made a wish he was barely aware of. Shaking off the abstract thought of Sia as more of a want than a wish, impossible either way, he pushed off against the post again.

He should never have extended this offer of fourteen days. He should never have allowed himself to get so distracted. He didn't care about himself but the others, they had so much more to lose and he would never put them in danger like that. Yes, they'd all agreed, but still. It had been his plan, his idea…and he'd been the one to push it. Sia was a threat to all of that. He thought of Sia's question earlier about what he saw when he looked at the painting. And then Sia's answer when he'd asked who'd stolen her passion. He shook his head. Strange that they had both fought the same demons for incredibly different reasons.

He was about to snag hold of his beer when a creak on the decking stopped the movement. Every inch of him surged, the hairs on his arms lifted, he swore he could hear the thud of his heart, the rush of blood in his veins.

'Go to bed.'

The command was gravelly and low even to his own ears. His eyes firmly on the horizon at sea, he knew, *knew*, that if he turned, if he caught sight of her there would be no going back.

'No.'

'You don't want this,' he warned.

'Who are you to tell me what I want and don't want? A thief? A liar?' Her words struck him like bullets.

'I have never lied to you.'

'Then tell me you're not attracted to me.'

He clamped his jaw shut but it did nothing to prevent the growl in his throat. Carefully and deliberately, he placed one foot and then the other on the decking and turned himself out of the hammock, his eyes neither on her or the horizon but somewhere in between. As if holding off the inevitable for as long as possible.

Finally, he faced her and he swallowed the curse on his tongue. The Prussian-blue silk negligée hung from thin shoulder straps, dipping in a Vee into a diamond panel that hugged her stomach beneath breasts so perfect his mouth watered. The bias cut ensured that the silk, shimmering beneath the moonlight, skated over the dips and swells of her hips and thighs, dusky shadows hinting at the secrets of her body. Long locks of rich auburn hair fell against the deep blue of the negligée, making her look more regal than any queen. But the look in her eyes as she took him in, running over his shirtless torso and snagging on the trousers hanging low on his waist, her pupils wide and shining in the moonlight...*that* was what nearly undid him. He fisted his hands at his sides and then forced them open.

'I'm not a Neanderthal,' he said, although it was quite possibly the first lie he'd told her. 'I can be attracted to a woman and not act on it, for God's sake.'

Sia was confused, hurt and more than a little frustrated. He'd made her want. He'd made her confront her feelings, her desire for him. And it was overwhelming and she ached. For him but just as much for herself. She *wanted* to be the passionate, bold person he had met at Victoriana, the woman who drank with billionaires, wore turquoise dresses, danced and laughed. But, more than that, she wanted to be the person who reached for what she wanted, for what she knew was right. But now he was refusing to let her. The playboy who had whatever he wanted, whenever he wanted, didn't want her?

'Why would you do this?' She couldn't help the tremor in her tone.

'I didn't do it for me, Sia. I did it for you,' he said, easing a hand over his face as if frustrated. 'So that you realise that it's okay to be a passionate, vibrant woman who owns not only her desires but has the courage to act on them *safely*.'

'And you're not safe?'

'Not to you.'

All this time she'd thought of passion as chaotic, scary,

unbalanced, but that was because of what her mother had experienced, how her mother had behaved—selfish and needy, it had all been about her. But also, Sia believed, because it had been one-sided. Her father hadn't loved her mother and it had made her crazy.

Sebastian *was* attracted to her, and she wanted to know what that was like, what it *felt* like. Because suddenly it seemed as if it would be something beautiful, as if it would be the coming together of two halves of a whole. What had he said? He didn't have to act on it. Perhaps they didn't, but she wanted so much just to allow herself to feel it.

'Would you...' she said, struggling to find the words to ask for what she wanted. 'Would you just stand here with me? No words. Just for a minute. I... I just want to know what it feels like.'

She thought she'd have to explain what she meant, but understanding shifted across his features and after a moment he nodded. She walked out onto the decking to meet him, not breaking the connection of his gaze. He watched her as if both wary and wanting.

She came to a stop a few inches from him, the distance greater than when they had danced together and yet so much more intimate. She tried to tell herself his body was nothing she hadn't seen before, in paintings, statues, pictures and even in person from the opposite side of the room. But being so close to Sebastian, his bare chest a study in perfection, was altogether completely different. Her pulse beat erratically and she inhaled slowly and deeply, attempting to soothe it.

She glanced at Sebastian, expecting to see a knowing, taunting gaze in his eyes but no, that wasn't what she found. Instead, he seemed to be watching everything about her, taking in as much as possible in exactly the same way as she had been and there was nothing remotely humorous in his gaze. When his eyes joined hers there was such a serious intensity there, something beyond words, beyond explanation or justification. She felt it in every single inch of her body, this strange sense of being known, seen.

And then, in a heartbeat, it changed.

It was as if a flame had been lit beneath their feet, licking up their flesh in an undulating tide, utterly overwhelming and urgent, demanding and angry almost. This time, when she caught his eyes, all she could feel was the power of just how much he wanted her and how much he fought it and it was incredible to behold.

She felt it, the moment he wanted to break the connection, the second before he would turn away.

'If I sleep with you, do you expect me *not* to go to the police about the painting?' she blurted out.

'What?' Sebastian replied, clearly confused at the turn of the conversation. 'Of course not!' he said, as if outraged by the suggestion.

'If I sleep with you, will you ignore my wishes, my words, if I say stop—?'

'Sia, no. There will be no—'

'If I sleep with you—'

'This is not a game Sia. This is—'

'My choice, is it not?' She paused, waiting for him to interrupt. When he didn't she pressed on, her breath high with hope in her lungs, 'If I say stop?'

'Of course I would stop,' he said shortly.

'So why won't you start?' she asked, trying to keep the desperation out of her tone.

'Because you're innocent, Sia. You don't know what it is you're asking.'

'Don't patronise me,' she replied and this time *she* was frustrated.

'I'm not,' he said sincerely. 'No one does. You don't

know what emotions this will bring, how you will feel in the morning. Better for it to be with someone who is in your life for the right reasons and for the long haul. Not...'

'Someone who has lost me my job and, in less than twelve days now, will leave and not look back? I know the deal, Sebastian,' she said, just as sincerely.

But she began to feel a little like her mother. As if she were desperate, dependent on him even. On the verge of begging, she hauled herself back from the brink. She wouldn't do that to herself, no matter how much she wanted Sebastian.

And that was when she realised that she wasn't like her mother at all and the release of the chains she hadn't re-alised were holding her back was so great that she felt as if she were soaring free. The light welling up within her, the power of it... She took a deep breath, allowing it to fill her completely, and she shook her head in wonder. Had her fear been holding her back all this time? Was this what she could have felt like—this powerful, this free all this time? Rather than feeling the loss, she marvelled at it and knew that she had Sebastian to thank. But in spite of that she also knew what she had to say, what she *wanted* to say.

'Despite what you think, I *do* know what I want. But I won't be like her. I won't beg and I won't be desperate.'

She turned to leave when his hand caught her wrist and spun her back round to face him.

'You're nothing like her,' he insisted in a deep growl.

'I know, because I *can* walk away.'

She easily pulled free from his grasp, turned and made it four steps back towards the cabin before he closed the distance between them. Bracing his arm against the wall, Sebastian crowded her from behind, feeling every inch of the Neanderthal he'd professed not to be. She stood loosely encased in his arms with her back to him, and he watched the rise and fall of her shoulders as she drew in breaths as deep as his own.

The heat rising from their bodies filled the space between them so much it was as if they were touching and he fought it. He fought himself. She turned her head halfway towards him, her eyes cast down as if just as reluctant as he, and he knew in his heart that if they shared a look it would all be over.

In the moonbeams he picked out the delicate eyelashes fanning her cheek, the hollow beneath her cheekbone and the slender curve to her neck, the slope of her shoulder and sweep of its blade. He studied every single inch of her in deep fascination, desperate to prolong the moment, to put off the final second of the internal war he was waging.

'You have to know that this has nothing to do with the painting,' he said, his defences weakening.

'I do,' she insisted quickly.

'I haven't finished,' he warned gently. 'Nothing to do with the painting, but time. This—whatever it is—can only be for the rest of our agreement. Do you understand?'

There was a pause before she responded and he was thankful for it. Because it meant she was thinking it through, truly appreciating that he meant there could be nothing beyond these twelve days.

'I do,' she whispered on an exhale.

'Then tell me you want this.' His voice was a harsh whisper as if he'd released the battle cry that had been sounding in his head.

'I want this.'

He placed his hand over hers, his fingers tangling with the silk and skin at her thigh. Her eyes drifted closed, her head slowly falling back in surrender.

'Promise me you'll tell me to stop if you want to stop,' he commanded in a whisper to her ear.

'I promise.'

And in that moment he knew he'd lost.

He'd lost the moment she'd had set her eyes on him, before he'd even looked across the bar in Victoriana.

He reached for her, turning her in his hands, her hips in his palms, sweeping her into his chest, and plundered a kiss from lips so soft and so open he thought he'd drown in them. The way she opened beneath him humbled him and he revered her with his hands and lips. The silk of her negligée skated over her skin beneath his palm as his thumb caught on her hip, pulling her into his body. His tongue delved into the welcome wet heat of her mouth and he wanted more. With a restraint and a patience almost unknown to him, he guided her through the doorway and walked her backwards to the bed without breaking the kiss.

Her hands roamed across his chest, leaving trails of branded skin, her short nails kneading into his arms and back, making him want to roar. Instead he pressed his lips against the curve of her neck, allowing his teeth to gently scrape against the sensitive skin there, relishing the shudder that shivered down her body and into his hands. She threw her head back in pleasure and he couldn't resist pressing open-mouthed kisses from her neck to her shoulder, gently moving the strap of her negligée aside, exposing just that bit more of her to him and drawing his attention to the way her taut nipples pulled at the silk across her chest.

Unable to stop himself, he took her covered breast in his hand, running his thumb over the stiff peak as he pressed kisses against the seam where skin met silk. She writhed like fire beneath his fingers and tongue and he wanted to consume every twist and turn of her, his pulse now like a drumbeat in his ear and mind.

She's mine, she's mine, she's mine.

Her own hand came up to the strap on her other shoulder, pulling at it, releasing the last thing holding up the silk between his skin and hers other than where it was caught in his hands at her chest. All he had to do was release her, release it, but he couldn't quite bring himself to do it yet. Her breasts, even covered, fitted perfectly within his hands, his mouth.

She shifted restlessly against him and he widened his stance as her legs instinctively slipped either side of his thigh. This time he couldn't help the growl that formed in his throat as she pressed against him and her moan sank into his skin. His hands flew to her shoulders, securing the straps beneath his palms, holding her back or drawing her closer, he didn't know any more.

His arousal pressed almost painfully against his trousers and he wanted nothing more than to tear the clothes from their bodies. But Sia was an innocent in the truest sense of the word and that meant that he put aside his own wants.

She looked glorious in his arms, her head cast back, the long trails of thick golden waves falling down her back almost reaching the base of her spine, her eyes having drifted shut as if lost in the sensual pleasure she was experiencing. He wished he could stop this moment in time, record the way she looked in this very moment. Because he had never seen anything more beautiful.

He couldn't help the curve to his lips as her eyes opened and she lifted her gaze to his. He gazed at her, trying to imprint this image on his mind, his memory, the gentle light cast by the moon shining on silk and catching in her hair. For a moment Sia seemed to study him in the same way and he wondered what she was thinking, what she was seeing. And then her hand came up around his neck and pulled his lips to hers and his mind went blank as he was lost to everything but the feeling of her tongue against his, her fingertips winding into his hair, the pull of his waistband from where her hand had sneaked between them.

Dios, he wanted her more than anything he'd ever wanted before. It was so much and so intense he struggled to keep the tremors from his touch. Finally, unable to take it any more, he released his hold on her arms and the straps caught beneath his palms and he watched, captivated, as the blue silk slid from her body and pooled at her feet, leaving her naked to the moonbeams and his scrutiny.

'I have no words,' he said, his gaze raking across every inch of beautiful smooth pale skin.

'You don't need words,' Sia said, reaching for the waistband of his trousers with a confidence that astounded him. Not because he didn't think her capable of it, but it was a confidence, a trust, that she had placed in him.

He caught her hand and held it against his chest for just a moment before he reached for her, picking her up and smiling as she instinctively wrapped her legs around his waist. He kneeled onto the bed, Sia still high in his arms, pressed against his chest, but able to look down on him, her hair coming about them like a curtain, cutting them off from the rest of the world.

He teased them both as he lowered her slightly, knowing she could feel the press of his erection through his trousers against her core. The way her eyes widened with expectation and want... He held her there until once again her eyes drifted closed and her body took over, her legs tightening their hold around his waist and leaning further into him to increase her own pleasure. The gasped inhale sharpened his arousal and he wanted to bury himself in her until he couldn't tell where he ended and she began. But Sia deserved, needed more than that.

Gently he laid her down, ruefully accepting the groan

of disappointment that fell from her lips. He leaned back enough to remove his trousers and boxers, feeling her eyes on him the entire time. He stood there for a moment, allowing her to take him in, taking her in, in turn and marvelling how she reminded him of a Dante Gabriel Rossetti—her flowing auburn hair, pale skin...

His lips lifted gently as he saw the moment she began to grow self-conscious beneath his gaze and looked forward to the day she wouldn't. Until he realised that in all likelihood he would never see it.

He ignored the way his gut clenched at the thought and turned his attention to her feet. Picking one up, he kissed the arch of her foot and nipped at the soft flesh there when he heard Sia giggle. He lifted her leg gently, smoothing his hands along her calf, guiding her legs to either side of his to make room for him. The laughter left her lips and her eyes grew heavy with arousal as his hands swept further up. He relished the hitch in her breathing, mirroring his own, as he gently drew her legs further apart and settled his attention on the dusting of auburn curls at the apex of her thighs.

'Sia, I will stop *any* time,' he promised.

'Thank you.'

It was an exchange, an offer that had been accepted and it felt as if it was weighted with a trust that stretched beyond this moment and Sebastian refused to squander it. He placed open-mouthed kisses across her hip and downward until he found the soft, wet, enticing heat of her.

His tongue swirled around her clitoris and her hips bucked beneath him in euphoria. He placed his forearm across her hips, gently holding her in place, and sucked against her just as he entered her with his finger. Sia's breathing became tinged with small moans of delight, which only served to spur him on.

Her body shifted to welcome more of him, more of the pleasure he was bringing her and he relished it. Her body, her pleasure…it was more to him than his own. He could tell that she was on the brink of orgasm—the flush of her cheeks, the unseeing gaze—there was just a slim tether holding her back and he resented it as much as he imagined she did. He deepened his kiss between her thighs, brought two fingers to her entrance and thrust into her as he sucked on her clitoris and nearly came himself when he felt her orgasm against his mouth.

Sia came back down to earth gradually, but beneath the flickering moments were the traces of a feeling that had overwhelmed her entire body. She felt outside of herself, a giddy joy that almost made her laugh to think that such a feeling existed. She watched Sebastian through heavy-lidded eyes as he leaned back from the bedside table with something in his hand.

He put it aside and came down to lie beside her, running his palm from her hip up to her ribcage, over her breast and nipple and towards her neck to smooth away her hair from her shoulder, before placing kisses on the exact spot that made Sia want to hum with pleasure.

She leaned into the kiss as his arm came around her, pulling her back against the length of his body and the hardness of his arousal. Shocked by how much it turned her on, she couldn't help but shift against him, loving the way it felt to have his body encompassing hers.

'We can stop.'

'I don't want to.'

He gently pulled her round onto her back and when she looked him in the eye she could see that he was studying her, trying to seek out any hint of doubt.

'Sebastian, honestly. Am I nervous? A little. Excited?

A lot. Scared? Not at all.' She reached up to cup his face, her palm against the slight stubble of his jaw. 'I want this,' she said before leaning up to place a kiss against his lips. And then another and another until mouths opened and tongues tangled and hands gripped and she was lost again.

Until she felt the loss of heat from his body and heard the tearing of foil even as he kissed her, his tongue filling her the way she wanted his body to. She shifted to welcome him between her legs and when his arms came up to frame her face she felt protected, cared for and she blinked against the sheen of tears threatening to form.

He kissed her then, long, slow and deliberate, easing away the last thread of nerves and distracting her with the sensual delight he was weaving between them. Seconds passed—minutes and time lost all meaning for Sia, who simply relished the power and passion of an endless kiss. Her body came alive, yearning and wanting, eager and impatient, her breathing quickened and her body flushed, heat tingling across her skin.

He positioned himself and gently pressed into her, gliding slowly deeper and deeper. She felt the unfamiliar tension of muscles building, the pressure strange and new, but his kiss was so different. He plundered her with his demanding tongue, filling her again and again with passion and power and it made her want more, need more. The aching desire building within her caused her to shift beneath him, to widen her legs, urging him deeper, harder into her so that his body would finally mirror his tongue, so that she would know what it felt like to be consumed by him completely.

Finally giving in to her desires, he pushed to the very depth and she felt him, all of him, and more, as if she no longer knew where he ended and she began. He withdrew and she nearly cried from the loss until he thrust back into her and she cried instead with pleasure. Again and again he thrust into her, her moans of ecstasy poured into him as he kissed her, their sweat-slicked bodies sliding effortlessly together, bringing them closer and closer to something unfathomable to Sia—a strange wordless moment that defied explanation. Each thrust took her nearer to the edge and further from rationality and she both longed for it and wanted to delay it because it would take her away from the sheer pleasure drenching her entire being.

Her hand slipped around Sebastian's waist instinctively, knowing what she wanted, pressing down against the base of his spine to hold him there, deep within her, as she shifted her hips, welcoming him further into her. His eyes grew wide, ringed with gold flecks that shone in the darkness, and in that second—the moment just before they both fell—they shared infinity.

CHAPTER EIGHT

SIA STIRRED, FEELING the warmth of a sunbeam against her skin, smiling to herself from the memory of the night before. She stretched out her legs, feeling the pull of unfamiliar muscles and the gentle hum of pleasure still in her body.

Reluctantly prising her eyes open, she spied the beautiful sunny day through the large open windows of the cabin. She also caught sight of a round table, pristine white cloth swaying in the breeze. From the bed she could make out platters of fruit, croissants and, thankfully, a large silver cafetière.

She realised that Sebastian wasn't there and was actually a little thankful to have just a moment to collect herself. She didn't for one minute regret what she'd done with him last night, but she was beginning to understand what he'd meant about unforeseen consequences.

The emotions that wrapped around how she felt about him and even herself were shifting in the sunlight like dust particles. There had been a moment last night when she had felt utterly connected to him. No masks, no lies, no secrets yet to be revealed. It had been just them and for a moment she'd thought—she'd imagined—they could have…

The rest of their lives.

And then she kicked off the sheets as if she could kick away the thought as pure fancy, even if somewhere deep in her heart she clung to the possibility. She had agreed only to the next twelve days—eleven now, she realised as she ducked into the shower and stretched beneath the soothing hot jets of water cascading over her skin. It shouldn't have been arousing, but the memory of Sebastian's hands and lips doing the very same thing heated her blood and she twisted the handle to cold, relishing the sharp shock and clearing the sensual fog from her mind.

Laughing at herself a little, she reached for a towel, dried herself and then took the silk robe hanging beside the shower. As she walked out towards the decking, fastening the robe at her waist, she took in the signs of what had happened last night. At the foot of the bed she picked up her silk negligée from the floor, running it through her hands as she looked out to the decking and the feast on the table. Condensation had formed on the glass jug of freshly squeezed orange juice and the pang in her stomach prodded her into action.

She sat in the place opposite a cup that still held an inch of rapidly cooling coffee, her frown dissolving as she bit into the most delicious flaky pastry, uncaring that she groaned out loud, especially with no one to hear her. Not even halfway through it, she was already eyeing another, contemplating just how wicked it would be to have a second. Sebastian had made her wanton and as her tongue flicked out to rescue a sliver of sweet almond she couldn't bring herself to care.

Although there was a slight sense of unease building as she considered the range of emotions Sebastian might be feeling. Did he regret it? Had it been *okay* for him? The wisp of concern at that thought was immediately soothed by the memory of the look in his eyes last night, the awe that she'd felt reflected back at her in his gaze... that wasn't fake.

She held the rim of her coffee cup against her lip, unseeing of the horizon or the beautiful blue sea peppered with boats at varying distances from shore until a small speedboat caught her eye. Not because of the speed at which it was going but the figure at the helm. Tall, proud and focused, there was something about the man that made her think of Sebastian as the boat cut through the waves.

Without thinking, she went into the room to retrieve the binoculars from the table and, returning to the decking, brought them to her face, startled by the detail she could see.

The wind rippled across his white shirt, flicked through his hair and pressed against his tan trousers, outlining powerful thighs. For a moment she was distracted by the sight, her senses still alert from the night before. Until her gaze snagged on two large dark shapes on the floor by his feet and she remembered the duffel bags they'd waited for at the airfield back in London.

Sebastian passed a catamaran and several jet skiers, ignoring their greetings, his focus zeroed in on a beautiful yacht way out in the distance, far enough for the two figures waiting on the boat to seem tiny even with the binoculars.

Unable to look away, it was some minutes before Sebastian met the yacht, pulling up alongside to pass something to them which could have been the duffel bags. After a brief exchange Sebastian manoeuvred the speedboat around and turned back to shore.

Sia put the binoculars to the side and picked up her coffee cup, her mind purposely blank. Automatically she finished the croissant, no longer under its sugary sway. She must have sat like that for quite some time because she stirred only when she heard footsteps on the pathway and saw Sebastian approaching the steps to the cabin.

His lips quirked into a broad smile and he removed the sunglasses to reveal eyes sparkling with sensual mischief. He closed the distance between them and before she could finish her breath had placed a firm kiss against her lips.

'I was hoping to find you in bed,' he said.

'I could say the same,' she replied, purposely keeping her tone neutral.

'Oh, that,' he replied as she saw his eyes skate across the table and over the binoculars. 'A couple of guys sailing the islands underestimated how much fuel they'd need. I didn't want to bother the staff in their preparations for the opening, so I headed out and gave them enough to get where they were going.'

'Very kind of you.'

'You sound surprised,' he remarked with a raised eyebrow.

'Not in the slightest,' she said, unable to resist the smile pulling at her lips.

He leaned in and stole another kiss. 'I don't believe you.' Grabbing an apple from the bowl, he took a bite. 'Finish breakfast because we have to get going.'

'Going where?' she asked, intrigued in spite of herself.

'You'll see,' he teased and disappeared inside the cabin, from where she heard the shower start. But out on the veranda the smile loosened its hold and a cloud passed over the sun, chilling the air, and Sia shivered.

Sebastian loved the speedboat. The feel of the engine roaring behind him, the feel of the wheel beneath his palm, the stinging heat from the sun soothed by the cool air buffeting them as they cut through the waves. And he wasn't the only one. The look of excitement in Sia's eyes, the exhilarated yell each time they crossed and crested a wave unexpectedly, the juddering bump both startling and delighting.

Everything he'd set out to achieve in the Caribbean was done. The party celebrating and thanking the hotel staff and contributors had been a roaring success. The feedback from the visiting staff had been not only good but useful and he had a team working out whether it should be an annual event for all staff and hotels.

And now he could put the business with the painting behind him. He was surprised to find a sense of relief. Perhaps that was what had been missing when he'd toasted Aliah in Victoriana. The line in the sand. Everyone now had their due and their own piece of revenge.

Not everyone, his inner voice chided.

Sia might not have a job or a career to return to when their time together concluded. Not that she should return to a company as rotten as Bonnaire's, but still.

'Fancy taking her for a spin?' he asked Sia, while wondering if perhaps there was something he could do about that.

'Really?'

'Sure. It's not as if there's a lot of traffic out here for you to hit,' he said, gesturing to the acres of crystal-blue sea around them. She practically jumped off the seat in her eagerness and Sebastian couldn't help but smile. When he'd returned to find her at breakfast, for a moment he'd wondered... There had been a look in her eyes, but it had disappeared since then.

Shutting that thought down, he brought her in between his body and the wheel, encasing her within his arms, and smiled when she looked up at him.

'What do I do?'

'Aim for that small island over there,' he said, placing her hands on the wheel. 'Have a bit of a go—*gently*,' he said as she squeaked and the boat veered off to the left. He guided the wheel back on course. 'You got it?' She nodded, her expression fierce with concentration, allowing him to stand back a little and enjoy.

It's just for now, he told himself. Just for the next two weeks. Because after that, whether she returned to Bonnaire's or not, whether she miraculously found either the proof or the painting, she'd be gone from his life. And he was happy with that, he told himself fiercely. He was good at indulging momentary pleasures and that was what Sia was. An incredible, impressive woman but she was only in his life for the next eleven days. He'd done serious, he'd buckled down when he'd needed to, he'd played the parent, even. And no matter what kind of promise he saw in Sia's eyes, he would not willingly return to that.

The wind whipped at the white linen top Sia wore over her orange bikini. He couldn't help but smile. That morning, when he'd presented her with it, rather than questioning it or hesitating, she ran her eyes over it in wonder, the smile pulling at her lips one of excited expectation. A look he wanted to see much more of from her.

'Sebastian?' Sia called over the roaring wind, pulling him from his thoughts.

They were approaching the island and he took the wheel, keeping her encircled in his arms. 'Perfect. Thank you, Chief Mate,' he said.

'If you expect me to say *aye-aye*, or call you Captain then—'

Sia broke off at the sudden, shocking heat in Sebastian's gaze that threatened to consume them both in its ferocity even as he powered down the boat.

'Really?' she teased. 'You want me to—'

And then all she could do was scream as he scooped her up in his arms and jumped them both overboard, the warm water soothing on wind and sun-kissed skin, his arms around her as he trod water to keep them above the surface.

'You look like a mermaid,' he said as she pushed the wet ropes of her hair back from her face, before putting her arms around his neck, leaning in and pressing her lips against his, the warm salty water making her bold. He held her against him, allowing her to explore him, her fingers travelling around his strong neck and shoulders, her legs around his waist, his thighs supporting her. She wanted nothing more, to think of nothing more, no doubts, no needs, just want. Just him.

He carried her all the way to the shore, where they had a picnic on the beach of cold potted shrimp with mango salad, bacon-wrapped crab bites, salmon rillettes, smoky seared octopus, fresh green lemony salad and beautiful breads with butter and a bottle of chilled white wine. They snorkelled, swam, laughed and kissed and not once did Sia think of Sebastian's morning boat trip, the lost painting or her job.

Because this loose and easy way of living… She was beginning to really fall for it.

INTERVIEWER ONE: *So let me get this right. You went to the Caribbean, where you attended a VIP party with no VIPs, went snorkelling, swimming and had a picnic? Did you even look for the painting? I mean, separate rooms at least would have allowed you some time alone—did you not investigate at all?*

MS KEATING: *I no longer believed that he had the painting with him in the Caribbean.*

INTERVIEWER TWO: *But did you ask him?*

Ms Keating: *If he had the painting?*

Interviewer Two: *No, about his mother.*

Sia followed Sebastian back to the cabin, her fingers tangled with his, her body happily exhausted from swimming and snorkelling and her heart satiated with happiness. She caught sight of a barbecue set up on the decking.

'I hope you don't mind. The restaurant is now closed so that they can prepare for opening next week. You're going to have to put up with my cooking.'

'You cook?' she asked, genuinely surprised.

'Not at all,' he said without shame, 'but putting a piece of meat on a grill and presenting dishes that other people have prepared is hardly cooking.'

She laughed at his honest response. She went to the shower to wash off the sea salt, strangely relishing the moments she had to herself. Having Sebastian intent on her in this way was overwhelming—and, she warned herself, temporary. Her empty fist clenched, remembering how good it had felt to her fingers entwined with his. She couldn't let this be more than what it was. She couldn't let herself feel more than what she should.

Determined to keep a little of herself back from him this time, Sia put on a bright smile as she made her way out to the decking. The dress she'd chosen was forest-green with a thin shoulder strapped lace bodice that stopped just beneath her breasts and fell down to her ankles with silky skirts. She felt both Grecian and bohemian, her hair drying in thick waves from the shower and her feet bare.

As she reached the decking, Sebastian had his back to her, focusing on the steak he was cooking. The marinade smelt incredible, making her mouth water just as much as he had in the shower.

'Would you pour the wine?' Sebastian said without turning.

She reached for the red, noticing the label.

'You know it?' he asked.

'Heard of it, never tasted,' she replied of the Tersi branded Pinot Noir.

'You couldn't be tempted?'

'I couldn't afford it,' she replied on a sigh as she poured out the light, fruity wine into two glasses. He really did live in a very different world to her, one that she doubted very much she belonged in.

She took a seat at the table, laid—as promised—with beautiful dishes, salads and vegetables, and smiled when Sebastian returned to the table victorious with two perfectly cooked steaks. Gentle conversation, the warmth of the wine, delicious food and the promise of later behind nearly every look or touch from Sebastian lulled Sia into a state of relaxed bliss.

As he gathered the plates and cleared the table, she looked out at the sun, lazily setting on the horizon, slashing ochre and burnt sienna across the division between sea and sky. It felt almost as if it could be just the two of them at the edge of the world. It was magical. And for the first time in what felt like years she had the urge to pick up a paintbrush. To capture the moment, the *entire* moment, the feeling as much as the view, the slight sense of tearing within in her between sadness and sheer joy.

'You okay?' Sebastian asked and she realised that he'd been sitting there for some time.

'Yes. A nearly perfect day,' she proclaimed.

'Nearly?' Sebastian countered, full of mock outrage.

She couldn't help but think back to the start of the day. To his trip to the yacht and his explanation. *I'm very good at spotting fakes.*

'What would your perfect day look like?' he asked, bringing her out of her thoughts.

'A private viewing of the *Allegory of Fame* by Artemisia Gentileschi,' she replied without hesitation.

'Really? Why that artist and painting?'

'The artist is my namesake.'

'Your full name is *Artemisia*?' he asked, the shock in his voice almost amusing.

'Yup. Try that on for size at primary school,' she said, the sting of childhood taunts still sharp years on. Even more so after her father's arrest.

'You don't like it?'

'Hardly. I consider it his worst act of parental cruelty.'

'Above getting arrested?'

'Absolutely. It was about *him*. *His* favourite artist. *His* arrogance and obsession with the greats.'

Sebastian looked out at the sea, a slight frown on his brow.

'You said your father named you after his favourite artist because of his arrogance?' he asked, and she nodded. 'Could it have been that he saw something in you, even as a baby, that reminded him of Artemisia?'

It was not something that Sia had considered before.

'You know her story?' Sebastian asked. 'What she overcame to become one of the most accomplished Baroque painters of the seventeenth century?'

'Of course,' she said, calling to mind the difficulties the artist had experienced, but also how afterwards she had thrived and flourished.

'Then is it beyond the realm of imagination that your father would name you after such an incredible woman because he sensed those same traits in you?'

Sebastian allowed her to sit with her thoughts while he rose to retrieve the wine and topped up their glasses.

'So, what is it about *Allegory of Fame* that is so significant for you?'

Pushing her musings aside, Sia couldn't help but smile as the image of a painting she knew like the back of her hand rose in her mind. 'It's a remarkable painting, but in a private collection even the Bonnaire's name won't allow me to access. Fame—depicted as a woman—isn't portrayed as being classically beautiful. She's not Titian, or half naked, she's not under some intense sensual sway or an object for male appreciation. She is handsome, powerful in her own right, and there's a look on her face... She seems to be watching something happening off the canvas and her acceptance of it is striking. As if it's shocking, sad, but also unsurprising.' She realised that Sebastian was looking at her in a strange way. 'Sorry, that sounds fanciful.'

'Not at all. It's your perfect day to do with as you please. Did you always want to be an art valuer?'

'I always wanted to be in the arts,' she said, skirting around his question. 'It was more than just following in my father's footsteps. I wasn't lying when I said it was in my blood; turpentine and oil paints flow through my veins,' she confided ruefully.

'Did you ever want to paint?'

'Yes,' she said, remembering her childhood obsession with colour, with recreating images in her mind, light and shade, depth and composition. The expression of meaning and emotion beyond language, which cried out and screamed in colour and texture. She could feel it rising within her now as if Sebastian had set off an avalanche within her and she was beginning to feel everything, feel too much.

'Why didn't you?'

'I...' Sia considered all the possible answers and felt a

wave of tiredness at constantly filtering her words as if
they might be used against her in whatever game it was
they were playing. She wasn't sure she wanted to play it
any more. So she told the truth. 'I was afraid. Of only being
able to copy artists like my father. Of not having any natural talent myself.' She realised then that it was a little like
her fear of passion…that she might have inherited both
her parents' worst traits. But hadn't Sebastian shown her
a way around that? To navigate that fear, access her own
passion and *not* be like her mother?

What might art school have looked like if she'd not let
her fears in there too? Unable or unwilling to face the answer to that question, she turned to him.

'What about you?'

'What *about* me? I have eleven hotels, a combined total
of seventy-two stars, many of which are Michelin—'

'I know,' she interrupted, slightly frustrated at his almost standard response. 'But…is this what you really
want? Please don't get me wrong,' she stated quickly, sensing that Sebastian was growing annoyed. 'I don't mean to
question you on it, but you're just going to keep opening
more and more hotels? Make more and more money? I'm
not disparaging what you've achieved, Sebastian, because
it's incredible and it has clearly supported your family to
a great extent. But—' she searched for something that
would pin down what she meant, what she was looking
for, his hopes and dreams, not obligations and responsibilities '—what did you want to be as a child?' she finally
asked. 'Astronaut? Deep-sea diver? Surely you wanted to
be more than…'

And then she could have bitten off her own tongue. She
genuinely hadn't meant to belittle his accomplishments,
as if somehow being a billionaire was distasteful, but she
couldn't shake the feeling that it wasn't, perhaps never

had been, what he'd intended to be. She took a mouthful of wine, hoping to swallow some of the guilt and shame.

'I was going to be a doctor. I'd got into Harvard Medical School.'

Her heart broke at the way he said it. As if he'd meant to pick something up on a shopping list and forgot it. No big deal. But it was precisely that which told her how much of a sacrifice it had been.

'After the exile I couldn't afford to go, and I wouldn't leave Maria. Eduardo was barely capable of holding his head up and Valeria was too busy bemoaning her fate of being married to an ex-Duke, so neither would have been able to look after her. Do you like the wine?'

The swift about-turn of the conversation nearly gave her whiplash.

'I do. It's delicious.'

'Theo will be glad to hear that,' he said before she could try and steer the conversation back. Instead, she let him have the space he needed.

'You know the vintner?'

'A very good friend of mine.'

'You have friends?' she teased, trying for levity.

'You seem surprised,' he observed wryly, taking a sip of the wine.

'No,' she replied easily. 'I'm just curious as to what they'd think of you stealing a painting worth one hundred million pounds.'

'Is that your question for today?' he replied around a smile.

'No,' she said, her tone suddenly serious, thinking back to what he had said last night. Was it really only last night? It felt as if so much had passed since then.

The look in Sebastian's eyes told her that he was thinking of the same thing. She heard his sigh taken away by the gentle breeze of the night and waited. Because she couldn't help but think that his response, *this* response, would be the answer to nearly all of her questions.

Sebastian knew what she wanted, knew that they would work their way around to this question at some point. It almost felt like a relief to finally address it.

'The first time I met Durrántez was in his studio. My mother had taken me. She'd just found out she was pregnant and, it's trite but true, she had this glow about her. Everything felt—' he shrugged '—bigger. Not physically, but her emotions. Her love. It was as if they had grown to encompass Maria before she was even there. And for those few months of her pregnancy I relished in it, rejoiced even.

'Durrántez was in his seventies when he painted *Woman in Love*. He had this full head of thick white hair,' he said, gesturing in the air with his hand as if frothing the man's hair in his imagination. 'Thick black-rimmed glasses and a blue paint-covered shirt. Half of his studio was a mess and the other half was almost military in its precision.'

'My father was the same,' Sia said, smiling as if she could imagine what he was remembering. 'He said it was the order that made the creativity possible.'

Sebastian nodded, thinking that it seemed to fit with Etienne's slightly erratic but always passionate persona.

'Even Durrántez seemed to have fallen under her spell. They would talk for hours about artists, arguing over who was the greater in each decade, first by painter and then by painting.' The memory of their voices, heated with passion and then deflated by laughter, rose up over the gentle cooing of Caribbean birds and he was back in Spain. 'I could see it, you know? In the way that he looked at her. It was the way anyone who loved her looked at her. As if my mother were not only the centre of the room but of

the universe. She had a laugh that would attract attention
and a way about her that would make her as amiable to
prince or pauper.'

'It sounds quite a bit like you,' Sia observed, her eyes
shining in the darkness.

Sebastian shrugged it off, half wanting to share something, anything, with his mother and half wanting to remember that ability as uniquely hers.

'I was ten at the time and it was during the summer
holidays. I had brought a book, expecting it to be boring
and dull, but I couldn't help but watch every minute of it.
And now I'm glad of it. My mother sat for Durrántez for
a total of seventeen hours and for every minute of it, like
Durrántez, I traced the line of my mother's smile, the curve
of her cheek, the warm blush of happiness and I assessed
the colour of her eyes. I'll never forget my mother's face,
even if my sister wasn't the spitting image of her.'

Goosebumps rose over Sia's skin as she realised what
Sebastian was saying and she felt tears press at the corners of her eyes.

'The painting was completed after her death. In the
sittings she'd been wearing a white dress. But in the finished painting Durrántez changed it to black. A mark of
respect, a mark of loss—his, ours, I'll never know, but it
was a mark nonetheless. It was the last painting that Durrántez ever painted.'

For nearly twenty years no one had identified the model
for *Woman in Love* and, for some reason, Sia found herself
wanting desperately to keep that secret. A sense of loss,
greater than she'd ever personally experienced, rose up
within her chest as she realised that his mother must have
died giving birth to his sister, perhaps only weeks or less
after she had sat for the painting. Loss of a mother, of a
muse for a painter, of a powerful presence who'd debated

great artists, the loss of a future that Sebastian had clearly wanted, because of his father's own stupidity.

'How did the Sheikh end up with the...?' She didn't need to finish the question. She began to see how the threads came together as if she had just unravelled a knot she'd been struggling with for days. 'The Sheikh was the business partner who convinced your father to invest his money and the money of others. Oh,' she said, the shock finally settling—the moment she realised that his father had used the portrait of his mother as financial collateral. The sense of betrayal Sebastian must have felt causing her to shake her head as if trying to deny such a thing.

'And Abrani never let you buy it? Even though he must have known how important that was to you?' Sia was no longer seeing the beauty of the sunset, the way the rich forest-green palms swayed in the breeze. She was forging pathways in her mind, making connections... 'So you got the painting back. But it wouldn't have been enough to steal the painting, would it? Because, although you *wanted* the painting, it wasn't really about that. It was about publicly shaming the Sheikh. Or perhaps giving him the choice?

'He could always have insisted that the painting was authentic, but he'd end up facing an investigation that could reveal his own duplicity in the oil deal ten years ago. Or he could accept the public shame for trying to sell a fake.

'But, in order to achieve any of this, the painting *had to be seen* as a fake. Otherwise, it would never have come back on the Sheikh.'

And it would have the double impact of punishing Bonnaire's for getting involved in backdoor auctions and dodgy dealings, Sia realised, her head spinning. Now that she could see the pieces, how they fitted together, emotions began to pour through the cracks. Her heart ached for the young boy who had first lost his mother and then later lost his home, his future. She could see the sacrifices Sebastian had made for his family and understood his penchant for indulgence now. She could taste a desire for revenge on her own tongue.

But what that meant for her, for what she was trying to do here... Her head began to spin.

'It is an interesting hypothesis,' he said, watching her very closely. And she knew why. She could feel it just as much as him. The turning point. The moment that would define their future. 'It is a shame that you've used up your questions for today and therefore I can't confirm or deny.'

His gaze locked on hers, as if both questioning and insisting. Sia nodded slowly.

She could walk away now. She might not have proof, she might not have even seen the painting, but she'd been wrong when she'd told him in Victoriana that she didn't care why he'd stolen the painting. Because suddenly the why had become the most important thing about this whole mess. Neither Bonnaire's nor Abrani *deserved* to have the real painting returned, so the only person to lose out would be her.

Or she could take Sebastian up on his offer. Remain in the game for at least another twenty-four hours, this strange bubble of hypotheticals that felt incredibly far removed from real life—real life with a horrible job she might no longer have, living in a miserable flat she'd never liked, hiding from a passion she had refused to acknowledge and a desire to do something...*more* than valuing paintings for other people.

She turned to Sebastian, away from the questions, away from the world outside. She wanted to feel his touch, feel the truth of it, because it was so much easier than working out the lies that had been told to her and that she had told to herself.

'Take me to bed?' she asked.

'Your wish is my command,' he said, taking her hand and kissing her palm. 'For as long as you will it.'

CHAPTER NINE

INTERVIEWER ONE: *Okay...so snorkelling—tick—sunbathing—tick—swimming—tick. Gorgeous food, stunning sunsets and walks on the beach—we get it. But we know you didn't stay in the Caribbean for the whole time.*

MS KEATING: *Really?*

INTERVIEWER TWO: *We are investigators.*

MS KEATING: *[silence]*

INTERVIEWER ONE: *When did you get to Italy?*

SIA HAD BEEN reluctant to leave the Caribbean but the prospect of going to Italy had her practically skipping down the steps of the private jet that had whisked them to an airfield just outside Siena.

'I can't believe you haven't been to Italy,' Sebastian said as if disgusted. 'It is a crime.'

'Your definition of crime might need to be looked at,' she replied around a smile.

'Anywhere you would like to go?' he asked, guiding her towards a beautiful grey convertible at the end of the tarmac. It was sleek and old-fashioned, the kind of car that made Sia want to run her hand across the bonnet to see if it was as silky as it looked, gleaming in the Tuscan sun.

'Is this yours?' she demanded, momentarily forgetting his question.

'Yes.'

'Can I drive?' she asked.

'Absolutely not.'

'But you flew the plane,' she said, knowing full well that she sounded like a stroppy child.

'Really? That's how you're going to play this?' Sebastian demanded, peering over the top of his sunglasses.

'Fine.' She relented long enough to return to his earlier question. 'I want to go to the Uffizi and the Galleria dell'Accademia in Florence. Definitely have to see the medieval frescoes in the Basilica di San Francesco in Assisi, and Michelangelo's *Pieta* in St Peter's Basilica in Vatican City—'

'Okay, okay, I get it,' Sebastian interrupted, putting the car into gear and pulling out of the airfield onto the road towards his estate just outside of Siena. 'You want to see everything.'

'If we can,' she said, a hint of reticence in her voice for the first time in days.

'We've got time,' Sebastian said, as if trying to convince himself as he shifted up to the highest gear and hit the accelerator.

The glide of the steering wheel beneath his hands as they took the familiar corners and bends in the road to his estate was strangely satisfying to Sebastian. It hadn't been that long since he'd been here, but for the first time it felt as if he were coming home. For so many years, on the move between his hotels all around the world, working every hour he could, it had been a place more for Maria than him. But, bringing Sia here, it felt as if he were revealing part of himself to her.

But only a part.

He could afford her this small glimpse into his life because she was going to leave it. They only had ten days left now and it was because he felt that time was running out for them that he'd decided to surprise her that evening.

He smiled, the prospect of it exciting him as much as he hoped it would delight her. He looked across to where she sat beside him. Having tied a scarf around her hair to stop it whipping about her head, she looked like a siren from the silver screen, the bright slash of red lipstick screaming from rosebud lips that he wanted very much to mess up with deep, hot, open-mouthed kisses.

She looked glorious. Alive and full of even more passion than he'd thought possible when he'd first met her in Victoriana. He wanted it, all of it. His fingers gripped the steering wheel and he wondered when this obsession with her would be done. His need for her was almost constant, but it was absolutely nothing in comparison with his awareness of what *she* needed and wanted.

'When was the last time you were home?' Sia asked in a half shout over the roar of the wind and the purr of the engine.

'I had a little lunch thing with the Queen of Iondorra and her husband,' he said.

'Did you just name-drop a royal?' she demanded.

'Absolutely,' he said, shrugging his shoulder, causing Sia to laugh. 'It's one of the perks of Theo's marriage.'

'Theo?'

'Tersi. The friend you were surprised I had?' He paused to take the last turn-off for the estate. 'We were checking out Maria's husband. Needed to make sure that he was good enough,' he said as he drove parallel to the boundary wall of his home.

'And was he?'

'Time will tell,' Sebastian replied, turning his mind away from Matthieu Montcour as he guided the car through the wrought iron gates and up the drive before pulling to a stop beside the steps leading up to the front door.

Sia took her time getting out of the beautiful sports car she'd enjoyed so much, partly because her legs felt a little unsteady and partly because Sebastian might as well have brought her to the house of her dreams. Only it was more of a grand estate than a house.

Two storeys high and what looked like at least six rooms wide, the beautiful stone building stood, box like, against a background of beautifully manicured greenery dotted with lazy bees and butterflies. She almost laughed. She needed someone to pinch her but wanted to stay in this strange place that she could so easily fall in love with. She feared falling back down to earth with a very harsh bump.

Sebastian had paused halfway up the steps and, perfectly framed by the three arched domes in the centre of the estate's façade, looked at her as if *she* were on display rather than his wealth, his home…his sanctuary.

She walked around the car, over to where his hand was outstretched, and braced herself for the tingles and shivers that his touch always caused. He led her through the front door and down a terracotta-floored corridor. Shafts of sunlight fell on the tiles from the door at the end, making the hallway feel warm and rich and welcoming. She passed an office on the right-hand side, just before a staircase that clung to the side of the hallway leading to the upper level. On the left, she could see a large living area with a fireplace and mantel that drew her gaze, but Sebastian kept on towards the door at the back and the moment that she followed him through the door she could see why.

It was spectacular. She felt as if she'd sneaked into paradise.

A table and two chairs in white wrought iron were set with lunch and a pitcher of what looked like cool lemonade, the scent of sweet citrus hanging in the air. The borders were lush with large evergreens in silver and blue, box trees had been proudly manicured into appealing shapes and large pots of bay created a path to where purple wisteria hung over a metal arch above the table to provide shade from the strong summer's sun.

'And this just happened to be here waiting for us?'

'Not at all. I would imagine my very good staff spent hours slaving over hot stoves to present you with this feast.'

They reached the table and she inhaled the beautiful scent of fresh garden herbs.

'Me?'

Sebastian grimaced. 'Are you happy to amuse yourself for an hour or so? I have business to attend to,' he said, cupping her chin with his hand, his thumb pressed gently against the centre of her bottom lip. In an instant the fire that was always there, waiting to be fanned into life, roared.

Reluctantly, he let her go. 'You can go anywhere you like in the estate, apart from the basement.' Then he kissed her on the forehead and, before Sia could even think to ask any questions, he disappeared.

It was the first time Sebastian had gone against their agreement. He'd promised her that nothing in his life would be off-limits, yet in seconds the excitement that she had felt at being in Italy, at being in Sebastian's home had turned to ash, making her stomach ache and killing her appetite.

It was that same seesawing feeling that she got when something was wrong. Like the way she'd felt when she'd seen Sebastian take the boat out to the yacht. She pressed her hand against her stomach, trying to soothe the feeling away with gentle circles.

Was it a double bluff, perhaps? Did he think that she was going to search the house for the painting? Did he *want* her to focus on the basement rather than another part of the house in the hope that she might miss something hiding in plain sight? No matter what happened between them, she couldn't lose sight of why she was here. Her job. Returning with the painting or with proof. Even if the lines of who was right and who was wrong had become blurred. Even if she thought Sebastian might have already stolen something far more precious to her than the painting.

Sia started on the second floor of the house and she couldn't help but remember doing the same thing in the house in Knightsbridge. Only this actually felt like a home. The colours were mostly earthy in tone, warm terracotta, soothing cream, soft greys from natural stone and wood. The fresh life-giving green from the outside had been brought inside by trailing indoor ivy in the bathrooms, which loved being near the large, bright, south-facing windows. The powerful midday sun beamed into spacious bedrooms, each taking their colour cues from one large dominant painting. It all called to an unknown yearning within Sia. A yearning for something so much like this.

The paintings reminded her of the ones by Astou Ndiaye, most by seemingly unknown artists but each were exquisite, stunning and mostly abstract, as seemed to be Sebastian's preference, and her mind began to wander away from Durrántez and instead to Sebastian. Was it jealousy she was beginning to feel as she wondered what it would have been like to be 'discovered' by Sebastian? To have a patron who believed in her art, in her and what she could achieve? But, even as she had the thought, she bit her lip and realised that perhaps she *did* know what that felt like—to be discovered by him, to be encouraged and championed, to be challenged and to rise to meet that challenge.

Not the challenge of this game they seemed to be playing. It went deeper than that as, no matter what might happen with the painting, Sia couldn't deny that she had been changed by him, made to question herself, her job, her choices. And rightly so.

She was about to leave the upper floor when the sound of wheels on the gravel drive drew her attention to the window looking out on the front of the estate. There was a large grey van and several men in uniforms stepped out and walked to where Sebastian was ready to greet them.

She couldn't hear what they were saying, but she could see them shaking hands and nodding. The uniformed men went to the back of the van and Sebastian stood back as they removed something. It was a reasonably small wooden crate, the kind used to store and move paintings. The kind that was the perfect size for the Durrántez.

Her heart clenched and her skin prickled painfully. Was he planning to sneak it into the estate without her knowing? Did he intend to keep it hidden in the basement or would he share it with her? And if he did, what then?

As her mind raced through the possible implications she realised that seeing the painting would make it real. That she'd finally have to make a choice. In the last week she'd been living out the most beautiful fantasy—one of incredible experiences and impossible pleasures. But it was just that. A fantasy.

But if he shared the painting with her then the fantasy

would disappear and she'd be forced to choose between him and the painting. And for the first time since this whole thing started she wasn't sure what to do.

She stood looking out of the window long after Sebastian had disappeared inside with the crate, after the men in uniforms had driven away and long after Sebastian's allotted 'hour or so' had passed as she contemplated whether the fantasy was one he'd invited her to step into or one he'd enticed her in to, to cover his tracks.

Sebastian felt a twinge of uncertainty. He'd not seen Sia that afternoon though, in all fairness, he'd been distracted by a minor wrangling in the New York hotel and by the time it had been resolved it was nearly five p.m. He'd thought she might have found herself something to do, or been resting, but as the day drew into dusk he couldn't quite shake the feeling that, despite his best intentions, the evening might not quite go as planned. He'd known that telling her an area of the estate was off-limits was a risk, but had decided it was worth it. Something he still believed.

When Sia finally arrived in the living room she took his breath away. The dress was of a similar style to the one she had worn in Victoriana, but this one was the colour of honey. Rich, alluring, evocative. As if she'd dressed with the sole purpose of driving him out of his mind. Which was why it took him a moment to see that Sia was braced, as if ready for some kind of hurt, and he couldn't quite tell why.

'Are you okay?' he said, fighting the urge to close the distance between them, instinctively knowing that it could cause her to flee.

'Yes.'

Sebastian bit his tongue. Clipped, one-word answers weren't Sia's usual style. Giving in to temptation, he crossed the room, stopping barely a foot from her. Sia couldn't meet his gaze and he closed down the bitter laugh he felt rising. He hadn't been exaggerating when he'd declared her a terrible actress. In an instant he knew what she had thought of his request, what conclusion she'd drawn. And could he deny that she was right to do so? Justified, even, after everything he'd done?

He took a breath. 'I had a plan. For how this evening would go. But…' He trailed off, realising that it didn't matter what he said, how he might explain things. The only way would be to show her. 'Come with me?' he asked, his hand held out just like he had done hours before. She nodded, only this time she didn't take his hand, leaving his fingers to close on thin air.

Pushing down on a feeling he refused to name, he led her to the door to the basement, flicking on the lights for the staircase and taking the lead. 'The previous owners converted the entire area into a *very* expensive wine cellar,' he said, all the while questioning why he was persevering with this. Anything he'd hoped to gain was now well and truly shot to pieces. 'But with a few tweaks I realised it would be perfect,' he said as he reached the bottom of the stairs.

'Perfect for what?'

'This,' he said, turning on the low lighting that instantly brought warmth and light to the cavernous underground chamber. The space stretched beyond the footprint of the estate, almost all the way to the boundary. It could have been a World War One weapons bunker for all he knew, but it had been exactly what he'd wanted for his collection.

He was strangely satisfied by the gasp of surprise that fell from Sia's lips. He'd fallen in love with it the moment he'd seen it and it had been the sole reason for buying the estate. Beautiful sand-coloured stone slabs made up the flooring that met aged brick, running along, up and over the walls and curved ceiling of the basement. Soft blond up-lighting mirrored the arches in the walls that led through to other rooms and areas that ran off the central corridor stretching before them. It was his pride and joy and he'd been so excited to share it with Sia, but the moment he'd seen that look in her eyes, the fear of what he might reveal to her, he knew he only had himself to blame.

The space was what Sia noticed first. The walls she noticed second. Paintings. Everywhere she could see. Paintings by unspeakably famous artists, some that she'd only ever heard of and some she could have sworn were hanging in museums and galleries visited by tourists every day. She left Sebastian to walk through the stone corridors and arched hallways, her mind lit with wonder at the most incredible private art collection she'd ever seen. There didn't seem to be a particular pattern, subject matter or epoch to curate the paintings, other than 'famous' and 'priceless'.

She noticed that the temperature wasn't cold, nor too hot, Sebastian clearly taking great care of a collection that's value increased with every single new painting she saw. It made her head swim.

Further into the space she came to a stop.

On the far wall was a small square of velvet covering a painting. There was even a little golden rope attached to it, as if for some grand reveal. Her pulse spiked and leapt, her heart thudding wildly. She was scared. Scared that it was the Durrántez, scared that it wasn't. Now the moment had arrived she still didn't know what to do.

There was a table in front of the painting and it felt strange, inappropriate almost. As was the bottle of champagne gathering condensation, waiting to fill the two empty glass flutes on the ivory tablecloth. The whole thing felt absurd, as if he were making even more of a joke of her and it hurt—the idea that whatever was behind the cover was some form of entertainment.

Sebastian hadn't said a word, remaining behind as if leaving her to face it by herself. Sia felt his eyes on her as she slowly walked towards the velvet cover, conscious of the way her dress shifted over her skin, the way the wedge of her shoe felt against the slight unevenness of the stone flooring, causing her hips to sway, the awareness straightening her spine, and she gently stretched her shoulders back as if determined to meet her fate head-on.

She reached for the golden cord and even before she'd pulled strongly enough on it to lower the velvet she knew.

It wasn't the Durrántez.

'*Allegory of Fame* by Artemisia Gentileschi,' she heard him explain unnecessarily as she took in the painting she'd always wanted to see.

It was breathtaking in the truest sense. Sia's eyes hungrily consumed every inch of the small painting—the richness of Fame's dress, the golden trumpet in her grip, the angle of her head as she leaned to one side... It sounded so mundane but in reality, in *person* it was incredible.

And it was not the Durrántez. No. It was the thing she had told Sebastian she would want for her perfect day. Which made sense of the table behind her, the chilled champagne, the exclusive, intimate private viewing of a painting that she'd always wanted to see. A painting that it must have, at the very least, cost a fortune to secure for even a single night—as she refused to contemplate the idea that he might have actually *bought* it.

She ran a hand over her face, unsure as to whether she was relieved or even more upset.

'I thought...' She trailed off, unwilling to say the words out loud.

'I know.'

She felt him come to stand behind her, the wall of heat at her back bringing her senses to life.

'Did you want it to be the Durrántez?' he asked, his tone so neutral she could have screamed.

'I don't know,' she replied honestly.

With one last look at the Gentileschi, she turned, still unable to meet his eye. 'I ruined this, didn't I?' she asked.

'Not at all,' he said lightly, handing her a glass of champagne.

'You're a terrible liar,' she said, the last word catching in her throat. She couldn't help the tear that escaped down her cheek. A tear that Sebastian swept away with his thumb.

The Durrántez would always be there. Coming between them. Until one of them broke. She just didn't know which of them it would be.

His thumb moved from her cheek to rest against the centre of her bottom lip, as it had done earlier that day. Instinctively, she gently bit down on the pad, anchoring it in place, desperate for anything that could connect them beyond the damn painting.

Her lips came around the tip of his thumb, so slightly sucking on it before letting him go. She turned away, still unable to make eye contact, to let him to see the shame she felt, the embarrassment that she had got it wrong. Got *him* wrong.

But his hand came up to her jaw, gently guiding her to face him. He waited for her to raise her gaze to his. If she'd expected censure, frustration or resentment she'd once again misjudged him.

Fire blazed in his eyes and it pulled open a door within her, creating a sudden backdraught of desire. A hot, twisting sensuality that she felt calling to her body from his. His eyes dropped to her lips and something wild and feminine cried out from her soul. In the days since they had first come together Sia had learned a lot about her body, her desires. He had taught her how to ask for what she wanted, how to listen to her body and know what that was. He had driven her to heights of ecstasy she could never have imagined in moments of beauty she could never have expressed to another living soul.

And after the agonising hours spent wondering and guessing she didn't want to think any more. To question any more. No, she wanted to drown in the way that Sebastian was looking at her. As if she were both his salvation and damnation.

Silently she dared him. Dared him to take what he wanted from her. To do as he willed, for as long as he willed it. She saw the moment he understood, the flare of surprise in his eyes, the sparkle of golden flecks bright against deep, dark, unfathomable eyes. His hand wrapped around her waist, drawing her chest against his. She let her head fall back in surrender, relaxing into his hold, and he feasted on her. Open-mouthed kisses sent shivers radiating across her skin from her neck that she felt in her very core, as if he were already there, consuming her from within.

His hand came up to her hair, his fingers sweeping into the strands and firmly guiding her head back to his, his eyes locked on her lips again for the barest second before he claimed them for his own.

And she relished it, the powerful exploration he made of her, the press of his lips, the way his tongue filled her. She clutched at his shirt, clinging to him, wanting more from him. She felt utterly enthralled by his touch, his kisses, his command.

She was barely conscious that with one free hand Sebastian pulled the chair out from the table and walked them towards it. He positioned them in between the table and chair, pulling her onto his lap as he sat them both down.

Her chest unfurled against him as she sought to press herself deeper into him. Her gasped inhale must have pleased him as she felt his hands fist against her backside, as she drew her knees closer to either side of his hips, ensuring that she brushed up against the length of him, the hard, powerful erection leaving her in no doubt as to his desire for her.

His hands worshipped her body, tracing invisible pathways from her neck, around her breasts, over her taut nipples and down her torso and abdomen to her hips, pulling her once again against him in a way that made her want, need their clothes gone.

As if he sensed her urgency, his hands slipped beneath her dress, came up and over her thighs, his fingers hooking into the elastic band of her panties, his thumb firmly pressing against her clitoris, drawing a moan from her which he consumed with the kiss he still devoured her with. She writhed against his hand, her body shaking with need and urgency. He lifted her slightly, manoeuvring the thin strap of her panties over one leg, then the other, before returning her to his lap and casting them aside.

Her hands swept to the waistband of his trousers, making quick work of the fastening and the zip, pushing aside his boxers to feel the length of him in her hands, hot and velvety. Her thumb danced gently over the tip before positioning him beneath her as she held herself above him.

Her tongue danced with his and she risked a glance, startled to find his eyes staring into hers. She gently drew the kiss to a close, wanting to focus on him, wanting to see what he saw, to feel what he felt when she lowered herself down onto his length.

As she did she watched a hot, heady blush rise to his

cheeks, saw the fierce control and concentration he was exerting over himself to allow her to take the lead in this. The way his pupils dilated to inky black depths drove her on. She held his gaze, the connection so focused it spurred her on, gave her confidence, made her want to relish the power he had given her.

She felt her muscles flex around him as the torturously slow way he filled her made her gasp again and again the lower she got, the skirts of her dress fanning out to cover where they came together, seemingly both indecent and discreet at the same time, adding a strange heady, wicked pleasure to their joining.

It wasn't long before she lost control of the devastatingly slow pace she had set, delighting in the way she could no longer tell where she ended. Her eyes drifted closed, finally severing the intense connection between them and her head fell back. Sebastian's arm came around her, allowing her to bend over it as he placed open-mouthed kisses on her breasts and his thumb swept beneath her skirts and found the apex of her thighs, pressing firm circles around her clitoris, bringing her closer and closer towards the most powerful orgasm she'd ever experienced. She wanted to tell him to wait for just for a minute, just so she could capture this feeling, this moment with him, to hold it to her and—

And then he thrust upwards into her and the stars fell from the sky, through the house, down into the basement and showered them with golden light that she consumed as she gasped air into her lungs and he pulsed within her, his own completion pouring into her making her feel more alive than she remembered ever being. And in that moment Sia knew that she would make the most of it. Whatever 'it' was, and for however long it was to last, she would see it through to the end.

CHAPTER TEN

INTERVIEWER ONE: *So, instead of making use of your time on his estate in Siena to search for the painting, you went on an art tour?*

MS KEATING: *It was Florence.*

INTERVIEWER TWO: *[whispers] Did you see David?*

'SO YOU'RE TRYING to tell me that between the Uffizi and the Galleria dell'Accademia, of all the things we saw, your favourite was the *Gates of Paradise* on the Baptistery of St John?' Sebastian demanded, staring at her with all the mock horror he could summon. Secretly he was pleased.

'Eyes on the road, mister.'

'That's Your Grace to you,' he teased, taking his eyes back to the sweeping road returning to the estate.

He'd been almost sure that she was leaving him the night he had the Gentileschi brought in. But the passion they had shared that night had been like nothing he'd ever known before. She'd surrendered to him and it had awed him—the trust she had placed in him. He wasn't sure he was worthy of it. But something deep within him had started to hope.

'Can we go back?'

'Now? Did you forget something?' he said, his hands pausing on the wheel and already scanning a turning point.

'No, I just want to see more of it. And some of it again. And that spaghetti… Sebastian, seriously, that most definitely has to be done again. So tomorrow? Maybe we could…?' The pleading in her tone was too much to resist.

'If you want to, I am yours to command.'

'Okay. But we should get up *really* early. I want to avoid the tourists.'

Sebastian couldn't help the belly laugh that erupted from his chest. 'We *are* the tourists,' he chided, and flinched as she slapped him on the arm.

'You know what I mean,' she threw at him.

'There's no reason we couldn't stay over.'

'In Florence?'

'Yes,' he said, mentally flicking through his contacts. 'We could stroll the Ponte Vecchio, have dinner on the other side of the river, looking out across at—' He frowned as his phone vibrated in his pocket and the ringtone he'd assigned his sister cut through the sound of the wind whipping past the car.

'Sorry, it's Maria. I have to take this.'

He searched for the headset but couldn't see it, immediate concern about the baby, about Maria firing in his blood enough for him to know it wasn't safe for him to be driving. Before the call could ring off, he saw a layby and pulled into it, ignoring the arc of sand and pebbles thrown into the air as he hit the brakes.

'*Estás bien?*' he demanded down the phone, as he turned off the engine and launched from the car. He knew that his reaction might be seen as extreme, but he also knew Maria. Knew how much she'd valued and embraced her new-found freedom and knew more than anything that this wouldn't be a social call.

'Yes, I am,' she replied calmly, as if having expected such a reaction. 'And you need to hear that because I really am okay, despite what I'm going to tell you.'

Sebastian took a breath, her words really not doing anything to assuage the fear he was feeling for his sister.

'I've left Matthieu.'

'What happened?' he growled.

'It's not important, but I wanted to tell you myself before you found out from someone else. I've already found a house in Umbria. It's a two-hour drive away from you—'

'I'm coming.'

'I don't want you to.'

'I don't care, I'm coming,' he said mulishly.

'Not if I don't give you the address.'

'Maria, we both know that I can find you in less than fifteen minutes if I want to,' he said. Realistically he only needed ten, but it was a Sunday.

'But you won't, because you're my brother and you will respect my wishes.'

'I'm going to kill him,' he promised through gritted teeth.

'You won't, even if I did consider letting you do it for just a minute. Because Matthieu is the father of my unborn child.'

'Come home?' he asked, knowing already that he was defeated.

'Sebastian, that's *your* home. It's time I found one of my own.'

After another five minutes of assurances that she was okay, she signed off. '*Te amo, hermano.*'

'*Te amo, hermana,*' he concluded, before disconnecting the call.

He stared, unseeing, at the range of dusty green hills beside the road, his hand white-knuckled around the slim phone.

'Are you okay?' Sia asked.

'No. And I won't be remotely okay until I have found Montcour and beaten him into a pulp,' he said, his anger finally taking hold, his tone harsh, his words yelled, and he cursed, throwing his phone on the ground in rage.

'Is this something you do a lot?' Sia asked from inside the car, her face turned to him, her eyes covered by sunglasses, her expression impassive.

'*Qué?*' he demanded, confused by her question.

'Perhaps I don't know you well enough to tell if this is your usual reaction to bad news, or if this is extreme. Either way, I can't say I'm a fan.'

'If you don't like it—' he said, the heated words coming out of his mouth before he could call them back.

'It's not a matter of like. You are beginning to scare me.'

The calmly delivered line was at complete odds with her words, but the thought that he might have been in any way making her afraid cut him like a knife. The excess adrenaline from his anger, from his need to fight for those he cared for crashed through him but he quickly got himself under control. He cast a hard glance back towards her, concerned that he had pushed her too far. As if sensing his need, Sia took off her sunglasses. The purity of her gaze, the honesty and concern—not fear—shining for him, for his sister struck him all over again.

'Your sister, is she okay?' Sia asked.

'No. She's eight months pregnant, alone and if anything happens to her—' Residual waves of helpless anger still lapped over him.

'Is she in danger?'

He forced himself to take a breath. 'No.'

Sia leaned over to the driver's seat and opened his door, inviting him back into the car. 'What about Eduardo?'

'What about him?' Sebastian asked, utterly confused about what their father had to do with it.

'Can he do anything?'

Sebastian sank into the seat of the sports car with a bitter laugh. 'He's been the dictionary definition of absent for Maria's entire life. I doubt very much that he's going to change now.'

Sia leaned back in the leather seat, tucking her feet beneath her, signalling her patience for an explanation. He nearly laughed. Somehow, the truest interactions they shared had become silent exchanges, no need for words or questions, their understanding of each other almost instinctive.

'It was one of the conditions of the purchase of their estate in Rimini. That Maria come to live with me.'

'How old was she?'

'Eight.'

Sia nodded as if beginning to understand and perhaps, given her own parents, she might just be able to.

'It was the only way to protect her. Even before our father lost everything in the deal with Abrani, he had removed himself from her, emotionally and physically. Maria is a study of my mother. Hair, eyes, nose, mouth, chin... an almost exact replica. And, much like everything else, Eduardo simply couldn't bear to be reminded of his wife. Because my father, despite all that he became after her death, had loved her so completely in life.

'So, even though it was unintentional, I had to stand by and watch while he broke my sister's heart, knowing that I wasn't enough to fix it and never would be. Because what she needed was her father.'

Sia's heart broke, knowing just how much that would have hurt Maria. Knowing just how much it had hurt her to be separated from her own father. But it also ached for the boy who had become a parent at such a young age. Not just to Maria, but to himself. Her heart melted for the man who would clearly do anything to protect those he loved, those within his purview. She'd seen that at the hotel. She saw it every day in the little things he did for her that she had almost stopped noticing. The way he would have spun the car round and driven back to Florence. The way he had arranged for her to see everything she could ever want in Siena and Florence, and further.

But Sia could see that he was still caught in the past, pulled by the negative tug beneath a tide of anger, and she hated the hold it had on him. And the only way he could move on was to change his thinking, to shift his focus. Torn for just a moment, she realised that the risk of hurting him was not enough to outweigh the gift of release if her plan worked.

'I agree that Eduardo should have stepped up. I'm truly sorry that he wasn't capable of it. You should never have had to do the things you did. But, because you did so, could it be that Eduardo didn't *need* to?' she asked gently, bracing herself for the reaction she knew would come.

'So I should have let the whole thing crash down about our ears?' he demanded hotly.

'No. But Sebastian, it's not about shoulds, coulds or might-have-beens. You *did* step up. And because of that Maria had a safe, loving, caring brother to look out for her. Which is exactly why she's going to weather the storm she's experiencing with her husband.

'Your father had a very plush roof over his head with his wife, and you found the strength to build an international hotel conglomerate that is worth billions,' she said, infusing her voice with all her awe and wonder that he had been able to do so. 'Something that might not have happened had your father managed to resolve even half of the emotional baggage he needed in order to be there for his children. And perhaps, rather than focusing on whether that *should* have happened or not, you could focus on the amazing things that resulted because you did?'

Sebastian resisted the urge to shake off her words. For so long he'd been looking at what he'd missed, what it had cost him to compensate for Eduardo, to assume the position as head of his family. But Sia was right. When he considered what he had gained, not money or things but security, emotional and physical, for his sister and, as much as he could, for his father and Valeria and even himself, that was so much more than where they could have ended up. And the hard work that he put into his company, it had allowed him to invest in his friends, like Theo, and staff, the people who worked for him. In fact, all those early years of struggle and hardship, the impossibly long sleep-deprived hours, they had brought him here, to a moment in time where the world was his oyster—he could now do literally anything with his life. And the sense of accomplishment that spread through him, the pride in his own hard work and achievements began to smooth over the harsh hurts of the past. Not completely, but in its own way it began a healing that took him by surprise.

He cast a look at where Sia was sitting beside him and all he wanted to do was haul her into his lap. As if sensing the train of his thoughts, she smiled, pure wicked deliciousness.

'I didn't pick you as an optimist,' he said, restraining that heat before he did something ludicrous that would have them arrested for public indecency.

'Oh, I am—which is why I know I'm going to get my hands on the painting,' she teased, and he wondered if she realised it was the first time that she'd made a joke, or even referenced the Durrántez since their first night in Siena.

Keeping his hands on the wheel of the car, and not all

over her body where he wanted them, he pressed a kiss on her lips, a promise of more to come. He turned the key in the ignition and guided the car back onto the road that would see them home.

In that moment Sebastian realised that Sia hadn't asked her question since that night either. Was it because she no longer wanted to prove that he'd stolen the painting? Was that a good or a bad thing? He couldn't tell. But now he had a different perspective on his past, along with the realisation that it wasn't that he didn't want a family or commitment in his future—but that *because* of his past he didn't trust that he could ever have such a thing. But Sia was making him want it. Want it with her.

As he parked up in front of the door, Sia was almost halfway out of the car before it had stopped. 'I'm going to stretch my legs before dinner,' she said with a smile on her lips and in her eyes.

'It's not in the garden,' he teased of the painting's location.

She shrugged and turned, walking away. 'But it is here somewhere,' she called over her shoulder.

Sebastian didn't see the way the smile slowly loosened on her lips, the way that Sia steeled her shoulders and spine before removing her mobile phone from her clutch, the way her jaw clenched as she checked the fourth message from Bonnaire's on her answering machine.

'Ms Keating. This is Michael. We've been trying to reach you for quite a number of days now. We have some questions to put to you and we would like to pin down a date for you to come in and speak with our investigative team. Especially given the company you have been keeping since your suspension. We expect to hear from you in due course.'

Her hand shaking, Sia deleted the messages before turning off her phone and slipping it back into her bag. They had suspended her for thirty days. She had been away less than half that. She had five days left of the fourteen that Sebastian had given them and her heart raced at the thought that time was running out. No matter how much she might want to, she couldn't hide out here for ever.

Dressed in Sebastian's shirt and an old pair of jeans she'd found in her suitcase, on bare feet Sia made her way out into the garden to a table laden with coffee, croissants and fruit. Smiling at the half-eaten croissant and half-drunk coffee Sebastian must have consumed in haste before heading out to see Maria an hour ago, Sia unfolded the English newspaper he insisted on having delivered to the estate for the duration of her visit.

Sinking into her seat, she poured herself a coffee, picked up the cup with both hands and inhaled the rich aroma as the heat from the china warmed her palms. It was already hot and barely into double digits, today was going to be...

Her thoughts trailed off as she caught sight of the image dominating the front page of the newspaper. A large black and white photo showed a handsome couple, heads bent, as the man stretched out his hand as if both protecting the woman and warding off the press. But it was the woman who caught her eye. Because Sia had seen her before and as her eyes skated over the accompanying article, the bottom dropped out of her world.

Abrani Heiress Weds Billionaire!
  Despite recent concerns over the attempted sale of a fake painting, things are beginning to look up for Sheikh Abrani as his youngest daughter Aliah surprises the world with a shock secret wedding!

Rumours about possible pregnancy are yet to be addressed by the royal family, but an official statement is expected in due course.

The Sheikh's youngest daughter might have been recently married, but less than eleven days ago she'd been sipping champagne with Sebastian Rohan de Luen, in a private club in Mayfair. 'An old family friend' he'd said, just before calling her beautiful.

Of all the people perfectly positioned to swap out the real painting for the fake, surely the Sheikh's daughter would be at the heart. Something caught in her mind, the memory of Sebastian's righteous recounting of the Sheikh's sins, the least of which was the fact Abrani had literally gambled her hand away in marriage…and that was considered a *good* thing.

All this time, Sia realised, she'd been focused on Sebastian but not the people who could have helped him—like the artist who'd created the forged painting. In her mind's eye she was back in David's lab, the night the fake had been damaged, scanning the painting, the remaining brushstrokes, the technique that…that…

Her mind leapt from one painting to another, but quite possibly by the same artist. Astou Ndiaye, the Senegalese artist who Sebastian had chosen to commission for his Caribbean island hotel. Because something Sia had seen in the two large canvases—a brush stroke, a colour combination—something even then had risen a flag to her visual senses and now she couldn't help but wonder…could Astou have been the forger? What had Sebastian called it? A recent commission.

She reached for her phone and pulled up the search engine. Ndiaye's website was the first hit and she flicked across the images of her abstract paintings, but further below were a collection of classically styled paintings, portraits and still lifes—certainly showing promise and a strong sense of the classical techniques that would have come in handy when trying to forge a Durrántez. Clicking through to her bio, Sia's heart plummeted as she discovered that Ndiaye grew up in Senegal but went to live in France after her mother, who had been a high-profile trader, had been forced to declare bankruptcy. Right around the time Eduardo's business deal had fallen through.

A wave of anger began to build, as if a way out from shore yet but coming closer and closer the more her suspicions grew. And she almost didn't want to look further because if she was right, if what she thought was true, it might break her.

Bracing herself, she pulled up a new tab and searched for the name Sabbatino. Headlines screamed back at her, laying bare the various secret assignations of the Italian brothers, one particularly insalubrious article saw a woman proclaiming to have spent the night with both of them. Ignoring the attention-grabbing reports, she instead clicked on the few images.

Pictures of the two handsome Italian brothers grinning at the camera, suave, sophisticated, charming and doing absolutely nothing for Sia until she caught sight of one particular image. She clicked on the thumbnail and used two fingers to enlarge the image on her screen. There they were, arms slung around each other as they stood in front of their yacht. A yacht they were currently sailing around the Caribbean.

A pit yawned open in her stomach and she pushed the phone away before she could see any more. Before she could hurt any more. It wasn't the proof that she needed. It was nothing she could take back to Bonnaire's. But that didn't matter any more.

She'd always known that he'd stolen the painting but at the very least thought she'd had his respect, his promise not to lie to her. He might have been a thief but she'd thought him truthful. Honourable. She'd been such a fool.

Sebastian had told her that his life was an open book and perhaps she couldn't say that he'd lied.

Because everything he'd done had been done in front of her, even from the first moment. Aliah in Victoriana—the thief imprisoned by her father and paid with, what, her freedom? Ndiaye's paintings in the Caribbean—the forger whose mother's career was ruined, and paid off with a massive commission. And the Sabbatino brothers? Who knew what they'd got or what even their connection was to the defunct oil deal. Did it matter any more?

She was devastated by the wave of hurt as it drew closer and closer, threatening to overwhelm her. Not because of a plan that had been put in place before she'd ever laid eyes on Sebastian Rohan de Luen, but the fact that he could do it under her watchful gaze and think he'd get away with it. Was he really that cruel? Had everything been a lie? *All* of it? Or was it just the painting?

The last time she had questioned his actions she had hidden in the fantasy. But she couldn't do it again. This time she couldn't ignore what was staring her in the face.

Sebastian returned to the house just as the sun was beginning to set, feeling much better than he had for a long time. He and Maria had spoken almost all day. He was surprised to find how strong she was. Hurt, yes, and for that he would most definitely make Montcour pay. But her determination to forge a future that would protect her and her child had made him proud for her.

For the first time he had seen her as more than his little

sister. He had seen her as an adult, a woman. A mother. It was incredible.

He took the steps to the house two at a time, excited and happy to be returning to Sia. He'd told Maria about her, of course. Not everything, and nothing about the Durrántez, but he'd explained that he was thinking about things differently. And he only had Sia to thank for that. He wanted to tell her, thank her for making him wait, for making him calm down. That as much as he'd wanted to step in and take control, Sia was also right in that Maria needed to do that by herself and she was flourishing.

In his enthusiasm it took him a moment to realise that the house was shrouded in darkness. Had there been a power outage? But as he headed further down the hallway he saw a light on in the corner of the living room.

He leaned against the door frame, his arm above his head, just looking at her. Curled up on a large cream armchair, her head turned to look out of the window, she was the most beautiful thing he'd ever seen. In a large oversized thick wool cardigan and soft silvery-grey lounge suit it shouldn't have worked with her golden Titian hair, but it did. She seemed regal almost, like a figure from a Renaissance painting—a silver angel with a crown of gold.

And then she turned to look at him and the sadness in her eyes cut him like a thousand knives.

'What happened? What's wrong?'

She ignored his question and asked, 'Is Maria okay?'

'Yes,' he assured her.

'Good,' she said, turning back to look out into the darkness beyond the window.

'She wants to meet you.'

Sia shook her head. 'I'm not sure that's a good idea.'

Something slithered in his stomach, making him nauseous. 'Why?'

'I have to go back to London,' she said, gently tapping her mobile phone against her knee.

'When did that happen?'

Instead of answering him, she nudged at the newspaper folded up on the table beside the lamp. While he scanned the headline, his gut clenching tighter and panic shooting through him like lightning, her gaze returned to the window.

'Did you know that the Sabbatino brothers have a yacht? And that Ndiaye once studied fine art at the Sorbonne? And that both had parents who were negatively impacted by undisclosed business deals in the same year that you were exiled?'

There were so many ways he could have responded to her question, but he finally settled on the truth. 'I did know those things, yes,' he admitted.

'What? You didn't want to know if that was my 'question' before answering it? Because it wasn't,' she said, shaking her head. 'That's coming, but not yet.'

Anger began to mix with the fear, creating a toxic concoction spreading through his veins. 'I thought we were done with that game.'

'It wasn't a game, Sebastian,' she said disdainfully. 'It was my job. My reputation. My career.'

He blanched. 'I can get you another job.'

'And the fact that this is your response goes to show how little you understand what I've lost.'

'Don't talk to me about loss,' he growled. 'My family lost everything—home, money, reputation.'

'The exact price that I am paying for your revenge,' she said, her voice so horrifyingly calm. 'Do you *care*?'

'Of course I care! How can you ask that?'

She shrugged indifferently. 'Because at every turn you give me two very different sides of the coin. The billionaire hotelier who throws a VIP party for his staff. The thief who will do anything to protect his co-conspirators. The brother who was more father to his sister than anything and the playboy who almost made me love him,' she choked as a tear began to roll down her cheek.

Sebastian experienced a tearing sensation as half of him soared with joy at even the possibility of her love, but the other—the half that registered the past tense, who caught the word 'almost' and who realised the depth of her sadness—felt the greatest loss he'd ever experienced.

'How could you have done that to me?' she demanded, unfolding from the chair and closing the distance between them. Her anger, her hurt, the thread of injustice vibrating in the air between them calling to him. 'How can you proclaim to care and yet wave *every* aspect of your thievery and falsehood in my face?'

The pain her words caused made him desperate. Unable to shake the feeling that the most precious thing he could ever know, ever touch or be near wasn't the millions and millions of pounds' worth of paintings in his basement but the woman who sat in front of him.

'You weren't supposed to be there. You *weren't*,' he insisted. 'It was supposed to be Sean Johnson, who came down with food poisoning the night before flying to see the Sheikh. It wasn't supposed to be you.'

'But it was,' she said simply. 'So my question, the one you promised to answer truthfully…' she said, piercing him with a look, warning him, begging him, and he felt it call to his very soul. 'Was it worth it?'

He flinched.

'Stealing the painting and all that it resulted in. Was it worth it?'

He reached for her then, crushing his lips to hers in a kiss that would brand them both. For a blissful moment she unfurled beneath his touch until he felt it, the second she regained her hurt about her like a shield and pushed him away.

'Was it worth it?' Sia demanded, her voice hoarse with pain. She looked at him, breathing just as hard as him, the look in his eyes unfathomable.

'Yes—but not because of the painting,' he rushed to add. But it was too late. His words had done the damage she knew they would.

'Sia, listen to me. It was worth it because it brought you to me.'

'And you expect me to believe that?' she cried harshly.

'You have to trust me,' he begged.

'I can't!' she yelled. 'I can't trust you at all. This whole thing has been a game to you. A con. An elaborate, incredible fantasy, but ultimately a ruse. When does it end? How will I ever know if you really do care about me or if you're just trying to get away with it?'

'Sia, I care you about you so much that I'm willing to let this go and that scares me so damn much. Everything I've risked, that other people have risked for this? I would give it all up in a heartbeat if you ask me to.' A part of her didn't want to believe him. In his eyes all she could read was sincerity, but could she really take such a gamble? 'But you won't. Because you're too scared,' he accused.

'I'm not scared of you,' she insisted.

'No, but you are scared of yourself. Terrified to reach for the things that you want, that make you unique and incredible. And until you realise that, until you face what it is you truly want, accept it and pursue it, you won't stop being scared.'

'And I suppose you think that what I want is you? Is that what your words are shaped to make me feel? To make me think?' she said, the way his words had hit home making her mean. 'I was so worried about passion, about falling into the hysterical love that consumed my mother that I missed the one real likeness we share. That you're just like my father. The forger, the con-artist.' For the first time that evening she felt a clarity descend over her—as if the ice around her heart was crystal-clear and on the point of breaking.

'But the biggest con you've pulled is on yourself, Sebastian. Because it's not me who can't trust myself and my wants, is it?' His eyes flashed a warning but she pressed on, her heart raging in her chest, aching for both herself and him.

'You say you would give it up if I asked, but it's not that simple, is it?' she demanded.

His eyes darkened, gone were the golden flecks she loved so much, gone was the gentle tease to soften the blow.

'To give it up, to give me the painting, you'd need my surrender.'

'No, it's not—'

'Is that not what you're asking? For me to tell you that I love you? For me to leave Bonnaire's, to give up my career, leave London and hang on your arm? Follow you around the world while you visit your hotel empire?'

'Would that be so terrible?' he asked, his tone halfway between sincere and teasing.

'Yes, if you were just playing some game, getting me to go along with what you wanted to get away with your revenge. And if I asked the same of you?'

'What do you mean?'

'If I asked you to give me the painting, to have your surrender before mine, would you?'

He held her gaze and this time the silence spoke volumes.

'You can't give me the painting until I tell you that I love you,' she said, her voice breaking on the last words. She felt his palm at her cheek, raised her eyes to his and gently leaned into his hand.

'And you can't tell me that you love me until I give you the painting,' he returned, the sorrow in his eyes finally matching hers.

Her heart raged in her chest, crying out that she was wrong, begging, pleading with her not to do this. Everything in her felt as if it were being torn in two and she drew in a jagged breath, trying to drown out the pain.

'I have to go,' she said, her mind severing connections her heart and soul weren't ready to yet, the well of ache— a hint of what was still to come—already building within her.

Sebastian nodded, but didn't move his hand either.

When his lips met hers, as they were always going to, she opened beneath them, pulled him to her as he sought to bring her to him, the thrust of his tongue claiming her in a way so primal, so pure, she knew she would never be the same again.

The feel of him, the taste of him, she imprinted them on her mind, on her heart, even as she was saying good-bye. She allowed herself that moment to absorb the heat and passion that pressed against her, her mind lost to all but sensations, wants and needs.

Until finally their kiss drew to a close and, without looking back, Sia collected her bags and left.

CHAPTER ELEVEN

SEBASTIAN RUBBED THE centre of his chest, where a dull ache had taken up residence the moment Sia left his estate in Siena. There was nothing dull about the pounding in his head though, which at this point either required extreme numbers of painkillers or simply more alcohol. He was leaning towards the latter.

At least the latter partly managed to limit the fragments of conversations with Sia which ran on a loop in his mind. The way that sometimes he would turn his head to the seat beside him, expecting her to be there, laughing at him in that way she did.

It was as if without her in his life there was suddenly very little to it. She'd made him see that he'd spent far too long actively indulging in his desires like a child throwing a tantrum. Yes, he'd had to work hard to protect his family, Maria…but, he finally acknowledged, he wasn't forced into that position. He simply took it. And would do it all over again.

But in the last three or so years, Sia had been the only person to challenge him, to make him look at what he was doing and want to be better, do better. He'd needed to impress her, he realised now. So dramatically different to the women who had graced his bed before, almost desperate in their attempts to impress him. Oh, he wasn't naïve enough not to realise that for the most part they were either after his money or his prowess, both of which were considerably well known.

But not Sia. She had wanted him against her natural inclination. And, in doing so, had made him look at himself through her eyes, had pulled him out of his selfish hedonism and reminded him that there was more to life. That there was her.

The woman he loved.

'Did you really punch Montcour?' Theo Tersi demanded as he stalked towards where Sebastian was sitting in the garden.

'I might have done. It's a bit hazy,' Sebastian replied without surprise at his friend's appearance, his hand lifting to gesture towards the bottle of whisky on the table.

Theo came to stand before him, hands on his hips, looking both disappointed and angry at the same time. 'And you didn't let me know so that at the very least I could be here to see it?' he demanded. 'Do you regret it?'

Sebastian reared back in offence. 'He broke my sister's heart. Of course not. Even if they have now made up and are back in Switzerland.'

'And Montcour?'

'Will get over it. If I'm honest,' Sebastian said, rubbing his stubbled jaw with his thumb at the memory, 'I think he let me.'

'Punch him?' Theo asked.

'Yeah.'

'Fair.' He nodded, shrugging a single shoulder as if in agreement with how things had played out.

'I think so,' Sebastian said, pouring whisky into the glass, passing it to Theo and holding the bottle to his lips. 'Drink. You've got some catching-up to do.'

Theo took a decent mouthful of his drink. 'Before we

get to the point where neither of us are able to focus, can I see it?'

'Yes,' Sebastian replied half reluctantly, hauling himself from the chair and leading the way into the living room, where he had placed the painting on the mantelpiece above the fire.

Theo came to stand beside him and they both studied the Durrántez in silence.

'So that it's it then.'

'Yes.'

'*Christos*, she looked like Maria.'

'Yes.'

'Very beautiful women in your family,' Theo observed.

Seb turned on him, and Theo raised his hands in surrender.

'Hey, I'm a happily married man, don't look at me like that,' he said, turning back to the painting. 'So. Was it worth it?'

'*Dios mio*, you too?' Sebastian demanded.

'Okay, this time I *really* don't know why you're looking at me like that,' Theo replied, the first sign of frustration written clearly across his features.

Sebastian passed a hand across his face, trying to wipe away the days of self-disgust that had gathered around him. 'It's a long story.'

'Best you get started then.'

The sun had set by the time Sebastian had told Theo all that had happened. Theo, in a strange turn of domesticity, had gathered a half decent meal together and the empty plates and coffee cups attested to the mostly successful sobering effect of the evening.

'Well, do you? Trust her?' Theo asked.

'It's not that simple,' Sebastian dismissed.

'That's a no then.'

'No, I do. It's just…' Sebastian trailed off, trying to find the right words. 'I've had only myself to rely on for so damn long.' Theo dramatically cleared his throat, and Sebastian tipped his drink towards him in consideration. 'For the most part, it's only been me. Because the trust I had in my father? That was the unknowing, unthinking, unconscious trust of a child to its parent. It was just there and when he broke that? I think he broke something in me.' Sebastian clamped his jaw against the wave of emotion that swept over him in that moment, the confession, torn from the depths of his past, almost as much of a surprise to himself as it was to Theo. 'The thought of being that dependent on someone again, I'm man enough to admit that it's terrifying. I'm not sure that I am capable of it.'

'Well, I guess you have to weigh it up. The suffering you are feeling now for what you *might* feel *if* it doesn't work out.'

'I'm not….' He was about to say *suffering* when an inner voice whispered in his ear.

Passion is a suffering that you take on yourself for what you want.

Only, rather than willingly taking it on, Sebastian had been pushing it away. Rejecting it, denying it. Denying what he truly wanted. Which wasn't the painting, which wasn't revenge. It was Sia. Only her. And if he had a hope in hell of getting what he truly wanted then he was going to have to put himself on the line.

He dropped his face into his hands, pulling at his hair in frustration. Oh, he'd been a bloody fool. The animalistic sound that emerged from his mouth was full of self-loathing and recrimination.

'There it is,' Theo said, half satisfied and more than a little patronising. 'Let it out.'

'Why do you get to be so smug?' Sebastian groused.

'I've been there.' He shrugged. 'You have a plan?'

'I think so,' Sebastian replied, staring into the flames twisting and turning in the fireplace before raising his gaze to the painting that had started it all.

Sia stared at the glowing red figures of her alarm clock and turned on her back, glaring up at the ceiling. The one-bedroom apartment had felt tiny and very, very dark since she'd returned from Siena. The minute hand ticked over and drew her closer to the interview with Bonnaire's scheduled for just a few hours' time.

She tried to call up some kind of emotion about it, but since she'd agreed to the meeting all she'd felt was numb. Which was distinctly better than the near constant ache that had sunk into her bones the moment she'd left Sebastian's estate. A dull agony had swirled in her stomach for the few days since then, ensuring that she couldn't manage to eat more than a few mouthfuls at a time.

She missed him. Terribly. Every time she closed her eyes she could see his smile. The way he looked at her when he thought she wasn't looking. The way it felt to have his gaze, his hands, his lips on her skin. The memory of it caused an aching arousal that led only to sadness and she had cried so much that her eyes felt constantly swollen and puffy, her heart just tired of hurting.

She had given herself two days. Two days to allow herself just to feel it. In that forty-eight hours she had asked herself time and time again why she hadn't just admitted to him that she loved him. Because, she reminded herself, unlike her mother, she *did* want more, she *deserved* more. She needed and wanted to be an equal in their love.

What had he said about not being a Neanderthal? He could be attracted to her without acting on it. Well, she could love him without being cowed by it or him. But, even as she thought it, she knew that didn't feel right for Sebastian. He would never have sought to dominate her. But the painting would have always been there. Hanging over both of them. An unanswered question, the only one she had never asked.

The other way she had spent those two days was to think about what he had said about her. That she had been scared to embrace her desires, her wants. With a long, hard internal look, she'd been forced to admit that he was right. She'd spent so long, too long, being thankful for things she shouldn't have been thankful for. The job at Bonnaire's, where they had treated her with little more than grim-faced tolerance. The obscenely expensive one-bed flat in Archway that was, in reality, hideous and oppressive, just so she could commute to work. The two things combining to ensure that she had absolutely no money or time to do anything else.

On the off-chance that Bonnaire's actually still wanted to keep her on, did *she* want to stay? Time and time again over the last forty-eight hours her mind had wandered to her uni things. The sketchpad full of drawings and plans, designs for paintings she'd never completed. She shook her head. Crazy thinking. As if she wasn't already in enough debt. But, rather than giving up on that thought, Sia had tested out a few options. Maybe going part-time? Maybe an internship or finding studio space she could share? Certainly moving out of the flat would be the first move. She didn't have to give everything up in one go. She could dip her toes in first.

The alarm finally went off beside her and she forced herself into the shower to wash away the exhaustion and heat from her overactive mind.

Half an hour later, dressed not in her usual office clothes but one of the summery creations Sebastian had given her, she was ready. It was a dress that she felt not only comfortable in but also a little glamorous and it was perfect for the gentle heat of London in July.

She grabbed her purse and stepped out into the street and almost smack bang into a man in a grey suit and carrying a black briefcase.

'Can I help you?' Sia asked over her shoulder as she turned back to lock the door. 'It's just that I'm running a little late...'

'Sia Keating?'

'Yes?' she replied.

'Can I see some ID?'

'Really? Can I see yours?' she asked, offended for a reason she couldn't quite name.

'Of course,' the man—Mike Newton—said amiably, showing his work ID.

After they had exchanged identification, he left her with the briefcase, 'With the Duke's regards.'

She stood in the doorway wearing a pretty summer dress, holding her purse and a black leather briefcase that seemed more than a little incongruous—especially considering the fireworks it set off in her stomach. Her hands shook as she lifted the briefcase in both hands to inspect it.

It couldn't be, could it? Her knees threatened to give way. Not because of the exorbitant value of what she thought the briefcase might contain. Not because of what she might do with it *if* it was what she thought it was. But because of what it meant for Sebastian to have given it to her. Her heart trembled as she caught sight of the car Bonnaire's had sent for her pulling up in front of her.

Sia was shown into one of the glass-fronted meeting rooms on the fifth floor. Two men sat on one side of the table, one on the large side, balding and slightly sweaty, and the other stick-thin, tall and with a rather abundant head of dark auburn hair.

Her mind had been a whirlwind the entire journey here and it wasn't until that moment that she realised that Bonnaire's had summoned her to the equivalent of an interrogation. On a good day there might have been something farcical about the two 'heavies' who had been sent to interview her about the painting. But Sia suddenly saw what this could have been like only weeks ago.

A junior member of staff pulled into an interview, two weeks into a suspension from a job she needed to pay bills, to pay debts, her career and future on the line…she would have said whatever they wanted her to say. Already she felt the weight of the threat hanging in the air. But, instead of making her scared, it made her angry. Angry that they thought they could do this, not just to her but to anyone they employed.

The large one gestured for her to sit in the one chair between them. She eyed it, not liking the way it would make her feel to be imprisoned between the two men at the head of the table. Instead, she politely declined and sat a few seats further up, on the side nearing the door. She was done playing other people's games. From now on, Sia promised herself, she would make her own choices and live with the consequences.

'Ms Keating, you understand that this interview is being recorded for internal Bonnaire's purposes only and that you do not need a lawyer present?'

'I'm afraid that hasn't convinced me that I don't need one,' she said lightly, relishing the new feeling of power coursing through her veins. Perhaps having a painting worth one hundred million pounds at her feet hidden in a briefcase did that to her. Or at least the possibility anyway. She still hadn't looked inside it yet.

'But you understand the statement that I have just made?'

'Yes,' she said, biting her tongue before she could accuse him of being a patronising Neanderthal.

'Then, if you would, can you please explain how you came to believe that the painting in question was a fake?'

And even though she could make everything all disappear, just by saying that she had changed her mind, that the painting had always been a fake, that she had made a terrible mistake, a proud, defiant part of her made her say, 'As I have already explained, the painting I assessed in Sharjarhere was most definitely *not* a fake.'

The two men proceeded to ply her with questions and Sia concentrated on answering them very specifically. The fact that Bonnaire's clearly wanted her to lie was making her much more determined to tell the truth. Just not *all* the truth. And she began to see how Sebastian had answered her questions not necessarily with the intent to beguile or deceive, but to protect. Protect the people who'd helped him achieve his goal, protect her to a certain extent, from exactly this situation.

'So, let me get this straight. The reason you didn't answer our calls was because you got on a plane with the man you believe to have stolen a painting from Bonnaire's and flew to the Caribbean?'

'I believe he stole the painting from Sheikh Abrani, but yes,' she clarified, strangely angry at the possessive view Bonnaire's seemed to have towards the painting they claimed never to have been in contact with.

It was strange to be recounting the last few weeks of her life to two complete strangers. But, as she told them in as little detail as possible about her time with Sebastian, she couldn't deny how it made her feel. She had to work hard to keep the smile from her face at the memory of him trying to get her to take control of the plane, of how much he loved his convertible sports car, of his delight in her joy at being able to see such incredible art in Florence, not even to mention the Gentileschi. At how he'd encouraged her to reach for whatever it was she wanted, how he'd allowed her complete and unfettered access to him, his body and the pleasure she could find there.

'When did you get to Italy?'

While her mind almost numbly supplied an answer, she realised that while there were a hundred different ways this could end, there was only one that she wanted.

'So you spent nearly two weeks with him and during that time…did you see the painting?'

'No.'

'And you don't know where it is?'

'No,' she answered truthfully because she didn't actually know for sure that it was in the briefcase.

'Because if you did see it—'

'Which one?'

'Excuse me?'

'Well, if you mean the forged painting, then I assume that is back in Sharjarhere with Sheikh Abrani. And you surely can't mean the 'real' painting because, according to you, that was never here as I was mistaken in my valuation.'

The stick-thin man started to go a little pink in the face.

'Because any other option,' Sia continued, 'would mean that the painting *was* stolen and replaced with a forgery under the watchful gaze of Bonnaire's. And that Bonnaire's was subsequently involved in a cover-up, which at best would be seen as perverting the course of justice and at worst would involve a much deeper criminal investigation into the practices of the auction house. It could even go back years. Who knows?' She shrugged with all the mock innocence she could muster. It wasn't hard because she suddenly felt the full force of disdain for a company that was clearly as corrupt as the Sheikh himself.

'That sounds very much like a threat, Ms Keating, which could end very badly for you. And you would be wise not to let emotions get in the way.'

Fury wound through her and for the first time, instead of shying away from it, she embraced it. 'You appear to be accusing me of becoming emotional? Well, you're right. I *am* emotional. Very, I'd say on reflection. There are quite a number of emotions running through me right now. Feelings of anger, righteousness, power, desire—desire to see justice done, even. Every single one of them not making me worse at what I do, but better.

'Just not better for you,' she stated, watching the two men become an interesting shade of puce. 'So I will be handing in my notice, effective immediately, and you will be paying me my last month's wages, in spite of the suspension. You will do this because I know, and you know, that Bonnaire's does not want me to pay a visit to the police. And,' she said, turning to the larger of the two, 'this is more than a threat. It's a promise. It is also the last time I will see you. Because next time? *You* will be the ones needing a lawyer.'

Her heart racing wildly but ecstatically, Sia left the building, her hands white-knuckled around the briefcase, feeling a kind of adrenaline high she'd never experienced before. She was thriving on a personal power she'd had no idea she possessed. Before Sebastian she would never have had the courage to do that. Everything in her knew that it was the right thing to have done. With Bonnaire's so insistent that she tell a lie to save them, they didn't deserve the painting. And she didn't deserve them.

She rushed out onto the front steps of the building, de-

termined to find Sebastian. Not because he'd helped her
to see the truth about the company she used to work for,
and not because he might have given her the world's most
expensive gift, but because she loved him. She'd known
it for days. But she wanted *him* to know it too. Perhaps if
she maxed out her credit cards she could get to Siena. A
last-minute flight might cost a fortune but it would be—

She came to a crashing halt, briefcase swinging by her
side.

There, parked highly illegally on a red line on Goodge
Street, attracting more attention than anyone had a right
to, was Sebastian Rohan de Luen, leaning against another
stunning convertible sports car, hands in his pockets, hair
a bit of a mess and with a fair bit of stubble, looking every
inch the disreputable playboy he was.

But he was hers.

For a second, she just stared at him. Her eyes raked
over every inch of him, searing the image onto her mind
and heart, delighting in the way he pulled his arms from
his pockets and crossed them over his chest, as if to stop
himself from reaching for her. The way his eyes lit on her
face and not once moved, not even to the briefcase dan-
gling at her side.

And then she felt a smile pulling at the corner of her
mouth, one that seemed connected to the endless joy, the
love building in her chest. It grew broader and broader and
the moment that he smiled back she launched across the
pavement, threw herself into his arms and when he picked
her up she wrapped her legs around his waist and kissed
him like she'd never kissed before.

'I love you.'

'Dammit,' he said, his lips still pressed against hers. 'I
wanted to say it first.'

'Tough.'

'Well, I'll just have to say it more. I love you. I love you. I love you,' he said, punctuating each one with a kiss.

'Not everything's a game, you know,' she teased as he lowered her down to the ground, but she refused to move from his hold.

'You still have the painting,' he said, his eyes still not leaving hers.

'Yes.'

'You could have given it to them if you'd wanted. I need you to know that,' he said with all the sincerity she could ever wish for, soothing away some of the hurts of their last encounter.

'Well, as you gave me the painting, I'm assuming I wouldn't have needed your permission,' she teased.

'Nope, absolutely not. I just…it's important to me that you know the painting is completely yours to do with as you wish. Because you are more important to me than the painting. Than anything.'

Her heart soared with his words and with wonder. He loved her. She shook her head a little. He'd given her so much. And the gesture that he had made, of love, of trust, that must have cost him so much emotionally, could only be matched by one thing.

'I'm not really that sure *what* painting you're talking about. Because I haven't opened the briefcase.'

'You haven't?' He pulled back, staring at her a little as if she had lost her mind.

'I didn't need to,' she said, reaching up to cup his jaw, relishing the feeling of the stubble tickling her palm. 'Whether this painting is the Durrántez, a Monet or a Pissarro, I love you and I trust you. And I want to thank you. Because you showed me that it was okay to be *all* of me. To want more, to *be* more, to be bright and shiny and powerful.' As she said the words she felt them working a magic within her. Not only knowing that they were true, but feeling it as well. 'That wanting to be more, wanting more, wouldn't make me selfish or mean, but that it would make me strong. And part of that strength is drawn from the love that I feel for you.'

Sebastian took her hand and placed it on his heart, desperate for her to know, to feel how much her words meant to him. 'And I want to thank you. You showed me how to make peace with my past, so that I could be free to make a different future for myself. A future I want to make with you. I want to have babies with you, to be a father to our children, a husband, lover and best friend to you.' Her beautiful blue eyes shone with tears of happiness and he hoped that she could feel his heart pounding beneath her palm. 'I want to fight with you, make up with you, laugh and cry with you. I'd personally prefer not to play games with you again...' he paused as she laughed '...because I'd lose. Every time. But even then I'd still die a happy man.'

Sia looked up at him, complete trust and love in her eyes, and he was humbled by it. He took the small black velvet box from his back pocket and, getting to one knee, ignoring the way people around them had begun to stop and stare.

'Will you, Artemisia Henrietta Keating, do me the greatest honour of being my wife?'

'Yes,' she replied, a happy tear sweeping down over her cheek.

Sebastian surged onto his feet, pulled her to him and kissed her with all the love he felt in his heart. It was only when the wolf whistles and cat calls intruded that he finally let her go.

'I do have one condition, though,' she said as he rounded the car to the driver's seat.

'Get in the car, Sia,' he mock-growled. He was genuinely not looking forward to the day she realised that he'd give her whatever she wanted.

'You don't want to hear my condition?' she said, her tone wicked and full of tease.

'I want to get you home so that I can make love to you. You can tell me the condition later,' he replied, loving the way her eyes widened and her pupils responded to his sensual promise.

'It's bad form to make agreements—'

He stopped her words with the first kiss of the many more they would share over the years. As Sebastian pulled away from Goodge Street, his future wife beside him and his past as a thief firmly behind him, he knew he'd stolen the most beautiful, most precious thing of all. Sia Keating's heart.

EPILOGUE

'MUMMY! MUMMY! MUMMY! Jacob is writing on the walls again,' cried Maria's youngest daughter, running into the garden where everyone was gathered.

'It's okay, my love. Auntie Sia has put special paper on the walls so that everyone can draw whatever and wherever they like there.'

Sia smiled at her sister-in-law's daughter. 'Would you like to have a go? Here,' she said, reaching for a spare set of pencils and sharing them with the girl, who looked very much like her mother and her grandmother.

'Thank you,' the girl replied and ran off to the large wooden workshop that had been built in the back of the garden for her to paint in. Sebastian had designed and constructed it the moment she'd expressed even the vaguest notion to return to her art and she was thankful each and every day for his unending support. She had returned to university to focus on the practice of her own art rather than the history and analysis techniques of others. She had built up a small but dedicated following, which kept her happy as it allowed her to find that magical line of balance between enjoying and delighting in her family *and* her passion for painting.

Sia couldn't help but laugh as Theo Tersi played out an invisible sword fight with his daughter and Sia and Sebastian's son Jacob. Lord knew where the other two of her sons were, usually hiding up a tree or swimming in the lake.

'I don't know how you do it with three boys,' Princess Sofia of Iondorra said.

'And I have no idea how you run a country,' Sia replied with a laugh.

'Oh, that,' Sofia said, swiping the notion away with her hand. 'I have people to help me with that.'

Ella came rushing over to her mother and pulled on Sofia's elbow, holding her hand in front of her mouth. 'Mummy,' she said in the loudest whisper, 'why is there a briefcase on the wall above the fireplace?'

Sofia looked up at Sia, and Maria looked at Sofia, each of the women smiling.

'It is a game Uncle Seb and Auntie Sia are playing.'

'What's the game?'

'Not to open the briefcase,' Sia replied with a smile.

'That doesn't sound like much of a game,' Ella said, frowning and then running off.

'I think it's crazy,' Sofia replied with a smile. 'Aren't you ever going to open it?'

'I don't need to.' Sia laughed.

'So the painting stays in the briefcase, hanging on the wall above the fireplace *like* it's a painting. A—' she dropped her voice to a real whisper, leaning forward '—one hundred million pound painting?' Sofia leaned back. The look in her eyes definitely said she thought they were crazy.

'I think it's romantic,' stated Maria firmly.

'You do?' asked Sia, relieved. 'I've not asked before, because I was worried you might—'

'I don't need to see the painting. It…brought you to Seb, *and* to us, that was all I needed it to do,' Maria said.

So much had changed in the last six years. Bonnaire's

had gone down in a hail of public scandal after several more dodgy deals had brought the attention of both Interpol and the British police. Abrani had been quietly removed from his position as leader of Shajarhere and the state had welcomed a new leader whose interest was focused on the betterment of his people.

Sia and Sebastian had made Siena their home, despite still travelling around the world to visit his hotels, but less frequently than he'd used to. Sebastian had taken a step back from his company to develop the vineyards at the back of their estate as well as working with a local architecture firm to explore eco-friendly social housing. He'd come to realise that he'd really loved the design aspect of his hotels and was enjoying exploring it in a way that could benefit the local community.

Sia felt a kiss pressed between her neck and shoulder and turned to find her husband's lips, eager to feel them on her own.

'Matthieu has invited us to Lake Lucerne next month.'

'You'd like to go?'

'Yes, I think he has a business proposal he wants my advice on.'

'Of course. Though it may be my last flight for a while,' she confided, one hand on his cheek and the other taking his and placing it on her stomach.

Sebastian's eyes widened with excitement. 'Really?' he said, the joy beaming from his heart straight to hers.

'Four? *Four?*' Theo demanded, joining the table.

'They're like rabbits,' teased Maria.

'You can talk,' Sofia teased Maria as Matthieu approached, looking like a giant with giggling children hanging off every limb.

'Who are like what?' he asked as everyone fell into laughter about him.

They sat, talked and ate long into the beautiful summer's evening, Sia feeling not only at peace with the love in her heart and the child growing within her, but excited by it. Her life had become something wondrous, bright, bold and beautiful and unknowingly she glowed with it.

She caught Maria staring and nudging her brother. Sebastian turned to Maria and then to Sia.

'What?' Sia asked, unaccountably feeling goosebumps rise over her skin.

'You look like her. Not physically, but there's something about you,' Maria replied with a smile, a glint in her eye both sad but full of joy.

'Like who?'

'A *Woman in Love*.'

* * * * *

THE VOWS
HE MUST KEEP

AMANDA CINELLI

For Keith, the hero of my own love story.

CHAPTER ONE

VALERIO MARCHESI AWOKE to the thunder of his own heart-beat, his senses taking in the complete darkness that surrounded him and the feeling of cold sweat on his skin. It was not the first time he had awoken in a state of panic in the past six months. His physician had called it post-traumatic stress, and like countless others had sympathised with him for his ordeal. He didn't want their damn sympathy.

Gritting his teeth, he fought through the fog left by the entire bottle of whisky he had downed the night before and reminded himself why he'd completely sworn off drinking in recent months. As he came fully to consciousness and tried to sit up, he became instantly aware of two things.

One, judging by the soft clearing of a throat nearby, he was not alone in the room. And two, he couldn't move his upper body because he had been tied to his own bed.

Any remaining effect of the alcohol in his system instantly evaporated. The room was dark, but he could just about make out the blurry outline of his luxury yacht's master cabin around him. Both of his wrists had been tied to the ornate wooden headboard on either side of his head, using what felt like soft fabric. He tested the bonds, black panic snaking up his back like wildfire, followed by the swift kick of fury.

He would die before he allowed this to happen again.

'Good, you're awake.'

A female voice cut across the shadows.

'I was just debating if I should throw some water over your head.'

The woman's voice silenced his growls momentarily as his brain scrambled to differentiate between the danger of his past and in the present moment. Drawing on some recent meditative practice, he inhaled deeply past the adrenaline, focusing his mind to a fine point. The woman's voice sounded familiar, but Valerio couldn't quite place it other than to note that it was English, upper class, and deathly calm. Nothing like the rough-hewn criminals from his memories, but one never knew.

'What the hell is going on here?' he demanded gruffly. 'Show your face.'

Heels tapped across the wooden floor, the dim light from the curtain-covered windows throwing her shape into relief. She was tall, for a woman, and had the kind of exaggerated full-figured curves that made his spine snap to attention. A knot of awareness tightened in his abdomen, catching him completely by surprise. At thirty-three years of age, he'd believed himself long past the kind of embarrassing loss of control usually attributed to youth. But it seemed he hadn't been around a woman in so long, apparently *anyone* was going to ignite his starving libido. Even someone who was possibly attempting to hold him hostage.

It was a strange kind of twist, considering his most recent brush with captivity had been the catalyst for his self-imposed isolation from society. Had his broken mind moved on to finding some kind of thrill in the possibility of danger?

He pulled at the headboard once again, a sharp hiss escaping his lips at the burn of the fabric on his skin. The sheet that only partially covered his nude body slipped further down the bed.

'You're only going to hurt yourself by struggling.'

'Well, then, cut these damn ropes off,' he growled, trying and failing to keep the edge from his voice. 'I don't keep money here, if that's what you are after.'

A soft laugh sounded out, closer this time. 'I'm not here to rob you, Marchesi. The ropes are for my own safety, considering the night we've just had.'

'Your safety…?' He tried and failed to process her words, feeling the tug of a memory in his mind.

He knew that voice.

Soft hands brushed against his skin as the woman gently adjusted the sheet over his body. Another shiver of awareness heated him from the inside out. It had been so damn long…and her familiar scent was all around him, tugging at those memories. He breathed her in greedily, feeling the warm blend of sweetness and musk penetrate his chest, melting some of the ice that seemed permanently lodged inside.

A soft lamp was flicked on beside the bed without warning, the sudden golden light making him wince with pain. The woman came into focus slowly, a watercolour of long ebony curls and flawless dark caramel skin. Recognition hit him with a sudden jolt, his eyes narrowing, and all anxiety was suddenly replaced by swift, unbridled anger.

'Dani.'

'Only my friends get to call me that, Marchesi.'

Daniela Avelar narrowed her eyes, pulling a chair closer to the bed and lowering herself down elegantly, as though sitting down to afternoon tea.

'You made it clear the last time I saw you that you are *not* my friend.'

Guilt hit him in the gut even as he fought to remain

outraged. Memories assailed him of the last time they had spoken. Six months ago he had delivered the most painful speech of his life, marking the death of his business partner at a memorial ceremony. His best friend. Her twin brother.

Duarte Avelar had been shot dead right in front of him, after they'd both been taken hostage after an event in Rio de Janeiro and kept at gunpoint for two weeks, deep in the slums of the city. The story had made global news. He'd been lamented as a hero for surviving. He alone knew the truth of what had happened.

He had forced himself to hold it together throughout his friend's memorial service on a rainy morning in the English countryside. He had tried to speak words that would honour the sacrifice Duarte had made to save his life. But eventually he'd lost his grip on control and had torn out of the church as if the fires of hell had been at his heels, needing to get away from all the sympathetic stares and unbearable grief.

But Dani had run after him, standing in front of the door of his chauffeur-driven car. Daniela Avelar—a woman who prided herself on being one of the best PR and marketing strategists in the business, and who had always seemed to look down her nose at him and his wild playboy lifestyle. She was a woman who never asked anyone for help, not even her own brother, but she had begged him to stay. She'd held on to his arm and begged him to tell her the truth of what had happened in Brazil…to let her help him.

He had scraped together enough composure to growl at her, telling her that knowing wouldn't make anything different. That it wouldn't bring Duarte back. Then he had got into his car and driven away, pretending not to be affected by the sight of the tears streaming down her cheeks.

Shame was a familiar lead weight in his solar plexus even now.

In the lamplit room, Daniela crossed her legs, drawing his attention to the spindly-heeled shoes on her feet. She had been working for Velamar as their PR strategist for years, so he was used to her trademark pinstriped trousers and perfectly pressed blouses, with their delicate ribbons tied at the throat. But on this cream-coloured confection the collar was undone, the ribbons hanging limp and creased as though someone had grabbed them and held them tight in their grip.

She looked tired, though she was trying hard not to let it show. But he could see the faint dark shadows under her eyes, the tightness around her mouth. He wondered if grief had stolen her perfect polished image and grace, just as it had stolen his carefree nonchalance.

'Do you have any idea how long I've been trying to find you?' She met his eyes without fear or hesitation—an easy feat considering she had him half naked and trussed to a bed.

'I'll admit that of all the ways you could have got my attention this is quite creative, if not a little insensitive.' He spoke easily, pulling at the bonds and feeling them slide slightly to one side. The knots were strong, but not strong enough. She might be about to inherit part-ownership of Velamar—one of the most exclusive yacht charter companies in the world—but she was no sailor.

Valerio ignored the pull in his chest at the thought of the brand he had built from the ground up, the work that had once given him purpose and pride. 'Did you ever think that maybe I didn't want to be found?'

'You walked away from your responsibilities, Marchesi.'

'My company is in good hands.'

'*Our* company is in brilliant hands—considering I've been running it alone for six months.'

She sat and surveyed him like a queen on her throne, which was not inaccurate considering the Avelar family name was practically royalty in their native Brazil.

'But your employees don't respond to my own particular brand of authority, it seems. They're practically begging for the return of their playboy CEO and his infamous parties.'

'Final warning. Untie me and get the hell off my yacht, Daniela.'

'You don't remember anything about last night, do you?' She raised one brow, watching him with curiosity and the faintest ghost of a smile.

Valerio looked around the room once more, the pain in his head sharpening. The last thing he remembered was storming out of his brother's sprawling villa in Tuscany after an embarrassing display of temper and popping open the first alcoholic beverage he could find. He'd drunk alone and brooded silently in the back of his chauffeur-driven car the entire way to where his yacht had been moored in nearby Genoa.

He'd always known that yesterday would be a difficult day, considering he'd avoided his family for so long, but he'd thought he'd done enough work on himself to get through a couple of hours in their company. He had expected pity and tiptoeing around him. He hadn't been prepared for their anger. Their judgement. They didn't know anything about what he'd gone through…what he'd done. All they cared about was the precious Marchesi image and the worrying rumours that he'd gone insane.

His rages were unpredictable, and tended to fog his memory, so he didn't remember much. But he was pretty sure he had smashed a few of his brother's expensive vases on his way out.

Wincing, he tried to sit up more fully against the

wooden headboard, only managing a couple of inches before he inhaled sharply against the sudden throb of pain that assaulted his cranium. What had been in that whisky?

'Don't move too fast. The doctor gave you a mild sedative.'

'You *drugged* me?'

'You tried to take on my entire security team one by one. You were in some kind of a trance. We couldn't...' She swallowed hard. 'You weren't yourself.'

Growling, he pulled hard against the bonds once more. A satisfying creak sounded from the wooden beam above him. He saw the first glimmer of unease flicker in her eyes.

'This was the only way I could think of to make you listen.' She stood up, her eyes darting to the door at the opposite side of the room. 'I didn't mean for it to go this far... I didn't think you were as out of control as your brother said.'

'You spoke to Rigo?' His brother—the damn idiot. He had promised Valerio that if he accepted the invitation he would keep his appearance in Tuscany to himself. But then, Valerio hadn't planned on causing such a scene. Once again, he'd lived up to his reputation of being the reckless wild-card Marchesi brother.

The shame burned his gut.

Daniela cleared her throat. 'Look, I've been patient. I've given you more than enough time, considering what happened, but now it's time for you to come back. The board members are not happy with my choices as acting CEO. There's a motion in place to sell off my brother's design projects and pull out of a large chunk of our charity commitments, and I'm the only one blocking their way.' She pinched the bridge of her nose, a deep sigh escaping her chest. 'This kind of unrest is bad news. With the pressure of the new *Sirinetta* launch coming up, I just don't have time for it.'

Her words rang in his mind, fuelling his anger and disbelief. Nettuno Design was Duarte's brainchild—an offshoot of the Velamar brand—and the maritime engineering firm had created the very first *Sirinetta* mega-yacht. It was the yacht that had launched their modest luxury yacht charter firm right up into the upper echelons of society five years ago. It had been the catalyst that had brought them in contact with figures of royalty and power across the globe, and wealth beyond their dreams.

'So you decided to kidnap me to tell me this?'

She narrowed her eyes on him with barely restrained irritation. 'A second meeting is being held the day after tomorrow in Monte Carlo, with more board members flying in. I have information that they are planning to vote me out.' She took a deep breath, meeting his eyes. 'I need your help. I need you to get over whatever this is and come back.'

'I know it's not technically official, but *I* named you acting CEO in place of both me and Duarte,' he gritted out, his friend's name sounding wooden and unfamiliar in his mouth. 'They can't vote you out. They're bluffing.'

'Considering Duarte is about to be declared legally dead, and what with all the recent rumours in the press about your mental instability... I'm afraid they can.'

Valerio froze, the news sending his blood cold.

Duarte's official death certificate had not been issued—he'd made sure of it. As executor of the estate, he'd specifically given the authorities more time before Daniela could legally inherit all her brother's assets.

And now she dared to barge on to *his* yacht and calmly make demands while she was sitting on a bombshell of this magnitude? *Dio*, she had no idea what this meant.

Oblivious, she continued. 'Apart from the fact that our reputation is being pulled under the proverbial bus...they know I'm not qualified. I mean, to be honest, I know it too. I'm a PR strategist—not a leader or a figurehead. I've never done this before.'

'Let me free,' he growled.

'Not until you agree to come to the meeting.'

She folded her arms under her breasts, the movement pushing up her ample cleavage and making the blood roar in his ears.

'Daniela... I'm warning you. You have no idea what's going on here, so let me off this bed right now.'

'I'm quite aware of what's going on in my own company. *You're* the one who's been MIA for months on end, and I can't risk you disappearing on me again.' She closed her eyes briefly, opening them to lock on his with intent. 'I don't care if you hate me for this. I will do whatever it takes to save my brother's legacy.'

She claimed that *he* was the only one who could save the company? The man she had once called a frivolous playboy? She had no idea what he had been uncovering over the past six months. Hell, he wasn't even sure *he* knew.

What he did know was that she wasn't the only one prepared to do whatever it took to save something. But the person he'd been trying to save seemed intent on putting herself in danger, again and again.

Anger gave him an extra spurt of energy, and the last knot that bound his wrists slipped free.

Like a coiled spring, Valerio launched himself off the bed.

Dani felt a shocked scream rise in her throat but she refused to let it free—refused to believe that this man whom she had known for almost half of her thirty-one years on the earth would ever actually harm her.

But this was not the Valerio she had watched from afar—the playboy reprobate who'd bedded half the socialites in Europe and charmed everyone he met with his pirate's smile and his wild thirst for adventure. It was as though any trace of light in his deep blue eyes had been snuffed out.

Before she had a chance to run, he had grabbed her by the wrists to stop her. He pulled her to face him but she shoved him back, the movement accidentally sending them both tumbling down onto the bed, with her body landing directly on top of his.

Large hands moved to grip her waist and she inhaled sharply at the feel of his skin as it seemed to burn through the fabric of her shirt. She shifted position, trying to stand, but her movements somehow only served to press her even harder against him.

'*Dio*, stay still,' he cursed, his voice sounding strangled and raw.

It seemed a lifetime ago that Dani had fantasised about exactly this kind of situation. Her foolish teenage self had once dreamed of having Valerio Marchesi look at *her* the way she had seen him look at a parade of beauties, while she'd watched awkwardly from the sidelines. But he had long ago made it clear that there was no way he would ever look at her as anything but his best friend's chubby, boring, know-it-all twin sister. The annoying third wheel to their perfect partnership.

No, there was nothing sexual that she could see in the barely controlled fury glittering in his eyes now, as he stared up at her. He seemed to inhale deeply as her hair fell over her shoulder, forming a cocoon of ebony curls around them. His hands flexed just underneath her ribcage, his eyes lowering to where the buttons on her blouse had come undone, revealing the far too large breasts threatening to spill over the plain white lace of her sensible bra. And still his hands tightened, holding her still and stopping her retreat.

'Let go of me. What do you think you're doing?'

She was furious, her knees moving directly towards the part of him where she could cause the most damage. Not that she *wanted* to hurt him, but he was being completely unreasonable—and she refused to accept that she had lost the upper hand now, after all her careful planning, simply because he had more brute strength.

He easily controlled her, pinning her legs with his own and pulling her arms directly above her head.

'What do *I* think I'm doing?' He repeated her question, a harsh bark of laughter erupting from his chest as he grabbed both her wrists and tied them to the headboard he had just freed himself from. 'I believe there is an English expression… Turnabout is fair play?'

Dani was breathing heavily with the exertion of trying to fight him. She didn't see his plan until she was already tied in place. Disbelief turned quickly to anger as she tried and failed to pull herself free.

'Thrashing around like that really isn't going to help either of us. Especially considering our position and my lack of clothing.'

Dani became completely still, looking down to where their bodies were melded together. Her legs in the dark wool of her designer trousers were wrapped around the bare skin of his torso. She felt her cheeks heat up, perspiration beading on the back of her neck. He said he was unaffected, and yet just a moment ago she had moved her hips and she could have sworn she'd felt…

Suddenly he moved. With an impressive flex of muscle,

he slid his large body out from underneath her with surprising ease, gently laying her down on the pillows before moving out of her vision.

'I understand that you have some anger towards me…' His voice sounded husky, and he was slightly out of breath from his exertions in freeing himself. 'But, whatever this game was tonight, know that it was out of line.'

'I'm not playing a game. I told you that I had to have you restrained for your own safety and mine. You were threatening to kill your own bodyguard, for goodness' sake, and we couldn't snap you out of it.'

She tried to lift her head to look at him, but on seeing a flash of tall, naked male, she returned her head to the pillows with a thump.

'Maybe so. But you're trying to manipulate me. To force my hand. Maybe in the past I might have seen the humour in all this…but I am not that man any more.'

'Where are you going?' she asked innocently, remembering that while she might have temporarily lost the upper hand in this battle, she was far from losing the war.

'I am going to walk out of here and leave you to think about your actions for a while.'

He flicked on the full lights in the room and she watched as he walked towards the doorway, then suddenly stood still. Her body tensed in the long silence, and she imagined the look on his face as he realised his mistake. Because they were not on his luxury yacht in Genoa. They weren't even on Italian soil.

He let out a dark curse in Italian and Dani felt an unruly smile threaten at the corner of her lips. She listened as his footsteps boomed across the luxury wooden floor of the cabin and out into the hallway.

He might not remember the events of last night but she did—with painful clarity. She remembered having

Valerio's own personal bodyguard help her carry his boss onto the brand-new, not officially launched *Sirinetta II* mega-yacht that she'd commandeered, and then sending the man on a fool's errand to the doctor in town so that she could order the captain to sail off into the night.

She waited for Valerio to return, realising that it was impossible even to attempt to look ladylike while she was sprawled face-down on a bed, her arms pinned at an awkward upwards angle as they were.

'Where the *hell* have you brought me?'

His voice suddenly boomed from the other side of the room and the door of the cabin banged open on its hinges, making her jump.

'Back so soon? I've had barely four minutes of my time out. Hardly enough time to think about my actions.'

He came to a stop beside the bed. Dani turned her head on the pillow and allowed her eyes to travel up his impressive form. Mercifully he had donned the clothing she had grabbed from his yacht's cabin during their swift exit. The dark blue jeans fitted him perfectly and the plain black T-shirt was like a second skin, moulding to his impressive biceps. The rumours of his mental state were yet to be confirmed, but he certainly hadn't stopped working on his infamous abs since he'd gone into exile, that was for sure. If anything, he'd kicked it up a notch.

'I'd say we're cruising somewhere near Corsica.' She met his intense gaze without showing her unease. 'I decided to multitask and give you a tour of the new model while we discussed our approach for this meeting. And before you get any ideas, the wheelhouse is locked down and the captain has been ordered to refuse entry without my passcode. Company policy.'

'You...' He took a step away, pinching the bridge of his nose. 'You had me drugged and loaded onto one of

my own company's yachts. And then you turned my own
crew against me?'

'*Our* crew.' She smiled sweetly. 'You forget that I've
got quite familiar with all the staff in our employ over the
past six months, *partner*.'

'Order them back to land. Now.'

He leaned over her, one hand braced on the headboard
beside her. His breath fanned her ear, sending gooseflesh
down her neck. Evidently being tied up and ordered about
was something her inner self got a dark thrill out of, re-
gardless of the fact that the man giving those orders was a
selfish bastard who had abandoned her when she'd needed
him most.

No, she corrected herself, he had abandoned *his company*. The company that *she* was going to inherit half of
once her brother's estate was released, as well as countless
other assets and properties—thanks to his death. And that
was without the inheritance she'd already got after their
parents' accidental deaths seven years before.

If she had still been the praying kind, she would have
thought that someone somewhere up above had really
taken a dislike to the Avelar family. But she no longer
believed in anything but cold hard facts, and right now
keeping her brother's prized Nettuno Design a part of the
company was what she needed to focus on.

Valerio and Duarte had had countless other investments,
but they had spent twelve years building Velamar from
the ground up. Was he just going to sit back and allow his
work to be poached by the vultures? Not on *her* watch.

'You can leave me tied up here as long as you like. I
won't make the order.' She flexed her fingers, feeling a
slight numbness creeping in from her position.

'Dani—'

'I told you not to call me that,' she snapped. 'Use my

proper name. You and I are business partners now and nothing more.'

'Do business partners usually tie each other up naked and watch from the shadows?'

'I wasn't watching you.' She bristled, hating the way that her skin immediately turned to gooseflesh at his words and hating the sinfully erotic image they created. She closed her eyes, praying he couldn't see. That he didn't notice the ridiculous effect he still had on her, no matter how much she'd believed she'd got past it.

'It's pretty clear that you were sitting there in the dark, waiting for me to wake up. What were you thinking about all that time, Daniela? The company? Or was there a small part of you that enjoyed having me at your mercy?'

He crouched low, sliding a lock of hair from her face, and waited until she met his gaze. Dani swallowed hard, fighting the urge to lick her suddenly dry lips.

'You shouldn't have followed me. You could have just emailed me the details of the meeting. But you didn't trust me to show up, did you? Bastard that I am...' He let his fingers trail along her face, smoothing her hair behind her ear. 'You found me and saw me at my worst. The runaway playboy, the raging madman in the flesh. Tell me that you didn't relish the opportunity to punish me, to ensure I didn't have an easy escape. Tell me you didn't enjoy it, Daniela.'

She bit her lower lip, knowing that he was just playing a game. Trying to make her uncomfortable enough to make her order the yacht back to land and let him cut his responsibilities all over again.

She turned her face, opening her eyes to meet his directly and summoning all the strength she had. 'There is nothing enjoyable about watching you give up and walk away from everything you've worked so hard to achieve,' she said boldly. 'You could have died in Rio too, but you didn't. I thought that might have made you see life as more precious than you did before, that you might take things more seriously. But you've just been running away, pretending that nothing's happened.'

Valerio's hand dropped as though she had burned him. In a way, she supposed she had. Guilt momentarily pulled at her subconscious, but she pushed it away, knowing that she was doing what she needed to do. Lucky for her, she knew exactly what to say to keep Valerio Marchesi at a distance in order to protect herself. She always had. But right now she needed him on her side more than she needed him to get away from her.

She felt his hands on hers as he silently loosened the ropes at her wrists. She worked herself free as quickly as she could, noting that his knots were skilled. He had been a sailor practically from birth, after all. The blood rushed quickly back into her hands as she sat up, rubbing at her wrists, and saw that he had moved to the other side of the room. He stood completely still, looking out of the window to the blackness beyond. There was no moon tonight—nothing to light their way in the night. Only dark clouds and the subtle sheen of the waves that surrounded them.

'I know all too well how precious life is, Daniela. If you think I've been running away, then you really don't know me at all.' Valerio's voice was cold and distant, bleak. 'If you think that I could ever hope to forget what happened… If you think I haven't gone over and over every single second…' He shook his head as he turned to face her, and a look of complete darkness seemed to cast a shadow over him.

Dani felt emotion burn her throat. She wished she could take her words back but knew it was done. Since Valerio had left her alone at Duarte's funeral all those months ago, she had been filled with a rage of her own. *He* had been the one to return from their trip alive after weeks of being presumed dead. *He* had been the one to refuse to tell her the full details of what had happened, only revealing that Duarte had been killed shortly before Valerio had escaped.

Her twin had been murdered and she'd had no idea. There had been no sudden shift in the cosmos, no supernatural feeling of loss or pain. Instead she had felt nothing. And that feeling of disconnected numbness had continued for the past six months as she had thrown herself into keeping the company running smoothly.

'I'm sorry. I didn't mean to be so harsh.' She breathed past the emotion in her throat, wishing she'd chosen her words more carefully. 'But it doesn't help that I don't know anything about what happened other than—'

'It doesn't matter.' He cut across her, pure steel in his voice. 'I'll be there at the meeting. I'll say whatever you want me to say.'

'You will?' She paused, struggling to make sense of his sudden shift from outraged to passive. Yes, her words had been harsh, but...

'I will come to Monte Carlo with you because it's what Duarte would want.' He took a step forward. 'But in return I need you to do something for me.'

'You're giving *me* terms?' She tilted her head. 'I should have known there would be a catch.'

He folded his arms across his chest in a pose filled with dominance and attitude, but his voice quavered slightly as he spoke. 'I have one condition, yes, and I need you to trust me that it's necessary and non-negotiable.'

'Is this a security thing?' She took in the tension in his posture, the way his fists were pulled tight by his sides. 'I have taken on board all the terms you laid down with that crazy security team before you disappeared. I never go anywhere without their protection.'

'You think I haven't been checking in over the past six months?' He shook his head, his voice deepening with some unknown emotion. 'I may not have been here, but I didn't run away. I need you to understand that. There were things I had to do before I could...' He frowned, turning slightly to look out across the murky water through the window. When he began speaking again, his voice was deeper. 'When we realised things were going to end badly in Rio... I made a promise to him that if I survived I would keep you safe.'

Dani felt a lump in her throat, but pushed it away, reminding herself that getting emotional would only put her in a vulnerable position. He wanted her to trust him? Valerio hadn't even tried to keep whatever promises he'd made—he had blocked her out and walked away at his earliest convenience, preferring to process his grief alone. Or more likely in the company of expensive whisky and a string of beautiful women across the globe.

She had learned the hard way that she could only rely on herself. Folding her arms tightly across her chest, she didn't bother to hide the ice that crept into her voice. 'Just outline your terms, Marchesi.'

His jaw flexed menacingly, and a hardness entered his gaze as they stood toe to toe in the darkness of the master cabin. When he finally spoke, the huskiness was gone from his voice and had been replaced by a hint of that sultry charm she remembered.

'The board believe that Velamar is weakened because of my absence...that I am unreliable and unstable. If you want my presence to be of any benefit, then we need to show them a better angle. If I get off this yacht tomorrow, my only term is that you stay by my side. That we stand together as a couple.'

'Of course. I'm the PR guru here. I can find a good spin for all this, if that's what you're worried about.'

She frowned at his use of the word 'couple'—a strange expression for their partnership. Still, she forced a smile, hardly believing the upward turn this venture had taken. An hour ago she had been terrified of what he might do after her actions tonight. She had taken a risk, forcing his hand this way. For now, she was happy to have him firmly on the side of the company and getting his mind back into the game.

'I presumed you would be more averse to the idea of us being together.' Valerio raised one dark brow, shrugging a shoulder as he moved to open the door. 'It's settled, then. We will announce our engagement first thing in the morning.'

CHAPTER TWO

VALERIO MOVED AWAY from Daniela's frozen form and walked quickly down the hallway. A part of him longed to turn around and reveal the full truth of their situation— the real reason he had promised to keep her safe, the truth behind his disappearance from society and the reason it needed to be this way. He had told himself he was biding his time, gathering all his facts. He hadn't expected the imminent issue of Duarte's death certificate to completely force his hand this way.

He focused on some deep and steady breaths as he emerged into the open-plan living space of the yacht's accommodation deck.

He remembered attending the initial meetings for the *Sirinetta II* just before they'd left on their trip to South America. It had been one of Duarte's most innovative design projects yet. His senses felt overloaded by the bright and airy interior, with its open-plan spaces and natural blond wood design. He knew from memory that the endless smooth surfaces were an illusion, and in fact filled with discreet touch cabinets and modern technological gadgets.

'What did you just say?'

Daniela's voice had risen an entire octave, and her flashing amber eyes filled with disbelief as he looked over his shoulder.

Her cheeks were flushed with the warmth of the force of her anger at his proposal. Well, technically he hadn't proposed so much as *declared* their engagement... He winced inwardly. Probably not the best way he could have done things.

Turning away from her, he touched a panel and grabbed a bottle of water from one of the discreet built-in fridges that slid out from behind the wood. 'We can make the announcement in the morning papers if you get on it now. You are the PR guru, as you said. I assume you have contacts who can word it to make it all appear as romantic as possible.'

'Valerio, we are *business* partners—our alliance is solid enough without turning it into some kind of media circus.'

'Did you or did you not say that rumours surrounding my disappearance from the public eye have cast doubt on my stability?'

'I—I am experienced with appeasing doubt.' She stammered a little over her words. 'It's been my job to control Velamar's public image for the past seven years and I'm quite good at it without resorting to outright lies and... and pageantry!'

'My terms are that we release the news that we are engaged. That is non-negotiable.'

He took a long drink of water, trying to shake off the feeling of adrenaline still running riot in his veins. He was always like this after a bad night—he felt on edge for days. But now, knowing that someone had pushed to have Duarte declared legally dead even when he had made every effort to hold it off... He had to act now. He had to be ready.

Dani was silent for a long time, a frown marring her brow as she shook her head slowly from side to side. 'I don't buy it. What aren't you telling me?'

Valerio walked out onto the open-air deck, gritting his

teeth at the sound of her heels as she instantly followed him. Of *course* she wouldn't just meekly accept his terms and move forward; this was Dani, after all.

He closed his eyes and inhaled a deep breath of cold sea air into his lungs. He wasn't ready for this—for any of it. He needed to get off this yacht and find some breathing room while he built himself up to step back into his old life. Daniela thought she knew everything he had been doing for the past six months. Yes, he was broken, but not in the way that she thought. Despite public opinion, he was far from losing his mind. He had never had a more single-minded focus.

But that focus was entirely set on revenge.

'Valerio…' She appeared at his side, her expression a mixture of confusion and concern. 'Talk to me. Please.'

She believed him to be mad… Let her think that. Maybe then he would be able to shield her from the true monster he had become. Before all this he had been a good man. He might even have deserved a woman like her. Not that he had ever truly considered having her. He had always known she was off-limits to him. His friendship with Duarte had been worth more to him than any pleasure he might have got from pursuing any inconvenient attraction he may or may not have had. She was and would always be his best friend's sister.

Untouchable.

Now he was just the man who had let her down in so many ways. He'd known that she disliked him before, but now that he'd abandoned her to run Velamar for months without explanation… It was his own fault if she hated him, and perhaps that was a blessing in disguise. The man who stood beside her right now was nothing but darkness and regret. If hating him would keep her safe from getting too close, he'd bear every moment of the burn from her wrath.

He turned away from her, bracing his hands on the railing and looking down at the inky foam of the midnight waves as they crashed along the side of the yacht.

'You made your demands, Daniela. Now I have made mine. I'm willing to forgive your actions tonight so long as you agree to my terms without any further questioning.'

'Your terms being the immediate announcement of a fake engagement?' She was incredulous, her chest rising and falling with outrage.

'Not just an engagement.' He turned to face her, noticing once again how much warmth her eyes held. He could almost feel the heat emanating from her, along with that intoxicating scent she wore. The galloping of his heart seemed to slow when he considered the deep golden-brown depths of her eyes.

'You will be my wife.'

As he spoke the words and saw the shock turn to anger in her eyes, he felt a strange calm settle within him. He had known for six months that it might come to this. He had known that she would fight him every step of the way. And now, seeing her ablaze with fury and outrage, he thought maybe she would withstand the burden of being tied to him. He had to believe that. He had no other choice.

Dani stood frozen, her mouth refusing to form words, as Valerio took a step forward.

'A long time ago Duarte told me to keep the hell away from you unless I planned to marry you.' Valerio shook his head, looking out at the darkness that surrounded them. 'I doubt he ever thought things would come to this.'

'This is ridiculous.'

Dani turned and walked inside, needing to move away

from him. He had no idea what he was saying. How hurtful it was on so many levels. Even when she'd moved back to London and become engaged to another man, she'd fought not to let herself think of him. She growled in her throat, marching into the living area and reaching for her laptop— only for a large male hand to close over hers, stopping her.

'Valerio, stop. Let me show you my plans and we can discuss this rationally.'

'Your brother knew the kind of guy I am. He knew the perfect way to ensure I would never touch you.'

'You never *wanted* to touch me!' She practically growled it. She felt heat rise into her cheeks at her own words... at the hint of years of hidden feelings under the surface.

He opened his mouth as if to speak, then paused. For a moment there was nothing but weighted silence between them and the sound of the waves outside the open door.

Valerio cleared his throat, waited until she met his eyes. 'The day before Duarte was killed, we planned an escape. He told me that if anything happened to him and I survived, I was to keep you close. To give you my name and protect you.'

'I don't need a husband for protection. That is *my* choice. Not his.'

Dani fought against the lump of emotion that tightened in her throat at the thought of her brother instructing his best friend to care for her. He must have known that she would never agree to this kind of archaic showing of duty, or whatever it was.

Valerio turned away briefly, pushing his hands through his hair. 'I swore to him. I promised that I would follow his wishes. And I spent the last six months...'

Dani looked up at him, seeing a strange look in his eyes. 'You spent six months...what? Trying to find a way out of it? *That's* what it was all about?'

'No…you don't understand.'

'I think I understand far more than you do, Marchesi.' She picked up a small bag from under the desk and threw it onto the low sofa between them. 'I'm done here. I apologise for wasting your time tonight. Believe when I say I wish I hadn't bothered. The code for the wheelhouse is in that bag, along with your mobile phone. Order the Captain to take you wherever you need, so long as you're off this yacht by morning.'

'This won't just disappear because you order me away. I'm coming to Monte Carlo. You say you need me for this board meeting, so I'll be there.'

'I'll find another way. I always do.' She fought to keep her voice level, to hide her hurt and anger under the professional veil she wore so well. 'Pretend tonight never happened. Consider yourself officially relieved of your duties to Velamar. To me. All of them.'

She didn't wait for his response before she walked away, not stopping to take a breath until she had her cabin door firmly closed between them and she was sure that he hadn't followed her.

Then she closed her eyes tight and sank back against the door, allowing herself a single moment to feel the blinding pain of knowing how little Valerio Marchesi had ever cared about her.

'I can't believe you didn't take a photograph. I'd pay good money to see either one of the Marchesi brothers all tied up.' Hermione Hall waggled her brows seductively from across the terrace table of their favourite little Monte Carlo café.

Dani rolled her eyes, playing with the remains of her omelette as she struggled with the knot that had formed in her stomach and had refused to shift since the night before. Her best friend of eighteen years usually always knew just how to pull her out of a dark mood, but her night with Valerio had shattered all the careful control she had worked so hard to achieve over the past few months. She felt completely off balance.

Hermione was no stranger to difficult situations, being the child of an infamous Los Angeles talent agent who had stolen money from half of Hollywood. They'd met as teenagers, on their first day at boarding school in England, when Hermione had stepped in to defend Dani from a group of name-calling older girls. Together they'd become untouchable, unrepentant overachievers all the way through college, supporting one another through the loss of parents, bad relationships and sanity.

Now that Hermione was one of the most in-demand personal stylists in Europe, they didn't get to see one another very often, but their emails were long and never short on salacious details.

Hermione called over a waiter and ordered a caramel-drizzled waffle from the extravagant dessert menu, declaring it a celebration after hearing Dani's heavily edited version of the events of the night before.

Dani shook her head. 'You're completely overlooking the part where he just assumed he could announce our engagement. Along with the rest of his little speech about keeping me safe by *marrying* me. I mean…who even *thinks* like that? Apparently "safe" is just another word for "away from my own sources of power and independence".'

'I don't know… Daniela Marchesi has got a nice ring to it.' Hermione smirked.

'You're taking far too much enjoyment from my outrage.'

'Sorry—a drop-dead gorgeous Italian, whom you used to have a gigantic crush on, is now back to run his own company, which might allow *you* to finally get back on track with starting your own PR firm.' She took a sip of her tea, her tone dry. 'Oh, and he apparently wants to marry you too. How utterly *terrible* all this is.'

Dani looked away from her friend, ignoring the tension in her body as she remembered that her own consulting work had come to a standstill since she'd taken the helm at Velamar. No one knew that she had signed a lease on an office in London just weeks before the awful news from Rio—that she'd finally been poised to quit her job at Velamar and launch her own firm.

But, truthfully, it had been easier to cancel all her plans and throw herself into the heavy workload that had come with being a stand-in CEO. There was less time to think, less time to feel…

Hermione continued to chatter, trying to lighten the mood in her usual way. 'With those eyes and that insane body… I wouldn't turn down *any* kind of dark and brooding proposal from Valerio Marchesi—that's all I'm saying.'

'I'm sorry that I don't share your love of dramatic romance. And I get it that he's a little paranoid since…since everything that happened in Rio. But I'm not in danger. This isn't Regency England and I am not on the market for a protector.'

She frowned as her phone buzzed with an email notification from the head of the Velamar events team.

Subject: You might be interested in this.

The email showed the guest list for the modest cocktail party she had planned for some select guests to get a sneak preview of the *Sirinetta II* later that evening. Dani frowned, her eyes scanning down the list with increasing disbelief.

A shocked huff of laughter escaped her lips. It seemed that Mr Hotshot CEO had decided to dive right back into work.

The numbers for the 'small and intimate' gathering had now tripled, and contained the names of some of the wealthiest people in Monaco, including philanthropists, celebrities and even a few members of European royalty. It was no secret that the Marchesi family had connections, but seriously...

The arrogance of the man! For him to just march over and amend details of an event that *she* had planned and executed without even asking...

The curse words that escaped her lips were very un-ladylike, sending even wild-mannered Hermione's eyebrows upwards.

'He believes he can just reappear and completely rail-road an event that I've been planning for weeks! I bet he doesn't even think he's done anything wrong.'

She stabbed her index finger at the phone screen, beginning to type an email to inform her team that she didn't need to see the guest list, as she wouldn't be attending. Let the returned 'Playboy Pirate' explain her absence to his guests—let him try to make the same kind of connections and collaborations that she did at such events. He thought he could just swoop in and do everything? She would leave him to it.

Hermione interrupted her thoughts, bending to look at the email over her shoulder and letting out a low whistle. 'That's a lot of prime potential new clientele. What are you going to wear?'

'I won't go.' Dani bit her bottom lip. 'If he refuses to treat me like an equal partner in this company, then I don't see why I should jump to host this event by his side.'

'Correction, you *will* go. Because you *are* an equal partner in the company and a professional one at that. You'll go and you will tell him exactly where he can stick his proposal. Along with giving him a clear outline of the kind of treatment you will be expecting from now on.' Hermione opened up her small tablet computer and began clicking rapidly. 'I've got the perfect dress I've been saving for you—you just need to get the perfect date. And before you ask, I already have plans tonight.'

Dani knew her friend was right. The problem was that Valerio would also know that she couldn't *not* attend, and that grated on her nerves. 'If I do go, I won't need a date. I was the one to plan the thing originally, so I'm technically the hostess.'

Hermione had a familiar glimmer of mischief in her eyes. 'You don't *need* one…but imagine what kind of statement it would make for you to walk into that party with the one man that Valerio Marchesi truly despises by your side.'

'You don't mean…?' Dani felt her eyes widen as she let out a puff of shocked laughter. 'I couldn't bring *him*. It would cause a riot. Besides, it's pretty late notice…'

'You think Tristan Falco isn't going to jump at the chance to gatecrash that party?'

Dani frowned, knowing her friend was right.

'You want to put Marchesi in his place, don't you?' Hermione waggled her brows. 'Time for you to introduce the ace up your sleeve. Show him that you're not playing nice. You make the call—I'll go and assemble my wonder team. That man has no idea who he's messing with.'

Hermione dropped a quick kiss on her cheek and breezed away, leaving Dani staring down at her phone, which was still open on the guest list.

She walked to the railing of the restaurant's terrace, looking out at the pink and orange clouds painted along the sky… The sun would start setting soon—she didn't have the luxury of waiting around. If she was going to put up a fight, she had to go to this event. Tomorrow she would come up with a new angle and figure out how to save Nettuno from being sold off. As for tonight...

She opened her phone and scrolled down to the name of a man she had never thought she would call again. A smile touched the corner of her lips as the number rang and a deep male voice answered. Within moments she had confirmed her scandalous date for the evening, silently marvelling at Hermione's evil genius.

It seemed that Cinderella *would* attend the ball after all, but she would not be waving the proverbial white flag and dancing with Prince Charming.

Tonight she would make Valerio Marchesi realise just how wrong he had been to underestimate her.

The paparazzi were gathered eagerly around the gates of Valerio's luxurious Monte Carlo villa, waiting for the first public photograph of the Playboy Pirate's return and an exclusive opportunity to see what had become of their tragic hero.

Valerio had planned to give them their show—to depart in his usual extravagant style, driving one of his prized sports cars. But at the last moment he had chosen to have his bodyguard drive one of the Jeeps, instructing him to exit the rear gate so that he could slip past the cameras.

He had told himself that he was adding to the mystery—that he was playing up to the media circus and fanning the flames of gossip. It was all good publicity, after all. He was building up to a grand return on his own terms. But the reality was that he had stopped himself from booking the first flight out of Monaco at least three times since walking off the yacht into the dawn light that morning. If it hadn't been for the threat to Dani, he'd have gone. But he knew he had to be here—knew he had to ensure her complete safety.

He had stood in the marina, looking up at the now unfamiliar city that had once been one of his many playgrounds, and he had felt like an impostor. He was playing the part of Valerio Marchesi, but he had no interest in that life any more.

It all seemed so hollow now, as he looked back at the way he had lived. He had gone from one extreme to the next, proving himself in daring sailing challenges, throwing the wildest parties and seducing the most beautiful women. Life had just been one big adventure after another, with nothing ever big enough to satiate his appetite for more. Until everything had suddenly become tasteless and the thought of sailing or seducing had seemed just a waste of energy better spent on his investigations.

His old life seemed like a distant memory—like the life of a stranger. But if he was no longer that version of himself…he had no idea *who* he was…

When he arrived at the party, his first priority was to ensure that Velamar's private marina was securely locked down. The elite security team he had hired six months ago had been expertly trained by the best in the business and they knew exactly where they needed to be. He stepped onto the main entertaining deck of the massive yacht to see that some of the guests had already arrived. A small swing band had set up on a small platform, and the intrusive bouncing melody of the music provided a perfect background for a night that would likely be filled with uncomfortable conversations and questions about his time away.

For the first time in months he wished he could down a few drinks as he was approached by several acquaintances all at once. But he'd long ago learned that drinking only made him feel worse. He needed to be in control of his senses, of his mind.

The party filled out quickly, and soon enough the entire room was watching him, the curiosity in their gazes mixed with the familiar sympathy he'd come to expect in the days immediately after his rescue. Hushed conversations began, ensuring that anyone who was *not* aware of the events that had put the scars on Valerio Marchesi's face and the growling darkness in his eyes was soon informed.

He had never lacked confidence about his looks—he knew that even despite the minor scarring and his leg injury he was still attractive enough. Some women would probably find it thrilling, seeing such a dramatic reminder of his fight for survival. They would build it into the fantasy of him as a rugged adventurer, like in the stories the media had loved to spread. But having so many eyes on him was a stark reminder of everything he would never outrun.

He would always be the scarred hero to them—someone both to pity and admire. None of them knew the truth of what had happened. None of them had lived through it.

But now was not the time to show weakness—not when he had important work to do. Being born a Marchesi meant he had been introduced to instant fame and pressure even before he could walk. He had chosen a different path from the family business, but he still used the lessons he had learned from his father every day. *When you feel weak, walk tall and look them in the eye.* So he met each set of curious eyes without hesitation, ignoring any mention of his absence and filling each conversation with talk of the latest yacht they planned to launch.

'Ah, here comes Daniela.' One of the members of the Velamar board craned her neck to look past him. 'Good grief—is that Tristan Falco on her arm?'

Every set of eyes in the small group around him snapped towards the steps at the opposite end of the long entertaining deck.

She wouldn't... Surely she would have the sense not to...

After seeing a series of nervous furtive glances towards him, Valerio gritted his jaw and turned to see for himself.

CHAPTER THREE

TIME SEEMED TO come to a standstill as his eyes sought Dani across the crowd. She was shaking hands with one of the politicians he'd invited, the wide smile on her ruby-red lips a world away from the indignant anger he'd last seen on her face.

He was powerless to look away, and the tightness inside his chest loosened as he watched her tilt her head back and laugh. She didn't even have to try to be the perfect hostess—it just came naturally.

As he looked on, the crowd tightened and gathered around her, vying for her attention. And even if he hadn't already been treading a fine line with his control, seeing Tristan Falco by her side had him fighting the insane urge to growl.

There wasn't a single person on this yacht who didn't know of his long-standing rivalry with the heir to the Falco diamond fortune. He shook his head, biting his lower lip to stop himself from laughing at such a deliberate power-play. Clever, infuriating woman. For some reason she was trying to provoke him...

As though she'd heard him, the object of his thoughts met his gaze across the sea of guests. Almost in slow motion, she raised her champagne glass in a toast, an unmistakable smirk on her full lips.

AMANDA CINELLI 41

Schooling his own expression to one of mild interest, he raised his own in response and began to move slowly across the deck towards her. He could see her eyes shifting towards him at regular intervals as he got closer, her hand moving first to push an errant curl behind her ear, then to touch the delicate necklace at her throat.

He noticed that she had trapped her ebony curls high on her head, only letting a few hang free. It was impossible not to see how the style accentuated the long, bare expanse of her neck and shoulders, but likely that had been her aim. She was a confident woman—surely she knew how her appearance captivated the crowd around her.

He didn't know much about fashion, but he knew that she had chosen perfectly in the emerald-green concoction encasing her curves. He felt his throat turn dry as the shimmering material moved, revealing a modest slit up to the smooth skin of one thigh. Reflexively, he forced his gaze back to her face. She seemed to sparkle in the light as she moved away from the small crowd around her, taking a few steps in his direction to close the final gap between them.

'My compliments on your stellar work today, Mr CEO,' she said tightly, her charming smile still firmly in place as she waved politely at a couple of guests who passed them.

'I assumed you wouldn't mind my input on this event's inadequate guest list, seeing as you were so eager to have me back.' He fought the urge to smirk as her eyes sparked fire at him.

She took a delicate sip of her champagne, giving him an icy glare over the rim. 'If you had given me your input *before* making your sweeping changes, you might have found out that there was a strategic, brand-specific reason for my tiny guest list.'

'If you'd answered any of my calls today, maybe I could have done that.'

'Well, maybe I was too busy recovering from your ridiculous...*proposal*.' She lowered her voice to a hiss, her eyes darting around as she uttered the last word as though it were some kind of demonic chant.

Valerio couldn't help it then—he chuckled under his breath. There was absolutely nothing funny about any part of their situation, but some long-buried part of him was really enjoying this verbal sparring.

It had always been like this between them—from the first time they'd met as teenagers, when she'd come to watch Duarte in a sailing competition at their all-boys boarding school. Even when she'd joined Velamar he'd used to start fights with her at events just to draw out this...*fire*. At one point he'd started to wonder if she was avoiding him, and that had only made him try harder to provoke her—before Duarte had mistaken his playful jabs at her as interest and moved the entire PR and marketing division to their London offices. He'd said it wasn't because of that, but Valerio had known better.

The terse silence between them was broken by the arrival of a wide-smiling Tristan Falco at Dani's elbow. 'Marchesi, you seem to have forgotten my invitation tonight. Luckily your partner was in need of a fine male escort.'

'I wasn't aware that you were in town.' Valerio extended his hand to the other man, not missing the way Dani's eyes widened with surprise. 'I've never had the chance to thank you since the last time we spoke.'

A serious look came across the other man's features. 'It was nothing. I hope you took my advice.'

Valerio exhaled on a sigh, reflexively crossing his arms over his chest as he nodded brusquely. 'I did.'

'Am I missing something here?'

Dani's voice was hard as stone between them. Her hand was on her hip, her eyes narrowed as she looked from one man to the other. Tristan was the first to speak, sliding his arm over her shoulders and pulling her in close.

'It's a private matter between us guys.' He smiled in his trademark way. 'I met up with Marchesi a couple months back while I was in Rio.'

'Rio?' Dani fired that amber gaze Valerio's way briefly, then turned back and fluttered her lashes up at Tristan. 'How lovely. What did you guys get up to in lovely Rio?'

Valerio tensed, hoping Falco would have the good sense to stop talking. Despite his invaluable help, the man was still a thorn in his side. Even looking at him now, with his big meaty arm slung over Dani's shoulders, it made him want to throw a punch in his pretty-boy face and launch him bodily off the yacht.

After a long, painful silence it seemed Dani had realised that neither of them planned to elaborate further on the matter. But she didn't fire off another smart retort. Instead Valerio watched as a brief glimmer of hurt flashed in her eyes. Her lips thinned for a moment and she made a big display of looking around the party. Then she smiled—a glorious movement of red-painted lips and perfect teeth that seemed to hit him squarely in the chest.

'Excuse me, gentlemen… Some of us have work to do tonight.'

Valerio was powerless to do anything but watch as she retreated in the direction of the bar, stopping here and there to greet her guests cheerfully, as though nothing had happened at all. He cleared his throat, turning back to see Falco pointedly raising one eyebrow.

'Why do I feel like I'm interrupting something?' the other man drawled.

'Just a professional disagreement.' Valerio cleared his throat and took a long sip from his glass. 'None of your concern. Also, she's off-limits to you.'

'Professional?' Tristan Falco laughed. 'Right...and that's why you looked like you wanted to throw me overboard when you saw her with me.'

'There's still time if you don't stop talking,' Valerio said, gritting his teeth.

Falco raised both hands in mock surrender, leaning back against the wall to survey the crowd in his usual calculated way.

Valerio tried to ignore the pang of guilt in his gut. He hadn't wanted Dani to find out that he'd been back to Brazil at all. And he certainly hadn't wanted her to find out like that.

She didn't know anything of the past six months of his life because he'd been trying to protect her from the worry that would come with the knowledge that he was still actively pursuing the men who had taken him and Duarte in Rio. That he had been knee-deep in a dangerous criminal underworld of corrupt politics and blackmail as he tried to piece together the events that had led to his best friend's death.

It had been pure chance that Tristan Falco had been in Rio at the same time. He'd saved Valerio from being arrested, drunk and ranting, after another lead had turned out to be useless.

The other man had cleaned him up and offered him some solid advice. *No more booze. Hire professionals to do the digging.* He'd also put Valerio in contact with a discreet and highly qualified clinician to help with the psychological aspects of his recovery. And he'd shared some of his contacts to help Valerio dig into the backgrounds of some of the men he suspected of involvement. The diamond heir had become an unlikely ally in his fight for justice.

Valerio took the first opportunity to move away in search of his unhappy business partner. He had made his peace with Falco, but that didn't mean he was suddenly able to tolerate his company for longer than necessary.

He moved through the crowd, hating how uneasy and wooden he felt when he stopped to converse with his guests. His smile felt too tight, his shoulders heavy. The old Valerio would have been in his element here, not counting down the minutes until it would be acceptable for him to slip away.

This conflict with Daniela had got under his skin. Clearly she was annoyed by his actions today—which, honestly, he'd expected. He hadn't planned to triple her guest list, but it added to his mission to draw attention to his social standing and good connections. An unstable CEO would hardly host a party for all of Monaco's elite, would he? Plus, he'd been frustrated at her reaction to his proposal. He felt an urgency to his plans now and he needed her to stop fighting him.

The trouble was, he didn't want to reveal the full truth of her situation and scare her away. He had planned to find a balance tonight, to give her just enough incentive to co-operate and accept his proposal. She was no fainting little miss, that was for sure—especially considering she had quite literally kidnapped him to ensure she got him to Monte Carlo.

But his plans for tonight had not involved having her completely furious with him. He needed her by his side. It was the only way he could keep her safe.

Discomfort had him running a finger along the rim of his collar, fighting the urge to rip off his tie and open a few buttons. He had chosen the open decks of the yacht deliberately, knowing that confined spaces were one of his triggers. But it seemed that even having the entire night sky above him was not enough to stop the familiar tingle of hyper-awareness from creeping up his spine. Every loud bark of laughter and clink of glassware brought a shot of tension painful enough to have him gritting his teeth.

A movement on the opposite side of the sea terrace caught his eye. One of Daniela's security men, conferring with the rest of the team with a worried look on his face. Valerio moved forward, the tension mounting in his gut like a furnace.

One brief exchange of words with the men was enough to confirm his worst fear.

She was missing.

Dani had moved away from the crowd initially just needing a moment to herself. That moment had turned into a quarter of an hour as she'd wandered through the yacht in search of privacy. Finally she'd emerged onto an open sea-view terrace at the stern, breathing a sigh of relief to find it empty but cursing herself for not grabbing another glass of champagne or some canapés. She hadn't eaten a lot after her brunch with Hermione, and already she could feel the buzz of alcohol in her head. She'd always been a lightweight.

From their current position, she could see the lights of Monte Carlo twinkling like fiery diamonds above the water. She could see the glow of the iconic Monaco Naval Museum and the Grimaldi Forum in the distance. Such beauty would usually bring her a sense of calm, but nothing seemed able to rid her of the restless feeling that had plagued her all day.

Her late entrance to the party had been calculated to ensure the maximum effect of the majestic, glittering emerald gown Hermione had provided. Its designer was a new hot name on the Paris runway, his trademark exclusive material a blissfully comfortable stretch velvet that had actual diamond fragments threaded throughout.

The piece was heaven for the more curvaceous women of the world, like her. It moulded to her body like a second skin and flared out slightly just below her knees in a delicate flounce. And the *pièce de résistance* to complement her perfect ensemble was the man she'd had on her arm.

What on earth had she been thinking, bringing Tristan Falco? Everyone else on the yacht had watched that ridiculous display of thoroughly masculine camaraderie between him and Valerio with a mixture of appreciation and curiosity. She had heard whispers—one person wondering if this finally meant a partnership of the two brands was in the works...another dreamily wishing that *she* could be in the middle of the two hunks.

Dani didn't know what bothered her more: all those women drooling over the two men or the fact that most of the guests would attribute any future partnership between Falco Diamonds and Velamar to Valerio's presumed genius.

Dani had been approached by Tristan numerous times in the past few months about a possible collaboration between their two brands. It was no secret that Valerio had firmly declined his numerous offers in the past, even though it made perfect business sense for the two to join forces, considering the strong history already present between Falco Diamonds and the other members of the wealthy Marchesi family.

The soft clearing of a throat brought her back to the moment. She turned, expecting to see that Valerio had followed her, but instead she was met with the sight of a thin man with a shock of salt-and-pepper hair that seemed vaguely familiar. There was a kind of meanness in the smile he gave her, and a shrewdness in the way he scanned the empty deck area with a seeming lack of interest.

'*Boa noite*, Senhorita Avelar.'

His voice was reedy, as though he smoked twenty cigarettes a day. A few steps closer and the odour that drifted off his expensive suit confirmed her theory. She held her breath as the man leaned forward to place the customary kiss on her right cheek.

'Angelus Fiero—I'm an old friend of your father's and a silent member of the board.' He smiled, extending a flute of champagne towards her. 'I hope you don't mind me following you?'

She accepted the glass, pasting a polite smile on her face and ignoring the shiver of unease in her spine. He took a seat directly across from her on a low cushioned bench that bordered the delicate curved rail of the deck.

'You seem to be taking your job as CEO very seriously. I have heard of your divine talent. Ruling with an iron fist and a perfect smile. Turning things from rotten wood into finely polished oak,' he said cryptically, with a strange glimmer in his eyes. 'Tell me…is it a new company protocol to bypass a direct order from the executor of someone's will?'

Dani paused, the champagne flute inches from her lips.

'I'd bet Marchesi has no idea that *you* were the one to apply for Duarte's death certificate, has he?'

Dani initially fought the urge to shout that Valerio was not her keeper. But then her logical brain processed the man's words and she didn't speak, her mind utterly frozen in confusion. Who *was* this man, with his all too knowing eyes and his knowledge of top-secret information?

There was no proof that she'd been the one to file the request for Duarte's death certificate—she'd used a notary and the company name as a group entity. Not that she'd been planning to keep it a secret—not until Valerio's furious reaction, anyway. She'd planned to tell him eventually.

She couldn't really explain her urge to have the limbo

of her brother's death put into legal black and white. It had been an intolerable hum of sadness and a slow bubble of frustration—like an itch under her skin that she couldn't scratch. She'd known she couldn't wait around for Valerio to return and decide to accept that Duarte's death was a reality.

But now, on this dark, secluded part of the yacht, a part of her became suddenly painfully aware of the fact that she had put herself in a vulnerable position, out here alone without any of her security team.

Fiero stood up, taking a few steps to close the gap between them. Dani fought the urge to stand and run, taking note of his distance from her and feeling the weight of the empty champagne glass in her hands. She was alone, but she was not incapable of self-defence. She straightened her shoulders, meeting his gaze with what she hoped was a perfectly calm expression.

'I came here tonight to give you a warning. If you value your life, stop digging into things that don't concern you.'

Dani inhaled sharply at the threat, watching as the older man turned to walk away.

His route was suddenly barred by the arrival of three security guards in the doorway and a thunder-faced Valerio, who took one look at Daniela's ashen face and immediately cornered their guest.

'Marchesi.' Fiero spoke calmly, placing a cigarette between his lips and lighting it. 'Nice to see you again. Is there some sort of problem?'

'I don't know yet.' Valerio looked the man up and down, his fists clenched at his sides. 'Daniela?'

Valerio said her name softly, but with a stern undertone that had her snapping out of the daze she was in. 'Everything is fine,' she heard herself say. 'Let him go.'

She was vaguely aware of Valerio ordering the security

men to escort Fiero back to the party and keep a close eye on the man. He waited until they were alone on the deck, then took a few steps towards her, crossing his arms in that way he did when he was intensely annoyed by something.

It amazed her that she could still tell his mood just by observing his body language, considering how little they had seen one another in the past few years. She was lucky he couldn't do the same with her, or he'd know just how absolutely terrified she felt. A shiver ran down her spine as she looked up at the thunderous expression on his face.

'Disappearing alone without protection—have you lost your mind?'

'We're on a yacht.' She rolled her eyes. 'Also, I'm a grown woman, Valerio. Not a child for you to keep track of and scold.'

'Even a child would know not to risk its own safety by wandering off alone into the darkness.'

He blocked her path when she tried to move away, placing one hand on her arm.

'Why did you come out here, Dani? What could Angelus Fiero possibly have to say to you?'

Her mind kept replaying those words over and over on a loop.

If you value your life.'
If you value your life.'

She felt the heat of Valerio's hand on her arm, sinking into her skin like a brand. She tried to draw on her anger at him for disappearing, for leaving her to run Velamar alone while she tried to hide her own grief. She shouldn't feel this urge to fall into the safety of him when he had done nothing but give orders and trample on her work in all his six-foot-four and ridiculously handsome glory.

He had kept his newfound peace with Tristan Falco

from her, and his apparent trip to Rio, and God only knew what else. He made her utterly furious.

She tried to remember all the reasons she might throw at him for why she had walked out…other than the fact that she'd needed to get away from him and the way he made her feel completely off balance. But now, with his simple touch burning against her arm, she was powerless even to control the erratic beating of her own stupid heart.

He frowned down at his hand on her arm, dropping it away as though he hadn't realised he was touching her.

'He was just expressing his condolences in person for our loss. He couldn't come to the memorial service.' Dani felt the lies fall easily from her lips, guilt pressing at her conscience as she turned and began walking back through the yacht towards the faint strains of the string quartet and the sound of laughter.

'Stop running from me. I need to speak with you alone.' He easily moved around her in the darkened study and blocked her way. 'You arrived here tonight with that womanising fool on your arm without any thought other than angering me.'

'Why would I care what you think, Valerio? You clearly don't do the same for me.'

'You don't see a slight problem with bringing a date to your *fiancé's* event?'

Dani froze in disbelief, the word 'fiancé' coming from his lips sending her blood pressure into overdrive. The man had lost his mind entirely.

'Again this ridiculous promise you made? Valerio… I've already made it quite clear what I think about your proposal. It's completely unnecessary.'

She took a step backwards, needing to put physical space between them. No one made her quite as angry as he did. No one else could manage to get under her skin and surpass her control.

'I'm not some damsel in distress who needs your protection. Until this morning I was acting CEO of the company we share equal ownership of. I've been at the helm of Velamar for six months while I gave you the time you needed to recover.'

'I don't think you're a damsel in distress. You are the strongest woman I've ever met. I just need you to trust me that we need to do this.'

'It doesn't make sense. I wouldn't let Duarte make this choice for me if he were alive. And I won't be accepting it from you, either.'

'This isn't about how capable you are. This is about your safety.'

Suddenly her anger fell away and she looked at him. Took in the tension around his mouth, the shadows in his eyes. She remembered his reaction when she'd told him that Duarte was soon to be declared legally dead. She had seen something entirely different then. He hadn't just been angry... He'd been afraid. For *her*. And then her mind replayed the look on his face as he'd arrived just now with the three guards in tow, asking her if there was a problem.

'Look... I haven't been truthful about what I've been doing for the past six months. You thought I was in hiding while I recovered and I let you believe that because it's partially true. I have been isolated and angry and dealing with...with what happened. Tristan Falco witnessed my own methods of dealing with it first-hand and gave me some good advice.'

'No more lies and avoidance. Tell me the truth. Why do you need me to agree to this so badly?' As she asked the question, her legs felt weak, and an odd twisting sensation started up in her stomach.

He smoothed a hand down his face, closing his eyes for a long moment as though fortifying himself.

'Duarte knew that he was in danger when he went to Rio alone. He didn't expect me to follow him. All I know is that he was being blackmailed. I couldn't get a full picture of who was behind it or what had gone down before I arrived and everything went to hell, but I do know that he was trying to neutralise an imminent threat…to you both.'

Dani felt the breath completely leave her chest as she sat down on a nearby chair, looking up at him with disbelief. 'If I'm in danger… If they've already got Duarte…'

'Daniela, look at me.' He knelt down, gripping her chin between his fingers and forcing her to meet his eyes. 'I won't let anyone hurt you. I've spent months trying to find another way to help because I knew you would hate this. The only thing I'm sure of is that it has to do with part of your inheritance. The land and properties in Brazil.'

'They can have it—I never wanted any of it.' She breathed in, feeling her pulse careening out of control. This was insanity—utter madness. She'd give everything away…every single cent. Nothing was worth the loss she'd endured. *Nothing.*

'I thought of that.' Valerio spoke softly, as though he feared he had fully tipped her over the edge. 'But it's complicated. We're talking about decades of your parents' work in creating affordable housing there. Tens of thousands of innocent tenants who stand to be displaced. Acres of protected land being put at risk.'

Tens of thousands… Dani closed her eyes and felt a tremor within her.

Her father had been an only child, sole heir to the wealthiest, most corrupt landowner in Brazil. When his old man had died, her *papai* had been newly married to his very liberal-minded English wife. Together they had wasted no time in setting out on a crusade to turn the majority of their expensive, undeveloped inner-city land into rent-controlled housing initiatives for disadvantaged families. It had been revolutionary, and it had angered a lot of wealthy developers by the time they'd started on the city of Rio.

'Dani…' Valerio said. 'As a married couple, we can create an iron-clad prenuptial agreement that ties all your assets to mine. We need to make them untouchable, so that there's no valid reason for anyone to target you. My family name, the legal power it holds… It's like a fortress. Duarte knew that. He'd planned for it if his efforts didn't succeed.'

Dani shuddered, the reality of her situation settling like a frost on her skin. She and her brother had been targeted for something they had no control over. She had never asked to be born into this life… She hadn't asked for her entire family to be taken away from her in a matter of years.

She felt her throat contract painfully as she tried to force breath in and out.

'Do you understand now why it needs to be this way?' he said softly, coming round to look into her eyes. 'I need you to stop fighting me on this. I need you to put your trust in me and let me keep you safe.'

She couldn't meet his eyes. This was all far too much to handle without the effect he had on her added to the mix too.

She simply nodded once. 'I'll do it.'

'I'm sorry I couldn't find another way.'

She tried not to wince at his words. Tried not to imagine his horror when he'd realised he was going to have to shackle himself in matrimony to a woman he could barely tolerate. A woman he seemed to actively avoid even though they'd been working for the same company for years.

'You don't need to pretend that this is what you want. It is what it is, Valerio.' She stood up, smoothing down her dress in an effort to compose herself even as her voice shook. 'We need to get back to the party or they'll start talking about us… Although I suppose I'm going to have to get used to that if I'm about to marry you.'

Something glittered in his eyes as she said those words. Whether it was relief or dread, she didn't take the time to find out. She needed to get away from the strange intimacy of being here in the darkness with him. Back to the safety of the party, to networking, putting on a show.

'You will have to get used to a lot of things.' His gaze drifted away, his jaw tightening. 'We both will.'

Dani smiled tightly, turning and walking along the corridor, then up the stairs to the entertaining deck. She heard him following silently behind her, but didn't pause until they were safely on the sidelines of the dance floor, where the music made it slightly harder to hear him without leaning in.

'I'm making our announcement here…tonight.'

His voice travelled slowly across the din of music and voices, and Dani frowned, his meaning taking a moment to sink in. Her eyes widened as he moved to step away, and her fingers clutched at the sleeve of his jacket to stop him.

'If you're talking about what I think you are…'

He moved close, dipping his head to speak close to her ear. 'We are on a superyacht, filled with the most famous people in Europe. If we want news of our engagement to travel fast, then there's no time like the present.'

Dani shook her head, hardly believing what a turn the evening had taken. 'Okay…but there's no need for it to be a big deal. It doesn't have to be a spectacle.'

'You know it does.'

He smiled, and for a moment she got a glimpse of his old self. Mischievous and eager to cause a stir.

'I'm going to make sure the whole world knows you are about to become my wife.'

CHAPTER FOUR

'OH, GOD...' DANI breathed, staring up into the azure blue depths of his eyes and praying that she could maintain her composure. She looked around at the beautiful people surrounding them, oblivious to the fact that her entire world had shifted on its axis. 'We can just make the announcement tomorrow somewhere...please.'

'This needs to be convincing, Daniela.'

His voice was gravelly and low in her ear, making her skin prickle. She knew he was right. This was the kind of guest list, with the kind of publicity reach, that could undo every single bit of questionable press Velamar had got in the past six months. It was the perfect way to take control of the media narrative while also taking steps to secure her safety. She tried not to imagine the backlash—the sniped remarks about why a man like him would choose her.

She prided herself on being self-sufficient. On having walked away from her ex because he'd assumed that she would change her iron-clad life plan to fit around him. And now here she stood, contemplating entwining her life and everything she owned with the one person she had sworn never to trust again. This wild, reckless playboy had somehow become the only solid land within reach in a dangerous sea.

She shook her head, hardly believing what she was

about to do. 'Okay, but…but you need to get down on one knee,' she breathed, hardly believing the words coming out of her mouth.

'Are you organising my proposal?' His eyes sparkled with mirth. 'Do you have a preference for which knee I use?'

'Be serious. Just… It's more romantic that way.'

One dark brow rose in disbelief, and for a moment she expected him to argue. But then he raised both hands in mock surrender and took a step backwards.

A single gesture to a nearby server gave a signal that he wished to grab everyone's attention. Somewhere nearby silverware was clinked gently against a glass and a lull fell over the party, the string quartet slowing their melody to a stop. Dani felt her heartbeat pound in her ears as Valerio met her eyes and then lowered his impressive frame gracefully down onto one knee.

Dani tried not to be hyper-aware of the dozens and dozens of stunned eyes and gasped breaths as everyone became glued to the tableau unfolding in their midst. It was one thing to be in business mode amongst them, but this was so far out of her comfort zone she almost felt like taking her chances overboard. Never mind her lifelong terror of swimming in the open sea—anything was preferable to feeling this exposed.

Valerio looked up at her, and for a moment, Dani forgot to breathe. This painfully gorgeous man was every woman's dream. It was almost too much to take in the sincerity on his handsome features as he cleared his throat and reached for her hand. And she had never understood the term *fluttering* when it came to heartbeats, but there was no other way to describe the strange thrumming in her chest as Valerio gently lowered his lips and pressed a featherlight kiss against her fingers.

'This will come as a shock to many of you, but Daniela and I have been keeping a large part of our life private for a long time now.' Valerio's voice sounded huskier, his accent more pronounced, and his eyes never wavered from hers as he continued. 'Darling, I know we said we would wait, but I want to share this moment with our guests. Daniela Avelar, will you do me the honour of becoming my wife?'

Dani was painfully aware of the silence around them. She nodded, her chin bobbing up and down like a puppet on a string, forcing a wide smile and praying that she didn't look as terrified as she felt. Applause began to resound around them as their guests cheered and fawned over them.

She swallowed hard, her eyes widening as she noticed the small velvet box he had produced from his coat pocket. The ring inside was an antique canary-yellow diamond that she knew instantly would match the gold heirloom wedding band she had inherited from her mother.

She tensed at the realisation that he had come so prepared for this moment. Had he been so sure that she would agree to this madness? Suddenly, the huge guest list made even more sense.

Her hand shook against Valerio's warm skin as he slid the ring onto her third finger. It was a perfect fit.

He stood, his eyes darkening with some strange emotion as he pulled her against his hard chest and buried his face next to her ear. 'I'm going to kiss you now, Daniela. Try to pretend you're enjoying it.'

His arm tightened around her waist as his lips easily found hers. The kiss was initially just a gentle press of skin against skin. Dani tried to remain impartial to the searing heat of the large male hand on her hip and at the nape of her neck, but she shivered reflexively at the contact. He was so...*large* all around her...he somehow made her feel small.

She was being ridiculous. She needed to keep a level head here. But when the delicious scent of his cologne enveloped her, she couldn't help her own reflexive movement and she traced her tongue along the seam of his lips. It had been so long since she'd been kissed that her body seemed to jolt with electricity as a mortifying groan emanated from deep in her throat.

Valerio seemed to stiffen at the noise, and for a moment she fully expected him to move away. He would know that she wasn't just pretending. But instead he pulled her even tighter against his body, deepening the kiss and giving back just as good as he got. His movements were much more skilful than her own shy ones, and his lips and tongue moved slowly against hers in such a perfectly seductive rhythm she quickly lost the ability to think straight.

She had never been kissed this way. It was as if she'd spent her life believing she knew all there was to know about her own body and now he was just tearing everything down.

Her mind screamed at her to slow down, to stop falling for this act they were putting on, but her body flat-out refused to listen. Already she could feel herself become embarrassingly aroused, heat spreading through her like wildfire. She reached up and spread her fingers through his hair, down to the warmth of his nape under the collar of his shirt, needing to feel more of him under her fingertips.

When her nail accidentally scraped his skin, the groan that came from deep in his throat shocked her to her core. It was quite possibly the most erotic sound that she had ever heard in her life.

Of course he would choose that exact moment to rip himself away from her. His eyes were wide with a mixture of shock and anger, and he watched her for a long moment, both of them breathing heavily as they became aware of their surroundings once more.

Dani fought the urge to pull him straight back, then felt her cheeks heat with embarrassment at how quickly she'd lost control. The whole thing had probably lasted no more than a minute and yet she felt as though time had ceased to exist.

The swing band resumed their music with a loud, jazzy celebratory number, and the guests began gathering inward, everyone bustling over to give them their good wishes. Flutes of champagne were handed out and soon they were swept away on an endless stream of toasts and congratulations.

And all the while Dani was painfully aware of the man by her side, of every small touch of his hand at her back or dip of his head to speak close to her ear.

She thanked the heavens when he finally moved away to another group of people, feeling as if she was pulling air into her lungs after being underwater. It had been far too long since she'd had any contact with a member of the opposite sex, she thought. She felt as though every nerve-ending in her body had been lit up like a firework. And now the mad urge to seek him out in the crowd every few minutes plagued her consciousness. She couldn't concentrate, couldn't relax with these knots in her stomach.

A few glasses of champagne later and she was significantly less wound up, but the exhaustion of the past twenty-four hours was crashing down on her like a freight train.

The more distinguished guests disappeared once they'd docked back at the marina, leaving a younger, energetic crowd, who seemed to be only just getting started on their evening of partying.

Just as she began to wonder if anyone would notice if

she slipped away to bed, she felt two warm hands slide around her waist from behind.

'I think it's time for me to take my fiancée home,' Valerio said, addressing the small gathering of remaining guests over her shoulder.

'No, I can go alone. You should stay—' She turned towards him, gently removing his hands from their possessive grip on her hips.

He simply tightened his hold, a low chuckle coming from deep in his throat as he leaned down, his lips so close to her ear it sent another eruption of shivers down her spine.

'That's not how a newly engaged couple should behave. At least try to act like you can't wait to get me to bed,' he said quietly, and then he raised his voice to address their remaining guests. 'I believe Falco mentioned wanting to host an after-party back at his place—isn't that right?'

Tristan Falco, who had been sitting with a beautiful blonde actress, stood up, a teasing smile on his lips. 'Considering I've just put in an order for one of these wonderful vessels, I think I'll stay on board tonight—if that's all right with you?'

'Stay as long as you need.' Dani smiled. 'If you have any problems, I'll be sleeping just down—'

'She'll be unavailable because we're going home.' Valerio cut across her, one hand caressing her shoulder as he spoke. 'Please take your time and enjoy the rest of your night.'

With barely a moment to protest, Dani felt herself deftly manoeuvred away from the group and across the empty entertainment deck.

'Valerio, I'm not going home with you. For goodness' sake...all my things are here,' she finished weakly, a mixture of champagne bubbles and exhaustion weighing heavily on her brain's ability to function.

'I've already had them moved to my villa.'

She paused at the edge of the dance floor, narrowing her eyes up at him. 'I get it that I should be grateful that you're helping me. But the next time you decide to organise something that involves my active participation and *my* personal things, I'd appreciate if you clear it with me first.'

'Dani...'

He began to protest, but she'd suddenly had enough of talking for the night. She stepped around him, moving down the lamplit ramp and into the dark confines of his chauffeur-driven car before he could see how completely unravelled she'd become.

If silence was a weapon, Daniela Avelar wielded it with damning precision. Valerio had spent the entire drive from the marina to his coastal villa on edge as she faced away from him. He'd expected her outrage at his heavy-handed behaviour, but this passive silence was something he had never experienced from her. It was unnerving. They still had things to discuss about their arrangement.

Once they were safely inside the foyer, he steeled himself for a showdown—but his housekeeper appeared and offered to show her to her room. Dani practically ran up the stairs away from him before he could wish her goodnight.

He fought the urge to follow her, to force her to meet his eyes. To acknowledge him in some way. They were about to be married, for goodness' sake, and she was acting as if he was some kind of villain, trying to take away her freedom. Didn't she see that everything he'd done had been with *her* at the forefront of his consideration?

And then there was that kiss...

He shook his head. He wasn't going to think about the

kiss. They'd both known it was just a part of the act they were putting on. It wasn't *her* fault that he'd responded as he had…like a starving man with his first taste of sustenance… He'd wanted to devour her.

His body responded to the memory so powerfully that he jumped when his phone began to ring and shook him from his erotic thoughts. Looking at the number on the screen, he steeled himself for more bad news.

The call from his private investigations team took less than five minutes and told him everything he'd already suspected. Someone on the board at Velamar had applied for Duarte's death certificate without any clearance from him.

He felt a sick twist of nausea in his gut at the realisation that someone close to Velamar was behind all this. He remembered the look in Angelus Fiero's eyes as he'd moved away from Daniela on that darkened deck earlier. How pale she'd looked. He needed to share this information with her…ask her if Fiero had mentioned anything suspicious.

He thanked his housekeeper as she locked up for the night, then shrugged off his jacket and folded it over a nearby chair before climbing the stairs. To his surprise, the door to the main guest room was slightly open, a glow of golden light shining out onto the darkened hallway. She was still up.

He paused outside. He needed to press her further about Fiero… He had a feeling that there was something she wasn't telling him. And it had nothing to do with wanting to ask her why she had kissed him back so passionately. Or the fact that the memory of the way her fingers had slid up through his hair refused to shift from his mind.

He knocked once on the door, opening it a little more, then froze as he took in the sight before him. Dani sat fully dressed on the chaise in the corner of the room, her tablet computer glowing on her lap but her head thrown back at an angle in peaceful sleep.

Guilt assailed him; she probably hadn't got much sleep with all the dramatics the night before. She must have been exhausted and yet she hadn't complained once.

She would ache in the morning if he left her in her current position... He took a few steps closer, clearing his throat in case he startled her. 'Dani...?'

She didn't move. She looked as utterly composed in sleep as she did when she was awake—no snores escaped her lips, and even her legs were tucked perfectly to one side.

He gently tapped her shoulder, repeating her name once more. She was completely out.

Making a snap decision, he set her computer aside and lifted her from the chaise, depositing her gently on top of the bed. Her eyes drifted open, her hands moving up to touch his face.

'You kissed me tonight...' she slurred softly, eyes half closed.

'I did,' he said stiffly, removing her hands and pushing her down to the pillows so that he could pull up the bedcovers and leave.

'I usually hate kissing,' she mumbled. 'But you're really good at it.'

'You're not so bad yourself.'

'It's okay. I know I'm terrible. I'm awful at everything bedroom-related—it's a curse of some sort.' She made a sound halfway between a giggle and a hum.

Valerio froze, staring down at her as he processed her nonsensical words. 'What makes you think that?'

'My ex was very honest. Oh, wait—you're supposed to

take off my dress.' She closed her eyes, raising her arms above her head. 'I can't sleep in it. Hermione will kill me.'

'I draw the line at undressing unconscious women, even to save a designer dress.'

He'd gritted his teeth at her mention of her ex, but now he sucked in a breath as her hands began pulling at the hem of the dress and moving it upwards. He averted his eyes, steeling himself against the flash of delicious caramel skin in the lamplight. A tiny squeaking sound caught his attention, and he looked back to find her trapped inside a swathe of green fabric, her hands fumbling over her head.

Of course she wore no bra.

Cursing, Valerio pushed her hands away, then gently pulled the gown the rest of the way up over her shoulders and arms. The tension in his body mounted with the effort of trying not to notice the delicious curves revealed with every pull of the fabric. He averted his eyes as much as possible, fighting the flare of heat in his solar plexus at an unavoidable glimpse of a tiny pair of lacy red knickers.

Biting his bottom lip, he quickly covered her with the bedsheet and sat back, his breath coming fast, as if he'd just run a marathon. He was not any better for that three-second sight of her naked breasts. He imagined they would spill over his palms, perfect twin globes, with dusky tips just begging to be kissed. His heartbeat thundered in his ears, a fine sheen of sweat was forming on his brow, and his blood pressure was likely rising through the roof.

But then Dani sighed, and he couldn't stop himself from looking down at her as she stretched out like a cat in sunshine. He had never seen her so still. The woman was a force of nature—always on the move. He wondered when she'd last taken a vacation, or even a day off.

He eased back, planning to slip out, but she opened her eyes again, narrowing them on him.

'I want to kiss you again.' She reached for him, her fingertips sloppily tracing the column of his throat where his shirt hung open.

'I can't tell if you're drunk from too much champagne or overtiredness.' He tried to ignore the rush of pleasure her words gave him, knowing that the sober Daniela would be mortified. 'I need to go.'

'Don't leave me.' She opened her eyes more fully, their whisky-gold depths suddenly shimmering. 'Just lie here for a little while.'

Valerio felt the air in his lungs go cold at the vulnerability in her eyes. He had only ever seen her cry once, in the entire time they had known one another.

He sat back down on the bed, taking her hand in his and pressing her fingers to his lips. 'I'll stay a moment if you promise to sleep.'

Her eyes drifted closed and she sighed, the evidence of her sadness trailing from the corner of her eyes and down her cheeks. 'Everyone always leaves...' she whispered, half asleep.

Valerio felt something deep inside him crack at the pain in her words and he reached down to wipe the moisture from her cheek. He closed his eyes, inhaling once before looking down at her sleeping form. 'I'm not going anywhere.'

He shed his shoes, wincing at the stiffness in his injured leg as he lay back on the bed alongside her sleeping form. His fiancée had revealed far more tonight than she would likely have preferred.

He thought of her words—'my ex was very honest'. His fists tightened by his sides and he resisted the urge to wake her and demand to know exactly what her idiotic English lawyer ex had said. He had never met the man, couldn't even recall his name, but he had heard enough from Duarte to know that Dani deserved more.

Still, the violence of his outrage on her behalf was enough to stop him in his tracks. But it was entirely appropriate for him to feel protective towards the woman he'd vowed to protect, wasn't it?

There had been nothing 'appropriate' about his reaction to their kiss earlier. Nothing innocent or protective in the way he'd fought the urge to haul her towards him and devour her. Claim her as his own in front of the entire party—including Tristan Falco.

But he knew that he was not the kind of man she deserved, either. She needed someone whole. Someone who didn't abandon her and keep secrets. He had always been happy to live the life of a bachelor, thinking that maybe one day he might settle down. But now he knew that day would never come.

He wasn't built for family life the way his father and brother were. The Marchesi men were known for their reliable leadership and level-headedness. Somehow Valerio seemed to have missed out on that genetic component and that had always been fine with him. He was the wild one...the joker.

Cursing under his breath, he closed his eyes and saw again Daniela's golden gaze meeting his as he slid that ring onto her finger. For that split second she hadn't looked as if she hated him quite as much.

They both knew that even if it was only a legal arrangement this marriage needed to look real. Neither of them could afford any bad press, and the distraction of their supposed romance would work in their favour. He needed to make sure she understood what that meant. He needed to know she understood that while she might deserve better, for now he was the only man she would be seen with.

Forcing himself to look away from her sleeping form, he rested his head back against the pillows. He would stay until he was sure she was asleep—surely he owed her that much?

Not for the first time since he had woken up to see her furious form twenty-four hours before, he wondered how on earth his life had become so complicated.

Dani awoke with the most painful headache of her entire life, inwardly cursing whoever had thought endless flutes of champagne was a good idea—then realised that it had, in fact, been her. She rolled over in the bed, freezing, and realised she was wearing only her underwear. Not only that—she wasn't alone in bed.

Valerio lay on his back, one arm behind his head as he slept. Fuzzy memories of him helping her to bed came to her, making her flush with embarrassment. She had practically ordered him to take her clothes off and then begged him to stay. Good grief, had she really told him about the things Kitt had said to her?

She stared at his sleeping form for a long while, noting the deep frown line between his brows and the sharp staccato of his breathing. There was nothing peaceful about the way this man slept—it was as though he were in pain. Even as she watched, he kicked out one leg at some invisible form, and a deep rumble sounded from his chest.

She sat up, clutching the covers to her bare breasts, and laid one hand on his chest. His hand shot up to grab hers so fast she jumped with fright.

It seemed one moment she was staring at him, the next he was gripping her shoulders painfully tight and pushing her onto her back. He loomed over her, caging her with his arms, and for a moment she felt a flash of unease at the zoned-out look in his eyes.

She pushed at his chest, feeling the silk of his shirt and the heat of his hard muscles under her fingers. It was like trying to shift a hulking great pillar of marble. Had he always been this physically defined? She tried to find words, only managing a tiny gasp in the tense silence.

He watched her through hooded eyes, barely controlled violence in the tension of his shoulders. But when she let out a small whimper from the force of his grip, something finally seemed to shift in his eyes, as if he had only just awoken.

'*Dannazione*…never touch me while I sleep,' he rasped.

'You…you're the one in my bed.' She pursed her lips, all too aware of her lack of clothing and the intimacy of their position. The thin sheet was the only thing covering her body from his gaze.

Her mind went back two nights, to when he'd attacked her bodyguards on his yacht in Genoa. He had been awoken from sleep then too. His eyes had been wild and unfocused, as though he had been possessed.

'Did I hurt you?' he asked quietly, his eyes scanning the bare skin of her arms as though he expected to see something terrible there.

She watched as he swept his fingers up her arms, seeing the faint red skin on her shoulders from his grip. He tucked his fingers under her chin, gently tilting her face up to look at him.

'No, you were just startled. It's fine,' she said shakily. 'I'm fine.'

His head momentarily sagged against her, his forehead pressing gently on her collarbone as he let out a long, shaky breath.

'Do you see now? This is why I stayed away for so long. Every damn time I feel like I'm getting it all under control…'

She felt every breath he took fanning gently against her skin. It was shockingly intimate.

All too soon she felt him pull away. He sat up on the side of the bed, leaving her shivering at the sudden loss of his heat. She wanted to ask him what he was talking about, if these moments of trance-like behaviour happened often. But she feared him shutting down, freezing her out again. She needed to wait for him to open up, no matter how much she craved to know what had happened to him during those awful weeks and the months that followed.

She sat up, moving beside him and fighting the urge to cover one of his large hands with her own. She couldn't stop wanting to touch him, to be near him. It was ridiculous—she was supposed to hate the man.

'Look…you don't have to tell me any details. But you didn't hurt me, okay?'

He stood up, hissing briefly as he straightened his leg. Avoiding her eyes, he set about buttoning his shirt. 'Those marks on your shoulder say otherwise.' He looked back at her, cursing under his breath. 'Don't worry. I won't let it happen again.'

Dani frowned, realising that was the opposite of what she wanted. She had been surprised to wake up to find him in bed beside her, but it had been the kind of surprise that sent shivers down your spine, not fear. She had worried that he might be able to sense her response to having him there with her, but stopped now she saw the familiar look of detachment cover his handsome features.

She could understand him being angry, and possibly embarrassed by whatever she had witnessed, but the complete blankness that had descended over him made her grip the blanket tighter across her chest.

'You'll join me for breakfast on the terrace.' He avoided

her eyes, and his words were more of a command than an invitation. 'I'll leave you to…get dressed.'

His movements were stilted, the injury in his leg more pronounced as he stalked over to the doorway and disappeared without another word.

CHAPTER FIVE

When Dani emerged from her room, she was freshly show-ered and dressed for the office in one of her favourite dusky pink shirts, which she'd paired with form-fitting, lightly flared dove-grey trousers. The meeting wasn't tak-ing place until late afternoon, but she had some files to prepare and some facts to confirm. Valerio's presence was only a small part of her attack plan. She never walked into anything without considering every possible angle, and today was going to be no different.

The housekeeper showed her out to an impressive mar-ble dining terrace, bathed in golden morning sunshine and surrounded by creeping vines full of beautiful spring wild flowers. Valerio was drinking a steaming cup of cof-fee and staring blankly out at the hustle of Port Hercules below in the distance. His dark brow was furrowed when he turned to acknowledge her, standing to pull out a chair. She wasn't used to such small, chivalrous gestures. It made her slightly uncomfortable. But she knew he'd been raised in Italian high society—it was likely just second nature.

She avoided his eyes, thanking his housekeeper with a wide smile when she appeared with a platter of fresh fruit and a fresh pot of water for tea before disappearing again.

'I remember you don't drink coffee.' Valerio looked across at her, his eyes slits of stormy blue under his fur-

rowed brow. 'I've had a selection of teas ordered in. I don't
know if they're any good.'

'Thank you. That was very thoughtful.'

Dani felt a glow of warmth bloom in her chest, then
instinctively pushed it away, remembering that she was
trying to keep her guard up. But a small part of her whispered that Valerio had never been purposely unkind to her
in the past—only indifference. It wasn't *his* fault that she'd
been attracted to him. If he was trying to make a gesture
of goodwill, she should accept it.

She made a show of admiring the fine bone china tea-
pot and selected her favourite brand of English breakfast
tea. They passed a few moments in companionable silence, with the buffer of the usual city sounds forming a
background.

'We need to discuss our living arrangements,' he said,
then waited a moment, frowning at her stunned silence.
'I'm aware that you haven't yet permanently occupied any
of the homes that will form your inheritance. My villa is
not the most convenient location, but it has a large study
you can use for your consulting work.'

Dani felt something tighten in her throat as she looked
down at the ring on her left hand. She had been so preoccupied with today's meeting she'd foolishly thought they
would just brush past the fact that they were now engaged
to be married.

'Valerio…we haven't even talked about the logistics of
this arrangement yet and you're already saying you want
me to move in here with you?'

'Yes—as soon as possible.' He looked away, his jaw
tighter than steel. 'Obviously we won't share a bedroom,
but living under one roof will be better for your safety as
well as for keeping the appearance of a normal marriage.'

Dani marvelled at the utter madness of his words. 'We

both know that there is nothing "normal" about this marriage. But from a PR point of view, I suppose I agree.' She sat back, running a finger along the filigree rim of her teacup. 'I've still got a lease on my apartment in London, but that can be easily fixed. And I won't need your study, as Velamar is my only priority for the time being.'

'Good.' He paused, meeting her eyes as he processed the end of her statement. 'Wait…you've stopped taking on any independent clients? Why would you do that?'

'It's kind of hard to be the sole leader of a global brand and still find time to fly around the world on consulting contracts with unpredictable time frames.' She squared her shoulders. 'I made a conscious choice to focus on Velamar for my own reasons.' She spoke with a clear edge to her tone. 'Just as I will continue to do so now that I'm inheriting the responsibility.'

Valerio pinched the bridge of his nose sharply. 'Dani, I didn't think through leaving you the sole responsibility of Velamar while I was gone. You have to know I would never have allowed you to sacrifice your own career in order to step in for me.'

'Well, then, it's a good thing I didn't need your permission, isn't it?' She cleared her throat, pouring more tea into her cup. 'I'm not here to discuss my career decisions. Please can we just continue with the discussion at hand?'

For a moment he looked as though he fully intended to start an argument. But then he exhaled on a low growling sigh and braced two hands on the balcony ledge. 'We will live here, then, for the time being. For obvious reasons, we will both need to remain unattached while this arrangement is in place. Will that be a problem?'

'*You're* the notorious womaniser.' She raised one brow in challenge. 'If anyone will struggle with discretion, it won't be me.'

He seemed annoyed at her comment, his eyes darkening to a storm. 'I'm not talking about my wife indulging in discreet affairs—I'm talking about you abstaining from them completely. Just as I will.'

She froze at his use of the word 'wife', baffled at the sudden intensity in his gaze and the effect it was having on the knot in her stomach.

She hadn't been trying to insult him—it was no secret that he liked to date a variety of beautiful women. He hadn't been photographed with anyone since the accident, but likely he'd just been discreet. She seriously doubted that his name and the word 'abstinence' had ever been uttered in the same sentence.

'Dani, you know how this needs to look to anyone who is watching. I wish that I could have found any other way...'

'Yes, yes—I get it that you're making a huge sacrifice by marrying me.' She was surprised herself at her own flash of annoyance, and saw his eyes widen in response. Softening her voice a little, she avoided his curious gaze. 'Fine. So I move my stuff in with you and there will be no sordid photographs in the press of me with a string of lovers. Understood.'

'Good.' He was still watching her, his strong, tanned fingers idly twirling a spoon through his second cup of espresso. 'I'm glad we understand each other.'

Dani ignored the flush of awareness that prickled along her skin at the effortlessly sexy tone of his voice. Being around Valerio Marchesi so much was already causing mayhem on her nerves and she was agreeing to *marry* the man? Suddenly she felt caged in by all the unknowns about this arrangement and her ability to survive it.

'Is there a time frame for all of this?' she asked as nonchalantly as she could manage. 'I mean to say…how long do we actually need to stay married?'

His eyes darkened. 'Already dying to be free of me, *tesoro*?'

She inhaled sharply at the endearment, noting that he seemed slightly unnerved by his own words as well. He pulled gently at the collar of his shirt as though it had suddenly grown too tight.

The tense silence between them was interrupted by soft footsteps in the doorway to the kitchen. His housekeeper moved towards them, announcing an urgent phone call from Valerio's brother on the landline.

'Take the call. I've got to get to the office anyway,' Dani urged.

'This conversation is far from over, Dani.' He stood, unbuttoning the top buttons of his shirt. 'I'll pick you up for lunch. You can brief me on the meeting.'

And with a barely audible curse under his breath, he excused himself, disappearing inside with swift, thundering steps.

Dani watched him go with a mixture of relief and disappointment. *'I wish that I could have found any other way.'* Just what every woman wanted to hear from her fiancé. He had sounded as if he was prepping himself for a walk to the gallows.

His brother had probably got wind of the news and was calling now to put a stop to such madness. She shouldn't be hurt by Valerio's coldness. This was business. This was a formal transaction—a professional arrangement and nothing more. From his standpoint this was simple and clear-cut. *He* wasn't tied up in knots by complicated feelings and emotions the way she was.

She thought back to all the times she had dreamed of her own wedding day. She cared little about the actual day itself—more what it represented. Commitment, love, a family of her own and a home filled with happy memories. Deep down she craved the love and devotion she'd seen while growing up.

Her parents had adored one another and had always put their children's welfare before their own. They'd traded in their lofty social scene in Brazil when she was ten years old for a simple life in the English countryside. She had always imagined herself doing the same for her own children some day—that was why she had said yes when her ex, Kitt, had proposed after only six months of dating... even when a small voice in her head had told her to slow down and think it through.

But when her career had skyrocketed, she had realised that the high-powered work life she craved wasn't easily compatible with the traditional family life she had once dreamed of. At least that was what Kitt had said when he'd given her his ultimatum. He'd told her that her ambition and refusal to compromise was ruining any chance they had of a future.

Maybe this kind of business arrangement was the closest thing she would ever get to a real marriage. Maybe it was time she faced the fact that her life was never going to be the stuff of fairy tales and maybe that was okay. She loved her work. She was committed to taking care of the legacy her family had left behind, to doing them all proud.

Faking a happy marriage to a man who would never see her as anything but an obligation was a small price to pay for her safety.

It had to be—she had no other choice.

The rest of her morning was a blur, starting with an unplanned meeting with her regional team about some issues that had arisen with their plans for the Monaco Yacht

Show. Usually she didn't enjoy playing CEO at meetings, but for once she threw herself into the role, thankful for a slice of normality.

Work had always been a source of calm for her during times of difficulty. Her parents had taught her the value of hard work, ambition and charity, ensuring that neither of their children became entitled trust fund brats. After Duarte had dropped out of college at nineteen, to live the wild life with Valerio, she had thrown herself into graduating with top honours and had then gone on to do the same in her master's degree in Public Relations and Strategic Communications.

When their parents had died so suddenly, in that car accident seven years ago, she'd jumped at Duarte's offer to be Velamar's PR and marketing strategist. She had been the one to help them turn their modest success into an empire. She was more than capable of public speaking and turning on the charm but, being naturally introverted, preferred to do her work from the shadows as much as possible. She did not possess her twin's natural ability to attract people to her with an almost gravitational pull. Duarte had been the wall she had always leaned on and hid behind.

Pushing away the overwhelming sorrow that always accompanied any memory of her twin, she threw herself into a few hours of preparation for the meeting that lay ahead, praying that Valerio would have the good sense to arrive early so that she could prepare him.

But afternoon came without him and she made her way alone to the large boardroom on the top floor of the building, frowning at the eerily empty space. Even the surrounding offices were empty. A feeling of unease crept into her stomach as she tapped a button on her phone, calling her personal assistant.

'Dani, thank God you called. I just saw one of the secretaries for two of the board members...' The young woman gasped, as though she'd been running.

'Are you okay? What's wrong?'

'They moved the meeting!' her PA exclaimed. 'They moved it to Valerio Marchesi's villa and deliberately chose not to pass on the memo to you.'

Dani felt her fist tighten on the phone until she heard a crunch. Thanking her overwrought PA, she slammed the device down on the table.

He'd moved the meeting and hadn't called her. Damn him.

She had asked him to do one thing—one simple favour... But, as usual, Valerio Marchesi did what he wanted to do and only ever on his own terms. Heaven forbid the man should ever take her advice or think of someone other than himself.

She wanted to fight—she needed a win of some sort. Maybe then she might start to feel something again other than this restless void of work and sleep.

Embracing the hum of adrenaline in her veins, she raced towards the elevators.

Valerio sat at the top of the long marble dining table and surveyed the six men and three women seated around him. He told himself that he'd chosen to change the location of the meeting to his own home at the last minute because it would give him an advantage—not because he needed the option of retreat if he lost control. And he knew the board members wouldn't be able to resist the chance to find out where he'd disappeared to. To discover if the rumours of his madness were true.

Just to keep a little mystery on his side, he'd spoken very little as they'd commenced their professionally catered lunch, and had given short, clipped answers to their many questions. But his unease had grown as the minutes had turned into an hour and there had been no sign of his fiancée.

Daniela was never late.

He wanted a single-minded focus on finding out who had pushed for Duarte's death certificate, but now he could hardly concentrate.

After ordering one of his guards to find out where she was, he sat back and tried to focus his anger on discovering which of these people, with their greed and lack of patience, had put Dani in danger.

But of course no one else knew the truth behind the seemingly random events that had transpired in Brazil. No one who was still alive, anyway.

Angelus Fiero stood up from his seat near the top of the table, slicking back the neatly oiled salt-and-pepper hair atop his head. Valerio had never met the man in person before last night…

'Marchesi, I'm afraid my flight plans have changed and I need to leave. I'm needed back in Rio sooner than I thought. But I believe I speak for all of us when I say that I'm very relieved to see you return to work.'

Valerio swallowed his final mouthful of crème brûlée, narrowing his eyes at the man with barely restrained menace. Around him, the other board members continued in their heated discussion about the success of their new Fort Lauderdale headquarters and their expansion throughout the Caribbean and South America.

Angelus Fiero had been their very first investor, back when they had started up and had needed capital to bulk up their fleet offerings. An old friend of the Avelar family, he had been trusted with managing the family's affairs in Brazil after their move to England.

'Please, allow me to see you out.'

Valerio stood, prowling slowly beside the table until he stood so close to the other man he could see a tiny vein throbbing at his temple. He had amassed enough experience over the past six months to know when someone wasn't telling the full truth.

As they walked side by side towards the entrance hall, Fiero made small talk about the latest yacht designs. Valerio barely heard a word—he was too busy mentally cataloguing what he knew of the man's character. He had briefly suspected Fiero's involvement in the kidnap after he'd returned from Brazil and started his investigations, but he hadn't found a single motive or link. The man was comfortably wealthy, he had no debts or enemies, and he didn't stand to gain anything from Duarte's death other than the headache of managing the company's reputation and a slew of uneasy investors.

'I was surprised that Daniela didn't join us for lunch today.' Fiero paused in the hallway to don his coat and hat. 'She has to know that half of the board are pushing to have her voted out.'

'Quite a stupid move on their part,' Valerio drawled, 'considering Daniela is about to become officially one of the wealthiest women in Europe, thanks to an anonymous push for Duarte's death certificate to be released. *You* wouldn't happen to know anything about that, would you?'

Another man might have missed the sudden flicker in Fiero's pale blue eyes. He masked it well, subtly clearing his throat and pasting a grimace on his face.

'You should direct your suspicions elsewhere,' he said. 'I've been a good friend to this family.' He shook his head in a perfect show of grief, placing one hand on his chest, where a small gold cross lay over his tie. 'I have information that the death certificate is to be issued at the start of next week. Quite unusual, considering they never recovered the body…did they?'

Valerio felt his fists tighten, and nausea hit his stomach as memories threatened to overcome him. The old man knew something—he could tell by the way he narrowed his eyes, tapping lightly on his hat as he moved towards the door. There was no way to know if he was on the right track, but it was enough for him to place Fiero firmly back on the list of those possibly involved.

He said goodbye to his newly reinstated suspect, closed the door and took in the violent tremor in his hands that had already begun to creep up his forearms at two words. *The body.* The memories were coming hard and fast. The sharp smell of gunpowder was in the air… Blood soaked the ground around his feet.

He swore he could feel every pump of blood in his chest as he started walking, counting backwards from one hundred. He never knew when one of these bouts of dreamlike panic would hit, and he'd long ago stopped trying to fight them off or cure them with whisky. Like his scars, he felt they were a permanent part of him.

He reached the nearest bathroom quickly, slamming the door shut just as black spots swam in his vision and forced him to his knees.

CHAPTER SIX

DANI SANK BACK into the alcove under the steps up to Valerio's impressive villa and cursed under her breath. Angelus Fiero had just disappeared into a sleek black car and driven off—which meant she'd likely missed her chance to talk to him. The rest of the board would still be inside, though. Likely being entertained by their prodigal playboy CEO.

Adrenaline fuelling her, she barely waited for the door to be opened by a member of staff before moving quickly through the house, following the sound of raised voices. At a set of large double doors, she paused, pressing her ear against the wood.

'I'm just saying the majority of our clients are male,' someone was saying loudly. 'They flock to us for the promise of the brand. The iconic image of two powerful, handsome playboys who never settle for less than the best.'

'Duarte and Valerio were the dream team…' A strong female voice sounded out above the others. 'I can't help but feel that Duarte's sister's talents are better kept…behind the curtain, you know?'

'We can't dispute the effectiveness of her marketing strategies—she's had some great ideas,' someone chided gently from further back in the room.

'Yes, but what good are ideas in a company figurehead when she has all the charisma of a wet blanket. She's *bor-*

ing,' a male voice sneered, inciting a rumble of laughter that Dani felt pierce through the thin layer of bravado she'd arrived with.

Any belief she'd held on to that only a small portion of the board wanted her gone instantly disappeared. She felt her cheeks heat, her heart rate speeding up in the uncomfortable way she knew all too well. Old scars burst open. Damn them for making her feel this way. Damn them for seeing her brother as perfect and her as a poor replacement.

Someone cleared his throat behind her, making her almost jump out of her skin.

'Eavesdropping, are we?'

Valerio stood braced against a door frame on the other side of the hall—how long he'd been standing behind her was anyone's guess.

She straightened, rubbing her palms on the front of her trousers. 'It's impossible to eavesdrop on a meeting I am entitled to attend.'

'I had the notification of the change in venue sent hours ago. It's not my fault you're late.' He glowered down at her, the expression on his face strangely blank, his eyes unfocused.

'Well, that "notification" was purposely kept from me.' She moved to sidestep him, only to have him hold on to her elbow and gently manoeuvre her back.

Something wasn't right, she realised. He seemed on edge. There was a sheen of sweat on his brow and he was just a little paler than his usual olive tone. She stopped herself from enquiring, though, remembering how defensive he had been about his behaviour that morning.

Her pulse skipped a little as she looked back towards the door, feeling dread creep in at the thought of walking in and facing those men and women after hearing what they really thought of her.

Valerio tipped his head slightly, listening to the voices still perfectly audible through the door.

'Daniela Avelar is not his usual type.' A man laughed. 'She's frumpy and she frowns too much. No sex appeal, you know?'

'He may be marrying her, but we need to make it clear that Marchesi alone as CEO is our best move forward,' someone else said, inciting a loud murmur of assent from the others.

Dani felt Valerio stiffen beside her, heard a shallow gust of breath leaving his lungs. Mortification threatened to overcome her, but she stood strong, plastering a smirk on her face as she turned to face him with a shrug.

'They've been singing my praises, as you can hear. Clearly they *adore* me.'

'Lose the sarcasm,' he gritted out, bracing one large hand on the door frame. Tension filled his powerful body, as though he were suddenly poised for battle. 'I'll put an end to this. I won't allow them to discuss you this way.'

'You assume that I plan to just walk away?' She raised one brow, stepping past him and inhaling a deep, fortifying breath. She disliked confrontation, but that didn't mean she was incapable of fighting her own battles.

Without warning, she slammed the door open and strode into the room, leaving Valerio momentarily frozen in the doorway behind her.

'Someone forgot to invite the boring temporary CEO to lunch, it seems.' She threw a glance around as she took a seat at the head of the table and folded her arms across her chest.

Multiple pairs of eyes landed on her, widening. Some looked down at the remnants of their coffee, spread out on the dining table along with their files and spreadsheets.

'I'd like to know who kept the change of venue from

me.' She spoke with calm assertion, narrowing her eyes as one of the men cleared his throat and sat forward.

'Miss Avelar, there must be some mistake...'

'There have been many mistakes made.' Dani shook her head, pursing her lips. 'Shall I begin listing them?'

She slid a folder from her briefcase, opening up the file she'd prepared in advance the moment she'd realised a coup was in the works. She had evidence here to remove at least four board members for a variety of infractions that violated the company's code of ethics. And as she read out her first statement, the room was completely silent.

Footsteps sounded from the doorway. Daniela paused for a moment, watching as the man most of them truly wanted as their CEO finally entered the room. All eyes shifted to him, as if silently begging him to intervene, to stop this woman from tearing apart their plans.

Dani swallowed hard as his eyes met hers across the room. The impressive expanse of his shoulders was showcased in a simple white shirt with an open collar. She felt a thoroughly inappropriate flash of lust and instantly chided herself. He *had* to know how impressive he looked, damn him. He wouldn't look out of place on a Parisian runway. She knew that her larger frame would *never* be compared to a supermodel, but she certainly wasn't frumpy.

She waited a heartbeat as he silently took a seat at the opposite end of the table, but instead of cutting short her speech, he simply nodded and motioned for her to continue.

A gruelling hour followed, during which four members of the board were put on temporary suspension and the table became filled with more tension than ever. Dani handed out sheets advising some further steps she wished to take regarding the future management of their design branches and charity assets, but decided to leave the actual decision making to a future meeting. Slow and steady was sometimes the best course of action.

Valerio had been reserved throughout the whole process, only answering when directly spoken to. A strange tension seemed to emanate from him, and every now and then she caught his eyes on her, burning with something dark and unrecognisable. Uncomfortable, she lost a little steam towards the end of her speech, and was almost relieved when he finally spoke up and commanded the room.

'I'd like to address some of the comments I have overheard,' he said. He spoke calmly, but with a gravelly hardness to his tone. 'Firstly, our brand is based on experience, reliability and being ahead of the market—not on a room full of aging business execs who have an opinion on the sex appeal or charisma of those who lead it. Secondly, you will not pass further comment on the details of my relationship with my future wife or debate the reasoning for our marriage. She may be graceful enough not to retaliate against such nonsense, but I am not bound by the same brand of polite restraint.'

Dani shivered as his eyes met hers for a split second.

Exhausted, she was relieved when Valerio began to take charge of escorting the others out. She walked over to the large windows and caught sight of her reflection in the glass. Her trousers were wrinkled and her wild curls seemed to have grown even wilder than usual, but she didn't care. She felt powerful after the surprising success of the afternoon, despite the awful comments she'd overheard.

It seemed like a lifetime ago that she had spent so much of her energy trying to reduce her curves and bumps, trying to squeeze into waist-slimming corsets and spending hundreds of euros on having her thick Latina curls chemically straightened. She'd been obsessed with looking like the hordes of slimmer businesswomen with their designer suits and pin straight styling.

After her failed almost-jaunt down the aisle and subsequent break-up with Kitt, something had clicked inside her and she'd started working to accept the body she had. The one she'd been born with. She was done with being shamed.

Valerio returned to the room, closing the door behind him with purpose. Evidently the meeting was not entirely concluded. She sat down again.

'That was very well done,' he said sincerely, bracing his hands on the dining table. 'But it makes what I'm about to say even more difficult.'

She froze, taking in the darkness of his eyes, and felt trepidation churn in her gut.

'I'll be stepping back into my role as CEO of Velamar and I want you to take a step back. Maybe recommence your plans to start up your own firm.'

Stunned, she met his eyes. 'What the—?'

'I asked you to trust me.' His voice was sincere. 'I need you to take a step back from the spotlight for a while... until I have a few things in order.'

'You mean you don't want me leading the brand either? What a shocker.' She fought the urge to slam her hand down on the table. 'I will not allow you to put my brother's legacy at risk with your own shallow prejudice.'

'*My* prejudice?' His brows knitted together. 'They're the ones with ridiculous closed ideas of sex appeal and whatever else. I defended you.'

'You might as well have agreed with them. You're doing exactly what they want—getting me out of the picture so they can start picking this company apart like a damn chicken bone. You can't do this.'

In one single sentence he'd washed away all her self-doubt and made her feel appreciated for her talent. And then he'd ruined it all by railroading over her authority and making decisions for her once again.

'I can.' He stood slowly, stalking towards her like a predator. 'I am the only legal chief executive of this company. I appointed you as temporary CEO in my absence and I have the power to revoke that appointment.'

'You. Bastard.' She stood her ground even as he towered over her.

'Perhaps.' He shrugged. 'But if you trusted me you'd believe me when I say I have my reasons.'

He allowed his gaze to wander down her face…and further. She felt the heat of his eyes sweep along her chest and abdomen, right down to her toes. She took a step back, the urge overpowering her.

'If you think I agree with any of the things they said about you and your…assets… Clearly you have no idea what the meaning of sex appeal is, either.'

Her breath caught in her throat. Her mind was whirring, trying to find a clever retort to his words. He had to be trying to unnerve her, to make her leave. She felt hot shame rise within her, along with that damn pulse of awareness that refused to leave her every time he was in her vicinity. He was a beacon of sexual energy and, like a pathetic moth to his flame, she was completely unable to stay away.

'I've just been informed that Duarte's death will be certified in a matter of days,' he said. 'We don't have time for this back and forth.' He reached for the remnants of his coffee, downing the last of the liquid with a hiss of satisfaction. 'I need our marriage taken care of and tied up legally before your inheritance is unlocked. We could be married in St Lucia by Monday morning if we leave tonight.'

'St Lucia?' She repeated the words slowly, her shoulders tensing as she began to prepare all the reasons why she couldn't just up and disappear to the Caribbean without making plans for the business.

Then she remembered he'd technically just fired her from the only job she currently had. She had no reason not to go.

'I'm not your enemy, you know.' He spoke softly.

'I know.' She sighed. 'Right, I guess we're eloping, then.' She made a weak attempt at a smile. 'We've got a new base being built there. I've been monitoring the building work remotely, via our management team on the ground, but I'd love the chance to go and do a walk-through.'

'Should I be offended that your first thought is how to turn our romantic Caribbean wedding into a chance to get some work done?' He seemed irritated, gathering papers from the table and then thrusting them back down with a huff of breath.

'It's not a wedding,' she said quickly, frowning at his strange change in mood. 'It's an elopement. I don't understand why you're on edge—snapping as though you're angry with me for all this.'

'I'm not angry with you, Dani…' he growled, turning to walk towards the door. 'I'm angry that you've been put in this situation. And I'm angry that you still refuse to trust me. But really I'm always on edge—so maybe you'd best get used to that.'

Valerio had just ended a painful phone call with his mother—his second family intervention of the day—when their car arrived on the runway beside the sleek Marchesi family jet. He felt a nervous twitch in his stomach as he watched Dani walk across the Tarmac ahead of him, in her perfect form-fitting trousers and flowy blouse.

She was polite, greeting the in-flight attendant as she

stowed their bags and accepted some light refreshments. He gestured to the seat across from him and noticed her face tighten as she moved into it, her posture screaming with tension.

Just as he planned to apologise for his abrupt behaviour after their meeting, his phone rang again.

Seeing his brother's name show up on the display, he cursed aloud and jammed his finger on the screen to block the call. Ramming one hand through his hair, he closed his eyes and huffed out a loud breath filled with frustration.

'Is there a problem?' his fiancée enquired with a raised brow.

For a moment he considered not answering her question at all. But then he remembered the promise he'd made to himself as they'd driven in silence to the airport—to at least *try* not to be so closed off and abrasive with her. She was going to be his wife... They were going to be sharing a lot more time together. He needed to put some effort in to his behaviour.

Reluctantly, he sat down across from her and met her eyes. 'You saw that I got a call from my brother earlier today, followed quickly by one from my mother? We haven't been on the best terms since I came back from Brazil. I've been distant, and now they've found out about our engagement through the media... Needless to say, my family are not happy about our elopement plans.'

Dani frowned. 'Of course they're not. I never even thought of how they might see this. Do they know all the details?'

He frowned. 'My brother knows a bit, but I've told him not to tell our parents the full truth. I can't tell them about the danger, not when my mother is such a worrier. They think it's a real marriage.'

He thought back to the sound of worry in his brother's

voice on the phone. Rigo Marchesi had never been one to give his little brother an easy time, but after the display Valerio had put on at that christening dinner... Well, he couldn't remember all the details, but he was pretty sure that he deserved the scorn in his brother's voice. His entire family had believed him dead for two weeks and had been overjoyed at his return—only to be shut out and ignored for months on end.

They didn't realise that it was better this way.

'I won't pretend to understand what you've been working through these past months, *fratello*,' Rigo had said, 'but this seems quite sudden. I've been around you and Dani many times. She hates your guts and she is possibly the only woman I've ever witnessed being utterly immune to your charms.'

'No one is immune to my charms.' Valerio had answered easily. 'It's not like that. It's more like a business arrangement between us.'

'Now, where have I heard that before...?' Rigo had laughed out loud.

Rigo and his wife, Nicole, had married years before, as the result of a media scandal. Rigo had sworn his marriage was in name only, and yet now they were the picture of married bliss, with two small daughters and another on the way.

Across from him, Dani cleared her throat, pulling him back to the present. 'Valerio, if this is causing problems for your family, we should find another way. We can find someone with similar financial power and influence that we can trust.'

'Someone like Tristan Falco?' The venom-filled words were out of his mouth before he could stop them.

'I wasn't thinking of Tristan, but now that you say it, he might be a good fit.'

Valerio tensed. *Over his dead body.*

'I wouldn't trust anyone else—and neither should you. My family will get over it.'

He stood up, stretching his lower back muscles and pouring himself a glass of cold water to try to calm his nerves.

He had to admit that not once had he thought of his parents' reaction to his sudden nuptials. Amerigo and Renata Marchesi were not fiercely traditional, and they had always pushed their sons to choose their own path in life. But his mother was understandably hurt.

Once again he was a disappointment. Even when for once he was being selfless in his actions. He had nothing to gain from shackling himself in marriage other than protecting Daniela from harm and fulfilling his promise to her brother.

A small part of him spoke up, pointing out that so far he seemed to have been a lot more preoccupied with their living situation and ensuring she was by his side. He should have been working more on investigating possible perpetrators—like Fiero.

He leaned down, pinching the bridge of his nose sharply. '*Dio*, why is everything so damn complicated?'

Truthfully, he'd been relieved to talk things through with his older brother earlier. Rigo had been by his side at every important moment in his life—the day he'd dropped out of college, the day he'd told his father that he didn't want to be a part of the family business, and the day he'd cut the ribbon on the first company premises. Rigo had always offered impartial advice and support. He had always been a rock no matter how heavy the storm.

But his father was another story. Amerigo Marchesi had always hoped his two sons would run the family business together, but Valerio had never coped well behind a desk. He had been a wild teenager and an even wilder adult, taking on whatever ridiculous challenges life threw at him. He had once thrived on adrenaline and risk—now he spent his days obsessing over one woman's safety. The irony was not lost on him...

When Dani suggested they talk through some of the details of the new base they were going to visit in St Lucia, he jumped at the chance to shut his brain off by listening to the progress she'd made on the project. It was impressive—more impressive than anything he and Duarte could have planned. She was a marvel at organising, and seeing details no one else did.

When she finally yawned, and said she was going to try to sleep for the rest of the flight, he almost asked her to stay and tell him more. Something about her presence soothed him and made him feel less adrift. But in the end he let her go with a single nod.

Once he was alone he felt a familiar restlessness settling into his bones. The last time he'd been in St Lucia had been a few days before the accident with Duarte. They had been finalising the purchase of their new premises there when Duarte had told him that he needed to go to Brazil for a couple of days to sort out some business. At the last minute Valerio had decided to follow him as a surprise, so they could celebrate their expansion plans.

Valerio tried in vain to shut himself off to the memory... tried to block out the anger and regret. He'd spent months torturing himself for not realising that something was up with his best friend, that the man had been preoccupied and taking mysterious phone calls in the middle of important meetings. He'd clearly been under some unseen pressure, but Valerio had believed his excuse that he was just 'in a situation' with a woman.

Duarte had been an intense guy at the best of times—

it had been easier for Valerio to look away and focus on growing their empire.

Regret washed over him, and once again he fought the urge to ask his fiancée to come back and discuss more business plans. She would likely jump at the chance. She loved to talk about work, and he could simply lose himself in her soothing presence.

Then he cursed himself for his own selfishness, hoping he might relax enough to sleep but knowing it was completely hopeless that he would ever feel at rest.

When Dani awoke, a number of hours later, she found Valerio sleeping soundly on his recliner in the main cabin. She walked over to stand beside him, fighting the urge to cover him with a blanket. He had told her never to touch him while he slept and she wasn't about to overstep that boundary, no matter how much she wanted to soothe the beast that roared in him.

Frowning, she took a seat at the opposite end of the cabin and successfully busied her fretful mind by reading over some of the finer details of their new Caribbean expansion. She might not be a fully active CEO, thanks to his demotion of her, but she had been the one to put the work into the planning of this base and she wasn't about to let him go in unprepared. She was able to separate her emotions from her professional work.

She thought of Valerio's urging her to focus on her independent contracts and how success had felt when it had been on her own terms. It had been hard work, a lot of travelling, and impossible to forge any kind of relationship in such a transient role. But that was what had drawn her to the work in the beginning—it had been the perfect balance. She had spent half her time working with her brother and the other half travelling solo.

But even though she had believed she was content, something had felt strangely lacking. The travel had grated on her sleep schedule, and she'd felt no desire to see any of the cities she'd landed in, preferring just to get her work done and sit in her rented apartment or hotel room watching romantic comedies and eating cold pizza from the box.

The lack of travel in the past six months while she had been running Velamar had been a welcome change of pace, but it still hadn't quite eased the restlessness that had long plagued her.

In the months before Duarte's death, she had been drawing up plans to start her own PR firm—something she had always dreamed of. Initially she had believed that she needed more experience or larger jobs—that no one would take her seriously until she had proved herself on a grand scale. But bigger jobs and more respect had come and still she'd held back.

Now she was about to be the co-owner of a global yacht charter firm and about to marry her business partner.

Unable to focus on work any more, she set about tidying away the items that Valerio had left out on the table. A photograph slid from his wallet onto the floor and she picked it up, frowning as an image including herself stared back at her. She remembered that day. The picture had been taken at the very first charity yacht gala she had planned six years ago. Just a few months before she'd moved to London and met Kitt.

Duarte stood centre stage, looking straight into the camera, while Dani and Valerio stood either side of him. Dani's hand was outstretched towards her brother's best friend as though she was mid-punch. She sighed, seeing that look in her eyes that she remembered so well. But she couldn't quite place the expression on Valerio's face...

Embarrassment, perhaps?

Had she been that obvious?

She scrunched her face up, cursing how terrible she had always been at disguising her emotions. Even now, did he know how utterly infatuated she had been with him? Could he tell that she still struggled with that pull of attraction?

She let her eyes wander from the photograph to the real-life, grown-up version of the man. He lay completely relaxed, his strong jaw in profile, showcasing the kind of chiselled designer stubble that most male models would have killed for. His arms were crossed over his broad chest, where the material of his shirt strained over the taut muscles that lay underneath.

She imagined what this flight might have been like had they been a real engaged couple on their way to a romantic whirlwind elopement. That version of her wouldn't have thought twice about sliding onto her sleeping fiancé's lap and running her fingers along his perfect jaw to wake him with a sizzling kiss... And maybe that kiss would have led to the kind of mile-high aeroplane chair sex she had only ever read about in magazine confession columns.

Just as she allowed herself to imagine the mechanics of such an act, the Captain chose to announce their descent. Valerio woke with his familiar knee-jerk rapid awareness. His eyes landed on her and Dani felt herself freeze as though she'd been caught with her hand in the proverbial cookie jar.

His gaze seemed curious, and she wondered if her erotic daydreams were somehow painted across her forehead. She felt far too warm as she cleared her throat and slid into the seat across from him, averting her gaze as she commented all too loudly on the picture-perfect view of the island of St Lucia below.

Their first stop was the office of a very prestigious local attorney, to ensure that the documents their company lawyer had filed in application for a marriage licence had been received. They were assured that all was going to plan, and that the short ceremony would take place in two days' time, as per the legal waiting period during which they must not vacate the island.

Dani ignored the twist of nerves in her gut at the idea that in a mere forty-eight hours she would be legally wed to the silently brooding man by her side. He had been distant since their argument, his brow permanently marred by that single worry line in the centre. At one point she had almost reached out to smooth it down—had even had to pull her hand into a tight fist and marvel at how ridiculous she was being.

They left the attorney's office and walked the short distance to the marina, where Velamar's sleek new Caribbean base was in the final stages of being finished. The building was single-storey, in traditional St Lucian style, with an enviable frontage of the large marina, which housed the beginnings of their sleek new fleet of charter yachts and catamarans.

'Well, what do you think?'

Dani crossed her arms as Valerio silently took in the bright, modern entrance foyer. The interior was still a mess of plastic coverings and unfinished paintwork, but the majority of the structural modifications had been completed exactly according to her orders.

Valerio was silent, his eyes seeming to take in every small detail as he moved around the large space. He craned his neck upwards to the feature chandelier hanging above their heads and let out a low whistle.

'I had it commissioned by a local artist.' Dani spoke quickly, before he tried to comment on the possible price of such a frivolous item. 'I used local tradesmen for everything—including furniture design. I figured it was good for our global image, as well as making a statement about our commitment to being a part of this community—not just another big company setting up shop.'

'It's genius. This design is the perfect blend of our brand mixed with a St Lucian flavour.' He shook his head. 'You're perfectly on schedule too, by the looks of things. We've never managed that on any of our projects before.'

She fought the impulse to make a snarky comment about how she *was* just that good—about how he was making a mistake by removing her from her CEO duties. Instead she let his compliment sit for a moment, then replied with a simple thank-you. It was very adult, for the pair of them. Very professional.

More than once she caught him watching her from the corner of her eye as she spoke to the small management team who had been running things on-site. They were jumping over one another, eager to show the progress that had been made in readying the base for the first launch in the upcoming season.

Valerio seemed oddly distant now, allowing her to take the lead on the walk-through while he stood to the side and listened.

She suggested they take the team to dinner, to show their appreciation of their hard work, and was delighted when Valerio booked a sleek little boutique restaurant on the harbour that served the most delicious lobster she had ever tasted. He stepped easily into the role of charming CEO as he regaled the small table with entertaining stories from the company's early days, starting up in Monaco, and the various catastrophes they had endured.

She felt an enormous sense of pride in her company— and then froze, wondering when on earth she had begun thinking of it as hers and not Duarte's. It was as if hearing that his death was about to be confirmed had forced her to start accepting that he was not coming back to claim what should have always been his.

She found herself struggling to keep up with the jovial conversation during the rest of dinner, and fell into silence on the short drive up the coast to the villa Valerio had leased for the weekend.

It was nestled high on the side of a hill in a small inlet, with a short private beach visible between the cliffs below. The house itself was a warm peach-coloured creation of concrete and salvaged wood, surrounded by beautiful potted trees. Wild flowers grew up its façade, along with green foliage along the windows.

She stepped out of the car, breathing in the warm sea breeze. There wasn't a sound around them other than the chirping of birds and the muted crash of the waves on the wind. It took her breath away. It was as if her own personal postcard fantasy of an island paradise had been dreamed into life.

But even such a spectacular panorama couldn't cut through the heavy cloud that had come over her. Grief was a strange thing. It seemed to disappear then pop back up when you least expected it.

She followed Valerio as he led the way past the front door, following a lamplit paved path around the side of the house. The manicured gardens stretched for what seemed like miles around them, sloping gently down towards a sharp cliff edge. Whoever had designed this space had ensured a perfect symmetry between the smooth curving lines of the house and the natural beauty of the landscape.

Her heart felt both happy and sad as she inwardly acknowledged that her brother would have loved it.

'This place is magical,' she breathed softly as she wandered around to a sprawling terrace at the rear of the villa, which stretched out from the cliff face on what seemed like stilts, dug down into the rock itself. It was quite literally as if you could walk right out into the clouds from here.

At this northernmost point of the island, the Caribbean stretched out endlessly to one side, the Atlantic Ocean in the distance on the other. On a clear day, she'd bet you could see all the way to the neighbouring island of Martinique.

'I'm glad you like it.' Valerio had a smile in his voice as he spoke, stopping at the polished wooden balustrade beside her. 'I was thinking that, instead of the courthouse, we could just get married right here.' When she was utterly silent, he continued awkwardly. 'I have my security team on-site… It would be easier to contain. Plus, I thought it might be a bit of a nicer view than stacks of paperwork and musty bookshelves.'

Dani felt every romantic cell in her body light up from the inside out, the idea of saying her vows in such a place making her eyes water. But then she remembered that they weren't real vows, and that she wasn't to be a real bride in this picture-perfect setting. That the reason he had to keep her safe was because someone wanted to hurt her.

She felt herself deflate like a helium balloon coming down from the heavens. As beautiful as this place was, no amount of dressing it up would make this wedding any less painful.

CHAPTER SEVEN

VALERIO WAS PUZZLED by the sudden change in Dani as she simply nodded and murmured something non-committal about his idea sounding 'nice'. He pursed his lips, ignoring the sinking disappointment in his gut at her reaction.

He wasn't sure why he'd hoped she would be happy with the setting—they both knew that this was just a quick formality that needed to be done. It really didn't matter if they signed their licence and said their vows by the side of a road—only that the legalities were seen to.

He watched as she wandered down the terrace, briefly taking in the impressive pool area, then moved inside the house to explore. Valerio kept a few steps behind her as she looked around, commenting on the vibrant colours of the potted plants and the flowers around each room. For the most part, the rented house was decorated in neutral tones of white and grey. It was lacking an owner's touch of personality.

The kitchen looked like a relatively new addition, as did the state-of-the-art surveillance system and security room. The privacy and safety of the house had been one of Valerio's main concerns when booking, and he had advised his two guards to take shifts in the guest cabin at the gate. He wasn't going to take any chances.

'I'm going to go unpack my stuff...maybe take a shower.'

She wandered away through the house and Valerio watched her go, a feeling of unease within him. She was unhappy—he had seen it in the set of her mouth all the way through dinner. He had respected her silence in the car with difficulty, wanting to give her space in whatever bothered her, but he had also wanted to stop the car and demand she tell him what was wrong.

But it wasn't his place. He wasn't the man for her to confide her innermost feelings to...to lean on when she was sad. If he started blurring those lines, who knew what would come falling down next? Distance wasn't just wise with Dani; it was absolutely necessary.

Ignoring the sudden increase of tension in his spine, he moved to the fridge and found it fully stocked, as requested. Fresh fruit and pre-cooked gourmet meals lined the shelves—enough to keep them going for a couple of days while they waited for the paperwork to go through.

Suddenly, the idea of sitting around waiting for the formalities of their elopement just didn't sit right with him. If they had any hope of making this work, they needed to get back on the same team. He needed her to trust him, and not to feel like a coiled spring in his company.

Suddenly, he knew exactly what to do.

The tiny beach restaurant was a hidden gem Valerio had heard about on the east side of the island. Dani had initially worried aloud that her simple turquoise shift dress might make her feel underdressed, but that had been before Valerio had revealed that he'd booked out the entire venue for their exclusive use.

'There's no one else here,' she whispered as they were seated at a small table overlooking a pebbled beach. Small lanterns lit the way down to the shore and a light scent of salt was in the cool night air. 'I understand we need to be cautious, but it's so quiet.'

He nodded towards an area at the edge of the deck and watched as she turned and saw the duo of island musicians setting up under a string of fairy lights. Soon the sound of a steel drum and a rhythmic guitar began to flow through the air. She smiled as she closed her eyes and swayed a little.

'You should do that more often,' Valerio said silkily, taking a sip of his soda water and lime to distract himself from the hum of attraction that had refused to shift since she'd walked down the stairs in that flowy knee-length dress. She shifted and crossed one leg over the other, revealing a long, smooth expanse of perfectly curved skin. He cleared his throat, looking up to her face and away from those damn thighs. 'I want you to enjoy these few days here. Take it as a chance to recharge before we have to return to reality.'

'Or at least the new appearance of reality.' She smiled again.

'Exactly.'

The corners of his mouth tipped up slightly and for the first time he felt the urge to laugh. It was enough to stop him for a moment, before he caught himself. He'd had a hard time too, he reminded himself. Maybe they both deserved to feel a little freedom while they were here.

'You're starting to look serious again,' she commented, one brow raised.

'I was just thinking…maybe it's time we called a truce. Let's enjoy a few days off the grid, so to speak. No arguments or work. No serious talk.'

A simple handshake sealed the deal and they entered into a pleasant flow of conversation until their food arrived then drifted into companionable silence as the delicious food and great music added to their lighter mood.

Their waiter was a kind-faced older man, who saw the ring on Daniela's finger and insisted that the band play a slow number for them to dance to.

Valerio stood, extending his hand to her and forcing a smile as she stood up and moved close. The music had a soft, seductive rhythm, and he found himself forgetting all the reasons why he shouldn't be enjoying this, why he shouldn't pull her close and pretend they were just another couple on an island adventure.

He breathed in the scent of her hair and heard the softest sigh escape her lips.

'I didn't expect you to be a good dancer.' She spoke near his ear, her breath fanning his skin. 'I should have known you'd be good at everything.'

'You think I find everything easy?' He subtly moved even closer, moving his hand on her back and leaning forward. 'I stepped on every dance partner's toes at events when I was a teenager. My mother made me go to dance lessons twice a week for six months. I was an embarrassment.'

She laughed deep in her throat as he dipped her into a flamenco-style twirl, tipping her back over his arm. 'Well, you certainly overcame your awkward phase.'

Their eyes met for a long moment, their breath coming a little faster from their exertions. Valerio found himself wondering if he should suggest they kiss, to maintain the appearance of being a happily engaged couple. But really he just wanted to kiss her again. Wanted to see if it was his sex-starved brain that had elicited that first reaction from him after their first kiss or…if it was just simply her.

As he began tipping his head down towards her, a shout from behind them caught his attention.

They both turned and watched as one of the security guards ran down the beach and into the water towards a small boat. A single man was in the vessel, a black box-like item in his hands. Valerio turned himself in front of Dani, shielding her with his body as he shouted for the other guard to follow.

After a few tense moments of shouting and confusion, it was revealed that the man was just a local fisherman who hadn't been told of the restaurant's private hire. The guards and Valerio quickly apologised to the man, and to the restaurant owner, who had been quite distressed by the commotion.

'Get back to the car,' Valerio growled, guiding her away from the dance floor by the elbow.

'Valerio, it's okay. It was just a mistake.'

'This entire impulsive evening out was a mistake.' He shook his head. 'I can't even keep you safe for one day. I need to get you back to the house now. Just...please don't fight me on this.'

Dani didn't fight him. She barely even spoke on the drive back to the villa, knowing that Valerio needed time to cool down after the adrenaline rush of the false alarm. She had been scared too, but he had moved swiftly from fear and protective mode to anger towards himself. She was beginning to see a pattern with him. Did he have a hero complex? Or was he hiding something about himself?

An email on her phone caught her attention as they entered the large open-plan living area of the villa.

'The board have accepted my plans for Nettuno and the charities.' She frowned. 'But I never got the chance to send them my files before you asked me to step back.'

'I sent them.' He turned to her, both hands in his pockets. 'I looked into your plans further after the meeting and

I knew they were the best course of action. You'll get full credit, and I'll keep you in the loop on everything regarding Duarte's projects.'

'Valerio...that means more than you know—thank you.'

'You don't need to thank me. I should be thanking you for being so good at what you do. I'm being honest when I say I wouldn't ask you to take this step back if it wasn't important.'

She nodded once. 'And you still won't tell me exactly why?'

Valerio's gaze became instantly defensive and he prepared to turn away.

'No arguments, remember?' she said quickly, knowing that she needed to take a different tack. This was a business deal, after all—why shouldn't she employ one of her oldest moves? Entertain the opposition...keep them close. 'I'm not going to launch into a fight, if that's what you're thinking. I want us to keep to our deal. A weekend of fun, starting now.'

She moved to one of the sideboards she'd investigated earlier, returning with a deck of cards. 'How do you fancy your odds?'

'Poker?' He raised one brow, picking up the deck and shuffling the cards with seasoned practice. 'You sure you're up to playing me?'

'You forget that I've been schmoozing your clientele in Monte Carlo these past few months. I've become quite a pro.'

'We don't have any chips.'

He shuffled the cards again, dancing them easily between his hands with the lightest touch. She watched his movements, transfixed by how effortlessly he manipulated the deck. The man was good with his hands...

Clearing her wandering thoughts, she sat up straighter.

'I used to play without chips with Hermione back in college. We sat up all night, creating this stupid game where you get a forfeit instead of chips, while we were supposed to be studying for exams.'

'A forfeit?' His eyes met hers across the table. 'Like Truth or Dare?'

'More like Truth or Lies. You have to ask awkward questions and try to get the other person to lie or refuse to answer. But be warned: I'm pretty good at this.'

The premise of the game was simple enough: a crazy mix-up of various card games that only Hermione could have concocted. Each player had the chance to steal cards by challenging the other to answer a question or make a statement, then determining if the answer was the truth or a lie. The problem was, as the game went on for a few rounds, Dani realised that some of the questions Valerio was asking were quite inappropriate.

'How many lovers have you had?' he asked boldly.

Dani answered honestly, praying she didn't blush with embarrassment as she admitted she had only ever been with Kitt. Valerio's eyes burned into hers, widening with disbelief as he declared it a lie, and she shook her head, taking her share of his cards as her forfeit.

'How many lovers have *you* had?' Dani asked when it was her turn, trying and failing to keep a straight face.

Valerio pursed his lips, counting the fingers on both hands, then reaching for a pen and jotting down some sums. 'Let me see. Carry the two...multiply by seven... Roughly in the low hundreds.'

'Okay, well, I'm just going to say that's true.' She shrugged, pretending not to care about his answer.

'Lie.' His eyes sparkled as he took her cards. 'I'm actually quite discerning about who I take to bed, despite the tabloid rumours. You have a low opinion of me.'

Dani smirked. 'Well, what *is* the number, then?'

'Ah-ah, that's not a part of the game.'

He laughed as she groaned her annoyance.

'What's your biggest fear?' he asked on the next turn, his gaze strangely focused on her and a slight curve to his mouth. He was enjoying this, she thought.

'That's an easy one. The open sea,' she said easily, schooling her features.

When he guessed that she was lying, she shook her head, grabbing yet more of his cards.

'You're serious? You work at a yacht charter company and you're afraid of the open sea?' He let out a bark of laughter.

'I'm just afraid of swimming in it—not sailing. I don't like to sail myself, but I trust the boats.'

She sat back as they played another hand, feeling his eyes on her the entire time. The next time her turn came up, she felt the effect of the wine kicking in, along with a new sense of bravado. She asked him some questions about his childhood, his decision not to join his father's company—everything she could think of that she'd always wished to ask.

'What's your most shameful secret?' he asked on his next turn, laughing when she grimaced at his question. 'You know the rules: you have to give an answer or you forfeit.'

'Well, unlucky for you, that's an easy one for me.' She met his gaze, throwing out her best poker face. 'I have never had a proper orgasm.'

His brow furrowed, his eyes narrowing on her for one intense moment before they widened in a mixture of surprise and anger.

'You have to say if you think it's true or false,' she said, but she was instantly regretting her flirty answer, wondering what on earth had possessed her. 'Or we can just move on.'

The air was still and silent between them, except for the sound of insects chirping and waves crashing against the cliffs nearby. She pursed her lips, sitting up and flicking her hair over her shoulder.

'Forget that one. I'll give you the cards and let's just move on.'

A long exhalation escaped Valerio's lips. Dani looked up to see his hands in tight fists on his lap.

'*Madre di Dio.* I knew that pompous lawyer was beyond useless. You actually believe that you are somehow defective because of that idiot?'

'It's not always the man's fault, Valerio. And it's kind of a sensitive subject,' she said tightly. 'Draw your next hand, please.' She heard the ice in her voice—it was a sore subject for her. But she wasn't about to discuss it over some stupid card game.

'Even if it's true—which is up for debate—you're telling me he made you believe that it was your fault? That you can't—?'

'I said draw your next hand.'

The next round was more heated, with Dani using her best tricks to ensure she won. She knew she was a damn good card player, even if it was an utterly ridiculous game.

She met his eyes across the table. 'Time for your most shameful secret, Mr Marchesi. And it had better match mine.'

Valerio sat back in his seat, still feeling the tension within him from her revelation. He wiped a hand down his face, wishing they'd never started playing this game. She was just giving him as good as she got—she had no idea how many secrets he held in. But she had asked to know before…about

Rio. Maybe this was his chance to share his burden with her. He only hoped she would be able to handle it.

'Valerio, you don't have to answer,' she said quickly, obviously taking in the change in him. 'I'll choose a different question.'

'You answered yours,' he said simply. 'I have no problem continuing to play by the rules. My most shameful secret is easy. Most people believe me to be some kind of hero, but the reality is that I'm the opposite. I'm a coward. It was my fault that your brother was killed and I will never forgive myself for that.'

'Valerio...' she breathed.

'No. You asked me for the truth once before, and I walked away. You deserve to know how he died.'

An unbearable pity was there in her deep brown eyes as she nodded once and gestured for him to proceed. He felt her attention on him like the warm heat of the sun, watched her delicate hands folding and unfolding in her lap as she waited. They both knew this wasn't just a game any more.

'I followed him to Rio when he asked me not to. We were attacked by a van full of men and taken,' he began, hearing his own voice sounding out perfectly clear in the night air, as somewhere deep inside his chest ached. 'I woke up in a shipping yard, surrounded by men in black hoods. They roared questions in a Portuguese dialect that I couldn't even begin to understand. Duarte was tied up beside me for a while but then they separated us. They were far more interested in him than me.' In his mind, he remembered the solemn look on Duarte's face as he apologised for dragging him into such a mess... He swore he would get them both freed. That he had a plan, but he made him vow to protect Dani if anything happened to him.

But for days on end they had tortured him and Duarte in turn, in front of each other, never allowing him to speak, only Duarte, using their loyalty to one another against them.

'Days passed... They tortured me for fun. I didn't have anything else they needed. I had already offered them money... After they broke my knee and I could no longer fight back, they got bored. Then they mostly just left me alone in the dark.'

He heard a sob and looked up to see that Dani had covered her face with her hands, but he had to finish this while he could. He owed her this story, even if he knew it might break her to hear it. He hoped she was strong enough.

'Eventually they lost their patience. A man brought Duarte in and held a gun to my head. Someone asked in English how much his friend's life was worth. But one of the guards who I hadn't seen before turned his gun on the others. He freed us both before they killed him. I had a gun in my hand but I hesitated. I had the chance to end it and I didn't. They shot Duarte by accident. I saw the panic in their eyes once they realised. They debated shooting me too but got disturbed by someone outside and just knocked me out instead. When I woke up, Duarte's body was gone and so were they.'

Valerio remembered staggering out of that shipping yard. He was found on the street. When the police came, they found tracks leading to the dock—evidence that a body had been dumped in the water. Washed out to sea. They'd dragged his friend's body away, denied him a proper burial.

He shook his head as if coming out of a daze.

'You know the rest.'

He felt a warm weight on the seat beside him and felt himself cocooned in the soft comfort of her intoxicating scent. She leaned her head against his shoulder, her sharp breaths telling him that she was crying even though she hid her face.

'Thank you,' she said simply, and then she allowed the silence to stretch on for a long while. She seemed to know instinctively that he couldn't speak any more, that he needed to just...*be*...for a moment.

No matter how many times he allowed himself to access those memories, they always seemed to hit him with the same force. The look on Duarte's face as he'd realised they weren't getting out of that shipping yard alive. The look of pure hatred in the masked men's eyes as they'd tried again and again to beat him into submission.

Every single moment was like a pinprick in his skin, every vision a reminder of what he might have done differently, how he might have saved his friend's life if he'd not hesitated that split second.

After a long time Dani sat up and turned to him, her eyes a mess of smudged make-up.

'Lie,' she said, an echo to their earlier game.

'Is that your attempt at a joke?'

'I would never joke about what you went through. You came back alive—you survived the unimaginable. But the way you tell that story... It's as though you feel you were to blame for my brother's death. As though you could have saved him if you'd done something different. You're lying to yourself. Punishing yourself for surviving.'

Valerio looked away, his jaw tightening with anger. 'You have no idea what you're talking about.'

'I know that you're a good man. That you would have done what you believed was right. You were under so much pressure—'

'Stop.' He stood up, fury and resentment choking him, making him want to lash out. 'You blame me for his death just as much as everyone else. Are you telling me you have never wondered how I survived when he was clearly the more experienced fighter? You think I don't know what people say about me behind my back? You've had the luxury of grieving him without knowing the details, without having them permanently etched in your memory as a lifelong torture. Do you think you can just pull me out of my life, tie me to a bed and order me to get back to work... go back to living my life? Do you think I can just switch any of this off?'

He laughed, harsh and low.

'I'm done with this game.'

Dani stood up, walking quietly to the door back into the villa. She paused, turning back for a moment to meet his eyes. When she spoke her voice was surprisingly calm and soft in the aftermath of all the venom he'd just thrown at her.

'Valerio... I know you're angry. But there is no luxury in grief, no matter what side you stand on. We both loved him. And I know that I pushed you to come back, but I'm not sorry. I get it that there are parts of you that are broken and scarred from your experience. But I just need you to know that I don't blame you for his death. I never did. And you might have wanted to die in that dark shipping container, but I am thankful every single day that you came back.'

The door to the house closed softly behind her, leaving Valerio to sit alone in the darkness, feeling the result of his own stupid temper and guilt surrounding him like a dark cloud. He took a step forward, willing himself to storm after her and demand that she be angry. Demand the hatred he deserved.

But he remained frozen for a long time, his mind fighting to swim up from the fiery pit of anger it had succumbed to. It was at times like this, when the blackness came over him, when he wondered how there was anything of him left at all.

Valerio kept out of Dani's way the next morning, not even passing comment when she holed herself up in the study at the villa and he spied her hard at work on her computer. She needed to take a break and some time to relax, but she wasn't going to listen to him—not after he had been his usual difficult self last night.

He hardly even remembered half of what he'd said, he'd been so set on telling her the story of what had actually happened in Brazil.

He found his own computer and sat down in the dining room, logging on to the Velamar system for the first time in months and taking in the vast amount of work he'd been neglecting. It was no surprise Dani hadn't had any time for her independent contracts—he'd left her alone to handle all this.

He spent the day through to the afternoon methodically sorting through emails and project outlines, sales projections and marketing plans. He immersed himself in the work, surprised when it fuelled the drive in him rather than making him feel trapped at a desk like it usually did.

His mind felt focused—as if he had unburdened it a little just by sharing his darkness with Dani. But guilt assailed him. He needed to swallow his pride and apologise for his behaviour. For all his behaviour over the past few days. He was about to be her husband, and even if it was in name only, he didn't want to let her down.

'I'm still committed to our agreement of a weekend off, even if you're not. So I'm going to go for a swim before it gets dark.'

Like a mirage, she had appeared in the doorway of the

dining room, a towel wrapped around her and the black strings of a simple bikini top visible at her nape.

Cursing himself for his instant flare of arousal, he glared down at his computer, waving a hand in her direction. He listened to her footsteps pad away, closing his eyes at the distinctive sound of a towel hitting a smooth surface before there was the splash of water.

His mind conjured up a vision of her smooth, dark curves gliding through the cool water in the setting sunlight. His groin tightened in response, all the blood in his body rushing south. He snapped the computer shut, looking up at the ceiling and shaking his head. This was what happened when he ignored his body for so long. He was like a teenager around her. She would be horrified to know of his lack of control.

He tried to get back into his work but his concentration was shot. So he sat in painful silence, listening to the sound of her moving through the water on the other side of the terrace doors.

Suddenly a muffled scream came from far away, jolting him from his thoughts. He frowned, tensing. When a second scream sounded out, he jumped from his seat and started running.

He reached the pool to see Daniela frozen in the centre, her eyes wide with terror as she pointed towards the wooden bridge over the water.

He followed her finger, his eyes instantly landing on what was possibly the most gigantic snake he had ever seen. The reptile was olive green in colour, with black markings along its length which almost matched the entire span of the bridge.

As Valerio watched, its heavy body moved and became partially submerged in the water towards its tail end. He looked closer, seeing a small alcove under the bridge filled with tiny movements. This mother snake was protecting her young. She didn't move again, but was clearly aware of the woman who had interrupted her peace. Tiny black eyes were focused solely on Dani, and Valerio felt his chest tighten at the sight of her fear.

'Do you think you can swim to the edge?' He spoke softly, ready to move if the snake did. Judging by its size, it was one of the island's native boa constrictors—non-venomous, but who knew how it might react if it sensed a threat?

Dani laughed—a panicked, breathy sound. 'I can't move at all. I've tried.' She groaned. 'It's watching me.'

'Okay, I'll come and get you.' He pressed his lips together, stepping out of his shoes. 'It won't hurt you. The only poisonous snakes on this island are a lot smaller than this large lady.'

'Lady?' she squeaked, incredulous. '*I'm* a large lady—*that* is a gigantic reptile. Seriously, I'm in mortal danger here and you're being *respectful* of that thing?'

Valerio waded into the pool with slow, purposeful strokes. He reached her side in seconds, placing a finger against her lips. 'Careful. She might hear you and take offence.'

'Stop messing around.' She clutched at him, her hands shaking as she latched on to his wet shirt and folded her body against his.

He felt a low groan escape his lips as his body roared to life at the delicious contact.

'I'm sorry... Did I hurt you?' she breathed, her attention still largely focused on the snake.

Get it together, Valerio.

He sliced at the water to move them both closer to the edge. Now was definitely not the time to be losing his grip on his rediscovered libido. She was afraid, and she was trusting him to get her out of the pool safely, so he was going to do just that.

He began to lift her onto the lip of the pool, then instantly regretted it as she froze and clung to him even tighter. 'Don't *lift* me!' She pushed a hand at his chest.

Valerio growled with irritation. '*Dio*, again with the worrying. I have lifted you before and, believe me, I was not even slightly hampered by your size. You honestly have no idea how perfect these curves are.'

Her eyes went wide. 'I meant…don't lift me out where the snake can get me.' She began to blush a bright pink, her body suddenly softening in his arms. 'But…thank you.'

He froze for a long moment, just looking into her brown eyes, feeling her heartbeat thudding against his chest through the wet fabric of his shirt. He was an idiot. An absolute idiot.

His forehead dipped to press against hers as he fought the insane urge to kiss her. But he knew that if he kissed her now he would want more. He would want as much as he could have of her…as much as she was willing to give.

And where would that leave them? He had promised himself that the first time had been the last, that this was how it needed to be. And yet every time they were alone together it seemed like the most natural thing in the world to have her in his arms.

Thank God for the water around them, or she'd be all too aware of the nature of his thoughts.

'Valerio…'

She shifted against him, her thighs tightening on his hips as she tilted her face slightly. Her lips brushed against his, soft and wet, and he felt the ravenous beast within him roar with triumph. Surely, if she was starting it, it would be rude to stop her?

His arms banded around her, pulling her chest flush

against him as he plundered her mouth, deep and hard. He felt her nails on his back as she moved against him, heard the sound of her groans as he pushed her back against the side of the pool.

With one hand he gripped her hair, tilting her head back and gaining deeper access, deeper control of the kiss. The darker forces in his mind screamed at him to take her right here in the water and to hell with the consequences. But it seemed Dani had different ideas. She stiffened in his arms, pushing him away with surprising force.

'I'm sorry…' he began, readying himself for the inevitable argument.

'No, Valerio… The snake moved again. I heard a splash.'

He turned, and sure enough, the reptile was now fully submerged in the water. He lifted Dani up with ease, doing his best to ignore the deliciously wet curves under his hands. Once he'd lifted himself out too, they both looked down at the impossibly long, dark shape in the water.

'I'll call Animal Control in the morning. Our snake friend has a nest of babies under that bridge that need to be taken somewhere a little bit safer.'

Dani shivered at the word 'babies', stepping backwards, away from the pool. 'I swear, I'll never swim peacefully again.'

That made two of them, he thought wryly, but for entirely different reasons.

The cool evening breeze cut uncomfortably through the wet fabric of his clothes. He needed a hot shower and a lot of distance between them to get his head in order.

Making a snap decision, he pulled off his soaked shirt and hung it over a chair, doing the same with his trousers. The outside shower was tucked into a wall on the terrace of the villa. It was fully stocked with toiletries and had a cabinet filled with towels. It seemed the rental company had thought of almost everything—except checking for hidden families of snakes, of course.

When he emerged from the shower, he hoped Dani would have gone inside. But she sat waiting for him on a sun lounger, with a towel wrapped around her body. A wet pile of fabric lay on the ground beside her. Her discarded bikini.

Valerio gritted his teeth, wishing he had taken his shower inside and then locked himself in his bedroom. Being a coward was infinitely preferable to this kind of sexual torture. If she had any idea what her mere presence was doing to him, with her damp curls hanging over her bare shoulders and the way she watched him through her lashes with a look of uncertainty on her beautiful face...

He tightened his fists, searching for control, hating it that she made him ache for all that he couldn't have. And he was finally admitting to himself that he did want to have her—not just because of sexual frustration or circumstance. He wanted *her*.

'You said you were sorry.' She spoke softly, standing up to face him. 'About that kiss. But I'm the one who kissed you this time. I didn't even ask. Surely I'm the one who should be apologising.'

'You don't need to apologise. I'm the one who needs to apologise. My behaviour towards you has been unacceptable from the moment I came home,' he said, cursing himself as her eyes widened and she took a step towards him.

He raised a hand between them, holding her at arm's length.

'I'm sorry for how I spoke to you last night. I'm sorry I can't be...what you need. But we both know why we need to keep things professional here. My priority is keeping you safe, and that includes keeping you safe from me too.

You've seen the way I am. I can't even be woken from sleep without becoming a danger.'

'That's ridiculous. You would never hurt me, Valerio.'

'You have no idea who I am. Not any more,' he rasped, his eyes lowering to take in the towel she clutched to her chest. 'I'm the man who promised to keep his best friend's sister safe. Then kissed her for the first time in front of an audience and had to stop himself from lifting her up like some kind of brute and carrying her off to the nearest bed. And if there hadn't been a damn snake in that pool, the same thing would have happened ten minutes ago. I have no control over myself around you.'

'Well…that would have certainly got everyone's attention…'

'This isn't a game any more. In two days you are going to be my wife…' He swallowed hard, trying to ignore the way her eyes darkened to deep burnished amber in the low glow of the setting sun. 'But I'm going to find the people behind all this, and once I'm sure you're safe—'

'What, Valerio?' She spoke quietly. 'You'll leave again? What a surprise.'

'I'll have our marriage annulled and you can get on with your life.'

'What life? I've spent the past two years working myself to the bone.' She ran a hand through her curls, taking a few steps away from him to compose herself. 'At least with you I feel…'

'What do you feel?' he asked, feeling himself itching to move closer, to coax this fire between them until it burned them both.

'I don't know…' Dani began, twisting the white towel in her hands, suddenly unable to look at him as she spoke.

Was she really going to be honest? She had kept her

feelings for Valerio Marchesi under lock and key for so long it would be no effort at all to lie and agree to his sensible plans for their sensible marriage of convenience.

But she was tired of being sensible. She was tired of putting on a show of being strong and self-contained all the time.

'I don't think I have ever heard you speak in so many unfinished sentences,' he said.

'You said that I have no idea who you are any more,' she said, standing up and looking down at him. 'I think we're both different people now. Changed people because of events that neither of us had any control over. We've both been alone and we've learned how to cope with the unknown in our own way. I don't want to be alone any more, Valerio.'

He looked up at her. 'You're not alone. I'm here with you.'

'You're not,' she said quietly, feeling her bravado falter slightly but pushing on. 'Not really. And if I marry you, that means sharing a home with you, sharing my entire life with you… I can't be around you all the time in these intimate situations and not be affected. I'm just not that good an actress.'

'Are you saying you don't want to be around me?' He raised a brow.

'I do,' she said quickly, looking down at the ground and cursing herself for how badly she was getting her point across. 'God, I really do… That's the problem.'

Valerio stood up, closing the gap between them with a single step. 'We're not just talking about marriage any more, are we?'

'Look… I understand that this has never been something you wanted.' Dani spoke fast, praying she wouldn't lose her nerve. 'But I need to be honest. I'm really attracted to you. More than I've ever been to anyone else. It's quite inconvenient, considering that we're planning a marriage built on nothing more than business and friendship, but… I just wanted to have that out in the open.'

His fingers pressed against her lips, silencing her. 'Are you proposing to amend the terms of our contract, Miss Avelar?' He wrapped his hand around the towel, pulling her towards him until they stood chest to chest. 'How much more do you want?'

'I don't know,' she said breathlessly. 'How much are you willing to give?'

He answered her with his lips on hers, his hands spanning her waist and pulling her against him—hard. '*Dio*, I thought I was already crazy with wanting to have you. But now…with this mixture of pretty blushing and the throwing around of business terms…'

His lips trailed down her neck, his hands sliding down to cup her bottom through the towel. Dani moaned low in her throat, the power of speech slowly leaving her.

'Do you want me to make love to you, Daniela?' he whispered next to her ear, his hands kneading her skin gently.

'Yes… God, yes.'

He pulled back, an expression of awe on his face as he cupped her jaw and looked deep into her eyes. 'This will complicate things.'

'Only if we let it.' Her voice shook as she spoke. 'We're both adults. We know what this is.'

'I don't have any protection.' His brow furrowed, his hands tightening on her as though he feared his words might make her run away. 'I haven't been with anyone since before Brazil, and I don't really go around carrying condoms in my wallet. But I've had my yearly check-up since and I know I'm clean.'

'Me too—and I've had an IUD for years.' She pressed her hand to his cheek, hardly believing they were having this conversation. 'I don't want to think about this as a complication. I don't want to *think*, Valerio. I just want to do what feels right.'

CHAPTER EIGHT

HIS EYES DARKENED, his hand moving to the front of the towel, spreading over it slightly. His fingers trailed over the bare skin of her stomach. 'Tell me…does this feel right?'

She answered with a moan.

He continued his exploration, his touch sending her skin into an explosion of sensation. Her legs felt weak as he reached the edge of the bikini bottoms she had yet to remove, smoothing his hand down over her sex through the thin, still damp fabric. She bit down hard on her lower lip, tilting her head back as he licked a path of fire along the side of her neck.

She had never enjoyed sex in the past—she'd always been so consumed by her negative body image and her pesky inability to reach an orgasm. But her mind seemed unable to worry about that now, as he slid his fingers under the fabric and along the slick seam between her thighs.

'How about this?' he murmured softly against her skin, his teeth nipping at the area just below her ear.

Her answer was incoherent as she clung to him while he performed some kind of magic with his fingers. She had never felt such intensity from a simple touch before. Every slide of his hand sent fresh waves of pleasure shooting up her spine and down her legs.

Soon she was moving against him, powerless not to join

his sensual rhythm. Her eyes widened in disbelief as she felt herself tightening around his fingers. The shock momentarily stopped her rhythm, her legs shaking beneath her as her mind got in the way of her pleasure.

'Do you want me to make you come, Dani?' he purred next to her ear.

'It's okay. I don't usually…' she breathed, her chest tightening. 'I mean, I've only ever been able to do it a few times by myself. And it takes far too long.'

Valerio pressed his forehead against her temple. '*Dio*, that image…you touching yourself… But right now I'm the one in control.' He continued to move his fingers in slow circles as he spoke softly in her ear. 'You're going to relax and come for me…right here. I won't stop until you do.'

Dani felt a breathless laugh in her throat at the thought that this arrogant man believed he could simply will her to orgasm. But, God, she loved it. This artful combination of being commanded and cared for so thoroughly…it was almost too much for her to take. Her body seemed to relax just with his sensual presence.

She shook wildly at the lazy thrust and curl of his touch, feeling the pressure within her rise once again. This time she didn't fight it, and she listened helplessly as he whispered all the things he planned to do to her, letting his words add fuel to the fire that was already burning in her, wildly out of control.

When the wave of pleasure finally reached an earth-shattering climax, she could do nothing but hold on to him as the waves took her again and again. The intensity of the orgasm was too much, and she buried her face against his shoulder, his name falling from her lips like a prayer. Still he kept it going, only slowing down as she shook and fell slowly back to earth.

* * *

'I think I've proved your theory incorrect.'

Valerio bit his lower lip as he took in the rosy flush of Dani's cheeks and the delicious pout of her lips.

'I can't even think straight.' She smiled, half hiding her face against his shoulder.

'I don't plan to stop until you've lost the ability to speak.'

He fought the edge of his control as he took her by the hand and guided her back inside the villa, stopping to light two of the lamps on the bedroom wall. Letting go of her hand, he sat on the edge of the bed, looking up to take in the beautiful silhouette of the woman in front of him.

This was a bad idea—she had said it herself. But he no longer remembered any of the reasons why. Nothing mattered any more other than having her body under his and taking the entire night to explore every inch of her silky caramel skin.

She stepped towards him, dropping the towel from the tight clutch of her hands, baring her body to him. *Dio*, he had never seen anything as erotic as the sight of her blushing. Her hands flexed as though she wanted to cover her breasts, then dropped slowly down to her sides.

He remembered her words from before—her belief that she was somehow less feminine because of her size and her competitive streak. Less desirable because she was so unlike most of the women in her social circles. She had no idea how much she had tortured him with this delectable body for years…sitting across a boardroom table in her smart skirts, commanding the room with her brilliance.

This powerful woman actually doubted her beauty. Doubted herself in the bedroom because of some unqualified idiot in her past.

He bit his lower lip, anger and desire making his pulse

pound in his veins. He would make it his personal mission to ensure she never doubted a single thing about herself again.

'Come here,' he rasped, gripping her hips and guiding her to straddle his lap.

Her breasts were the perfect size for his hands. He took his time, trailing his lips and tongue across one delicate dusky nipple before moving to pay equal attention to its twin. The soft moans that escaped her throat made him so hard it took all his willpower not to just do away with the idea of going slowly. The thought of burying himself inside her made him feel primal...on the verge of losing his mind completely.

But if this kind of sensual control and skill was all he had to offer her, then he was damn sure that he would prove his worth. He thrust out his hips, his erection straining against the front of his towel. Dani gasped, her eyes darkening as she followed his rhythm, grinding against him. She moved like a dancer, her hips rolling effortlessly in time with his. *Dio*, it felt so right, having her against him.

Then she stopped her movements, bracing one hand against his chest. 'Lie back.'

'I was wondering when you would start fighting me,' he breathed, following her command without question.

He lay back on the bed, raising both arms over his head in a display of submission. He watched as she positioned herself at his knees, untying his towel and pulling it away inch by agonising inch. She worked slowly, deliberately drawing out her movements as she bared him. Her hair brushed over the skin of his thighs and abdomen as she ran one finger down past his navel. His manhood pulsed, straining towards her touch.

'I've never done this before, either,' she admitted huskily, meeting his gaze with no embarrassment, just trust. 'Tell me if I'm doing it wrong.'

'*Tesoro*, I don't think you realise how effortlessly sensual you are...'

He breathed the words as she freed him and ran her fingers over his hard length. He closed his eyes for a moment as the tip of her tongue moved against him in slow exploration as she figured it out for herself. Opening his eyes against a wave of pleasure, he looked down to see her taking him all the way past her full lips, his girth disappearing into the molten heat of her mouth.

There was no way he would withstand this kind of pleasure for very long without bringing things to a very abrupt ending.

He thought about it as he watched her take him, and he imagined letting her bring him to release right here. The image sent an electric pulse up his spine, but he sat up, cupping her cheek with one hand and drawing her up along his body until she lay flush against him.

'I wasn't finished.' She smiled that slightly awkward smile he had come to recognise as a sign of nerves.

'I promise to have you in that exact position again before tonight is over, but right now it's taking all my control not to end this before we've even begun.'

Her eyes widened with understanding, a smug smile spreading across her lips as she lowered herself down to kiss him. Valerio took advantage of her position, pulling her close before rolling them over on the soft pillows so that she lay in the cage of his arms.

'My turn.'

He moved down the sun-darkened valley of her breasts, following the path of her ribcage until he reached the gentle curve of her stomach. She writhed with every touch against her skin, her honest reaction to his kisses sending him back to the brink of release once again.

'Tell me what you're thinking about,' he growled against the silky skin of her upper thigh. And then with both hands he spread her legs wide, settling his shoulders between them.

'I've…fantasised about you doing this…'

Her words came quietly from above him, spurring him on as he dropped featherlight kisses against the neatly trimmed downy curls that covered her. God, but she was perfect here too. She writhed, moving her hips against his mouth, begging him to stop his sensual torture.

He barely touched her for a few moments more, then surprised her by spreading her wide and moving his tongue directly against her in one slow stroke. She went wild, a sharp curse escaping her lips.

'Are you going to come for me again?' he murmured huskily against her skin.

'I can't…' she breathed, her head moving against the pillow with each stroke. 'Oh, God, stop—it's too much.'

He paused, only to have her hands grip his hair, as if begging him to keep going. Valerio smiled against her as he continued to stroke, again and again, keeping a smooth, firm rhythm. But the power he felt in bringing her to this point of madness was too much—he needed to have her soon.

She gasped in shock, beginning to approach another climax under his tongue, and he wasted no time in moving over her, spreading her legs wide and looking into her eyes as he entered her in one hard, urgent thrust.

He needed to be inside her as she came apart more than he needed to breathe. The time for taking it slow had passed, and he had burned out every last scrap of his control. He felt her inner muscles continue to tighten around him, heard her breaths coming in short gasps as she met the strength of his thrusts. She pulled his face down to her own, crushing her mouth against his so sweetly as her climax hit. And Valerio felt his own pleasure reach an unbearable peak, felt fire spreading up his spine and consuming him. He closed his eyes, pressing his forehead to hers as he came apart, joining her in mindless oblivion.

Dani stared out at the hazy darkness of the moonlit night spilling in through the open terrace doors. Valerio's gentle snores sounded in the bed behind her. He had fallen asleep after another round of intense, earth-shattering sex. But she lay awake, wondering what would happen once he woke up and properly talked about what they'd just done.

She was afraid to move, as his arm was draped over her, pulling her tight to his chest. And something within her ached at the wonderful feeling of being in the cradle of his strong arms, even knowing it was only temporary.

She sighed. If she could just stay in this bed for ever she might imagine that things had deepened between them. If they never had to leave this magical island they wouldn't have to confront the reality that they shared a company together. That this was an arrangement, not a love match. That, while he was apparently attracted to her on a physical level, he would probably never feel even a fraction of what she felt for him.

She paused. What exactly *was* it that she felt for him?

Frowning, Dani slipped gently free of his embrace. Sitting on the side of the bed, she looked down at the strong profile of the man who was soon to be her husband. The engagement ring on her finger felt heavier than ever, its cool metal shining in the light of the moon.

She had agreed to live with him, share her life with him and trust him to keep her safe from the unseen danger that was closing in. But what were they to one another without this arrangement? Would he ever have fallen into bed with her if he hadn't been facing possible years of celibacy as her convenient husband?

Cradling her face in her hands, she breathed deep and tried to calm the anxiety within her. She was about to *marry* him—she couldn't have this many complicated feelings warring within her. She was falling into dangerous waters and it was clear she would be the only one hurt when it eventually came to an end.

She needed to keep her feet firmly on land—starting right now. Sleeping together in one bed seemed a step beyond sharing the occasional romp in the sheets, so surely leaving now would be a firm message to show she wasn't getting the wrong idea from what they'd done?

She stood up, pulling the comforter from the edge of the bed, and walked to the door, turning back just once more to look down at Valerio's sleeping form. She could do this—she could have what she wanted of him and still keep herself above water.

She went into her room and stepped straight into a hot shower, feeling the spray hit muscles that she hadn't used in years. She lathered soap across her skin, feeling her body tighten at the sensation, imagining it was Valerio's hands touching her, caressing her...

God, she'd had him three times and already she was fantasising about the next time.

Resting her forehead against the cool tiles, she breathed in deeply, calming her racing heartbeat. She sent up a silent prayer that she wasn't in completely over her head. They could mix a little pleasure into their arrangement and not risk ruining everything, couldn't they?

Before she could finish that thought, the shower door slid open and Valerio's broad naked form appeared through the steam as if in slow motion. The man was built like a prize fighter, and the shadow on his jawline made him look rough and dangerous. He didn't speak—just pulled her into his arms and kissed her as though he were a drowning man and she was his first gasp of air.

His hands tangled in her wet hair as the spray of hot water cascaded over them both. Framing her face in his hands, he looked down into her eyes, a wicked smile on his sinfully full lips. 'You left before I was done with you.'

'I'm just… I have no idea what this means. Us being together. I needed some space to think.' She met his eyes, feeling her heart still beating so hard she thought it might explode from her chest. 'What are we doing?'

'I have no idea, but I can't seem to stop.'

Dani felt her mind go blank as Valerio moved closer, kissing her worries away. There was comfort in knowing that he was just as powerless against this insane lust. She would worry about the consequences tomorrow. Tonight she would just live in the moment. In this perfect moment with him, with the steam of the water surrounding them, slickening their skin as the heat rose even higher.

He stopped for a moment, his eyes serious as he looked deeply into hers. 'How on earth did you ever think you were bad at this?'

Dani felt a blush creep up her cheeks. 'Um…let's just say when it comes to sex, it's the one area where I've never been an overachiever.'

He pressed the length of his erection against her, leaning down to nip gently at the sensitive skin of her collarbone. 'I strongly disagree, Miss Avelar. You're a natural.'

'Well, you're the first guy to ever get me to…to finish the race.'

He bit his lip, and something deep and dark glittered in

his eyes. 'Look at me. And if some idiot in your past told you it was a race, then he was playing the wrong sport.'

He dropped down onto his knees before her, framing her thighs with his strong hands. She shivered as his lips touched her upper thigh and began to kiss inwards.

'You should have been given more than a thousand orgasms by now. You've been robbed of years of pleasure,' he growled. 'I plan to set that right.'

Dani closed her eyes, trying to remain upright as he kept his promise again and again.

CHAPTER NINE

DANI AWOKE TO the sun streaming through the terrace doors and the glorious scent of coffee teasing her nostrils from somewhere in the distance. She sat up, momentarily disorientated as she looked around at her unfamiliar surroundings. It felt like a dream that she'd spent half the night experiencing the kind of orgasms and intense sexual chemistry she'd only ever read about in the books she'd devoured in her college dormitory. She'd never believed it could ever be for her.

Every encounter with Kitt, her ex, had been prearranged—no surprises. Even down to the type of underwear she had worn. Comparing her ex to Valerio now, after last night, was like looking at discount price wine after drinking a vintage reserve Chianti. It left a sour taste in her mouth and she knew she was worth more. But of course Valerio wasn't truly hers. He was just acting the part.

She quickly shut off her ridiculous thoughts with a bracing shower, throwing on her silk robe while she applied various beauty products and let her curls air-dry. She'd promised not to do any work, but nabbed her phone from the nightstand, telling herself she would just take five minutes to check the most important emails.

Twenty minutes later she was engrossed in a text conversation with an insanely curious Hermione when Valerio appeared beside her and snatched the device from her fingers.

'I was in the middle of reading something,' she squeaked, jumping up to grab the phone back—only to have him hold it further out of reach.

'You are technically on vacation, Miss Avelar.' He tilted his head to one side, lazily looking down over her scantily clad body. 'I'm demanding that you actually take the day off.'

'I can't just switch off like that. There are things I need to check on with the new plans…things that need my attention even while I'm relaxing.'

'So you don't trust the relevant teams to perform their jobs?'

She huffed out a breath, knowing he was right. She was checking on them for the simple reason that she wanted to. She couldn't let go of the relentless force telling her to keep on top of everything, to make sure nothing was missed.

'Well, since you can't control yourself, I'm cutting you off.' He smirked, tucking her phone into his back pocket. 'If you want this back, you're gonna have to work for it.'

She felt heat creep up her spine at his words, her nipples instantly peaking at the suggestion he'd created in her mind.

He raised a brow at her, evidently noticing her physical reaction. Suddenly shy, she closed her robe a little tighter and turned around in a pretence of opening up her small case and organising her clothes. When she looked back, a shadow had crossed his features, but he quickly disguised it with an easy smile.

'Get dressed quickly. We leave in fifteen minutes.'

'Leave…for where?'

She froze in the middle of selecting a T-shirt. His eyes twinkled with the kind of mischief she hadn't seen on his face in years. He was up to something, and it made her both nervous and strangely excited.

'We're going on an adventure. I plan to make a pirate of you yet.'

Valerio was stubbornly silent as he waited for her at the end of the wooden deck, and only gestured for her to follow him down the rocky steps in the cliff face towards the tiny bay below. He carried a small bag over his shoulder and stopped occasionally to help her down as the steps began to grow steep.

He tried and failed not to be distracted by how carefree she looked in simple knee-length capris and a tank top. She hadn't got a scrap of make-up on and her curls were tied back from her face with a colourful silk scarf she'd found in one of the kitchen drawers.

He'd been unsure of what she was thinking from the moment they'd spoken that morning, so he was glad he'd arranged today's trip before the events of last night.

It sounded so simple...calling it 'the events'. As if it was a small blip they could just forget about and move on from. But maybe that was what she wanted?

The thought caught him unaware, making him almost miss his footing on the steps.

She'd been skittish around him all morning—maybe she was having second thoughts? Surely if that was the case he should be relieved. And yet the thought of her drawing a line under whatever this was before he was ready made something tighten in his gut.

It was simply pride, he assured himself. No man wanted to feel rejected—especially not by the woman they were about to marry.

They emerged through the foliage onto the most beautiful little pebbled beach. The gentle curve of the land had created a perfect shallow pool where they could see tiny fish swimming.

Valerio gestured towards the end of the inlet, where a small wooden dock had been erected. The dock housed a single sleek black speedboat. 'I had this skippered over from the marina—figured I'd take a chance while we're here to get up to speed on our latest toys.'

'Oh, I see how this is. You get to do some work but I'm not allowed to?' she jibed, accepting his hand as she stepped down into the boat.

'This has never been work to me.' Valerio inhaled deeply as he fired up the engine and set his hands firmly on the wheel. '*Dio*, I forgot how good this feels.'

She sat back, watching the waves while he focused on pulling out from the small dock and gathering speed as they moved out onto open water. The boat was effortlessly smooth, and Valerio knew he was an expert at the helm. The familiar feeling that he had every time he was out on the water washed over him. It was as though he had finally come home.

He'd always had this affinity with the sea, this soul-deep connection. It was the thing that had bonded him and Duarte—their passion for sailing and exploring the world without fear.

Something within him stilled as he realised he had barely given his best friend a thought since the night before. Perhaps it was just the natural evolution of grief—the intensity of the pain wasn't any less but the frequency was bound to change and lessen. Guilt threatened, but he pushed it away, refusing to sully what he'd shared with Dani. He refused to mark it as wrong, somehow, when it was possibly the most right he had felt in a long time.

'Where are we going?' Dani moved to sit beside him,

speaking loudly above the noise of the speedboat crashing its way through the waves.

'You'll find out soon enough.' He smiled, his hands moving to take hers and place them on the helm. 'But for now it's time to ease you into your new life as an explorer. Step one: you will now captain this boat.'

She shook her head. 'No! I've never had the first idea how to drive one of these things. Take it back.'

She squeaked as he took a step away, leaving her alone and holding on for dear life.

'Just relax and feel the power in your hands. Feel the hull slice through each well.' He spoke next to her ear. 'Keep your eyes straight ahead. Brace your body and move with the water. Don't fight the current... Ease against it.'

Impulsively, he gently kneaded the tension in her shoulders. 'You're fighting it, Daniela. Breathe in deep and exhale... Lean into it.'

She rolled her eyes, doing as she was told, loosening her grip and easing forward. Her resulting smile was dazzling as she moved the boat over the swell without any tensing at all.

'Careful, now—I might start to think you're enjoying yourself,' he teased.

'I'm just very eager to earn that phone back.'

She pursed her lips against another smile as his hands covered hers on the wheel, joining her as they navigated over the water together.

Valerio had congratulated himself on his innovative idea of getting Dani to drive the speedboat to their surprise diving lesson excursion in Rodney Bay. But once he'd achieved the task of getting her out in the open water with their instructor, she had asked a million questions. The man had explained that this kind of diving was called Snuba—a cross between snorkelling and scuba diving—and that they would be connected to a small raft by air lines and safety lanyards the entire time.

Valerio tried not to laugh as Dani finally finished wrestling with the large diving mask on her face and took a long look at the depth of the water before them.

There was no certification required, because it was quite safe, but Dani still looked terrified now, as she stared down over the side of the boat.

Valerio advanced on her, his own mask making his voice sound muffled. 'We can just go back to the marina if you want?'

As he'd expected, she narrowed her eyes on him in challenge and turned to the instructor as he finished securing her weight belt, regulator and air line to the small safety raft. But as she moved to ease down the metal ladder on the side of the boat, her foot slid and she tumbled rather ungracefully sideways into the sea.

Valerio felt a shout leave his throat, moving to dive in after her, but the diving instructor stopped him with a hand on his chest, showing him he had a firm grip on her safety harness.

Sure enough, Dani emerged instantly and grabbed on to the large blue-and-white water tank floating beside the boat, pulling the regulator from her mouth and letting out a strangled cough that Valerio felt deep in his chest. He watched with awe as she gasped, holding on to the safety lanyard as she tried to adjust the mask on her face and remove the water.

'See, I'm a natural!' she shouted nervously. 'Well, Marchesi, are you coming in, or are you having second thoughts?'

Valerio finished his own set-up and eased down the ladder. They followed the guide's instructions, paddling out a specific distance from the boat before preparing to dive down. It had been a long time since his own deep-water scuba diving days, but he still felt the thrill of being out in the depths, with nothing below them but glittering blue adventure, pass through him.

He had only dived down about a metre when he looked to his side and realised Dani hadn't come with him. Using his own natural buoyancy, he kicked his way back up to where she still clutched tightly to the safety lanyard on the raft.

'Okay, so I was bluffing. You go ahead. I'll just watch from here!' She spoke over the noise of the waves.

'What about adventure?' He popped his own regulator out and pushed his mask up on his forehead, looking into her eyes. 'What about trusting me?'

'I do trust you. We both know that *you* can do this. You've always been brave and fearless. So don't let me hold you back. Go...please.'

'While you just wait around up here in the safe zone? Is that it?' He hardened his gaze. 'And how much happiness has *that* got you so far, Dani? All that fear and tiptoeing around...not taking any risks.'

'It's kept me alive, hasn't it?' she retorted, then gasped at the realisation of what she'd said, shaking her head. 'I'm going back to the boat. I'm sorry.'

'Look at me.'

He pulled her towards him, the water lapping at them on a light current. He could see the instructor watching from a short distance away. He didn't care—he wasn't letting her go without saying what he needed to say.

'There's a difference between actually feeling alive and just going through the motions of life. This, right here, being so far out of your comfort zone, is where you'll find the former.'

'What would you know? You've practically been a ghost for six months. Are you telling me that *you* feel alive?'

He took the hit of her words, knowing they were the truth. 'I deserve that. But the truth is I forgot how this felt—how healing it is to let yourself just be free. These past few days you've brought a part of me back to life that I'd thought lost for ever. I just want the chance to push you to do the same. The way I should have done the first time you asked for my help.'

She frowned, her bottom lip quivering slightly. For a moment he worried that he'd gone too far and opened too many old wounds. A part of him hoped that she would just swim away from him—that was what he deserved. Maybe it was just too little, too late, as the old saying went.

But, as usual, this woman had far more strength than anyone gave her credit for. She steeled her shoulders, taking one hand off the raft and extending it to him. 'I'll need your help. I'm shaking too hard to let go.'

For a moment Valerio stared down at her hand, shocked at such an open show of vulnerability and trust. Then, once she had the regulator in her mouth, he grabbed hold of her, feeling the tremors in her fingers vibrating against his own. He grasped her tightly, embracing her for a long moment as he pulled her bodily from the raft.

She stiffened, then moved with him, following his guidance as they trod water together in an easy rhythm. Valerio locked his eyes with hers, gesturing with the fingers on his free hand as he silently counted down from five and they slowly dropped below the surface together, hand in hand.

Daniela remembered, as a child, running after her brother through the gardens of their country home and always stopping the moment she got as far as the black gate that led into what Duarte had christened 'the haunted forest'.

It had been just a normal country wood, but the trees had been so dense it was almost pitch-dark once you were a few steps in.

Her brother would assure her it was okay, but her fear would always stop her from stepping nearer the shadows and into the unknown beyond. She'd needed to see safety ahead—not jump in and think later, the way he had.

Now, even as an adult, she trod softly and kept to her plans. She was fearless in the boardroom, and fearless in what she wanted for her career, but deep down she sometimes felt that she was still that child, staring at the line between safety and the unknown and keeping herself stubbornly behind that line.

But once she'd emerged from the water with Valerio's hand still in hers, she'd finally had a taste of what it was that pushed him to test his boundaries the way he did.

Pushing past her own fear had been terrifying, but that fear had got less and less as she'd dropped down into the ocean and seen the wonders that lay below the surface. Schools of tiny, vibrant coloured fish had danced through the current, and as Valerio had guided her deeper, she'd been entranced by the play of light on the seabed. She'd watched tiny creatures as they scuttled in between rocks and coral, and had spotted a couple of spiny lobsters locking claws with one another. The highlight of the dive had been the moment a sea turtle had swum nearby, its graceful body turning in the water and reflecting glorious beams of turquoise and blue light.

Dani had been utterly charmed by the world below the surface, filled with such simple quiet wonders. Wonders that she would never have seen from her spot on that life raft. She was grateful that Valerio had pushed her. Clearly he had seen something missing in her life—something she had never known she needed. And he was right. This feeling of adrenaline and triumph was healing.

She felt free. She felt as if she could take on the whole world.

The feeling carried on for the rest of the afternoon as, back on the speedboat, Valerio unveiled a small picnic lunch which he'd had delivered from a local restaurant. She knew he was still worried about her safety, and was thankful for the time he was giving them alone together, without their security detail.

Valerio took them out to a remote spot along the coast of Rodney Bay, from where they could view the impressive length of Pigeon Island in the distance. The food was from one of the finest chefs on the island: a delicious spread of green figs and fresh lobster, followed by a dessert of banana cake—a special St Lucian recipe that was deliciously spiced and sweet.

They talked for what felt like hours and she remembered exactly why she had always liked talking to him. He didn't just listen and nod; he gave his full focus to her—just like with everything he did.

She found herself telling him how she'd been relieved to cancel her plans for her own firm and how fear had always held her back. He seemed surprised at first, then quietly pensive as he listened to her ramble.

For the first time ever, she admitted out loud that it had been a need for comfort and closeness and safety that had driven her to work at Velamar after her parents had died. Then, when success had come upon her, she'd found excuses to not run on ahead into the unknown. She had held on tight to her position at Velamar, holding herself back by only taking on short-term outside contracts.

In turn, he told her of his decision to drop out of college and how disappointed his parents had been—how he had almost gone back just to please them. But he had known he would never have been happy in the perfect corporate tower with his perfect brother, as much as he wished he could have been. There had always been something wild in him—something that needed the open sea and the pull of adventure.

Sailing had always been his first love, so he'd bought his first yacht, and the tabloids' 'Playboy Pirate' had been born—a result of uncertainty and youthful pride.

A companionable silence fell between them and Dani realised that she'd always known there must be a lot more to Valerio Marchesi than anyone saw. He wasn't just the party-mad reprobate the media painted him as. Perhaps on some level he had purposely harnessed that image as a means to control his fall from the supposed grace of the Marchesi dynasty—to defend himself from the possibility of failure. It was strangely comforting to think that perhaps she wasn't completely alone in her fears.

Dani watched as Valerio began to pack away the remains of their food and tried not to focus on the swirl of emotions warring inside her. She was grateful to him for giving her this perfect day, but it wasn't gratitude that had her skin heating as he lay back on the blanket and let out a deep sigh of satisfaction.

They hadn't really talked about the night before and what it meant. Suddenly she found herself wondering if maybe he wanted to draw a line and leave it as a one-night stand. It would be understandable, considering the complications that carrying on would mean. But seriously… how was she ever going to look at him again without remembering all the things they'd done?

His body was an impossible distraction. He already looked more tanned and vital after only a few hours in the strong afternoon sunshine, and the pale blue linen shirt he wore only served to draw more attention to the impressive power of his shoulders and biceps. A memory of having those arms around her the night before rose up, her skin tingling with an electric current as she forced herself to look away.

'You have the most expressive features—did you know that?' He spoke softly, with a smile in his voice. 'What were you thinking just now?'

Dani looked back to see his sunglasses were off and the sun and sea were reflected in his cobalt-blue eyes. She cleared her throat, finding her mind blank and all her snappy retorts having deserted her. This man made her brain malfunction. She should be furious—should use that anger to stop herself from diving into this crazy fire that felt as if it was just waiting to explode between them again at any moment.

They were going to be married, for goodness' sake. This inconvenient attraction was fast turning into something deeper. The man was a drug—one taste and she couldn't think of anything but her next hit. But she couldn't torture herself like this. That way lay only danger and pain.

She bit her bottom lip, standing up and climbing down to the cockpit to grab a bottle of water in a vain effort to cool herself down. She heard him approach from behind.

'I told myself I'd let you lead the way—but, *Dio*, Daniela… I want to kiss you again.' He spoke softly. 'I haven't been able to think of anything else all day. Have you forgotten so easily?'

Her breath was shaky as she braced her hands on the smooth surface in front of her. 'I don't think I'll ever forget…but we both know this is a bad idea, Valerio.'

Warmth pressed against her from behind…the barest touch of strong, calloused fingers on her hips through the fabric of her dress. She closed her eyes, preparing herself to turn round and tell him that they had to be sensible. Then his lips traced featherlight kisses along her nape and she felt her traitorous body leap to attention. She pressed back against him, feeling him hard and aching, exactly the same way she felt deep inside.

She turned in his arms, her mouth finding his like a homing beacon, needing to taste him, needing all of him.

After a minute they were both frantic with need and tearing at one another's clothing. Her brief, momentary panic at being out in the open, where anyone could sail past and see them, was quickly overcome by his wicked whispers to enjoy the risk. So she did.

She leaned back against the side of the boat, spreading herself wide for him, letting him know that she was his for the taking. She was *all* his.

His guttural groan was almost enough to push her over the edge as he grasped both her thighs, his fingers like a brand on her skin as he forced her even wider to accept his length. His lovemaking was primal, and frantic with longing, as though he too felt as if at any moment one of them would come to their senses and bring things to a halt.

She felt the swaying movement of the boat underneath them as he thrust hard and fast, taking her closer and closer to heaven. As she came, she looked up at the sky and let out a sound of pure abandon, not caring who heard her.

After a second, slower exploration of one another, Valerio helped her back into her clothes and insisted she sail them back to the small dock at the villa. His powerful body behind her guided her the whole way. And as she helped him gather their things and finish docking, she felt laughter bubbling in her throat at the fact that not only had she sailed a boat and deep-dived off one in a single day, she had also had two very public orgasms on it too.

'Something funny?' He raised a brow, offering her his hand as she stepped off the wooden pier onto the soft pebbles of the beach.

She smiled. 'I can't remember the last time I just felt… happy.'

'I'll never look at that boat again without remembering you, spread out against the mahogany deck with the glow of another orgasm on your skin.' He pulled her close. 'How many is that now? Not nearly enough yet.'

His use of the word 'yet' seemed to break a spell of sorts. It seemed that both of them had remembered there was a time limit on whatever it was that they were doing. She bit back the words on her tongue—the urge to ask him when it would be enough. When it would be over.

They both knew that there was no room for casual sex in their arrangement, that they had to get a handle on this. Besides, she wasn't sure 'casual' even began to describe the need she felt when he touched her.

She had agreed to share a home with him when they got back to Europe—but to sleep in a bed alone, knowing he was separated from her by only a thin wall. She shut her eyes against that unwelcome reminder of reality.

'I'm not ready for today to be over yet,' she whispered against his chest as she listened to the sound of the waves crashing against the pebbles on the shoreline.

'Who said it was over?' Valerio smiled. 'You may have tackled your fear of open water, but you have far from learned your lesson about pleasure.'

'I'm pretty sure I have bite marks on my neck that contradict that statement.' She laughed as they began the tortuous climb back up the cliff steps to the villa.

'Not all pleasure is sex, Daniela,' he scolded, his eyes wicked and full of mischief.

He smiled down at her as they reached the top step,

then turned to look up at the house—and his entire body suddenly froze.

Dani bumped straight into his muscular back, clinging to the material of his shirt to stop herself from toppling backwards, down the way they'd come. 'Valerio, what on earth—?'

She gasped out the breath she'd sucked in, and then followed his narrowed gaze to see a small gathering of people on the upper deck, peering down at them with interest.

'Is that your brother up there?' Dani spotted Rigo Marchesi, smiling down at them, and by his side she was pretty sure were Valerio's mother and father.

Valerio cursed something in fierce Italian under his breath, gripping her hand tighter and hauling her up by his side. 'We might have to hold off on the pleasure. It appears that my family have invited themselves to our wedding.'

CHAPTER TEN

IT TRANSPIRED THAT his family, namely his mother, had arrived to perform an intervention of sorts.

Valerio held his annoyance in check by a thin thread, his gaze anxiously seeking out his fiancée throughout dinner as she was practically interrogated over their sudden alliance and why they'd selfishly kept it hidden for so long. He felt the tension building between his brows as he watched his mother and sister-in-law fawn over Dani's engagement ring at the opposite end of the table. The three women had barely stopped talking—and his mother was asking question after question about what exactly they'd planned for the wedding. He had been a fool to think that Renata Marchesi would pass up the chance to be mother of the groom a second time.

His father had been his usual reserved self throughout dinner so far, but Valerio's brother, Rigo, had more than made up for it with his subtle ribbing about how relaxed and well-rested Valerio looked.

'I hope we haven't interrupted anything here between you and your fiancée?' Rigo said now, raising one dark brow as he took a sip of red wine.

'Should your wife be flying all this way at this stage in her pregnancy?' Valerio changed the subject swiftly.

'She's still in her second trimester. We decided to have

the older girls minded and treat ourselves to a romantic weekend before the baby arrives.' Rigo raised his glass to his wife, meeting her eyes across the table for one heated moment.

Valerio cleared his throat pointedly. 'A pity you couldn't have taken your romantic weekend somewhere else, rather than ruining my private elopement,' Valerio said, feeling a strange mixture of discomfort and awe at the fact his family had taken the time to fly all this way.

Nicole Marchesi stood up and moved to take the seat beside her husband. 'Dani's friend Hermione has already told us the truth about your trip here.'

Dani froze at the end of the table. 'Hermione has spoken to you?'

'She styled our wedding years ago, and we've kept in touch. She's horrified about the whole thing. Really, Valerio, I can't believe you.'

Valerio felt heat creep up the back of his neck. 'You don't understand the whole situation, and I didn't want to worry you.'

'I understand very well.' His mother stood up, censure in her tone. 'Romantic elopement? You didn't even book a proper venue to say your vows, for goodness' sake. It's a disgrace!'

'Papà thinks you've got your fiancée pregnant.' Rigo's eyes twinkled.

Valerio exhaled slowly and saw Dani's shoulders drop with relief. Her friend clearly hadn't told his family the whole story—just enough to ensure this intervention of sorts.

'I know my son.' Renata turned to Dani, shaking her head. 'He's an impulsive fool, which might seem romantic right now, but he doesn't think things through. *Per l'amore di Dio*, I don't care if she's pregnant or not. You're on one of the most romantic islands in the world and you were going to get married in a courthouse?'

Valerio had tensed at the word 'impulsive', hating it that his family fully expected him to be running off for a shotgun wedding. Clearly they still painted him as a wild fool. But they knew nothing of his life—only what he allowed them to see.

'Daniela is not pregnant. We were just trying to keep things small and intimate.'

He groaned inwardly, knowing that calculating look in his mother's eyes all too well. She wasn't deliberately trying to be unkind. She was big on creating memories, ensuring beautiful moments were made at important events. To Renata Marchesi, very little would seem more important than ensuring her second son got married in a way that befitted their family name.

'Small and intimate?' She nodded. 'I can do that. Just give me twenty-four hours.'

As his brother let out a bark of laughter, Valerio pinched the bridge of his nose between his fingers. He should have expected this. His parents' wedding was still talked about and they had been married for thirty-five years. They had stood together to watch their oldest son say his vows in a spectacular ceremony at a French chateau, and were now feeling the joy of welcoming grandchildren into their growing family.

How could he tell them that he didn't want an audience for what was only going to be a short-lived venture—another perceived failure to add to his ever-growing list? He couldn't tell them about the nature of his marriage to Dani without revealing the danger she was in. Maybe some day he would tell them the truth, but right now he had no choice but to go along with the charade.

The evening wound down in companionable conversation, with Rigo taking a moment apart from the others to quietly update him on the plans he'd put in place to tie up Daniela's inheritance and ask what progress had been made on the investigation.

After a while they joined the women on the terrace, and Valerio was once again drawn back into the charade of normal family life. He rested his arm across Dani's shoulders, feeling her settle her weight against him.

Across the table, Nicole announced that the baby had started kicking that week. Dani's eyes lit up with wonder as she asked if it hurt, at which Renata laughed and said that some day soon she might find out for herself.

He felt her tense against him, moving away ever so subtly. Dani's withdrawal got under his skin for some reason. As did the way his brother interacted so easily with his family, making jokes and talking about plans to build a tree house during the summer.

He had never before been jealous of the pressure Rigo had been put under as heir to the Marchesi fortune. But right now, seeing his brother rest his hand possessively across his wife's stomach, he felt an uncomfortable tightening in his chest. Needing to excuse himself, he stood and moved inside the house.

In the master bathroom, he splashed cold water on his face and glowered into the mirror. *Get it together, Marchesi.*

Dani appeared in the doorway behind him, her eyes filled with concern. God, she was so beautiful. It almost hurt to look at her without touching her. He wanted to take her, to consume her until the emptiness inside him was full of her laughter and her brilliance.

It was hard not to feel as if he was using her like a drug when the effect of just being in her company was so addictive. And it wasn't just the sex, either. He enjoyed being

ent looking

with her...found himself looking for ways to make her smile. What was happening to him? They had agreed on a time limit for whatever this thing was between them. And neither of them was interested in risking their business partnership over a fling. And it *was* just a fling.

A fling that was about to escalate into a marriage.

Valerio turned around and leaned back against the vanity unit. She didn't move closer and he told himself he was relieved. If his face showed anything of the chaos of emotions warring inside him, she would probably turn around and call off the whole wedding.

She *should* call it off. She deserved so much better than this. She deserved more than a brief few days of hot sex with a man who didn't come close to deserving her. She deserved the wedding of her dreams with a good man who was reliable and logical and safe—everything he could never be for her. And this fictional perfect husband would make her happy—he would be with her as she carried their perfect children and lived her life in blissful happiness.

Valerio was shocked at the swift kick of jealousy in his gut.

'You left the table so suddenly I was worried.' She stepped forward, reaching out to touch his arm in a soft caress. 'What's wrong?'

Her gentle touch was more than he could process. The pressure in his forehead was close to the breaking point and he couldn't seem to gather his thoughts.

'You shouldn't have followed me.'

Even as he said the words, he knew he didn't mean them. He knew he wanted nothing more than for her to keep looking at him that way, caring about him.

A look of uncertainty flashed in her beautiful eyes and she quickly removed her hand. 'I'll get back to the others, then.'

'I'm fine.'

He turned away from her, splashing water over his face again and avoiding her burning gaze.

'Before I go, I want to talk to you about this whole ceremony thing.' Dani cleared her throat to try to stop the sudden shake in her voice. 'The flowers...the violin players...'

'My mother enjoys making an occasion of things, and I can't deny her after the year she's had. I hope that's okay?'

He was watching her reflection in the mirror, clearly waiting until she nodded.

'They're all expecting to see a happy couple saying their vows, so that is what we will give them. We have no other choice.'

Dani felt his words hit her somewhere in the chest with all the subtlety of a sledgehammer on porcelain. She had followed him expecting him to have been set a little off balance by this sudden seismic shift in their plans. But this... It was as if shutters had come down over his eyes, blocking her out.

Confusion mixed with hurt, and anger rose briefly, before she shut them down tight and stretched her lips into a smile.

'If anything, it will add to the authenticity of the whole thing,' she said, and a breathless ghost of a laugh escaped her lips, seeming to bounce off the bathroom walls, mocking her. 'I'm a little jealous that I didn't think of it, to be honest.'

He turned around and stared at her, a muscle in his jaw beginning to tic rather menacingly. She waited for him to speak, in her own foolish mind still clinging on to a thread of hope that he might have something good to say. Something that wasn't about the coldness in his eyes, the detachment.

'We have no other choice,' he'd said. As if he'd already been forcing himself to do this and now it was becoming an unbearable spectacle.

The fact that she had felt so connected to him for a moment just now only served to cheapen things further, making her feel weak and used even though he'd made it quite clear where he stood when it came to any feelings between them.

She felt the shameful threat of tears building in her eyes and turned quickly towards the door.

'Dani, wait.'

She turned back, swallowing hard past the lump in her throat and pasting on another bright smile. 'Yes?'

'I… I just wanted to say that I don't regret this weekend,' he said stiffly, his expression hard and intense. 'I don't regret whatever this was between us.'

'Neither do I.' She smiled—as though her heart *wasn't* breaking into a thousand tiny pieces at his use of the past tense. 'It was…exactly what I needed. Thank you.'

She turned away again before she completely lost her composure and moved to close the door softly behind her. She wasn't prepared for him to barge through it, bearing down on her in the hallway.

'"Thank you"?' he growled quietly, eyes glinting like sapphires in the evening light.

'What do you *want* me to say?' She felt her head shaking, her insides trembling dangerously. She needed to get away from him—get some breathing room before she totally embarrassed herself.

'I didn't do this as some sort of *service*, if that's what you're telling yourself.' His voice was low and gravelly, his eyes refusing to leave hers. 'The marriage is one thing, but let there be no misunderstanding that this…whatever this energy is between you and I…was just for us.'

'Valerio…' She bit her lip as he moved towards her and flattened his hands against the wall on either side of her head.

'Tell me you don't want me,' he whispered. 'Even just one more time.'

'Why don't you tell me what it is that *you* want, Valerio?'

She heard the longing in her voice. Felt the choking fear of this coming to an end and the foolish desire for him to offer her everything she dreamed of. She didn't just want one more time. She couldn't bear the idea of accepting whatever little offering he wanted to give to get her out of his system and move on to someone else. She wanted it all and it terrified her.

'Right now? I just want you to kiss me,' he murmured huskily.

She reached up, her lips seeking his. Her hands dug into his hair and pulled him close. The growl he let out in his throat sent heat flooding straight to her groin. God, would he ever stop setting her off like this?

But he had never given any indication that he thought of this as anything more. He remained rooted firmly in the present, refusing to think ahead, to see the risks. She couldn't ignore the red flags any longer—she couldn't place all her faith in blind hope. She was no longer just falling into dangerous territory with this powerful, fierce warrior of a man. She had plummeted right into the unknown.

She was in love with him.

She broke the kiss, closing her eyes tight against the realisation, her throat convulsing wildly as his breath fanned her cheek. His delicious scent was everywhere, his warm body so close, and she could feel his eyes on her. But she had a feeling that even if he wasn't right there she would still feel him. He had climbed his way into her chest, folding himself around her heart.

What had she got herself into?

'Are you crying?' He held her chin, tilting up her face with a deep frown.

She swiped the tears from her face, forcing herself to meet his eyes even as she felt her heart break. 'Valerio... let's not make this harder than it needs to be. I don't think either of us are ready for the fallout. I think...this needs to end now. While we can still go back to being friends and partners in this arrangement.'

Footsteps sounded in the hallway, and without warning, Valerio's mother advanced on them, a phone hooked in between her ear and her shoulder. Dani scrambled to rub the moisture from her eyes and regain some composure.

'Daniela, I just wanted to check if you prefer white roses or...' Renata paused, taking in the sight of the two of them standing stiffly side by side.

Dani groaned inwardly, knowing her nose was likely bright pink and her feelings completely obvious. She prayed that the smile she forced would be convincing and mumbled something about adoring white roses before quickly excusing herself and going back into the bathroom.

She slid the lock closed before moving to the mirror and grabbing a wet flannel to scrub at the slightly smeared mascara under her eyes. Mortification crept up her chest and heated her cheeks.

Closing her eyes, she scrambled for her phone and hit the button to call Hermione, but was greeted by her friend's voicemail. She compensated by sending a single text, all in capital letters, asking what on earth she'd been thinking to tell Nicole about their elopement. No reply came.

Eventually she was going to have to leave this bathroom

and face her fiancé. It was no big deal, she told herself, and
straightened her shoulders and took a few deep breaths.
She was in the business of presenting an image of what
people wanted to see. She could do this—she could pretend to be his adoring fiancée for the rest of this trip. She
could stand by Valerio's side and vow to love and cherish
him as his wife without falling to pieces, couldn't she?

She sucked in a sharp breath. No big deal… No big
deal at all.

CHAPTER ELEVEN

THERE WAS NO opportunity for Valerio to continue their conversation, as they weren't given any more time alone together. At the insistence of Renata, the men were hurried away to stay in one of the new yachts on the marina for the night, while the women stayed at the villa.

Valerio had explained the heightened security presence as his own need for protection, which his family had accepted with a slight look of worry. In the short time since Dani had come crashing back into his life, he had almost forgotten that the world still presumed him mad with paranoia.

Now Valerio stood alone on the bow of Velamar's brand-new luxury mega-yacht and tried to ignore the sense of restlessness that had hounded him since leaving Dani at the villa. His father and his brother had gone ahead to create an impromptu bachelor party, promising that it wouldn't involve anything inappropriate but that he would need his wits about him.

Valerio looked at his watch. He had another five minutes before they expected him to follow. He guessed it would involve gambling of some sort. His father was an avid poker player and was known for his skill. He sighed. Even the thought of a night of mindless gambling wasn't enough to calm the irritation brought by how badly he had handled things earlier.

She had *thanked* him for bedding her, as if he had been doing her a service. As though he had been trying to assuage his guilt by giving her orgasms as penance? His jaw tightened with anger at how little she must think of herself if she believed such utter nonsense. There was nothing charitable about his behaviour towards her.

If he'd been a better man, he would have kept his attraction under control. He wouldn't have complicated their arrangement and risked the fragile friendship they had formed. He had played with fire and ignited a full-blown blaze. He should be thankful that she'd seen sense and ended things.

But even now being away from her felt wrong, somehow, even though he knew she wasn't any safer with him by her side. He had left his two best security men with strict instructions to ensure she was completely secure. He had finalised all the necessary arrangements for the surprise he'd planned for her tomorrow. He'd wanted to see her face when she saw it, but it was probably better if he kept his distance until the ceremony. He wished they hadn't had that argument…that his family hadn't arrived and set off all alarm bells in his mind.

But above all, he realised a part of him missed her, needed her company, as if they had spent years of this fragile new intimacy together—not just a few days.

He frowned at the thought. He *didn't* need her—he had always made sure he didn't need anyone. He was Mr No Strings. They had just both been celibate for a long time, so it was only natural that it would add to the kind of explosive sexual chemistry they had… It was a recipe for this addictive feeling. But he was not going to become hooked. They'd had one amazing weekend of blowing off some steam and that was over.

Gritting his teeth, he closed his eyes and focused on the sound of the sea lapping against the stern to try to unwind the tension in his gut. Maybe having his family here planning this wedding had got under his skin? There was no other explanation for the crazy thoughts he had been entertaining since he'd left the villa.

He knew that someone like him could never have the kind of stable, normal lifestyle his father and brother enjoyed. It was utterly ridiculous. Did he actually think he could give a woman like Dani the life she deserved?

He had already resigned himself to being alone until he found out who was behind Duarte's murder. He hadn't thought further beyond that. It was hard enough just getting through each day with his rigid handle on his PTSD intact. He was broken. His body and mind had been damaged and scarred and, no matter how hard he tried, he would always have to bear the reminders of what had happened in Brazil—a catastrophic event that he had caused by being his usual impulsive, reckless self.

His head security guard appeared, snapping him out of his thoughts. 'Mr Marchesi, there's a man here to see you. Says it's urgent.'

It was his private investigator from Rio, Juan, his face looking entirely the worse for wear and his clothes dishevelled.

'You didn't answer my calls, so I put a flight on your tab.' He stepped forward, placing a tablet computer in his hands. 'You can thank me later.'

The man sank down onto a nearby lounger as Valerio's eyes scanned the file, seeing Angelus Fiero's name. He felt anger begin to surge within him, expecting the worst. But the contents of the report were so far from what he'd expected that he found himself needing to sit down.

'Get me Fiero on the phone—now.' His voice was a dry rasp.

'He's currently in an operating theatre after sustaining a gunshot wound.' Juan sat forward. 'He'll survive. He went after them himself, it seems. The politician who ordered the kidnapping is dead and all evidence of the blackmail material he'd been keeping about Duarte has been destroyed, thanks to Fiero's clever manoeuvrings over the past few weeks. I believe the threat to Miss Avelar has been neutralised.'

Valerio felt the air leave his lungs. Angelus Fiero had been on their side all along. 'How do we know there aren't still others who are waiting to take over? How do I know she isn't still in danger?'

'Fiero has used his intel to turn the tables on a few other corrupt individuals linked to the Brazilian government. He's had the Avelar land and properties in Brazil made untouchable. They can only be used for charity, so they're worthless to any other money-grabbing corrupt developers now. As is every other piece of her inheritance. She's safe. I'm sure of it.'

Valerio nodded slowly, wondering why he didn't feel a sense of elation at the news.

He thanked Juan, and instructed his security guard to ensure that the PI was paid handsomely for his efforts. Alone again, he debated heading straight over to the villa and telling Dani the news. Telling her everything. But it was late…and he didn't want his mother to overhear their conversation.

Renata Marchesi was going to be upset enough at the cancellation of her dream island wedding ceremony. Because if there was no longer a threat, there was no longer any need for a wedding. He could tell his family what had happened—why he had been so secretive. Maybe one day they would all look back on this and laugh.

They would have made one another miserable anyway... he and Dani. But, then again, maybe they might have found some way to be happy in their arrangement...

He stood still for a long time in the dark, staring out at the inky black waves as he imagined what his life might have looked like if things had been different.

After a fitful night of sleep, alone in the bed that still smelled like Valerio, Dani barely registered the conversation at the breakfast table. It was dawn, and the whole house was buzzing with activity in preparation for the wedding. Renata and Nicole were talking about the details of the ceremony planned for that evening—a sunset wedding, followed by an intimate family dinner prepared by a world-famous chef who lived on the island.

The moment she was able to, she slipped away and wandered out onto the deck, staring at the glorious sunrise as it kissed pink and orange along the waves and wondering how on earth she had managed to get herself into such a mess. It was her wedding day and she was utterly miserable. If she'd been the brave, fearless type, she would have just run away. She almost smiled, imagining herself commandeering Valerio's boat and sailing towards the horizon.

Heels tapped across the deck towards her and she inhaled, turning and preparing herself to tell even more lies to this wonderful family who had made her feel so accepted.

But it wasn't Renata or Nicole who stood in front of her.

'Jeez, this place is locked up tighter than a prison.' Hermione smirked. 'I had to show my ID and video-call your fiancé just to get his goons to let me past the gates.'

Dani's mind had barely recognised her best friend's smiling face before she launched herself full force into Hermione's arms. It was as though all the pressures of the day had been released, and she did nothing but hold her tight for a long time.

When they finally separated, she took a step back and lightly punched Hermione in the bicep.

'Hey, is that how you thank me for blowing off a job with royalty to come and be your maid of honour?'

'I wasn't planning to have an elaborate wedding at all until *you* intervened!' Dani said under her breath. 'His family aren't supposed to know anything about what's really going on here.'

'By that you mean the fact that you're having hot sex with your soon-to-be husband?' Hermione said dryly. 'That's utterly scandalous, Dani. How will they ever recover?'

Dani suddenly regretted the instant messages she'd been firing back and forth with her best friend. 'Be serious. It's not a real marriage—none of this is real—and it's only going to hurt them once they find out it's all lies.'

'*Is* it all lies, though?' Hermione asked softly. 'Because the look on your face in that picture you sent me of you two out on the boat… It's the first time I've seen you look happy in a long time. Does he make you happy?'

Dani swallowed hard, turning around to hide the sudden flood of wetness to her eyes. Yes, he made her happy. He made her feel stronger than she'd thought she was capable of being. He made her feel beautiful and powerful and utterly devastated all in the space of one day. He made her feel far too much for it not to be utterly catastrophic to her soul once he eventually walked away. Because he didn't feel anything for her other than a fleeting physical attraction and a responsibility to keep her safe.

'Dani...' Hermione spoke softly, laying a hand on her shoulder. 'Did I mess up here? I just thought of the wedding you lost out on before, and the awfulness of the past few years, and I wanted something beautiful for you.'

Silence fell between them. Then Dani exhaled a slow, shaking breath and turned to press her face into her friend's shoulder. 'Thank you. I'm really glad you're here now.'

They were interrupted by the arrival of Renata and Nicole, holding champagne glasses. Sharing a pointed look with Hermione, she joined their toast to a beautiful wedding and a happy marriage to follow.

'I'm sorry now that I didn't buy a proper dress.' Dani frowned, realising for the first time that the simple beige linen dress she'd packed was really not going to be appropriate any longer. She watched as the three women exchanged a look of pure mischief, and then Hermione leaned towards Dani's future mother-in-law and whispered in her ear.

'I asked these ladies to wait until I got here to surprise you,' Hermione said, and smiled, pulling her by the hand towards the house.

Dani followed Hermione upstairs to the master bedroom—Valerio's bedroom. At some point it had been filled with boxes of flowers and small bags bearing designer labels. Hanging on the frame of the four-poster bed was a large white garment bag.

Dani felt time stop as Hermione slid the zip downwards and revealed the most spectacular blush-coloured gown she had ever set eyes on. It was the dress Dani had pointed out to her friend at a fashion week over a year ago, when she had confessed that her ex had influenced the choice of her first traditional white wedding gown, which she'd had to embarrassingly return when he jilted her.

Hermione had been outraged, but had never brought up the conversation again. Clearly she had not forgotten.

In a blur, Dani was undressed and zipped into the gown, awed at how it fitted perfectly to her body like a second skin and flowed in all the right places.

'You remembered... How did you get this?' she breathed slowly, her hands stroking the material with awe. It was the same one. There was no doubting it. Even down to the hand-sewn rose-shaped gathering on the bodice.

'Your fiancé called my office yesterday, the moment he realised the wedding was going to be more than a simple affair. He asked me to choose the perfect dress as a wedding gift—and to bring myself, of course.' Hermione moved beside her, tipping her face up and wiping away a small errant tear that had slipped out. 'This is a *real* wedding, Dani. You both just haven't realised it yet.'

Dani thought of Valerio's thoughtfulness in helping her tackle her fear of the ocean. The way he'd held her as he told her how beautiful she was. The way he'd looked into her eyes as they made love. The sense of overwhelming rightness between them.

Now she was being told that he had gone so far as to make sure she had her best friend here, to obtain her dream dress... It was more than anyone had ever done for her before... It was too much.

She was overcome with the need to know what it all meant. What they meant to one another.

'I need to go to him.' She turned to Hermione and saw her friend's eyes light up with glee. 'There's no way I can marry him without laying everything out on the table, consequences be damned. I'm done with being afraid.'

'I like this change in you.' Hermione hugged her close. 'And I hope that man knows how lucky he is.'

They both knew there was no way Renata would allow

Dani to leave without asking a million questions and worrying, so Hermione offered to spin a story and cause a distraction while Dani slipped away.

She briefly considered the speedboat, and a dramatic exit, but she wasn't quite that adventurous yet. So she walked up the driveway to the small hut that housed the two security guards and turned on her best smile, matched with her most authoritative tone. She didn't have time for any of their safety protocol nonsense.

'I need to see your boss. Right now.'

Valerio had just stepped out of the shower when he heard the door to the master cabin burst open. Like something from a dream, Dani walked into the bathroom, her eyes filled with blazing emotion.

'You're wearing the dress…' His voice was somewhere between disbelief and wonder, and a part of him was cursing fate for throwing this vision at him when he had been preparing to go to her and call off their entire wedding. 'Why are you here?'

'I had a whole speech planned on the drive over…' Her voice shook as she looked down and realised he only wore a towel. 'Oh, God… I should go.'

Valerio gripped her wrist and pulled her back towards him. 'Don't.'

She moved closer to him, her eyes filled with a look that both terrified and delighted him. A look he had no right to see. She needed to know all the facts. She needed to know that she didn't have to trust him or rely on him any longer. That she didn't need him.

'I need to talk to you before…' She paused, one hand reaching out to lay against his bare chest. 'Before we go ahead with this.'

'I need to talk to you too.' He inhaled deeply, glad that

they were alone for this moment. That he could give her privacy, away from prying eyes and ears.

'I lied,' she said suddenly. 'I don't want things to end. The thought of not being with you again is unbearable.'

With disbelief and shock, he pulled her closer until they stood chest to chest. 'I've hardly been able to stop thinking of this...of what you do to me. It's like I have no control when it comes to you.'

'Me too.'

Her voice was a husky whisper as she pressed herself to him, her eyes widening as she brushed against the hard ridge of his erection. The look of instant heat she gave him was enough to bring him close to the edge as his lips lowered to hers in a fury of urgent need and frustration.

The sound she made against his mouth was half surprise and half seductive whimper as she slowly melted against him. His hands cupped the delicious curve of her behind, grinding her against the unbearable hardness that ached to be inside her.

Dani felt the urgency in him like a rising tide as he walked her backwards until she was pressed against the cool tiled walls. His eyes glimmered with intent as he slowly raised the full skirt of her wedding dress up her thighs. The material was light, and easily folded around her waist. She worried for a split second about crushing the fabric, but then decided it would be fine.

He moved to touch her, to feel how slick and hot and ready she was for him. His eyes darkened to the colour of a raging storm.

Her white lace underwear refused to stay to one side, and he let out a low growl, tearing at one side and throwing the scrap of lace to the floor. She bit her lower lip, feeling a thrill go through her at such a primal display. His lips nuzzled against her neck, biting softly.

'*Dio...* I need to be inside you right now.'

'Yes...' she breathed, feeling his hands grip the curve of one thigh and lift it so she was spread wide for him.

He dropped his towel and slid into her easily, her body singing out in sweet relief at being filled with such perfect hard heat. His thrusts were demanding, but his rhythm was just what she needed—she needed to feel that warm tension building deep inside her.

Every hard stroke brought her higher, and she clamped a hand over her mouth as she fought not to moan. They were far enough away from anyone else on the yacht not to truly risk being caught, but the thrill of it only added to her arousal.

Without warning, he gripped her other thigh and lifted her against the wall for even deeper access. She stiffened and tried to stop him. He shut off her protests with his mouth, the urgency in his body telling her he was far from burdened by her size. He pulled at one strap of her dress with his teeth, freeing one dark nipple above the fabric and taking it greedily into his mouth.

With his head bent low she could clearly see the reflection of him taking her in the mirror on the opposite wall. He followed her gaze, his eyes wicked as sin as he quickened his pace, giving no mercy as he took her over and over until she cried out against her hand.

'Just look at you,' he growled, his eyes almost reverent. 'Do you see how beautiful you are?'

She looked at the flush on her cheeks as she felt pleasure mounting, at the plump swollen flesh of her lips. She looked like a stranger.

She felt utterly weightless in his arms as she rode out her climax, feeling it crest and take her like a rush of electricity until her entire body shook. He was right there with her. A few hard thrusts and he came hard inside her, his head tilted back and eyes closed tight as though he were in pain.

After a moment he stepped back and grabbed a towel from the rack, wetting it and kneeling down to cleanse her. The movement was so caring she felt her throat clench. He didn't meet her eyes, however, as he stood up and put himself to rights. Then he reached down to grab her torn underwear from the floor and stared at it with such ferocity that she inhaled a sharp breath.

'I didn't mean for that to happen.'

He spoke with his jaw tight, and there was a sudden tension in him that made Dani feel the need to reassure him.

'Well… That's not exactly what I came here for, either.' She forced a small laugh, still slightly out of breath as she pulled her dress down.

'What *did* you come here for, then?' he asked roughly.

'Because I was just on my way to see you.'

She tried not to read into his words, into his implication that sex was all they had. Even though he had told her that was all he was capable of giving her. They'd agreed to end things, but here they were after ten seconds alone together, panting in the aftermath of what had possibly been the most intense lovemaking she'd experienced with him. That had to mean something, didn't it?

'I came here to say that I'm not going to marry you today without telling you how I really feel.' She inhaled once more, fighting the twist of anxiety in her stomach at the leap of faith she was about to take. 'I can't pretend to be your wife, Valerio. Because I'm in love with you, and the only way I'm marrying you today is if it's real.'

Silence stretched between them for a moment, and she felt her heartbeat racing wildly in her chest. She forced herself to stand tall and meet his eyes, knowing she owed herself this moment of risk. She knew she would never regret giving him her heart, even if he handed it right back and walked away.

'I don't want to be your wife in name only. I want it all. I want everything that you said you can never give me.'

'What if I told you there was no need for us to get married any more?' He spoke quietly, his eyes stubbornly refusing to meet hers.

'What do you mean?'

'The threat to you has been neutralised.'

'You should have come straight to tell me. How long were you planning to keep this to yourself?'

'My private investigator informed me late last night. I waited to confirm the details myself and it's true.'

He told her of Angelus Fiero's involvement, about the blackmail and the corrupt politician. He went on laying everything out on the table until his head hurt and she sagged back against the wall, her face filled with disbelief.

'You said you were coming to see me this morning,' she said. "Were you planning to call off the wedding?'

'Yes, of course,' he said quickly, then caught her sharp wince. 'I mean... I was going to tell you everything. We both agreed that this marriage was just for your protection, but now...there is no more danger. Does that not change things?'

She nodded once, her lips pressed into a thin line. 'Of course... It changes everything. I just wish you'd told me before I came here.'

'Dani, wait.' He placed his arm on the wall to stop her leaving. 'I've told you who I am... I've told you that I'm not the right kind of guy for you. You need to go and find out who you are and what you want without the threat of danger influencing you.'

'Valerio. I just laid my entire heart on the line.' She

flashed him a deep look of disdain. 'My feelings for you never depended on you being wrong or right for me. I accepted you for the man you are—not the one you think you should be.'

'I don't want to leave things like this.' He frowned, hating it that he was hurting her but knowing he had to let her go.

'If you don't have anything else to say, then I'm going to leave, before anyone sees me in this dress.'

She waited another moment, refusing to look up at him, before disappearing quickly through the doorway and out into the hall beyond.

He let her go, telling himself that it was better this way even as everything in him fought to follow her. As though distance might help, he launched himself into the first speedboat he could find in the yacht's docking bay, pushing the vessel to its limits, needing to feel the lightness that always came with being on the water.

The lightness didn't come.

After a while he gave up punishing the boat and cut the engine, bobbing in the open water as he watched the sun rise higher in the sky. He could be selfish, he thought. He could follow her and take all that precious love she'd offered for himself. He could pretend she wouldn't grow to hate him, even though everything in him knew she would. He wasn't built for the kind of love she needed.

She would move on from this and start anew...find someone better. As for him... He wasn't so changed that he would pine over a woman, was he? He cursed aloud, slamming his fist against the wheel. He couldn't feel any pain, but the awful emptiness in his chest was a different matter entirely.

CHAPTER TWELVE

THE AIR IN Rio de Janeiro was warm and heavy as Dani walked out of the airport and into a waiting car. Blissfully, the chauffeur was not eager for conversation, so she had plenty of time to rest her eyes and prepare herself for whatever lay ahead.

Heartbreak was just another inconvenience right now—along with Angelus Fiero, who had refused to stop calling her every day for the past week until she'd reluctantly agreed to book a flight to Rio and hear him out.

It wasn't that she didn't feel gratitude for the part the older man had played in bringing justice against those who had been responsible for so much pain and loss. But something about coming back to Brazil felt wrong, somehow.

It was as if she was adrift amongst the old shadows of a life and had no idea how to navigate. The last time she'd set foot in Rio, she'd had her parents and her brother by her side, her family unit intact. Memories of her childhood were just as foggy as the cloudy sky above, which threatened to spill with rain at any moment.

Dani frowned as her car came to a stop outside wrought-iron gates and looked up at the concrete façade of the Avelar family villa for the first time in over two decades. It seemed like a lifetime ago that her ten-year-old self had said goodbye to the palatial mansion just outside the city, as she was torn away from the only home she'd ever known and forced to start over in England.

Was it any wonder that she had clung to her twin amidst all the constant change in their lives over the past two decades?

As she stepped out into the warm afternoon and told the driver to wait, Valerio's words rang in her ears. *'You need to figure out who you are and what you really want.'* The trouble was, she *had* figured it out. She had told him exactly what she wanted and who she wanted.

The memory of Valerio's eyes before she'd walked away from him seemed like a dream. She shook her head. Had it really been a week since she'd seen him? It seemed as if only hours had passed since St Lucia. Since he'd held her hand as they dived into the depths of the ocean together... since he had looked into her eyes in Monte Carlo after he had kissed her for the first time in front of all those people...since she'd felt the heat and power of his body as he'd turned the tables on her that first night and tied her to her own bed.

Anger fuelled her as she dug through her bag in search of the old brass key. She rubbed roughly at the space in the centre of her chest, refusing to give in to another bout of tears and self-pity. She had done enough of that in the days after she'd returned to London.

She'd left St Lucia a week ago, returning to her tidy white apartment in Kensington and immediately sending a formal letter announcing that she was completely removing herself as an active partner of Velamar. Valerio had not attempted to contact her, but she'd told herself she didn't care that he was glad she wouldn't be working alongside him. It was irrelevant, and it wouldn't change her own course of action in finally taking the plunge and launching her firm. She should have done it years ago.

It stung like a fresh wound, entering what had once been her family home now completely alone. The air was dry and utterly still inside, where white dust sheets covered furniture like old-movie-style ghosts. A shiver ran from the base of her neck down her spine. But she surprised herself with how boldly she stepped over the threshold and laid her bags on the floor.

A quick scan of the barren downstairs space had her chest tight with emotion, so she distracted herself by opening shutters and windows, bringing light and much-needed fresh air into the stagnant dark rooms.

When she next looked at her watch, she was shocked to see that almost an hour had passed. She was covered in dust, sweat glistening on her brow, but something warm and precious hummed within her that felt suspiciously like relief.

It had never sat well with her to leave this beautiful house closed up and vacant. Her parents would have been happy to see it being taken care of, to see their daughter reconnecting with her roots in the home that held such precious memories.

She cleaned herself up as best she could and then set out for the hospital, to find out what exactly it was that Angelus Fiero simply had to tell her in person.

Two hours later she finally emerged from Angelus Fiero's hospital bedside onto the street, her legs feeling as if they might give out at any moment. It turned out the man had a very pressing reason for bringing her here. One that involved a web of secrets and strategies that her brother himself had created. Once she was safely alone in the dark interior of the car, she fought the urge to give in to the hysteria and tears threatening to burst free from her chest as she processed everything the old man had revealed. But one fact shone out high above the others.

Her brother had survived.

Duarte was alive. He'd been recovering from severe brain trauma and was being kept in a secret location, but he was alive.

A thousand thoughts flew through her mind at once, but one drowned out all the others. She wished Valerio had been there with her for this. She wished she hadn't been alone to take the hit of a bombshell of this magnitude.

She was hardly aware of the drive back to Casa Avelar. Her brain was stuck somewhere between numb shock and trying to analyse what the logical next step might be. But there was nothing logical about any of this. Nothing at all.

Stepping out of the car, she paused as she noticed that the lights in the villa were all blazing bright and a sleek black car was parked at the top of the driveway. She paused on the stone steps, her senses on high alert. The front door opened and she felt the tightness in her chest released on a heavy exhalation of breath.

Valerio.

His shoulders filled the doorway, the light grey material of his silk shirt making him seem ethereal, as if she could reach out to touch him and he might not even be there.

'You didn't answer my calls.' His voice was low and effortlessly seductive, with just a little hesitance thrown in.

'So you flew to Rio? You could have just left a message with my PA.'

She fought the shiver that ran down her spine as he held her in place with that intense gaze. The look in his eyes startled her. It was how she imagined she must have looked every day for the past week.

Miserable.

She needed to tell him what she'd just found out—that

her brother was still alive and had been kept hidden somewhere in Brazil. But a part of her wanted to know why he was here, how he felt about her, before he knew about Duarte.

Had he missed her?

The look in his eyes was almost enough to tip her over the edge of control and send her melting into a puddle at his feet. Was it simply regret at the loss of the precious friendship he'd spoken of? She held back, schooling her features as much as possible. Once burned, twice shy might not apply to every situation, but that didn't mean she should dive headfirst into this particular fire without thinking it through.

She crossed her arms and allowed the silence of the evening air to fall heavily between them. He moved first, taking a few steps down the gravel driveway with ease, showcasing long, powerful legs encased in worn designer denim. Of course he *would* look more delicious than ever, she groaned inwardly, imagining how awful she must look in comparison.

'I spoke to Angelus Fiero.' She tried to control the wavering of her voice, determined not to break down in front of him but desperately needing to unburden herself. 'He told me that Duarte is alive.'

Valerio froze. 'That's impossible. I saw him die.'

Dani opened her bag and handed him the folded hospital document as she relayed the information she'd been given of Duarte's injuries and rehabilitation in a facility deep in the rainforest.

For a long time Valerio just stared at the piece of paper in his hand.

'I thought about what I would say for the entire flight here...' He spoke softly, his hand moving for a moment as though he wanted to touch her but decided against it.

'I didn't plan on you telling me any of this. I'll come with you. We will find him together.'

Dani nodded thankfully, letting the silence pulse between them before she spoke. 'Valerio…why did you come if it wasn't to hear what Fiero had to say?'

Valerio hesitated, then seemed to make a snap decision. 'I came for you, Dani. I should have come sooner. I should have followed you the minute you left my yacht. I told myself I should be relieved that everything had changed, that you were free of needing me, but…' He shook his head, looking away from her.

Dani felt something in her heart stretch—something that felt foolishly like hope blossoming. 'You were scared,' she said softly, a thrill of electricity shooting through her when he looked up and met her eyes.

'I'm known for taking risks and following my instincts, even if it leads to trouble.' He shook his head. 'But the things I've done in the past…risking my safety and my wealth on crazy ventures… None of that scared me. I never truly valued my own life. I always saw myself as dispensable.'

She shook her head, ready to launch into a vehement protest, but he reached out a hand, stopping her.

'I thought that risking our friendship and disrespecting the promise I'd made to Duarte was what terrified me. But seeing this paper now…knowing he's alive out there somewhere… It doesn't change anything for me. We will deal with that as it comes.' He took a deep breath, laying the document down on the step behind him. 'Dani…look at me. I now know I was just afraid of what I felt—not the consequences or the risks. I don't need anyone's permission. Letting you move on without ever telling you how I feel is no longer an option.'

He laid his hand over hers, turning it to find she still

wore the diamond engagement ring on her finger. She hadn't been able to part with it just yet. He looked down at her, meeting her eyes with such reverence that it took her breath away all over again.

'I think I've been slowly falling in love with you since we were teenagers and I didn't have a clue. So I ignored you—I ran away or I provoked you. I'm far from perfect, and I'll probably make mistakes, but I'm asking you for a second chance.'

She felt emotion clog her throat as she fought to formulate the words rushing through her head. In the end she just threw her arms around his neck, burying her face in his shoulder.

Eventually she leaned back, looking into his eyes and seeing the relief and emotion there. 'You put far too much effort into playing a part and worrying about what others think...but I see a man who is so much more than a playboy pirate. You put me first every single time, and I...' She felt her throat catch. 'You told me that if you want something you just have to take a deep breath and dive... So I knew that I couldn't walk away without telling you how I felt. Without telling you what you could have if you were only brave enough to take a risk of your own.'

He closed the small distance between them with lightning speed and pulled her up into a kiss that made her entire body shake with emotion. His hands entwined with hers, coming up to press against his thundering heartbeat.

Dani smiled against his lips as he devoured her. He kissed her until she was kissing him back with every ounce of love she had...until she felt the breath sigh from her and her entire body melt into his arms. Only then did he pause for breath, burying his face in her neck and exhaling on a deep, primal growl.

'Sorry, I'm not good with pretty words or speeches,' he

said softly into her hair, his hands still clutching her tightly against him, as though he feared she might run away if he loosened his grip.

'That was pretty eloquent, I think.' She bit her bottom lip, feeling as if there was a hint of magic in the air—as if this couldn't be real, this perfect moment. But the smile that spread across his full lips mixed with a look of fierce possession told her everything she needed to know.

She gasped, looking down as he slid her engagement ring off her finger with one smooth movement. Silencing her with a finger on her lips, he took a step back and slowly lowered himself down to one knee.

'I know I've technically proposed already, but I feel the situation requires a do-over.' His eyes met hers with intense heat and emotion. '*Tesoro*... I want to be your husband and your partner. I want us to create a family and a life together. I swear I will spend the rest of my life giving you every single thing you desire if you'll have me.'

'I've never wanted anything as much as I want to be your wife for real. I love you. I want us to live together, work our crazy schedules around each other. I want to have your babies, Valerio Marchesi. I want all of it.'

She took a deep breath, fearing her heart might actually burst out of her chest with the effort of getting the words out. She felt shivers run down her spine as he slid the ring back onto her finger and stood up, pulling her into a tight embrace.

She felt a calm settle over her like nothing she'd ever experienced before. Despite the unknown of what might lie ahead of them, she knew he would be by her side. Together they would dive headfirst into whatever adventures lay ahead, and as long as she had her hand in his, she knew things would be okay.

EPILOGUE

THE NOVEMBER RAIN poured down on his face as Valerio raced across the busy rush hour streets, narrowly missing a black cab as he finally reached the door of the hospital. He barely stopped to announce himself at the desk, his breath crashing in and out of his lungs as he took the stairs two by two.

The prestigious London hospital was a maze of corridors as he passed by door after door, finally finding the one he was looking for. The one he'd been inside every day for the past week. He came to a stop inside the brightly lit room—only to see an empty bed, perfectly made up with white linen. Fear closed off his air supply for a long, panic-ridden moment, before a woman entered the room behind him, wearing bright blue scrubs and a white mask.

'Mr Marchesi, you're just in time. Your wife is in Theatre.'

He was rushed down to the emergency operating theatre and handed a bundle of scrubs to change into. His hands shook as he pushed open the door to the bright surgical space and saw Dani's beautiful face, white with fear, as she lay surrounded by doctors and nurses and the rhythmic beeping of medical equipment.

'Valerio!' Her shout of relief was palpable as she reached

out to clutch at his sleeve and pull him close to her face. 'I can't believe this is happening. It's too early!'

Valerio steeled himself at the anguish in her voice and murmured words of encouragement in her ear, his hand gripping hers tightly as the surgeons performed their work on the other side of a blue screen.

It seemed as if hours passed before the doctors announced that the baby was out, then spent a while bending over Dani with furrowed brows. Moments later a loud, healthy infant's cry erupted in the room and he felt his shoulders sag with relief as he pressed his forehead to Dani's and let emotion take over.

After a flurry of movement and various checks, the doctor assured them that their daughter was perfectly healthy and didn't need any care other than her mother's skin.

A nurse placed the tiny form on Dani's chest and Valerio felt his heart swell with love and gratitude as they both cradled and stroked their child's glorious head of jet-black curls.

'What do you think Leandro will say when he finds out he got a baby sister instead of a brother?' Dani asked softly, her eyes filled with laughter.

Valerio winced, thinking of the serious-faced three-year-old at home in their town house, being spoiled by Nonna and Nonno Marchesi. Leandro had been quite clear that a baby brother was the only thing he would tolerate.

'I'm sure we'll figure out a way to bring him around,' he said, and smiled, leaning in to brush a kiss on his wife's forehead.

Once the surgical team had finished the aftercare for her emergency caesarean procedure, Dani was returned to her comfortable private room, where she promptly fell asleep.

She awoke a short while later, to the sight of her husband cradling their infant daughter in his strong arms.

She was quiet for a while as she watched them, her heart threatening to burst with joy and relief that they had been blessed with a healthy child for the second time.

Their firstborn son had been born exactly on his due date almost two years previously, on the day of their second wedding anniversary. Valerio had joked that he was just like his mother: shockingly efficient and punctual.

The comment had turned out to be quite accurate. Leandro *was* just like her and Duarte had been as children, in spirit and in looks—apart from the brilliant Marchesi blue eyes that accompanied his rather serious gaze. She thought of her twin brother, feeling an echo of that old sadness mixed with relief. Her relationship with her twin had been strained for a time once they'd found him and discovered the depths of his ordeal and the web of deception behind it. But now...now she could hardly believe her luck at having so much family around her.

'I'll have to tell Duarte he won our bet,' Valerio murmured, looking at their daughter. 'I thought we'd have all boys. This girl is definitely going to steal my heart.'

Dani laughed. 'What are we going to call her?'

'I was thinking... Lucia.' He turned brilliant cobalt eyes on her.

Instantly Dani's thoughts travelled back to the island where they had fallen in love, said their vows, and where they'd returned every single year since, to the villa they'd now bought together.

'Valerio...' She felt her throat close with emotion. 'That's perfect.'

'*She's* perfect. Just like her mother.'

He placed their daughter in her small crib, his movements careful and confident. She had almost forgotten how natural he was with babies. He had been the one to show her tricks to get Leandro to sleep for longer and to bring his wind up, while she had been a shivering mess of nerves for months.

She sighed and leaned back on the pillows. He moved to sit alongside her, being careful of her tender abdomen and the tubes still attached to her arms.

'I have never been more afraid than when I walked into that room today and saw an empty bed.' A frown marred his handsome brow as he looked down at her, stroking one hand across her cheek.

'I was terrified too, once I realised something was wrong and they wanted to get her out so suddenly. I was so worried that you wouldn't get here in time. But I swear I could hear my mother's voice in my head, telling me to breathe. And I knew that we would all get through it okay.'

'You were amazing. You are a goddess of a woman—have I told you that?' He leaned forward, his lips brushing across hers softly, one hand cradling her neck. 'Your strength never ceases to amaze me. How on earth did I get so lucky?'

'I love you so much,' she whispered against his lips. 'But all this sweet talk isn't going to make me want more babies.'

'You said the same after the first one.' He smiled, nuzzling her ear. 'But two is perfect for me. I think your staff will kill me if I keep getting you pregnant—that company of yours is skyrocketing and they need their fearless leader.'

'Motherhood only adds to my superpowers.'

Dani smiled, thinking of the perfect top-floor London offices of Avelar Inc.

She had done it all—her own company, her perfect home in the English countryside and her wonderful family. Valerio had promised he would give her everything and he'd stood by her every step of the way, giving her his full support as they juggled their work and home lives together as a team.

'Lucia Marchesi...' Dani smiled down at her sleeping daughter. 'I don't think the world could handle another Riviera pirate—especially if she looks anything like you.'

'If she's like me she'll need to find the right person to balance out her wild spirit.' He leaned back, draping an arm carefully over her shoulders and dropping a kiss on her collarbone.

Dani leaned back into the power of his embrace, letting out a soul-deep sigh of contentment and happiness. 'This is quite an adventure you've taken me on.'

'We've only just started, *tesoro*.'

* * * * *

MILLS & BOON

Coming next month

AN HEIR CLAIMED BY CHRISTMAS
Clare Connelly

'I will never understand how you could choose to keep me out of his life.'

Annie's eyes swept shut. 'It wasn't an easy decision.'

'Yet you made it, every day. Even when you were struggling, and I could have made your life so much easier.'

That drew her attention. 'You think this is going to make my life easier?' A furrow developed between her brows. 'Moving to another country, *marrying* you?'

His eyes roamed her face, as though he could read things in her expression that she didn't know were there. As though her words had a secret meaning.

'Yes.'

For some reason, the confidence of his reply gave her courage. One of them, at least, seemed certain they were doing the right thing.

'What if we can't make this work, Dimitrios?'

His eyes narrowed a little. 'We will.'

It was so blithely self-assured, coming from a man who had always achieved anything he set out to, that Annie's lips curled upwards in a small smile. 'Marriage is difficult and Max is young—only six. Presuming you intend for our marriage to last until he's eighteen, that's twelve years of living together, pretending we're something we're not. I don't know about you, but the strain of that feels unbearable.'

'You're wrong on several counts, Annabelle.' He leaned forward, the noise of his movement drawing her attention, the proximity of his body making her pulse spark to life with renewed fervour. 'I intend for our marriage to be real in every way—meaning for as long as we both shall live. As for pretending we're something we're not, we don't need to do that.'

Her heart had started to beat faster. Her breath was thin. 'What exactly does a 'real' marriage mean?'

'That we become a family. We live together. we share a bedroom, a bed, we raise our son as parents. It means you have my full support in every way.'

It was too much. Too much kindness and too much expectation. She'd thought he would be angry with her when he learned the truth, and that she could have handled. If he'd wanted to fight, she could have fought, but this was impossible to combat. The idea of sharing his bed...

'Sharing a home is one thing, but as for the rest—'

'You object to being a family?'

He was being deliberately obtuse.

She forced herself to be brave and say what was on her mind. 'You think I'm going to fall back into bed with you after this many years, just because we have a son together?'

His smile was mocking, his eyes teasing. 'No, Annabelle. I think you're going to fall back into bed with me because you still want me as much as you did then. You don't need to pretend sleeping with me will be a hardship.'

Her jaw dropped and she sucked in a harsh gulp of air. 'You are so arrogant.'

His laugh was soft, his shoulders lifting in a broad shrug. 'Yes.' His eyes narrowed. 'But am I wrong?'

Continue reading
AN HEIR CLAIMED BY CHRISTMAS
Clare Connelly

Available next month
www.millsandboon.co.uk

COMING SOON!

We really hope you enjoyed reading this book.
If you're looking for more romance, be sure to
head to the shops when new books are
available on

Thursday 12th
November

To see which titles are coming soon, please visit
millsandboon.co.uk/nextmonth

LET'S TALK
Romance

For exclusive extracts, competitions
and special offers, find us online:

- facebook.com/millsandboon
- @MillsandBoon
- @MillsandBoonUK

Get in touch on 01413 063232

For all the latest titles coming soon, visit
millsandboon.co.uk/nextmonth

JOIN US ON SOCIAL MEDIA!

Stay up to date with our latest releases, author news and gossip, special offers and discounts, and all the behind-the-scenes action from Mills & Boon...

 millsandboon

 millsandboonuk

 millsandboon

It might just be true love...